Sherlock Holmes and The Missing Authors Trilogy

The Adventure of the Grinning Cat
The Nautilus Adventure
The Round Table Adventure

By Joseph W. Svec III

Hardcover ISBN 9781787053328

Published in the UK by MX Publishing
335 Princess Park Manor, Royal Drive,
London, N11 3GX www.mxpublishing.com

Cover design by Brian Belanger

The author may be contacted via his web page, www.pixymuse.com or via his Facebook page www.facebook.com/sherlockgrinningcat

Dedication

This book is dedicated to my loving, magical and gifted wife, Lidia. Thank you for your continued encouragement and traveling this curious and enjoyable journey with me.

Acknowledgements:

I would like to acknowledge and thank the following wonderful people for their assistance in making this book possible.

First, I would like to thank my wife Lidia for being an integral part of the writing of this book.

I would like to thank my son Joe for introducing me to the Amador County Holmes' Hounds Sherlockian Society which provided my first exposure to the adventures of Sherlock Holmes.

I would like to thank my daughter Leedia for listening to a reading of this book and providing comments.

Thank you very much to Linda Hein and Beth Barnard for reviewing the manuscript and providing most valuable input. It is very much appreciated.

Thank you to the Amador County Holmes' Hounds Sherlockian Society and Baker Street West of Jackson California for excellent inspiration.

Book 1

Sherlock Holmes and The Adventure of the Grinning Cat

Table of Contents:

A Note to Readers:

The following manuscript and cover letter was found in the belongings of Dr. John Watson, M.D. after he passed away in the early 1900s. You may recall that besides being a war veteran and a well-respected surgeon, Dr. Watson was also noted for being the close friend and biographer of Sherlock Holmes, the world-famous consulting detective. Dr. Watson recorded the more interesting and challenging of Sherlock Holmes' many cases and adventures propelling him into the spotlight.

Sherlock Holmes was world renowned for his uncanny skills in perception, logic and deductive reasoning, as well his astute knowledge in many unique subject areas. He was especially noted for seeing the minute details that were invisible to everyone else. In addition to his solving the most baffling and difficult cases that vexed Scotland Yard he had also published numerous technical papers on a wide variety of arcane subjects, many of which are mentioned in this story.

Per Dr. Watson's written notes in the cover letter, this manuscript apparently was set aside for 25 years as he requested, but then was lost over the passing decades until it was recently rediscovered. As the requested amount of time has more than passed, it may now be published without concern and the reader may judge for his or herself. Be prepared for a very strange and most curious tale.

Prologue

Memorandum:
To: Whom It May Concern From:
Dr. John Watson M.D.
Subject: Sherlock Holmes, The Adventure of the Grinning Cat
Date: February 1898

First let me state unequivocally that the events described below really did happen. As utterly improbable or even impossible as they may seem to you as you read this, they really did occur exactly as I have described them. I recorded the details of this very strange adventure almost as soon as it was complete so that I would not forget even one fantastical aspect of this amazing experience. If you have read my previous accounts of the great consulting detective, Sherlock Holmes, then you will see at once how utterly different this adventure is from each of his previous exploits. In all my years spent accompanying Sherlock Homes in his cases, I have never experienced one like this. My mind still reels in wonder when I think back to it all.

Yet as true and real as it was, I must take Sherlock Holmes' advice and ask that its publication be postponed until 25 years after my passing. After all, I must consider my reputation as a medical practitioner as well as the confidence of my patients, not to mention the reputation of Sherlock Holmes himself. Upon reading this, it is entirely possible that one may question the sanity of the author. I must confess that I questioned my own sanity several times during this adventure.

However, I must also ask that the reader refer to the rather odd newspaper article in the February 5, 1898, London Daily Times that is referenced within the manuscript, and then you may make your own judgment. Either way, your compliance in this request is greatly appreciated.

Dr. John H. Watson, M.D.

Sherlock Holmes,
And the Adventure of the Grinning Cat

Chapter 1.

A Very Strange Visitor (Now that's rather unusual.)

It was a cold and foggy February 4, 1898, rather typical for that time of year actually, but most untypically, Sherlock Holmes was not quite his usual self that day. No, not at all. Not in the least. And I must confess that even after all of the unusual and quite incredible adventures we had shared up until the morning of that very strange visitor, I was rather beside myself as well.

Countless times I had witnessed Holmes solving a multitude of odd and unusual cases without the slightest bit of hesitation or difficulty. He had applied his uncanny senses of observation, logic and deduction to disprove vampires, phantoms, demon dogs, and more. He had written volumes of scholarly papers on the most arcane and esoteric of subjects. Yet on that particular day, there he sat in deep concentration, just staring. Now this was not at all his normal mode of deep concentration in which he sat in silence puffing away incessantly on his pipe until the room was filled with noxious fog or playing his violin until one's nerves cringed, and one could not stand another shrieking, blood curdling note. No, this time he just sat there completely still as if in a trance and stared intently at the very strange visitor sitting in the chair across from him. Now, it is also very true that we had never before had a visitor or client quite like this, so I would imagine that Sherlock's behavior is somewhat understandable.

He had been staring at him, or should I say "it", since just after it appeared that morning in the study. We had come down for breakfast as usual only to find a cat sitting in the chair across from Sherlock's. It was a rather large cat with big green eyes and a grayish coat that suggested bluish black stripes.

"Hello? What's this? What are you doing here? How did you even get in here?" Sherlock wonderingly asked, never expecting a reply. But then the most unimaginable thing possible happened: The cat broke into a very wide grin and while gazing in the direction of the front door, replied, "Hello to yourself Sherlock Holmes. I am here to engage your services, and I came through that door".

We stood there rather shocked for a moment before I addressed Holmes asking, "Did that cat just talk to us?"

To which the cat turned and looked directly at Sherlock and replied while nodding its head in my direction, "Not very observant this one, is he? Or is he just hard of hearing? Now I know why you're the detective."

Sherlock broke into a wide grin himself and slapped me on the shoulder saying, "Good job Watson! After all these years, you have finally managed to pull one over on me. I really did not know you were into ventriloquism. How long have you been working at it? You did an excellent job you know! Just smashing! And how on Earth did you manage to get the cat in here? I was up rather late, and I locked the door myself last night. There were no cats here in the study when I went to sleep."

The grinning cat then jumped off the chair saying, "My dear Mr. Holmes, this has nothing at all to do with ventriloquism. Your friend Watson could not throw his voice even if he had a catapult." At which point its grin grew impossibly wider, and it laughed: "Get it? A 'catapult'?? I'm a cat??? Never mind. I know you are not noted for having a sense of humor. As I was saying, I came 'through' that door."

At that point, the cat casually walked towards and then completely through the solid wooden door vanishing right before our eyes. How in the world could it do that? Were we seeing things? I was about to ask Sherlock if he had seen the same thing I did, when there was a considerable amount of loud scratching on the other side of the door and we were able to hear a cat mewing outside of the door as well. However, before we could react, the cat's wide smile and piercing eyes appeared on the inner surface of the wooden door winking at us. This was immediately followed by the rest of its head (minus the body mind you!) reappearing on our side of the door, saying, "See? Like I told you, I came 'through' that door. I can do that, you know. We Cheshire Cats are noted for such things. "Seeing our shock, he added, "Really, we are. I could do it again if you don't believe me."

It then continued coming 'through' the door, completed reforming the rest of its body, slowly crossed the room, taking particular care to rub itself several times against Sherlock's pants leg, leaving a good quantity of cat hair as it did, jumped back up on the chair, sat down and stared at us. Sherlock brushed the cat hair off of his leg, very carefully examining it with the hand microscope he had removed from his pocket. Although one might not expect it, Sherlock Holmes is quite the expert on cat hair. He had once written a monograph on the subject. I think it was titled: *Determining Human Disposition to Violent Behavior Based on the Nature and Quantity of Cat Hair on Clothing,* or something like that. Sherlock then crossed the room, slowly seated himself into his chair right across from it and commenced staring at the cat.

This had begun at about 7:00 am, and the clock was now already near 9:00 am. Nothing had been said; neither one had moved. They sat quietly staring at each other the whole time. Just out of curiosity, to answer a question that came to mind while I was waiting and observing, I had gotten up, opened the door, looked at the outside of it, verified the brand-new scratch marks on the outer surface, closed the door, and sat down again. Now that I think about it, I recall Sherlock writing a paper on identifying scratch marks as well. I think it was called: *Identification and Classification of Mammalian Species Based on Scratch Marks on Wooden Doors.*

At one point, I had considered throwing a blanket over the cat to remove it from our sight, but just at the time that I was considering that, it turned and looked at me with its impossible grin as if to say, "Watson, you know that would not accomplish a thing. I would simply dematerialize and let the blanket pass right through me, re-materialize, and be sitting right here still waiting for Sherlock Holmes to say something."

But Holmes did not say a thing. He continued sitting there staring at the cat. I could almost see the gears and cogs of his analytical thinking process as he considered, reconsidered, analyzed, and then eliminated one explanation after another for our very strange visitor. I am sure each possibility was more bizarre than the previous. Yet in his mind logic *must* prevail. There is always a simple explanation if one can get one past the confusing distractions. As Sherlock had admonished me so many times previously, "After eliminating the impossible, whatever remains, no matter how improbable, must be true."

Finally, close to 10:00 am, with a long deep sigh, he shook his head, stood up, went over to the breakfast table, poured a saucer of milk, apparently for the cat, poured for me and himself two cups of tea, brought them back into the study, and set them down. He looked at the cat intensely and said. "All right. Against all rational logic, probabilities and likelihoods and as completely strange as it may seem, you really *are* here. Have a bowl of milk. Now tell me, how can I possibly be of any help to you? I am sure you are not here to read my paper on *Malfunctions, Breakdowns and Misdirection in the Feline Homing Instinct.*"

Chapter 2.

A Very Strange Tea Party (Now it's really getting unusual.)

The cat's grin softened somewhat as it looked towards the direction of the tea service and replied, "Actually, I would prefer some tea with that milk, if you don't mind." Turning back to Sherlock, it pointed out. "You know, it only took you three hours to eliminate all other possibilities and determine that, as completely improbable as it may seem, I truly am sitting right here in front of you. That is quite good. You really do live up to your reputation."

He turned, nodding in my direction and commented, "You could learn quite a lot from this one, Watson. You really must pay closer attention. However, it does appear that your stories of his exploits and adventures are not exaggerated in the slightest."

Then turning back to Sherlock, the cat requested: "Well, you can start by adding some tea to my milk-- Earl Grey, if you have it-- pouring two more cups of tea and answering the door." At which point there immediately commenced a loud thumping at the door. While Holmes went to get the additional tea, I strode towards the door, opened it and found myself, if at all possible, even more dumbfounded than I already had been with the day's proceedings. For, there before me standing upright on its hind legs, was a large white rabbit wearing a blue waistcoat and holding a large gold pocket watch in his paw, asking repeatedly, "Are we late? Are we late? Oh, I do hope we are not too late!"

Standing beside him stood an extremely short and oddly dressed fellow with shocking red hair, and an enormous brightly colored top hat on his head that was almost as tall as its wearer, and an equally large polka-dotted bow tie. With a grand flourish and much waving of his hands, he bowed as he introduced himself and his companion: "The Hatter, at your service." Straightening up and reversing the flourish of his hands so that they ended up pointing towards his companion, he very formally stated, "Allow me to present Mr. White Rabbit, Esquire." At which point the White Rabbit again implored, “Please tell me we are not too late! Are we too late??? I really do hope we are not too late! I don’t know what we would do if we were too late!”

Felling completely confused, looking back and forth between them, I bewilderedly replied, "No, I don't think so. Late for what exactly? I am not quite certain or sure about anything at this point."

"That’s wonderful!" cried the Hatter, as he followed by the White Rabbit marched past me into the room. "That makes two of us. You know that I am never *really* quite certain or sure of anything myself, except Tea Time of course, so I do think I could possibly use a cup of tea right about now. Yes, that would probably be most lovely."

I closed the door behind them and wondered how the ever-so-logical-and-grounded-in-reality, Sherlock Holmes would respond to these new and even more bizarre visitors. They were certainly much stranger than the cat that was sitting there. But having already given the cat some tea to go with his milk, and holding a cup of tea in each hand, he looked at them and calmly asked, "Does the Reverend Charles Dodgson, better known by his pen name, Lewis Carroll know that you three are here?"

"That's the problem!" they all three exclaimed at once. "Or least that's the second half of the problem," said the cat, "Lewis Carroll is missing!"

All three commenced to vigorous nodding, agreeing and bemoaning the fact that Lewis Carroll was indeed missing, and that it was most assuredly the second half of their very serious problem. Holmes held up his hand to gain their attention and get the conversation back under some semblance of control if that was at all possible, and asked them, "So tell me please, what exactly is the *first half* of the problem? You do know I wrote a paper once on *Analysis, Determination, Division and Classification of Issues in the Hierarchy of Problem Identification and Resolution.*"

"Alice is missing from Wonderland!" they all exclaimed together, then adding, "And so is the March Hare! Where can they be? What *are* we to do?" And once again they commenced to nodding at each other lamenting, agreeing and wondering what on earth or in Wonderland could possibly be done. The cat again interjected. "That's why we came to see you, Mr. Holmes. After all, you are known as the world's foremost consulting detective this side of Wonderland, and we really don't have any consulting detectives on that side of Wonderland. And besides, even if we did have, they too would have probably vanished by now. You simply must help us find Alice and the others before we disappear as well. All of Wonderland depends on you!"

Holmes gestured for the new guests to sit down, handed them cups of tea and slowly asked them, "Why don't you tell me your story and start at the beginning, when you first noticed something strange going on?" Looking at the three of them and considering the peculiarity of the situation, he paused for a moment, and added, "Or at least stranger than a talking cat that can dematerialize, a talking rabbit in blue waist coat and...," Once again, Holmes hesitated, looking directly at the Hatter who smiled at Holmes raising his tea cup in a salute. Sherlock nodded his head and raised his tea cup in return and concluded, "And him, who I am at a loss to describe."

All three looked at one another for only a moment glancing back and forth and once again began talking and gesturing all at once until Holmes again held up his hand and interjected, "If you please! One speaker at a time!"

The Cheshire Cat taking the lead and gesturing towards The Hatter, stated rather matter-a-factly, "Since I am a cat, and you know that cats can never be entirely trusted, and he's mad as a hatter, which is to be completely expected since he is one, why don't you explain it to him Rabbit? You know that rabbits are considered to be quite trustworthy, as well as very cute and cuddly, and after all, it did all begin when Alice followed you down the rabbit hole."

The Rabbit shied backward with a look of surprised indignation exclaiming, "Cute and cuddly? I am certainly not cute or cuddly! I am m-most assuredly distinguished looking, and I paid dearly for it. Do you know what this jacket cost? I assure you, Cheshire, no one thinks of m-m-me as cute or cuddly! Cute and cuddly indeed!" Then realizing that everyone in the room was staring at him, he cleared his throat, looked around rather nervously, straightened up, and began his unusual tale.

Chapter 3.

A Very Strange Tale (Can it get any more unusual than this?)

"A-a-actually, I think it may have begun when Lewis Carroll took that boat ride with Alice Liddell and her sisters and first told them about Wonderland. Or perhaps it began when he wrote it all down for her. It could have been something in the ink or the paper, or m-m-maybe it was just his will to create that somehow brought Wonderland and all of its inhabitants to life. M-m-maybe even Alice and her cats as well since they are part of the stories. I really don't know for certain. All we know is that since that day when she first visited Wonderland, we have been truly alive. We have been living in Alice's Wonderland adventures along with her and continuing living on each day in between Alice's visits and adventures.

“It has not been just her adventures down the rabbit hole and through the looking glass, but her newer adventures as well. Sir, you can't imagine the noise from all of those musical instruments playing at the same time when Alice visited Orchestra Land. And that trip she took to the m-m-moon? Why that was really incredible! I m-must say though, I enjoyed that cheese she brought back from the m-moon. I know some people have said the m-m-moon is m-made of cheese, but I never really believed it for m-myself until I tasted it. Have you ever tasted green cheese from the m-m-moon sir? It really is quite delicious. Now some of her adventures I unfortunately did m-miss because I was a bit too late, but we did have so many wonderful adventures together, all of us. Oh, I do hope we are not too late. Are we too late M-Mr. Holmes?”

As his ears twitched repeatedly, the Rabbit glanced nervously at his watch, took a deep breath, and then continued. "One day, Alice just disappeared from Wonderland. That is to say, she did not show up for our regular Wednesday afternoon tea. And I m-must tell you sir, Alice never m-m-misses tea! She is always there precisely on Wednesday afternoon for tea. Why, if my watch kept dates instead of time, I could set my watch by her. We have such lovely tea parties, all of us together. Every Wednesday…"

Standing up and striking a formal public speaking pose, the Hatter interjected, "Rabbit, you have most certainly established that Alice was regularly there for tea on Wednesdays. What happened next? We may not have much time left."

Glancing at his watch in fear, the Rabbit continued. "Three weeks ago, Alice did not show up for Wednesday afternoon tea as usual. We thought that m-m-maybe she had been caught up in a game of chess or a Wonderland croquet m-m-match, or something. M-Mr. Holmes, do you know how challenging it can be playing croquet with flamingos for m-mallets, hedge hogs for croquet balls, and wickets that get up and switch their positions on you?"

Sherlock shook his head sideways and replied, "No, I can't say that I do. But I did once write a magazine article on *The Logic and Geometry of Lining up Croquet Shots for Maximum Efficiency.* But as I recall, the wickets involved were all quite stationary."

The Rabbit gestured widely, pointing his paws all over the room, "What with the wickets continuously getting up, running around, switching their positions and charging all over the croquet court, a croquet m-match can sometimes take all day. In fact, I remember one m-m-match that lasted three whole days. The wickets wandered off into the forest and got lost. We had to send the Griffon out to go find them and bring them back."

The White Rabbit was glassy eyed and staring off in the distance for a moment until he went on: "The way those wickets are always shuffling here and shuffling there, one would think that they are a deck of playing cards… Oh! Wait a minute…" He slowly exclaimed as if deeply lost in thought. "Now that I think of it, the wickets really *are* a deck of playing cards! Yes! That would explain everything."

Holmes cleared his throat again, raised a pointed finger, and interjected, "Yes that would explain about the croquet match, but I believe you were talking about Alice."

"Oh, yes. Yes, I was. She m-m-missed the following Wednesday as well. And after that, this last Wednesday the M-March Hare was m-missing too. And he has always been there for tea! He m-may be m-m-mad as a M-March Hare and a wee bit hard on the tea service at times, but he has never, ever, ever m-m-missed tea. That is when I went to visit Lewis Carol m-myself, which was no easy task, m-mind you. I was chased by some horrible cats. No offense, Cheshire." He added glancing at the Cheshire Cat, who nodded while sipping his tea, and smiled at the Rabbit. "None taken, Rabbit. Please do go on."

Continuing, his strange tale, he went on, "I had rocks thrown at me by some m-m-monstrous little children, and, when I finally reached Lewis Carroll's front door and knocked, do you know what happened? Do you know what *happened*?"

Sherlock replied rather a-matter-a-factly, "Actually, I wrote a whole series on *The Determination of Impact and Effect of Rocks*

Thrown Based on Their Starting Location and Trajectory, Divided into Sedimentary, Igneous and Metamorphic Classes of Rocks."

With his eyes wide and his ears quivering, the Rabbit paused again and looked around as if frightened. "I'll tell you what happened. When the m-m-maid opened the door, she took one look at me, and screamed! 'Oh no! Not *another* one! Quick, hide the tea service!' and she slammed the door in right my face."

Holmes cocked his head sideways, turned to me and commented, "I can't imagine why she would do that." Turning back to the Rabbit, he asked, "What do you suppose she meant by 'Not *another* one?'"

The White Rabbit glanced nervously at his watch, before answering, "I am not certain. I can only imagine that perhaps the M-March Hare m-may have been there before m-m-me. You know, he is a bit hard on the tea service. I did not stay to find out. But as I was leaving, I did hear someone inside say if only Mr. Dodgson were still there, he would know what to do about all of the strange creatures showing up at the door, and something about, when is Sherlock Holmes finally going to arrive? Did you tell them you were coming for a visit? It sounded like they were *expecting* you."

Looking rather startled, Holmes shook his head slowly and replied, no, he most certainly had not indicated to anyone at Lewis Carroll's house that he might be going there, and it was rather a surprise to him. Sherlock had been so busy working on an important project over the last three weeks, that he had not spoken to anyone outside of 221-B or even read a newspaper.

The White Rabbit again glanced around nervously, looked down at the floor, and then concluded, "I am afraid that is all I can tell you sir. Alice and the M-March Hare are m-m-missing from Wonderland, and it sounds like Lewis Carol is m-m-missing from here. What are we to do? Can you help us?"

Holmes looked at me and said, "Well, Watson, from what I have just heard, I believe we need to take a trip to visit Charles Dodgson's home in Guildford. I don't think they will slam the door in our face."

Chapter 4.

A Very Strange Journey (And somewhat unsettling.)

Of all the journeys that Sherlock Holmes and I had ever taken while working on a case, this was to be one of the strangest. Not only were we going to visit a renowned author, mathematician, and logistician, but we had in tow a semi-intangible talking cat, an overly nervous talking rabbit in a blue waist coat, and a very odd little fellow whose hat was almost as tall as he was.

Now, that would have been strange enough if the three visitors weren't well known characters from a famous children's novel, but they most certainly were three very well known, yet very *imaginary,* literary creations who were sitting right there in Holmes' study, very much alive, drinking his tea, eating his tea cakes, and talking, usually all three of them at the same time. How could that be possible? Before today, if anyone had even suggested the possibility of this, I would have laughed at them, and Sherlock would have dismissed them from the room. Yet, there they all sat. It was very strange indeed.

Utilizing his contacts and referring to his original copy of *An Alphabetized and Cross-Referenced List of Reliable Carriage Drivers in Greater London*, Holmes was able to hire a trustworthy carriage driver who was willing to drive us the 32 miles to Guildford, as well as to not ask any unnecessary questions about his three unusual passengers. However, the driver did raise his eyebrows considerably as we all climbed aboard, and I do recall him muttering something about, "What does he think this is, Noah's Ark or a circus freak show? But I will say that is a very cute and cuddly rabbit." The White Rabbit cringed noticeably, but wisely did not say a word.

As Sherlock handed the address to the driver with an additional Five Pound note, he thought he glimpsed an unusually large-winged reptilian or bird-like creature lurking in the shadows of a nearby building. He asked me if I had seen it also. I had to confess that I saw nothing in the dense London fog, and when he looked again, it was gone. Sherlock muttered something about wishing he had his *Guide to Unusually Large-Winged Avian Species Native to London and the Surrounding Area* handy.

Sitting down in the coach, he asked our strange guests if perhaps any other Wonderland inhabitants had come to London, at which point they all began gesturing, shaking their heads every which way and answering all at the same time.

"No, no of course not, not at all", Grinned the Cheshire Cat. Adding, “It is not very likely, so I wouldn’t think so.”

The Hatter held up his head and profoundly announced, “I am not really certain. But then you know I am never really quite certain or sure of anything.”

The cat, now squinting as if it were closely examining something slowly added, “Well you know it may just be possible, but I couldn't really tell for sure.”

The White Rabbit, with his ears twitching, fearfully murmured, “But it could very well be. One never knows. If that is the case, who could it possibly be?"

And finally, with its eyes opened wide and an even wider grin, the cat proclaimed, "Why now that I think about it, yes, it is entirely possible."

Sherlock looked at me, sighed and commented, "I really must reconsider the way I ask these three a question." Adding under his breath, "Watson, I can see by the morning's proceedings this is going to be a very long and *very* strange day."

Little did he know it would be much longer and far stranger than even he could imagine. The journey began as a fairly normal carriage ride considering the three passengers. The sounds of the street were muted by the wisps of fog that curled and floated through the half-light that made up the cold, grey London morning. The clip-clopping of the horse's hooves on the cobblestones seemed to fade into nothingness as the shapeless mist rolled by the coach's window, when suddenly a dark black shadow fell over us, and the coach lurched as if it had been grabbed or snatched from above by something very large and powerful. At the same time, we heard the voice of the coach driver yelling frantically about dragons, demons, never touching whiskey again, and leaving the country. His voice then faded away, as if it was receding far into the distance.

All was silent except for what distinctly sounded like the flapping of a very large set of wings. The motion of the coach became quite smooth and fluid, almost as if we were floating. Not knowing what to expect, I opened the coach window and stuck my head out to see what exactly was going on. What I did see made me quickly pull my head back inside. It was not possible! It could not be! With a look of pure terror on my face, I said to Holmes, "Sherlock, you are not going to believe this, but I think this coach is airborne, and I feel like I am going to be sick."

Sherlock, sticking his head out the window to assess the situation himself, asked me to pull myself together. Meanwhile, our three visitors started screaming. "It's the Jabberwocky"! The Cheshire Cat wailed.

"Where's the Vorpal Sword?" demanded the Hatter. "We must have the Vorpal Sword!"

"It's too late! We're doomed!" muttered the White Rabbit with his ears twitching wildly.

Knowing Sherlock Holmes as well as I do and having seen his smooth and confident responses in the most challenging of situations, I can say that it is difficult, if not impossible, to rattle him. However, after pulling his head back into the coach, he certainly appeared more intense and focused than I had ever seen him before. I would even say that he was somewhat unnerved. However, with his usual cool and calm demeanor, that is typical of Sherlock Holmes, he addressed me. "Congratulations Watson, I do believe that this time your observations are actually correct. We are most definitely airborne, and the creature that is carrying us is stranger looking than all three of our guests put together. I shall certainly have to write a paper on *The Aerodynamics and Suitability for Air Travel of the Various Types of Cabs and Carriages in Greater London.*"

I began to pull out my service revolver, when Sherlock interrupted me and warned, "We don't dare shoot it, or we'll be in for a long fall back down to the ground."

Turning to the three Wonderland inhabitants, he asked them, "Would any of you happen to know exactly what creature has us in its clutches?" And recalling their usual habit of all talking at once, he added, "Again, if you please, only one at a time."

The Hatter responded by simply pulling his huge hat completely over himself and quivering; the Rabbit with his ears twitching madly, dove under the seat, screaming, “It’s too late! We're doomed! We are all doomed"; the cat meanwhile simply vanished into thin air.

"Wonderful!” cried Holmes. "Now what?"

Truthfully, I must confess, I was too overwhelmed to even consider an answer. I had no idea what we were going to do, when we slowly began to experience a gentle downward sensation, followed by the firm but controlled thud of our contact with the ground, and then silence.

I finally managed to pull myself together and ventured, "Why Holmes, I do think we are once again on the ground," and looking out the window I added, "And it looks as if our carriage is parked in the middle of Charles Dodgson's front yard. If this is Lewis Carroll’s house, that was the fastest trip from Baker Street to Guildford in history. Although I must say, I wouldn’t want to do *that* again."

Holmes, nodding his head in agreement opened the carriage door. "Yes, Watson, that was quite the ride. It was most engaging actually. We are indeed at Dodgson's house, and we seem to have lost our driver and horses somewhere along the way. If we had been set down any closer, we would be inside the house, or at least on top of it. This case is turning out to be most singular and fascinating. I think I would call it 'curious'," he said with a wry grin.

At that point, a local constable came charging through the front gate of the property crying out, "Now see here! You can't park that carriage on a front lawn. Carriages are supposed to stay on the..."

He never did finish his sentence. His jaw dropped, his eyes grew wide, he feebly held up his nightstick in a gesture that was more quivering than threatening and realizing the absurdity of the situation he dropped the club, turned, and ran back out the gate screaming something about dragons, the gates of hell being unleashed, not ever having signed up for anything at all like this, and moving to France.

As I climbed out of the carriage and looked up at what had caused such fear, I must confess that I almost followed behind him. Sherlock Holmes was completely accurate as always in his assessment that the creature perched on the roof of the coach was most definitely stranger than all three of our visitors put together. In fact, it was stranger than every other bizarre thing I had seen in my entire life combined into one abomination. This was, without question, a creature from one's worst nightmares. I can speak with authority on the subject, having read Sherlock's *A Discussion on the Use of Logic and Laudanum to Analyze and Classify the Intensity and Severity of Nightmares.*

It indeed looked much like a medieval winged dragon or perhaps a giant bat with chicken legs and a long snake-like neck that was as long as its scaly tail. Its claws looked as if they could rip the carriage into splinters without even trying, while its jaws worked like a bear trap. The creature's large eyes were a brilliant bright red, and if its appearance wasn't already strange enough, it was wearing a tweed vest. However, as frightening as it was, it did not appear to be menacing us in any way. It seemed to be preening in a very proud fashion, as if to say, "Wasn't that the fastest carriage ride you have ever had in your whole life? Who needs horses when you have me? We could do it again if you would like. Really we can!"

Sherlock stood his ground before the terrifying creature and boldly addressed it, "Jabberwocky, if you had wanted to kill us you could have easily done so in more than a dozen ways. And I would know, as I wrote a whole series on *The Analysis and Classification of the Number of Ways that Someone Can be Killed in Any Given Situation*, so I deduce that your intentions are not hostile. That, and the fact that you have provided us the fastest journey possible from London to Guilford, although a bit unsettling, tells me that you are as concerned about the current situation as our three guests, *if they would care to come out here*," he added raising the level of his voice so that they could hear him.

Hiding completely under his enormous hat and shaking like a leaf in the wind, the Hatter tiptoed out of the carriage and quickly ran to hide behind a tree, while the White Rabbit took a step outside, looked at the Jabberwocky, and promptly fainted. The Jabberwocky looked at the White Rabbit commenting, "Oh what a cute and cuddly rabbit. Do you think he will be alright?"

The Cheshire Cat, however, materialized his head only on a nearby tree branch and addressed the creature loudly in a rather formal voice: "Jabberwocky! Greetings oh great, manxomeous and winged one! We thank you for the timely transportation. It is most gracious of you."

In a booming, burbling voice the creature replied, "We are all in this together, most nebulous and translucent one. I too am aware of what is happening in Wonderland. The Tweedles, the Door Mouse, and the White Knight have all vanished. Even parts of the royal chess board have started to disappear. Soon there will be nothing left. I see that none of you are brandishing a Vorpal Sword, so I felt safe in providing assistance with the transportation aspect of this adventure. Time *is* of the essence, and nothing can compare to air travel."

Gesturing with one of his long claws in the direction of Sherlock, the creature pointed out, "You are very wise in seeking the assistance of this logical and deductive one. I can tell by his demeanor that he sees a great deal more than most anyone else. Looking into his eyes, it is obvious that he understands the meaning of what he sees more clearly than everyone else."

The Jabberwocky, twisting his snake like neck so that his head faced in front of Sherlock and looking straight into his eyes, went on, "I see too that he unquestionably deduces the implications of what he sees and the significance of what he understands more completely than anyone I have ever met. I believe he would make a really great detective. I am talking 'world class' here. He could become truly legendary. I imagine they will write volumes of books about him if he doesn't plunge to his death over a waterfall or something like that. I shall like to engage him in a game of chess, should we bring this conundrum to a positive conclusion. In the meantime, let us not lose our heads over it all."

Sherlock, meanwhile, had casually taken his clay pipe out of his jacket pocket and was filling it with tobacco as he carefully studied the beast and listened to its conversation with the Cheshire Cat. The Jabberwocky pointed a long claw at the pipe and in an equally casual voice, commented, "I *can* light that pipe for you, oh deep and contemplative one, but you would probably want to stand several feet away from it while I do. You may want to keep a bucket of water on hand as well, but I would still recommend staying away from waterfalls. They can be dangerous, you know."

Sherlock hastily returned his pipe to his jacket pocket and replied, "Ah, no thank you, most scaly and undulating one. That's quite all right. Perhaps now is not the best time for a pipe. But if you can explain your presence here and that most exhilarating ride, it would be much appreciated."

The Jabberwocky peered directly at Sherlock and started to explain that not only were the inhabitants of Wonderland starting to vanish, but parts of Wonderland itself were disappearing along with the boundaries between London and Wonderland. Just the other day, as he flew above the Tulgey Woods, he thought he had seen, sticking up through the clouds, a large tower with clocks on it. I knew he must have been referring to Big Ben and wondered what was going to happen next.

Before the creature could go on, however, the front door of Charles Dodgson's house slowly creaked open and a white-haired butler wearing a black suit and waving an envelope in his hand stepped out nervously and announced, "Well, it's about time you arrived, Mr. Sherlock Holmes." Looking towards the White Rabbit, he added, "My goodness this certainly is a cute and cuddly rabbit you have here." Returning his gaze to Sherlock, he went on. "I was not sure whether our chinaware could hold out much longer. I am James, the butler, and I have a letter for you from the late Charles Lutwidge Dodgson, who passed away just three weeks ago. I have instructions to invite you in for tea, with what little tea service is left. However, you, fine and scaly sir," and he pointed at the Jabberwocky, "will have to sit on the front porch and perhaps stick your head through the window into the tea room, if that is acceptable. And as we do not have any tea cups suitable for something of your size, would a large beer stein work for you as a tea cup?"

The Jabberwocky's eyes lit up considerably and he responded that the arrangements were quite satisfactory as long as the tea was Earl Grey and that there was plenty of cream. He cheerfully volunteered to quickly fetch a cow if necessary, to which the butler assured him that it, was not.

Holmes looked at me as if deep in thought and commented, "This sadly answers the question regarding the whereabouts of Lewis Carroll. I have been so involved in that project these last three weeks that I never saw the news of his death in the papers. This is still a most curious and unusual case, Watson. I am sure it will be one for your journals, although I seriously doubt anyone would believe it. You may consider postponing its publication for quite some time if you value your reputation as an author or continued future as a practicing doctor. Shall we go inside and have some tea and see what the late Charles Dodgson had to say to me? The presence of that letter tells me that he had some idea of what exactly is going on here, and we may receive more answers. Also, if you could rouse the rabbit and extract Mr. Hatter from his hiding place, that would be excellent."

Chapter 5.

Another Very Strange Tea Party (I guess it can get more unusual.)

A multitude of wild thoughts and questions ran through my mind as we entered the house of the late Lewis Carroll. How could he have possibly known three weeks in advance that Sherlock Holmes would be calling for him? What was in the letter, and how would it affect the outcome of all this? How was it possible that the imaginary characters from his books had actually come to life, and what was happening to them now that he had recently passed away? What must be going through the ever-so-logical-and-practical-mind of Sherlock Holmes as all of this unfolded? And finally, where in the world would this incredibly strange adventure lead us to next?

The answer to my last question was quickly forthcoming, as we were directed into the tea room, where a table with scones, tea sandwiches, tea cakes, and other savories, along with several pots of tea, a mismatched set of chipped tea cups, and one large beer stein were waiting for us.

Entering the tea room, I noticed that the Jabberwocky had already curled itself up on the front porch outside the window, with its long scaly neck and arms extending into the room. It was resting its head on the back of one of the stuffed chairs and addressing the butler. "You know, if you need help preparing more tea sandwiches, I could fetch a lamb or a goat and roast it in a jiffy," The Jabberwocky was telling the butler, while the butler did his very best to assure the creature that it would not be necessary. The Jabberwocky replied, "Suit yourself, oh ancient and laboring one."

Emptying an entire tray of tea sandwiches at once into its wide-open jaws, he handed the empty tray back to the butler commenting, “Hmm, pickled herring! Those are some of my favorites. Might you have any more of them? Oh, and I will take that stein of tea now, if you please; Earl Grey, if you have it."

The Cheshire Cat with its typical wide grin was casually enjoying its cup of tea with milk, while the White Rabbit appeared to be trying to hide behind his tea cup with very little success, finally abandoning the tea cup for a somewhat larger tea pot. The Hatter was no longer hiding inside his enormous top hat but instead was devouring tea cakes from a three-tiered tray.

As Holmes and I settled into our own tea and scones, the butler cleared his throat and made an announcement: "My dear guests” - And I did notice a slight hesitation at the word 'guests'-- "The night that Rev. Charles Lutwidge Dodgson, better known as Lewis Carroll passed away, he gave me this letter with instructions that it should be delivered into the hand of a Mr. Sherlock Holmes when he arrived here, of which the Master assured me that Mr. Holmes eventually would. The Master did mention that we might first experience a few 'odd' visitors prior to the arrival of Mr. Holmes, which we also have. He did not, however, mention exactly how odd the visitors might be or that we would experience a significant decrease in the amount of usable chinaware as a result of any such odd visitors."

At that point, the White Rabbit straightened up and exclaimed, "Then the M-M-March Hare was here before I arrived! That explains a part of it, or at least the condition of the china." Looking nervously in the direction of the Butler, the White Rabbit slouched down and resumed trying to hide behind a tea pot.

The butler looked downward at the White Rabbit and muttered, "Indeed!" Looking directly at Sherlock Holmes, he went on, "The Master seemed to feel that after you read the letter and figure out exactly what to do, the problem will be solved, and all will once again be back to normal. However, I am not certain that 'normal' will ever be truly normal again. He instructed me to invite you and who or whatever is with you in for tea."

Pausing and looking around the room with a skeptical gaze, he continued, "Here is your letter. Tea has been served. I will leave you to your discussions. Please ring if you need more tea or sandwiches."

At that point, the Jabberwocky waved another empty sandwich tray in one claw while vigorously ringing the bell rope with the other. The butler retrieved the tray and exited the room muttering something about certainly checking to make sure his next position was not working for an author, while consoling himself that at least he had not worked for Mary Shelley or Bram Stoker.

As the door closed behind the butler, Sherlock Holmes gingerly held up and examined the letter from the late Lewis Carroll. The envelope was pale lilac in color and of a heavy stock with a dark wax seal upon it as if it contained news of impending doom. He looked from the envelope and stated, "Did you know Watson, that last year I wrote a paper on *The Identification of Stationary Manufacturers Throughout Western Europe Based on Color, Texture and Weight of Envelopes*? I can tell you who manufactured this envelope, where it was made, what day of the week it was produced, and whether the machine operator was right handed or left handed."

I replied that none of that was really important and asked why he doesn't just read the letter as this case was getting stranger by the minute. Sherlock conjectured that he didn't think it could possibly get any stranger than it already was, and he proceeded to tear open the letter and read it.

As he read the letter out loud, I realized that, contrary to Holmes' comment, it was indeed getting much stranger than either of us could have ever possibly imagined.

Chapter 6.

A Very Strange Letter (And rather cryptic at that.)

"My Dear Mr. Holmes (and you too, Dr. Watson) as well as any of my dear and wonderfully strange creations who might still be there with you:

“I offer you this letter as a last resort to help preserve my legacy and the lives of all those whom I have brought into being through the writing of Alice’s Adventures in Wonderland.

“If there is anyone who can work though the strange logic and cryptic nature of this situation, it is you Mr. Holmes. For without question, next to me, you are the most logically-minded person in the world. I have read your landmark monograph on *The Value of Observation, Deduction and Logic in Determining Hidden but True Facts Versus Obvious but False Facts.* Yet I assure you, that to solve this puzzle, you will have to call upon the very illogical creatures whose existence must seem so unlikely and improbable to you. You truly must embrace the reality of them in order to succeed."

At that point, Holmes had to temporarily interrupt his reading of the letter to deal with a strong hug from the Hatter and the nuzzling from the head of the Jabberwocky while at the same time trying to reason with them and extricate himself from the Cheshire Cat’s tail which was wrapped around his neck, as the cat had apparently materialized on top of Sherlock’s head.

"All of you please contain yourselves!” He exclaimed. “If any of you were really listening, he asked me to embrace your *'reality,'* not all of you physically! You must trust me. As odd and unusual as this is, I accepted the reality of this highly illogical and most improbable situation exactly two hours and twenty-three minutes ago. The sooner we complete this puzzling, paradoxical prospect, the sooner we can, all of us, return to some semblance of normality, or whatever it is that stands for normal where you come from. Now let us continue reading the letter."

Nodding affirmatively, the Jabberwocky withdrew his head and voiced his agreement. "Yes indeed, most logical and far seeing one. We must continue the reading of the letter. This is quite wise as one would expect from someone as analytical and rational as yourself, even if you don't appreciate a fond, friendly embrace."

The Hatter returned to his tea cakes while the Cheshire Cat mostly dematerialized leaving only a wide smile looking rather like a glowing halo above Sherlock's head as he went on reading the letter.

"My story begins like so many often do, at the very beginning. But the question is: Where is that beginning? The answer is that it has been lost, and you must find it. You must return to the exact moment that Wonderland came to life, so to speak; for it is there that you will be able to correct the problem at hand. Time is running out!

"I must stress that time is of the essence, but not time as you know it. Most people look at time as a river flowing in one direction in which we are all swept along with no control whatsoever over our direction or destination. But you must believe me, this is false. I have discovered it is possible to step out of the river of time on to the shore of a reality that is outside of the boundaries of time. One can walk upon that shore in both directions, forward or backward, and then step back into the river at any point of their choosing. I have done, it Mr. Holmes, and I assure you that you can do it as well. And you must do so in order to set right what has gone so terribly wrong."

The serious tone of the letter caused the Hatter to lose interest in his tea cakes, while the White Rabbit stared at his watch so intently I thought he was going to burn a hole into it. The Cheshire Cat's smile meanwhile, had vanished from above Sherlock's head. The entire cat reappeared sitting upright upon the fireplace mantel with its tail hanging downward and swishing back and forth like the pendulum of a clock his eyes looking back and forth to the right and left in coordination with his swishing tail. It felt as if, with each second that passed, we were coming closer to a horrible conclusion.

Continuing the letter, Holmes read on, "While it is possible to step out of the river of time, it is not without its complications or ramifications. There are Time Guardians who closely control the manipulation of time, and they are the most logical of creatures in existence. Any time one steps out of the river, the Time Guardians are watching and waiting, ready to pose logic puzzles to any who dare choose that path. And with each additional instance a person attempts time travel, the Guardians create more complex and convoluted logic puzzles.

"When I first stepped out of the river of time many years ago, their logic puzzles were mere child's play to someone of my skills in logic. I felt so confident in my ability to solve any logic puzzle they could come up with, that I convinced them to agree to a wager. To me, the risk was more than worth the gain. What I gained in the wager with them, was life for Alice and all of the creatures of Wonderland, as well as Wonderland itself. What I risked was the loss of Wonderland and everyone in it if the

Guardian's final logic puzzle could not be solved in the time period provided. I was certain that I had all the time in the world required for solving their final enigma of logic, for like you, Sherlock, I am a master of logic and deduction. However, the one thing I could not predict was the failure of my health. I am dying, but Wonderland and all of its marvelous and most unusual beings must not die with me. With each passing day, the borders that contain Wonderland grow weaker, and more and more of its inhabitants will find their way to earth and whatever awaits them here, or they will just plain disappear.

"You must figure out how to step outside of time and then solve the final logic puzzle before February 5. Per the rules set forth by the Time Guardians, I myself cannot tell you how to step out of the river of time, but I assure you, there are horrendously great wells of possible ways to do so, and each one is unique to the individual. Once you have done so, it is then that you must solve the world's greatest logic puzzle, and Wonderland, with all of my most illogical of creations, will survive.

Sincerely yours,
Charles Lutwidge Dodgson, or to my friends, and I do count you as a friend, Lewis Carroll"

Chapter 7.

A Very Strange Discussion (Well, it's about time.)

In the profound silence that followed, I noticed several things: The White Rabbit was staring out the window in a daze, not even noticing that his pocket watch was immersed in his cup of tea, and the Hatter was sniffling and blowing his nose using the window curtains as a handkerchief as he moaned, "That was the most touching, saddest letter I have ever heard someone read." To which the Cheshire Cat responded, "Hatter, you know very well that that is the only letter you have ever heard someone read. I am not saying that you are not well read; in fact, your nose is quite red at the moment. Why it is almost bright red enough to read by. But I will agree that it was quite touching and more than a bit sad. Would you care to use the table cloth as well?" The Cat then proceeded to yank the entire table cloth off the table without upsetting a single thing upon it. He handed it to the Hatter who promptly used it to blow his nose, which sounded something like a donkey with a sore throat braying through an out of tune trombone.

The Jabberwocky, meanwhile, was contemplating his empty tea stein, woefully wondering how much time, if any, was left and whether or not there was enough time for more tea sandwiches. Deciding there was, indeed, enough time, he began vigorously pulling on the bell rope -- unfortunately pulling it right off the ceiling -- and then wondering out loud, "Now how are we to get refills?"

I myself was wondering what on earth we were going to do next. I had not seen any clues in the letter about how to step out of the 'river of time', as he called it. He had made it very clear *what* to do, but with no real instructions about *how* to go about doing it. We were no better off than before we arrived. I voiced my thoughts to Sherlock who had remained in a contemplative silence since he finished reading the letter. In his usual form, he immediately admonished me for my lack of vision and understanding.

"Oh Watson, my dear short-sighted friend, have you learned nothing at all from our many adventures together? Have you not read my report, *On Listening to What Has Not Been Said to Determine What Has Actually Been Said in Any Given Statement?* Did you not listen to the letter I just read? Were you not paying attention? In any logic puzzle, there are rules, spoken and unspoken. Some things must be inferred, while others are clearly given. Some clues are revealed, while others are hidden. One must analytically examine the information provided to reveal the answer. In any collection of information, there is the obvious background material, and there are the less than obvious real facts hidden between the lines. The ultimate logic puzzle itself will only be given to me when I reach the reality outside of time."

"But how are we to do that?" I exclaimed. "Dodgson said there are many possible ways to do it, but he did not mention a single one of them. He did not even provide any clues! We are no better off now than we were before we arrived."

"Ah, but he did Watson, old boy; he most certainly did. Think back for a moment. He did not say there are many possible ways. What he was *most* specific to say is that 'There are horrendously great wells of possible ways'. Do you not see it, Watson? 'Horrendously Great Wells', *H. G. Wells*! He is the author who recently wrote a novel about time travel. 'The Time Machine', I think it was called. It must be Wells that Dodgson is referring to.

He will be our next destination in this most curious and strange adventure. We must go see him immediately."

I was thunderstruck! I could not believe what I was hearing. "Holmes!" I cried, "What *are* you thinking? Have you completely lost your sense of logic and reason? How can you even suggest that we go chasing after the author of some fictional story about time travel? He is not a physicist or even a scientist. All he did is write a fictional novel about a completely imaginary machine that somehow travels through time. How is that supposed to help us?"

Holmes spread his arm in a wide circle as if to encompass all of the creatures in the room and answered me, "Look around you, Watson. We are surrounded by completely imaginary creatures that somehow really do exist and are right here in this room with us. How do you explain that? You and I saw with our own eyes as the Cheshire Cat walked through a solid wooden door and left real cat hair on my pants leg. I examined the cat hair and verified it was real."

The Cheshire Cat interrupted licking his paw, and grinned, "I may be able to pass through solid wooden doors and vanish at will, but I am still a cat. What can I say? Like it or not, cat hair goes with the territory, so to speak."

Sherlock ignored the Cheshire and continued, "The Hatter and the White Rabbit drank our tea and ate our teacakes. The tea and cakes had to go somewhere. They didn't just magically disappear from the table. You know there is no such thing as magic, but as strange as all of this seems, what we have been experiencing here is real. Of course, I shall have to rewrite my paper on *The Examination, Determination and Validation of Reality From Multiple Visual Perspectives, With an Emphasis on the Unreal.*"

Pointing towards the Jabberwocky, who cheerfully waved an empty sandwich tray back at him, he asked, "And him? How would you explain him and the near instantaneous ride from London to Guildford? Watson, we are in entirely new territory here. The old laws of reality and logic simply do not apply in this adventure."

At that point, we were interrupted by a timid knock on the tea room door as the butler opened it bringing in more refreshments and saying, "Excuse me sirs, but there is a Unicorn here demanding to see you. He insists that it is most urgent."

A *Unicorn*? This was the final straw. I threw up my hands in surrender and told the butler to send him in, but the Unicorn had apparently not waited for a formal invitation into the room and came trotting in past the butler, nearly knocking the food tray from his hands, and commenting as he went by, "I do hope there is some plum cake on that tray or at least some good brown bread."

I could not believe my eyes! A Unicorn had just walked into the room like it had belonged there. Imaginary or not, the creature was truly magnificent! One could not help but be in awe of its majesty. Its coat was whiter than the proverbial newly fallen snow, or for that matter anything else one could think of to compare it to. It was as if the Unicorn was the very definition of the color white, and every other thing that aspired to be that color was just a pale imitation.

Looking towards Sherlock Holmes, the Unicorn pointed his beautiful spiral horn directly at him and spoke: "You must forgive your friend, Mr. Holmes. All the years of working with you and recording your unerring logic and deduction functioning like clockwork has jaded his point of view. He still does not understand that true logic looks at every possibility, even the impossible or illogical ones."

Turning to look at me, the Unicorn rested its glowing horn upon my shoulder and in a timeless voice said to me, "*Believe,* Watson. Just *believe*. I really am a Unicorn. I really am standing right here in front of you. Your friend Sherlock Holmes is truly headed in the right direction. He is on the path to his destiny."

The peace, warmth and for lack of a better word 'light' I felt flowing through my entire body on that day was so beautiful and utterly beyond description, I know I shall treasure and remember it always…

However, the wonder of the moment was particularly short lived, as the Unicorn then quickly emptied the nearest three cups of tea and stated to no one in particular, "Now, can we can have some of that plum cake before we leave for Mr. Wells' home? My long-time sparring partner, the Lion, has already vanished, and I really do not want to be the next one to disappear."

Turning back towards Sherlock, he pointed out: "You are absolutely correct, Mr. Holmes. We must quickly go to the house of H. G. Wells. He published his work, 'The Time Machine' as a fictional novel, but I tell you he really has created a device for traveling through time. With all due modesty, Unicorns are faster, more nebulous and much more transitory than even Cheshire Cats. No offense Cheshire." To which the Cheshire Cat simply grinned and winked. "And I have been to the house of H. G. Wells and seen his Time Machine for myself. This is indeed the next truly logical step in this journey."

Holmes simply nodded in agreement and smiled as he put his arm around my shoulder saying, "So you see, Watson? You have a real live Unicorn telling you that a visit to the time travel author is the next *logical* step. What more proof could you want?"

What could I possibly say to him? I broke down and agreed that we should go to Wells' home. Then the White Rabbit, roused from its deep concentration, waved its pocket watch in the air and voiced its approval adding, "So it *is* about time. I suspected that all along. I just hope we are not too late."

The Hatter giggled and replied, "You all know that I am never really quite certain or sure of anything, but I would almost feel relatively safe to say that between having the undisputed master of logic and deduction, a Jabberwocky that can fly a coach from London to Guildford in record time, and a real live Unicorn, we stand a fair to moderate chance of not being too late. In fact, we *may* even be on time, but don't quote me on that. If you do insist on quoting someone, quote the White Rabbit. You can tell him, that I said it is perfectly fine with me."

The Cheshire Cat rematerialized on the brim of the Hatters top hat swishing its tail in the Hatter’s face mewing, "Don't forget about me, Hatter. I was the one that found Sherlock Holmes and convinced him to help us. Nothing gets one’s attention like phasing through a solid wooden door. Of course, some well-placed cat hair always helps. I am quite good at that also.”

Sherlock interrupted and pointed out that Lewis Carroll had clearly stated that we were all equally important in this endeavor; however, if we really didn't want to end up being too late, then we had better leave soon, at which point, the tea party adjourned, and we headed back to the coach

Chapter 8.

Another Very Strange Journey (And this time quite a bit more unsettling.)

As we exited the house of the late Lewis Carroll, we thanked the butler for his hospitality and the lovely refreshments. We tried to apologize for the condition of the bell rope, curtains, and table cloth. But he said not to worry, everything was just fine, and do come back soon, any time, but please check first as he may be leaving town in the near future. In fact, he may be leaving the country in the near future. As I recall, he said something about going to somewhere far away from libraries and authors.

I noticed that when we did finally leave, he was in a heated discussion with a bed of talking flowers that had suddenly appeared on the front porch and were trying to find a way into the house. I recall him saying something about never, in all his years as a gentleman's butler, had he ever had to try and reason with roses, bicker with begonias, or debate with daisies, and what *was* this world coming to when a butler had to be zoo keeper, a gardener, and serve tea to a dragon, (I am assuming he meant the Jabberwocky), all in the same afternoon.

In order to get back to London as soon as possible, we agreed that the Jabberwocky would again carry the coach with us all except the Unicorn, who knew the way to Wells' house and would guide the Jabberwocky from the ground. We did have to break up a minor disagreement about who was actually faster, with Jabberwocky saying that Unicorns were no faster than drying paint, while the Unicorn commented that he had already been there and back again three times in the time it took the Jabberwocky to finish its sentence.

Sherlock pointed out that if they wanted to be precise on the subject they could consult his report on *The Speed of Drying Paint in Varying Temperature and Humidity Conditions with an Emphasis on the Viscosity of the Paint;* however, they had better come to some sort of an agreement very quickly, or it would not matter who was the fastest, because they would both disappear quicker than he could say, "On your mark, get set, go!" That did get their attention.

Once again, the carriage flew through the dreary fog-bound skies of London in the claws of the Jabberwocky; however, instead of a relatively smooth Point-A-to-Point-B, straight-as-the-crow-flies (or in this case straight-as-the-Jabberwocky-flies) type of flight path as we had previously taken on the way to Guilford, we were subjected to a flight path that closely resembled a Tasmanian Devil let loose in a labyrinth.

While the Unicorn was incredibly swift, indeed faster than the wind, unfortunately, it did need to follow the surface roads and streets, which it accomplished at speeds far beyond anyone's imagination. The creature was capable of turning 90-degree corners, of which there were a great many, in a quarter second or less and then taking off again at speeds even faster than it had approached the corners. It would not have been so bad had the Jabberwocky not tried to follow the *very same exact path* as the Unicorn. Needless to say, being in the coach, we felt as if we were inside of a box tied to the back of a mad bull with firecrackers attached to its tail as it crossed the English Channel in a small craft during a full gale.

In the split second that we took off, covering three miles and navigating the first eighteen corners almost instantaneously, several things inside the coach happened at once. The Cat vanished into thin air, the Hatter seemed to fold himself up into his hat, which was bouncing off the walls of the coach, and the White Rabbit leaped into my arms crying, "Save me! Save me!"

Sherlock and I held on to the coach for dear life, as the coach did its best to hold on to itself for dear life and remain intact despite the wild ride. It almost succeeded in doing so, but if you recall the newspapers of the next day, February 5, 1898, there was a brief article about it raining wagon wheels from the sky in various parts of London. Authorities were most perplexed, and Sherlock made a note to provide extra compensation to the coach driver should he ever turn up.

As one would imagine, we did get to H. G. Wells' house in record time. Of course, it was minus the coach's wheels and various other odd parts, I am sure. As we stepped out of what little remained of the carriage, the Unicorn was casually waiting next to the front steps of the house, inquiring, "What took you so long?" to which the Jabberwocky responded, "We could have made it in half the time had you not taken the scenic route."

While I myself thankfully and unsteadily set my feet back on solid ground, the White Rabbit leaped from my arms to the ground kissing it and crying, never again would it even think of air travel. The Hatter extracted himself from his battered and bruised hat and crawled to the ground with a huge sigh of relief and a groan. Meanwhile, in his usual indefatigable and stoic manner, Holmes merely brushed off his sleeves saying, "You know, Watson, once the kinks are worked out of it, I do believe that there is a solid future in travel by air. Yes, a really solid future." At that point, the Jabberwocky released its grip on the coach which completely collapsed into a pile of wood and leather. Looking back at the pile of debris, Sherlock added, "Like I said, it does need to have a few details worked out." Then as an afterthought, he added, "Watson, do remember to remind me to make arrangements for a replacement coach for our driver whenever we find him. I believe this carriage has definitely reached the end of its useful life."

The Cheshire Cat, with its eyes looking a tad greener than usual, but with its characteristically wide grin unfazed, faded back into solid form sitting on top of the remains of the coach, and stated, "I say, fellow sky travelers, once we resolve the current uncertainty at hand, we should start a sky tour company. I can see it now! *See all of London in less than a minute! (Having lunch or dinner beforehand definitely not recommended. Not for the squeamish or faint of heart.) This is a once-in-a-life-time experience*!"

"That is because once anyone has done it, they would never ever want to do it again," groaned The Hatter. "Not to mention you would need to replace the coach after every flight!"

"Well, yes, you may have something there," acknowledged the Cat as it surveyed the ruins of the coach.

The door to the home opened and out stepped H. G. Wells himself. Surveying the odd group of travelers and the remains of the demolished coach in his front yard, he smiled and said, "Do come in. I have been expecting you."

Chapter 9.

A Very Strange Meeting (Maybe H. G. Wells does have the answer.)

In response to the invitation to enter the house, the Jabberwocky raised a claw and posed a question: "Greetings, oh chronologically gifted one. I was wondering whether or not that invitation included me. You do understand, considering my size and all, I would be quite happy to rest out here on the porch as long there is an open window in close proximity to the gathering room and reasonable access to refreshments."

Wells replied that either way was fine, as both the doors and the sitting room were large enough to accommodate all of them. The Jabberwocky burbled his enthusiasm and galumphed up the stairs, into the house, and directly into the sitting room finding an open place in a corner not far from the refreshment table sighing, "Ah, Earl Grey, and pickled herring sandwiches, my two favorites." The rest of us followed him into the room and found seats, except for the Unicorn, who chose to remain standing on the other side of the refreshment table closer to the tea.

Wells entered and began with the question, "Would anyone care for tea and refreshments?" To which everyone but Holmes, the Unicorn, and the Jabberwocky cried out in unison, "No thank you! Not just yet if you don't mind," with the White Rabbit adding, "Please! Can we first let the ground stop spinning?"

Wells again nodded affirmatively and smiled, giving me the opportunity to observe him. H. G. Wells at the time was 32 years of age, of medium build, with dark hair and a drooping mustache.

He had been a struggling writer for some time, and the sudden success of his novel, The Time Machine, three years before had set quite well with him with several more literary successes following since then. With a soft smile he addressed the group.

"Gentleman and visitors from Wonderland, your reputations precede you, and I am honored to be in your company. Mr. Holmes, your fame as the world's foremost consulting detective and master of logic and deduction is without equal. When I heard of the passing of Lewis Carroll, I knew it would not be long before you would be calling on me. That and several sightings of a Unicorn in the vicinity of my house told me that you would soon be here to discuss the possibilities of time travel. Am I not correct, Mr. Holmes?"

Sherlock nodded and agreed with him adding, "Indeed, Mr. Wells. We are here to talk about time travel and logic puzzles. I can see by the flower in your lapel that you are experienced in time travel, as that particular botanical specimen is not to be found In London at this time of year, or for that matter, anywhere else on the planet in this particular time period. I shall have to add it to my *Guide to Identifying Flowers Originating Outside of this Reality*. Recalling my paper on *The Analysis, Identification, Verification and Determination of the Origin of all Soils to be Found in London, England* and looking at the soil residue on your shoes tells me that it did not come from anywhere in London. I can also see that a large device was recently dragged from your garden into what I presume is your laboratory. I won't bore you with the details from my *Analysis of Drag Marks Based on a Scientific Study of 11,373 Objects Categorized by Size, Shape and Density*. Also, your complexion tells me that you have recently been in sunnier climates than London in the middle of winter."

I then jokingly added, "Or sunnier than London most any time of year, for that matter. I don't need a technical paper to tell me that. One hardly ever sees the sun any more it's been so foggy these last few years."

Wells responded affirmatively, "Yes to both of you. The soil residue and flower you speak of, Mr. Homes, are not at all from this time period, and Dr. Watson you would be amazed at the climates I have experienced up until recently."

The Hatter taking the pose of a public speaker offered, "As uncertain as I most always find myself, I am quite sure it was sunny the last time I was in Wonderland. But who knows if the sun is still there. If the sun is gone, that means there are no more Sundays. Can you imagine *two* Mondays in a row?"

The Unicorn then commented, "It was still there when I left yesterday, and the letter stated that Mr. Holmes had until February 5 to complete the logic puzzle. But if that is the case, then why are the inhabitants of Wonderland already vanishing?"

"That is because the time frame to complete the logic puzzle is nearing its completion," stated Wells. "The framework that holds Wonderland together is weakening and the boundaries are failing. Once the puzzle is solved, I am certain that Wonderland will return to its original state with all of its inhabitants, but I am getting ahead of myself."

The Cheshire Cat, now just a floating head with a wide grin, then interjected, "Well, that would give you a healthy "head" start in any kind of a race, wouldn't it? You could even "head" them off at the pass so to speak."

Holmes responded by pointing out to the Cat, "Cheshire, I really do accept your presence here, as highly improbable as it may be. However, that does not mean I have to accept your completely illogical musings."

Rotating his head completely upside down, the cat replied, "Would you prefer illogical mewing? As a cat, I am entitled to mew all I care to, logical or illogical." Cheshire started mewing both forward and backwards as well as upside down until Sherlock stepped directly in front of it, cleared his throat loudly and asked me if I happened to have my service revolver handy. The Cat then immediately ceased its mewing and vanished leaving a tail waving a white flag.

Sherlock then turned to Wells, and said, "Please do continue and hopefully without any more nonsensical interruptions."

Wells began his story in earnest. "My personal experience in time travel began several years ago. It was while I wrote my novel, The Time Machine, which as I am sure the Unicorn has told you, is based mostly on fact. Although I was able to successfully build a time travel device, I knew I could never let the public or the government know that such a device really exists. So, I wrote my story as a fictional novel. Society has made such a complete mess of things on their own; I shudder to think what they would do with the power the Time Machine could provide. I created the device because I thought I could find a different time period where my views were more common and the society that lived by such views would be perfect, but alas, I discovered that no such time frame exists.

"Returning to time travel itself: While I focused on a mechanical-crystal-driven approach, in my brief acquaintance with Lewis

Carroll, I discovered that he had utilized an optical mirror-based approach to time travel. He briefly alluded to that in a roundabout way in his story, *Alice's Adventure Through the Looking Glass.* By the way, Mr. Holmes, I did read your article on *The Optical and Refractive Properties of Looking Glasses Based on Temperature of Formation with an Emphasis on Polishing Compounds Used.* That was quite interesting, and I was not aware of the significant difference between polishing a mirror clockwise and counter-clockwise.

Wells resumed his explanation: "Each person's approach to time travel is unique and individual, suited to their own abilities and inclinations. I am sure that yours would be logic based, Mr. Holmes. The secret is to truly believe, with every fiber of your being, that you *can* step out of the river of time and create the methodology or mechanical construct required to make it happen. It is entirely up to you how you do it. Once you achieve success, it is then that you will meet the Time Guardians.

"As time is a logical progression of events, the Guardians are the most logical beings. While some randomness in time is normal and to be expected, the Guardians exist for the purpose of maintaining order in the flow of time. Whenever someone randomly steps out of the river to time travel, that person must answer a logic riddle or puzzle to be able to continue. The more one-time travels, the more challenging the puzzle becomes. If one cannot solve the Guardian's puzzle, they will be returned to their own time period, never to time travel again."

Wells paused for a moment with a look of sadness before he regained his focus. "I myself am now finished with time traveling. The logic puzzles have reached a level far beyond my capabilities, so sadly my device no longer functions for me. Lewis Carroll was a master of logic. He was so certain that he could solve their ultimate logic enigma, that he not only risked his continued ability to time travel, but the lives of all of Wonderland as well. The arrangement he made with them was to bring Wonderland into existence and give life to all its inhabitants, but if the ultimate logic puzzle was not solved by the fifth of this month, which is tomorrow, then Wonderland with all of its inhabitants, will vanish forever."

"Tomorrow?" the White Rabbit loudly exclaimed. "Did you say we are all going to vanish TOMORROW? We're all doomed! It's too late! I knew it. I knew we would be too late." The White Rabbit sadly placed his gold watch back in his pocket, slumped down in his chair and slid to the floor ending up under the table as Wells resumed.

"It *may* not be too late, my friends. You see the importance of your presence here, Mr. Holmes. You must go against the very foundation of your logic and reason to embrace the reality of all of this, as impossible as it all seems," he made a wide sweep of his hand, "in order to call upon that very same logic to solve the world's greatest logic puzzle. It is indeed a conundrum."

The room was utterly silent as Wells completed his story, poured a cup of tea for himself, and sat down in one of the chairs.

Sherlock Holmes sat as if in a trance for the second time that day. Once again, I could almost see the gears of logic, reason, and deduction turning inside his brain. I myself still saw nothing that he could do to resolve the situation. I did raise the question if it were possible for another person to use Wells' time machine, someone other than himself, who was not yet bound by the restrictive rules of the Guardians.

"That is an excellent question, Dr. Watson," he replied. "But who would be willing to risk using the creation of another person's mind to travel to an ethereal-other-worldly place that, in all practicality, logically does not even exist? My mind, intellect, reasoning, and thinking process are an integral part of the functionality of that Time Machine. How would another person's thinking and reality interact and function with it? There's really no telling what would happen. They might get permanently lost in time or possibly even end up on the planet Mars! Who knows? I have no idea if it would even function for someone else."

At that very moment, the whole room started to tremble and shudder slightly, and the lights began to flicker. We all looked around at each other wondering what was going on when H.G. Wells' eyes grew wide in shock and fear as he exclaimed, "My Time Machine! Someone is in the laboratory using my Time Machine!"

In a panic, we raced down the hallway to his laboratory to see the White Rabbit his ears twitching wildly, sitting in the velvet passenger seat of a beautiful brass and varnished wood sled-like device with a large spinning disc on the back of it and a series of blinking lights on the control console in front of the seat. The rabbit's paws were firmly clutching the crystal control lever.

"No!" cried out Wells, "It's too dangerous!"

"But we are out of time!" screamed the White Rabbit as he frantically pulled down on the crystal control lever.

"Somebody stop him!", exclaimed Wells.

As the machine began to blur growing more intangible by the second, Holmes, the Hatter, the Cheshire Cat, the Unicorn, the Jabberwocky, and myself all made a frantic leap for the machine to try to stop the Rabbit. We all made contact with the Time Machine, but it was too late. In a blinding flash of light, everything seemed to blur, and the room disappeared completely.

Chapter 10.

A Very Strange Side Trip (Who would have ever imagined this?)

We clung frantically to the Time Machine as it whirled through space and time taking us to who knows where. This time I had to agree with the White Rabbit and felt that we were all doomed. I was sure there would be no return from this journey. An unending array of lights and scenes raced past us in a multicolored kaleidoscope of blurry images. As we rushed past the moon, it seemed as if I could have reached down and touched it. I had never in my life seen the stars so huge and bright. A comet with a glittering tail of ice crystals and glowing dust particles streaked by so close I thought it would hit us. Where was this infernal machine taking us to?

I looked down towards the control console and saw Sherlock reaching desperately for the crystal lever. He was trying to maintain his grip on the machine and, at the same time, gain control of the device. At last he was able to get his hands on it and gradually pull the lever back to the stop position. The sounds and lights had ceased as the spinning disc gradually had come to rest and we finally stopped. But where in creation were we?

"Where *are* we?" queried the Hatter? "This time, I really am sure this is not Wonderland or Londonland or any other land that I can recall visiting. And I am typically never really quite certain or sure of anything."

The Cheshire Cat piped in: "That's because you have never been to anywhere other than Wonderland or Londonland, as you call it.

Unless you want to count the visit to Lewis Carroll's house in Guildford as a separate land since we did actually 'land' there after our carriage flight. That was a quite an *uplifting* experience. It's too bad the carriage did not survive. Once this adventure is brought to a successful conclusion, if I want to travel by air again, I guess I will have to just '*wing it.*' Ha! 'Wing it' get it?"

Ignoring the Cheshire Cat, I looked around at the desolate barren landscape with a reddish hue that stretched for miles around us and wondered the same thing. Where are we?

Sherlock looked out at the terrain, examined the reddish soil at our feet, scrutinized it with his pocket microscope, sniffed at the air, stuck out his tongue and tasted it, and then slowly addressed us. "At least we are all alive for the moment, but for how long, I cannot guarantee. The local atmosphere of this place is very weak. Based on my work, *A Study of the Chemical Composition of Various Atmospheric Environments and Their Ability to Sustain Human Life,* it may not sustain us for very long. I am afraid with so many different minds influencing the Time Machine at the same time; we overloaded its functionality and standard operational process. We completely bypassed the time travel limitations maintained by the Time Guardians. It seems that the machine took us to the last thought that went through H. G. Wells' mind before we disappeared. Fellow travelers, we are on the planet Mars."

A stunned silence fell over our group, and the White Rabbit with his ears completely dropping tried to hide beneath the seat of the device. "I was only trying to help." he whispered. "M-M-Mr. Wells had said we were out of time, so I thought I had to do something. The Time M-M-Machine seemed to be the only answer."

"Something, yes. But not launch us clear off the planet, my cute and cuddly friend," voiced the Cheshire Cat. "You could have at least sent us to the moon where we would have had some green cheese to eat. How are we to prevent Wonderland from disappearing from way out here?"

The Hatter quivered and seemed to be shrinking into his oversized hat as he pointed a shaking hand toward the horizon and proclaimed, "I am not quite certain or sure, as is typical, but Wonderland may be the very least of our problems. What is that tripod-looking thing coming this way?"

Off in the distance, a tall three-legged machine was striding towards us. It was a gigantic, metal mechanical walking device with three articulated legs attached to a central pod or body that had flexible mechanical arms extending from each side of it like the tentacles of an octopus. I had never seen anything like it before. It was intimidating in the least. One of the arms seemed to be holding a separate device of some kind. I was wondering what it could be when a beam of intensely bright light burst from it and scorched a furrow into the ground not too far from us. The device fired a second time striking even closer to our group.

Sherlock quickly took control of the situation declaring, "Well, that answers the question of whether or not the natives are friendly here. They most definitely are *NOT!* Unicorn, Jabberwocky, can you do something about that machine?"

The Unicorn reared up on its hind legs striking a regal pose for just a moment and then raced straight towards the Martian machine, stopping in plain view directly in front of it. It struck the ground in front of the tripod with its hooves as if to say, "Here I am, you mechanical monstrosity. Try and catch me!" The Martian aimed and fired its heat ray weapon, but the Unicorn had already vanished from the spot and was taunting the machine from the other side kicking at the tripod's mechanical legs. The machine turned and tried to follow the Unicorn, firing its weapon wildly, but as I have already described, the Unicorn was so incredibly swift that the there was no possible way that the machine could catch it or focus its beam weapon on it.

The heat ray flashed to the left and to the right ripping scorch marks across the Martian terrain as it tried to fire at the Unicorn to no avail. While the machine's occupants were focused on the Unicorn, the Jabberwocky swooped down on it from behind and grabbed the heat ray device in its claws, struggling with the tentacles for control of it. The Jabberwocky finally gained control of the device and turned it back towards the central body of the machine. The heat ray sliced directly through the center of the machine, and the tripod crumpled to the ground with a loud crash.

Unfortunately, though, during the struggle for control of the weapon, the Jabberwocky had received a wound from the heat ray. As he returned to the ground in front of us, I could see the bloody laceration. I was at a complete loss as far as what to do, as I didn't have my medical bag with me. Not to mention I had no experience treating Jabberwockies. The Unicorn however raced up to the Jabberwocky and laid its spiral horn directly on the wound. There was a soft silver glow, and within seconds the wound had completely healed.

"That was amazing!" I exclaimed. "What a doctor you would make!"

The Unicorn replied with a sideways shake of his head saying, "No thank you. I make a much better Unicorn. Not to mention, I get the attention of all the fair maidens and princesses. But I do have to be careful these days. Unicorn hunters have started to use fair maidens to try and lure me into traps. I really need to be cautious of that."

Sherlock applauded the Unicorn and Jabberwocky saying, "Excellent work! Now we must get off of this planet before any more of these things show up."

I agreed and pointed out that it had better be quickly, as it appeared there were two more of them over near the horizon coming this way. Off in the distance, I could see them as they quickly clanked their way towards us making great strides with their long mechanical legs. The two new tripods came to a sudden stop when they saw the destroyed remains of the first machine. They seemed to be assessing the situation and communicating between themselves.

Sherlock explained to our group, "If we somehow travelled to Mars by overloading the Time Machine's operating system, then I deduce that it is only logical that we should be able to return home by doing the exact same thing again."

The Martians, meanwhile, had come to some sort of conclusion about the situation and had begun deploying a new and different weapon. This one was a long metal tube that fired a grey canister a great distance from where they stood. The first canister fired fell short, but it burst into a dense black smoke cloud that quickly spread over the terrain in all directions. It curled and bubbled as it crawled out across the Martian ground. I wasn't certain what it was, but somehow, I knew it was deadly. I pointed at it and advised, “That does not look very healthy at all. It’s probably some type of poison gas. We have got to get out of here.”

Sherlock hurried back over to the Time Machine, sat in the passenger seat, turned on the controls and directed us. “There is no time left. Everyone quickly, I want all of us to touch this machine together, and as I push the lever forward, let us all think of home. Ready? *Now*!”

Chapter 11.

Yet Another Very Strange Side Trip (But not unexpected all, things considered.)

Sherlock thrust the lever forward, and once again, the air around us exploded into a burst of light and color. It felt like I was inside a giant kaleidoscope that was being rotated in a whirlwind. The motion was horribly nauseating. It seemed as if the Time Machine also was weakening under the strain of transporting all of us at the same time. It creaked and groaned while the disc whirled madly away. Just as I thought I could no longer stand the motion, Sherlock finally pulled the lever to a stop, and the machine came to a halt on what looked like the remains of a giant chess board surrounded by a field with a large red castle off in the distance. In unison, the five Wonderland inhabitants cried out together "Home!"

I looked at Sherlock in disbelief. While Holmes and I had both thought of Wells' home, the rest of them had thought of their home in Wonderland, and there were five of them compared to the two of us. I imagine it was an honest mistake. Sherlock really should have been clearer in his instructions. You know what they say: '*Always be precise in your directions.*' But we were under a great deal of pressure at the time with the additional Martian tripods approaching us and that nasty looking black smoke weapon.

"Are we r-r-really truly home?" The White Rabbit questioned as he looked around in disbelief. "Is it still here?"

"You all know that I am never really quite certain or sure about anything," replied the Hatter also looking all around. "But this time I think it may just be possible we are home again. What do you think Cheshire?"

Before Cheshire could answer, a shrill, shrieking voice from somewhere nearby cried out, "Off with their heads! *Off* with their heads! All of them, off with their heads! And be quick about it. I want to see some headway here."

The Cheshire Cat dematerialized his body, rotated his floating head upside down and replied, "Yes, I am quite certain that we are home. That must be the Queen of Hearts. I would know her screeching, caterwauling voice anywhere. And I am not talking about cats on the wall. Her voice makes bag pipes sound positively sweet and finger nails on a blackboard sound absolutely soothing."

Sherlock expressed a note of surprise. "Why that is a remarkable coincidence, I published a detailed study on *An Annotated Comparison of Bag Pipe Music to Finger Nails on a Blackboard Focusing on All the Major and Minor Keys in 4/4 Tempo.* By the time I had finished with that paper, I was able to play *Scotland the Brave* on a blackboard just using my finger nails. Isn't that just fascinating? I am surprised, though; no one really wanted to hear me play it."

We all then turned to look in the direction of the shrill voice and saw a column of oversized playing cards sporting human heads, arms and legs come marching towards us at a quick pace. They were dressed in red and white displaying the Hearts suit and carrying spears and halberds or other nasty looking medieval weapons. They did not look friendly at all.

At the back of their column, regally dressed wearing a ruby studded golden crown, marched what appeared to be the Queen of Hearts. She was short and stocky, attired in a red and black playing card Hearts motif and carried a royal scepter. She looked less friendly than her army of playing cards.

"Who dares to trespass on the royal chess board?" she demanded. "There is so very little left of it there is no room for intruders, not even cute and cuddly rabbits. We shall have to have their heads for this. Guards, head them off, and then off with their heads. And remember, this time to use your heads. The last time you brought me heads of lettuce while you let the prisoners escape."

The White Rabbit's ears stood straight up and quivered when he heard "cute and cuddly" yet again, but most wisely, he refrained from saying anything. Drawing on his skills of observation, logic and deduction, Sherlock assessed the situation, boldly stepped forward and addressed the Queen: "Why, your Majesty, how could you think we are intruding when we are the chess pieces? We most certainly belong here. The rabbit in the blue coat is the pawn. The Unicorn and Dragon are the knights. This fine gentleman and I are the bishops. How dare you question us being here? It is you who are not prepared for a game of chess. Everyone knows that you don't play chess with a deck of playing cards. That would be almost as foolish as playing croquet with playing cards. If you persist in this folly I shall demand that you forfeit."

The Queen's face turned redder than her outfit. "What kind of nonsensical logic is that? How can you demand that I forfeit when it is obvious that I only have two feet? Do I have to put my foot down here? You wouldn't have a leg to stand on. Not only that, you are being very impertinent. And what folly would you prefer me to persist in? The folly only runs twice a day and the morning folly has already left. Are you trying to derail this conversation? We must stay on track."

Sherlock firmly stood his ground and replied, "Your Majesty, if you are the Queen, then you can order a special folly any time you wish, to carry you anywhere you want to go. I am not suggesting that you get carried away here, but if we don't complete our task, then Wonderland and all of you will vanish forever. You would have no one to rule, and those are the rules.
Trust me, you can ask the Time Guardians yourself."

The Queen hesitated for a moment looking rather perplexed and responded, "What are you talking about? I have never seen a time garden. I imagine it would be full of tics as well as tocs. Not to mention, the garden would be full of time flies. Why would anyone even give it a second thought? However, if as you say, there is not a minute to waste and the hour is at hand and as you said, since I am the queen, I can order a special folly. I hereby command a special folly." Then with a flourishing wave of her royal scepter she added, "Now!"

Much to my surprise, a vehicle looking something remotely like a trolley came clanging and banging in from the distance on tracks that somehow appeared on the ground in front of it as it approached us. When I say that it looked like a trolley, that is an exaggeration. It was more accurately something that looked like it might have wanted to be a trolley but could not quite make up its mind on the details of subject. It had wheels and seats and polished brass poles and most everything else a normal trolley would have, but none of them were where they belonged. It was as if someone took all the parts for a trolley car, mixed them up, threw them in a pile and they stuck together. It was a true folly.

The bizarre looking vehicle rattled up to us and screeched to a halt with its bell ringing the entire time. The Queen and her army of playing cards then boarded the folly. She gave a twirl of her royal scepter and commanded, "Off and ahead. Off and ahead!"

The trolley, or folly, or whatever you want to call it, clanged and banged its way "off and ahead" into the distance with the bell constantly clamoring until it faded away.

The Cheshire Cat reformed its body, smiled and sighed. "It's so good to be home and see that things are still on track. You certainly engineered a clever way out of that situation. That was using your caboose. When the Queen showed up with her army of playing cards, I thought the game was over for us all. That it was check mate so to speak. So, what do we do next most logical and deductive one? Would you like me to catch a few time flies?
They might possibly be able to help us return quicker and save some time."

The Hatter raised his hand, struck a public speaking pose, and pronounced, "I am almost sure you all know, that time flies like an arrow, but did you know that fruit flies like a banana."

The White Rabbit meekly responded, "And butter flies like a flower."

To which the Unicorn added, "Don't forget, horse flies like a barn."

The Jabberwocky concluded the discussion by interjecting,
"And dragon flies like a knight. They are rather tasty you know."

Sherlock looked at the Jabberwocky and asked me if I had a Vorpal sword handy, to which the Jabberwocky replied, "I was joking, oh deep thinking and humorless one. I make no bones about it. That was in poor taste. I shall have to eat my words no matter how tasteless the comment. Might you have any pickled herring sandwiches to go with them? That would help immensely. Why I would be speechless with appreciation. Some tea would also help if you have any."

Sherlock shook his head, sighed and countered, "Watson, we have got to get out of this place before they drive me crazy."

Nodding in agreement, I turned to where the Time Machine had been sitting, but to my surprise and dismay it had vanished! It was nowhere to be seen! "Sherlock!" I exclaimed, "How are we to do that? Now the Time Machine has gone missing. And there are no signs of where it went."

Chapter 12.

One More Very Strange Side Trip (And this time some talking flowers.)

Sherlock spun around quickly to see and verified that the machine was indeed gone. Where its battered remains had previously stood, there was nothing but an indentation in the ground.

Sherlock turned to the group and was about to speak when the White Rabbit held up his paws and loudly exclaimed, "It wasn't m-m-me. I didn't do it! Really, I didn't. I was here in front of you the whole time. You can ask my watch."

Sherlock answered saying, "Don't worry, Rabbit, no one has said that you did anything *this* time. I want to ask, if any of you saw anything while the Queen of Hearts was leaving on the folly?"

In a panic, the group began answering in their typical fashion, of all of them speaking at the same time, starting with the Cheshire Cat shaking his head, "No, no, not at all."

Jabberwocky looking to the right and left repeatedly voiced, "I didn't see anything. Did you see anything? I really did not see anything!"

"But I wasn't looking in that direction," implored the White Rabbit.

In his speaking pose the Hatter declared, "I am not really certain or sure, and you know I am never really quite certain of *anything*, but I will say it certainly *looks* like it's gone."

"But how could it just disappear?" the Cat wondered while rotating its head. "Wasn't anyone watching it?"

The jabberwocky raised one claw and questioned, "Maybe it left on its own. Did anyone turn it off?"

The Cat reversed the direction of its spinning head, demanding, "How could it just *disappear*? I'm the only one that can disappear. Cheshire Cats can do that you know."

Dropping his gold watch, the White Rabbit slouched down to the ground with his ears and his whiskers drooping. "Now we are really out of time. We're doomed. We're DOOMED!"

The Unicorn then suggested, "Why don't we just follow the footprints?"

"Footprints? What footprints?" cried Holmes. "Watson, you said there were no signs."

"Well I did not see any," I replied rather embarrassed. "I did not see anything useful. Why don't you come take a look? You're the detective. This is your area of specialization."

This entire mad tea party adventure was beginning to get to me. Normally I could handle Sherlock's superiority in everything related to his cases, but here nothing was as it seemed, and everything seemed so strange and unreal. It was as if logic and common sense had been turned completely upside down. Yet, somehow Sherlock had still maintained his rational composure. How does he do it? Sherlock walked over to where the Time Machine had been standing and examined the area carefully. He took out his pocket magnifying glass, got down on the ground and studied certain areas with even more scrutiny. I watched him closely but could not detect what he was looking at, so I just waited until Sherlock stood up. “Well?” I finally asked him, “What did you find?

Sherlock stood there looking down at the ground and answered, “I am not quite sure yet. There are two distinctly clawed footprints that don’t go anywhere, and I am not at all surprised that they are not to be found in my *Complete Guide to the Identification of the Footprints of All Living Creatures on the Planet Earth.* It is obvious that a winged creature landed here briefly. Only long enough to snatch the machine and fly off with it. What it would want with the Time Machine, I have no idea, unless it wants the parts for its nest. It must be quite a large creature to be able carry off a machine that big.”

Looking at the group of Wonderland inhabitants, Sherlock started to ask them a question but stopped, turned and looked at me and asked, “Do I dare?”

I shrugged my shoulders and replied, “Really, what choice do you have?”

Sherlock sighed, “You’re right.” slowly turned back to them and asked, “Would any of you happen to know what creatures here in Wonderland would be large enough to carry off the Time Machine?”

As was quite typical he received a multitude of wildly different answers.

“The Jubjub Bird!” whispered the White Rabbit looking fearful.

“The Griffon!” called out the Cheshire Cat. “He has wings and claws.”

"I am not really certain, but you already know I am never really quite certain or sure of anything," offered the Hatter.

"We're doomed!" cried the White Rabbit.

"*The Jabberwocky*," stated the Jabberwocky quite straight forwardly.

When Sherlock gave him a puzzled look, the Jabberwocky countered. "YOU specifically asked what creatures in Wonderland *could* have carried off the Time Machine. I assure you that I am quite capable of carrying off that machine." He then twisted his long neck to stare directly at Sherlock. "I also assure you that it most certainly was not me."

He then withdrew his head from in front of Sherlock and proceeded to, one by one, examine his long, sharp claws.

Sherlock raised his eyes, shook his head back and forth and acknowledged, "Yes, Jabberwocky. Trust me. I am quite certain it was not you." Turning back to the group he asked, "Any more suggestions?"

"The Monstrous Crow?" offered the Hatter to which the Cheshire Cat replied, "Hatter, the Monstrous Crow has not been seen in Wonderland for ages. No one as seen him for quite some time, even before Wonderland residents started disappearing."

Finally, the Unicorn suggested, "Could it have been the Bandersnatch? She is certainly capable."

"The Bandersnatch!" All the rest echoed at once, "Yes… the Bandersnatch. She is very frumious, most frumious indeed. It could very well have been Bandersnatch."

Sherlock looked at them and answered, "I am *so* glad that I asked. Who or what is the *Bandersnatch*?"

The White Rabbit raised a trembling paw, leaned forward, looked to the left and to the right, whispered in a low voice, "The Bandersnatch…" and promptly fainted.

The Unicorn, however, once again explained, "It is a fierce flying creature with very long legs, a long neck, and snapping jaws."

"Why that sounds almost like me." offered the Jabberwocky proudly.

Ignoring the Jabberwocky, the Unicorn persisted with his description of the Bandersnatch: "It is quite fast, but I assure you nowhere near as fast as I am. It is noted for being quite frumious, which is to say both *fuming* and *furious* at the same time. What it would want with the Time Machine I can't imagine."

Sherlock exhaled and stated, "If we are going to ever get out of here, we will just have to find out now, won't we?"

I was perplexed. "But how are we to follow it if flew away and there are no more than two footprints?"

The Jabberwocky flexed its wings and stated, "We don't need to follow it. If it went home, then we know where it went. Its home is in the Tulgey Woods not far from where I live. I can be there in no time at all."

The Unicorn, of course, replied, "In the time it took you to say that, I have been there and back several times. She is home in her nest, and so is our Time Machine."

"Excellent!" said Holmes. "Do you think you and Jabberwocky can get it back?"

The Unicorn shook its head, "That may be a tad problematic. I think you should come with us."

The Cheshire Cat, grinning widely as usual chirped in, "A 'tad' did you say? I know a swamp where we can find some tad poles if we need any. They are very useful if we need to vault any tads. That was an exciting event at the last track and field competition - Tad Pole Vaulting -- almost as much fun as the High-and–Go-Seek Jump."

Needless to say, I didn't inquire as to what the "High-and-Go-Seek Jump" could possibly be.

The White Rabbit had regained consciousness, and Sherlock addressed the group. "Apparently, I will be needed in retrieving the Time Machine, so I have to go with them. Hatter, Rabbit, and Cheshire, if we leave you here, do you promise not to move from this place? We will be back as soon as possible and hopefully with the machine."

"I am absolutely glued to the ground," The Hatter assured us.

The eyes of the White Rabbit, however, grew very large, and he started quivering as he exclaimed, "You're leaving us?" At which point he again fainted and fell to the ground.

The Hatter looked at him and stated, "It doesn't look like he is going anywhere. And as I said, neither am I. My feet are *glued* to the ground. I think I may have stepped in some tree sap or something. My feet really *are* glued to the ground. I knew this would turn out to be a sticky situation. But don't worry, I will stick to it."

"Sort it out while we are gone, Hatter, and make sure the White Rabbit doesn't run off anywhere." Turning, he addressed the cat, "Cheshire keep an eye on both of them if you please."

The cat grinned, blinked and snickered, "Well it's a good thing I have two eyes, since there are two of them. At least we are seeing eye-to-eye on this. I can't imagine how 'eye' would manage if there were three of them."

Sherlock turned to the Unicorn and asked, "Since you are so swift, can you take Dr. Watson and myself to the Tulgey Woods one at a time?"

At that point, I wasn't sure what was happening, but all of a sudden, it felt as if the Unicorn was materializing directly beneath me, picking me up on its back. I frantically wrapped my arms around its neck and held on for dear life as it took off like a bullet.

The few trees I was able to see in the blur I remember of that ride seemed to spring up in front of us and instantly vanish just as quickly. Several times, I shut my eyes fearing we were certain to crash into a tree. But before I could react, I found myself sitting on the ground near a forest, with the Unicorn and Holmes astride him standing nearby. The Jabberwocky was complaining to the Unicorn, "I really don't see why you got to give both of them a ride."

Sherlock motioned them to be quite and pointed towards the woods. In the branches of one of the trees was precariously perched the Time Machine along with numerous other loose branches, bicycles, brass beds, bits of old machines and other miscellaneous objects. Our machine was a part of a nest. Sitting in it was the Bandersnatch, a creature even stranger looking than the Jabberwocky, if that was at all possible.

The Bandersnatch had very long spindly legs and a long neck. Its wings were folded up, so I could not see them well, but the claws and jaws that I could see were fearsome and ferocious. Its arms seemed to be of an average length, if there is such a thing for a beast such as that. The creature was a greenish-golden color that blended in well with the trees. Its eyes were purplish, and they darted back and forth as it continuously looked around the forest presumably guarding its nest. Somehow her eyes had a very sad and lonely look to them.

I looked at Holmes, the Unicorn, and Jabberwocky, and whispered, "Now what do we do?" I had envisioned an all-out assault on the creature in an attempt to get our machine back, but I was surprised when Jabberwocky took control of the situation, rising up and openly galumphing toward the Bandersnatch. Jabberwocky made a formal bow to the creature and addressed it in a burbling voice, "Greetings Lady Bandersnatch, most spindly and golden-green one. I bring you pleasant tidings this brillig and Frabjous day."

The creature's long neck and head spun swiftly towards the Jabberwocky and it answered sharply, "You mean you bring intruders here, you scaly, chortling beast. I see the other three with you. What are you doing bringing humans and a Unicorn here to my nest? No one comes here except to do me harm."

At that point, Sherlock stood up, walked towards it, bowed gracefully and spoke. "We mean you no harm, green lady of the woods. We are on an urgent mission to save Wonderland and all of its inhabitants including yourself. If we do not complete our task by the end of the day, this entire place and everything in it will cease to exist."

It careened its neck toward Sherlock. "Really? Is this true? How do I know you are telling the truth?"

I was going to mention Sherlock's famous paper on *Determining Whether or Not Someone is Telling the Truth by Observing Breathing Patterns, Eye Blinking, and Sneezing*, but I thought it best not to interrupt.

"And if you are telling the truth, what are you doing here instead of being somewhere else off saving Wonderland? Either way, I think you should leave. You are intruding, and the only thing intruders want to do is run around swinging Vorpal swords and slicing off heads. No one comes here just for a friendly chat over a cup of tea. Go on. Off with you, or I shall have to get frumious. Trust me. You really don't want to see me when I am frumious."

At that point, the Unicorn elegantly stepped forward and gently addressed her. "Verdant creature of the trees calm yourself. Be not concerned. I can vouch for this human and the other one as well. They have risked their lives repeatedly to save Wonderland and all of us in it. You *know* that Unicorns are completely truthful, and I say that everything he says is true and accurate. The reason we are here in Tulgey Woods is because our transportation device is somehow in your nest. We don't know how it ended up there, but we desperately need it back to complete our task to save Wonderland."

The Bandersnatch's eyes flared, and her claws flexed. "Ha! I knew you were after something. They are always after something. A great number of odd and interesting things end up in my nest. Which object might be your transportation device?"

The Jabberwocky flapped its wings and rose to the level of the nest and pointed a long claw. "It is the brass and wooden device with the large disc on the back end. If you would return it to us, we would be happy to replace it with something else even more interesting and enjoyable."

The Bandersnatch recoiled its neck and head in surprise. "Do you mean you want to actually *give* me something? No one has ever given me anything before. That is why I collect odd and interesting things to keep me company. Why various odd things find their way to my nest. Yes, yes, you may take it. It was in rather poor condition to begin with. If that pathetic thing is your transportation device, then Wonderland still may not have much of a chance."

The jabberwocky extended its claws and delicately snatched the device out of the nest and lowered it to the ground in front of Sherlock. It was fortunately not in any worse condition than before it had disappeared, which isn't really saying much, as it was just barely in one piece to begin with.

The Bandersnatch, with her eyes wide open, was really enthusiastic at that point. "All right, what are you going to bring me? I do love surprises, or at least pleasant surprises. You can't take the travel device until you bring me something. What do you have for me?"

I was at a loss for what to do next, as we didn't really have anything with us to give to the Bandersnatch. At that point, the Unicorn blurred, vanished, and then reappeared with an uprooted clump of brightly colored flowers held gently in its teeth. It pawed a hole in the ground directly in front of and beneath the nest of the Bandersnatch. There it delicately placed the flowers in the ground and carefully replaced the dirt around them. The Unicorn addressed the flowers encouraging them, "Okay, Snapdragons, welcome to your new home and your new friend."

The Unicorn looked up towards the creature's nest and called out, "Bandersnatch, come down and meet your new companions. You stated that no one ever comes just to talk or chat, so I knew you must be lonely. Here are talking Snapdragon flowers to keep you company."

The Bandersnatch cautiously descended from its nest to the ground and looked at the flowers quizzically. "Talking flowers?" she asked, "What a novel idea. Who would have thought of such a thing? It certainly isn't very logical. It sounds like something from a literary nonsense tale. The next thing you know, you'll be telling me that Time Machines really exist." Sherlock and I looked at each other and both of us decided not to comment.

The Snapdragon flowers took one look at the Bandersnatch and all cried out in unison, "Mummy!" and they all began talking to her at the same time. The Bandersnatch lowered its head to the ground in front of them beaming and was immediately lost in conversation.

Sherlock smiled and asked, "Jabberwocky, can you transport our machine back to the rest of the group while Unicorn transports Dr. Watson and I?"

Who would have ever believed what had just occurred? I was ready to launch an attack on the fearsome creature, and we ended up leaving it engaged in conversation with a group of talking Snapdragons. It's no wonder they call this place Wonderland.

Now if only the three visitors whom we had left behind were still waiting for us, we would have been able to get back to the business of saving this strange and unusual place. As I was soon to find out, however, that was a very big "IF".

Chapter 13.

A Very Strange Discovery
(And not surprisingly Sherlock had already written a paper on it.)

I will spare you the details of my second near instantaneous Unicorn ride other than to say that when the Unicorn dropped me off to go retrieve Sherlock, it took me over a minute before I dared open my eyes. To this day, I still have nightmares of near collisions with trees at speeds that you could not possibly imagine. When I finally did open my eyes though, the Rabbit, Hatter and Cheshire Cat were nowhere to be seen. What could have happened to them? We really weren't gone all that long. Jabberwocky had replaced the Time Machine exactly where it had previously been and was airborne looking to see if they were anywhere in the surrounding area. Sherlock was already on his hands and knees examining the vicinity for clues. It may sound odd, but imaginary or not, I was concerned for our missing travel companions.

"Have you found anything?" I asked worriedly. "Do you think they may have already vanished from Wonderland like all the others?"

Sherlock stood and looked at me. "Well they are definitely gone and not here, but they are not *gone* gone, if you know what I mean. You know, this really is exactly the phenomena that I addressed in my paper on *The Analysis and Classification of Transitory States Based on Observable Side Effects Upon the Surrounding Environment with Particular Emphasis on Rabbit Hair.* Since we have been here, Watson, I have discovered that when something or some creature disappears from Wonderland, there is no trace of it whatsoever left behind. They are truly gone. But if you look closely, you can see here where the White Rabbit fainted and fell to the ground; there are still some of his white hairs present. If he had actually vanished from Wonderland, there would be no white hairs or any other evidence of his previous existence. If you understand what I am saying, he would be *completely* gone."

Sherlock moved slightly over to the left, bent down, and pointed at the ground. "The same goes for the Hatter. He had said that he had stepped in some tree sap and was literally stuck to the ground. You can see that the grass is torn away from where he had last been standing when we left them. If he had vanished, then the grass would not be disturbed. Wherever they went to, you will see blades of grass still stuck to the Hatter's shoes. It is all part of proper observation, Watson. I assure you that, while they are not here, they are definitely somewhere."

Standing up and moving back to where the White Rabbit had been laying on the ground, he bent down again and looked even closer. "And if you look very closely, you can see a slight indentation in the dirt on either side of where White Rabbit had been laying. That clearly indicates to me he was picked up by a very large claw. The Hatter was standing, which is why there are no claw indentions in the ground. But as I mentioned previously, the grass that was stuck to his shoes was pulled away and torn from the rest of the field. I am positive they were both picked up and carried away by a very large-winged creature."

"That would probably be the Jubjub Bird," the Unicorn offered. "He is a nasty one."

"What about the Cheshire Cat?" I asked Sherlock. "What do think happened to him?"

"Now, that is an entirely different situation. Since he can dematerialize at will…"

"Actually, I can dematerialize not just at 'Will', but at anyone I choose to, which by the way, is a very good thing. That Jubjub Bird really gave me the Willies." Much to our surprise, the Cheshire Cat suddenly faded back into view close to where Sherlock was standing.

"That was a very astute explanation, most observant and comprehensive one," the Cat grinned. "You explained it exactly as it occurred. Just a few minutes after you four left, the Jubjub Bird swooped down and snatched the White Rabbit and the Hatter from where they were and flew off with them in that direction."

He pointed a paw in the direction of the Queen of Hearts' Castle and went on: "I was able to dematerialize, so I did, and the bird was not able to touch me. I believe that we may need to pay a visit to the Queen if we want our friends back."

"But why would she do that?" I wondered out loud. "I thought Sherlock had made it very clear; if we did not complete our task, then Wonderland, her Majesty the Queen, and her entire kingdom would disappear forever. She seemed to have understood when she left in the folly."

"Maybe she had a change of heart," suggested the Cheshire Cat. "For all of her playing card army and all that, she can be pretty heartless you know. There is no use having heart-to-heart conversations with her. She does whatever suits her. It's all in the cards, as they say."

"We will have to get them back," said Sherlock. "But we need to leave someone here to guard the Time Machine. We certainly don't want it to disappear again."

"Or we could all go together, and the Jabberwocky can carry it to the Queen's castle," I suggested. "That way when we retrieve the White Rabbit and the Hatter, we can all leave as soon as possible and get back to Wells' house, so we can finish this madness."

"And continue with the previous madness?" the Cheshire Cat grinned widely. "It's really no use. We're all quite mad here."

"Actually, Watson, that is not a bad idea, if you do not mind carrying the machine again Jabberwocky." Sherlock asked as he turned to the creature.

The Jabberwocky, however, was beaming with pride. "Of course, I don't mind. Did I not mention that I was more than capable of carrying the Time Machine when you first asked what Wonderland creatures were able to do so?"

"Excellent!" said Holmes. "Cheshire, can you ride in the machine with the Jabberwocky while Watson and I ride with the Unicorn to the Queen's castle? That is, without touching any of the machine's controls, of course."

The Cat vanished from where it had been sitting and reappeared floating just above the chair of the Time Machine. It gave a sly grin and nodded to indicate that it was in the Time Machine, but obviously not touching anything. "Why of course, most curious and cautious one. I would not even think of touching the controls. You needn't worry. I have everything under control or actually under me as I just happen to be floating above the controls. I can do that you know. We Cheshire Cats are noted for that."

I was not very enthusiastic about the idea of another high-speed ride dodging trees on the back of the Unicorn, but I knew we had to complete this as soon as possible, so I tried to prepare myself. I had just closed my eyes when I felt the Unicorn's close presence beneath me again. I experienced a whirling rush of wind and the notion of trees flying past me at impossible speeds, when I suddenly found myself standing on the lawn in front of the Queen of Heart's castle.

A croquet court was laid out on the castle lawn with nine playing card soldiers bending over acting as the wickets. The White Rabbit and Hatter were tied to poles on either side of the Queen of Hearts' throne, which seemed to be placed in the position of the starting post of one side of the croquet court. There was a sudden scrambling and shuffling around of the playing card wickets changing their locations after the Jabberwocky had set the Time Machine down, and it was somehow sitting at the exact opposite end of the court in the position of the other starting post.

Behind the Queen's throne perched a particularly vicious looking oversized bird in a vibrant red and white plumage. I was sure that this was the feared Jubjub Bird. I did not have a good feeling about this whole arrangement at all.

Chapter 14.

A Very Strange Game of Croquet (Only Sherlock Holmes could have managed this one.)

Standing next to me were Sherlock and the Unicorn, and in front of her throne was the Queen of Hearts with a very angry expression on her face.

"I don't know who you are or what your game is, but I can certainly see that it is a foot. I have tried to keep you at arm's length, but I need to hand it to you, you certainly know how to keep ahead of the game. You stated that Wonderland and its inhabitants are disappearing, and you are absolutely correct. I am not sure how you managed to do it, but all of the hedgehogs and flamingos have simply vanished from Wonderland. Now how am I supposed to play croquet?" she screamed while gesturing wildly.

Pointing a finger at Holmes she carried on, "I am positive that you had a hand in this, so rather than take up arms against you, you have left me no other option than this. Whether you have the stomach for it, or not, I must put my foot down. It's quite simple. If you want your companions back alive, you will play this croquet game against me per the following two rules:

1. The first player to maneuver his or her imaginary croquet hedgehog, using imaginary flamingo mallets, across the court to the opposite post wins.

2. All shots must be accurately described by the player and conform to the Standard Queen's Rules of Wonderland Croquet."

The Queen turned and pointed to a nearby pedestal on which there sat a book that must have been at least twelve inches thick. It was titled, *The Standard Queen's Rules of Wonderland Croquet: Abridged Edition.*

"If you win, you get your friends back alive and you can all leave. If you lose, you and all of your friends remain here playing croquet until Wonderland vanishes and the game is over for good. Those are my rules."

What was she talking about? This was insanity. Every second we lost could spell the difference between life and death, or at least disappearing forever, for all of them, and she wanted to play imaginary croquet?

Much to my surprise, Sherlock walked to the pedestal, leafed casually through the pages of the huge rule book, stepped forward, took some imaginary back-and-forth swings of a mallet and said, "I accept your Majesty. But you should be aware that, in addition to having written my magazine article on *The Logic and Geometry of Lining up Croquet Shots for Maximum Efficiency,* I have also published an entire series on *The Manipulation and Coordination of the Sensory Perception of Imagined Physical Actions on a Playing Field with Particular Emphasis as it Pertains to the Game of Croquet.* I am so experienced in this, that I have played and won entire matches of imaginary croquet with my eyes imaginarily blind-folded and one hand imaginarily tied behind my back. Allow me to demonstrate."

Sherlock walked over to the Time Machine, which served as the starting post for his side of the court, turned to the Cheshire Cat, held out the up-turned palm of his hand, and stated, "A Hedgehog if you please."

The Cat, of course, made the motion of handing Sherlock a Hedgehog, which he pretended to hold up for the Queen to see. Sherlock bent over, placed the imaginary Hedgehog on the lawn, loosened up his legs and arms, performed an elegant backswing with, of course, the imaginary flamingo mallet, and followed through with his swing.

To my astonishment, as the imaginary flamingo hit the imaginary Hedgehog, there was a very unimaginary and audible sound of the two making contact.

"Ah Ha!" cried Sherlock. "It went right through the first two wickets, bounced off of that pebble in the court right there, proceeded to go through the third wicket, hit that clump of grass, reflected backwards off of it and lined up perfectly for the fourth and center wicket. I now have three shots available."

That was amazing and quite creative on his part. I was sure that Sherlock would have this nonsense wrapped up in no time at all. The Queen of Hearts, however, had other thoughts on the subject.

"Guards!" she called out, and the center playing card wicket quickly straightened up and was about to run off, when the Cheshire cat pounced on it and forced it back into a hoop position. Sherlock quickly made a backswing and swung his imagined flamingo, and again there was an audible clunking sound of it contacting the imagined hedgehog.

"Straight through again," he calmly stated. "And this time that gust of wind, caused by the Jabberwocky's wings, has blown the ball back and to the left to place it right in front of the fifth wicket. Of course, that was perfectly legal per the rules; if you check *Section 3, Sub-section 8.5, Paragraph 2 on Atmospheric*

Conditions and Effects of Wind Naturally Created or Otherwise."

"GUARDS!" the Queen screamed again, but this time even louder. "Do something!"

The fifth playing card wicket that had been caught off guard jumped up to the upright position and was going to spear Sherlock's hedgehog, when the Unicorn stepped in front of it, bent its head down, and with a sharp twist of its horn, knocked the spear well off into the distance where it impaled the side of a tree. The Unicorn pointed its glowing spiral horn at the playing card and asked: "Now would you like to end up in the same position as your spear, or have I made my point?"

The playing card wicket took one look at the Unicorn's glowing horn and immediately dove back down into the hoop position trembling as he did.

The Unicorn smiled at him adding, "Good choice. It would have been pointless to resist."

Sherlock, meanwhile, had taken his next shot and launched the envisioned hedgehog towards the fifth wicket; however, a wall of playing card soldiers had taken a defensive position in front of the wicket to prevent the hedgehog from getting past. The Cheshire Cat, not to be out done, came bounding towards their direction, leaped at them, and in midair dematerialized its body so it was just a head crying out, "Heads up everyone!" crashing into the left side of the row of cards and knocking them all out of the way.

"Excellently done, Cheshire and Unicorn," Sherlock nodded as he walked over to the new position of the fantasized hedgehog, which apparently had followed a perfectly curved furrow in the lawn that had been created by the Unicorn to place it directly in front of the last two wickets.

*"**GUARDS**!!!!"* screamed the Queen yet again. "I will have your heads for this!"

The remaining two playing card wicket soldiers struggled desperately to escape but were firmly held in their position by the claws of the Jabberwocky, who smiled and casually voiced, "I do believe it is your shot, most accurate and croquet talented one. The path is clear." Sherlock was in the process of swinging his imagined flamingo for the final shot to end the game when the Jubjub Bird, with a hideously shrill scream and its claws viciously extended, came diving straight towards him.

"Look out!" I cried, but they were too far away, and I could not reach my service revolver quickly enough, so there was nothing I could do. I thought Sherlock was done for, when suddenly the Bandersnatch came swooping in from the opposite direction, grabbing the Jubjub Bird in mid-flight and flinging it out of the court and against the wall of the castle where it crumpled to the ground in a flurry of feathers. Sherlock was able to complete his shot, and he raised his arms in victory.

The Bandersnatch landed in the croquet court and congratulated Sherlock: "That was an excellent shot, most truthful and vouched-for one. I had just wanted to come by and say thank you again for my wonderful new Snapdragon friends. They are so delightful and that was most kind of you. I simply had to find you all to say thank you again. It looked like that bird-brained combination of nails on a chalkboard and a moldy feather blanket was going to interfere with your game, so I got rid of it for you. But then what can you expect from birds? They are so aggressive that one would think they were related to dinosaurs. And I am sure you all know how that turned out."

The White Rabbit and the Hatter both gave a loud cheer as an audible clink of a make-believe hedgehog struck the Queen's throne and their ropes fell to the ground, freeing them. The Queen of Hearts stepped forward, curtsied and, most surprisingly, in a very calm and formal voice stated, "I must congratulate you sir. That was an outstanding game of croquet. It would have even been great standing inside. In fact, you are certainly standing in good standing inside or outside. It was quite excellent, really. The best game I have had in years. You must come back sometime again for a rematch. It's the Queen's prerogative you know. It is in the rule book. You *do* have to return for a rematch." Sherlock bowed and replied, "Yes, I know. It's on page 753, paragraph 5, sub-section 2, *The Queen's Prerogatives on Rematches.* When my current task is through, I shall endeavor to return for a rematch. But I really must be going now, Your Majesty."

"Well, then be off with you!" she commanded. "And not just with your heads. All of you be gone!" And with that she turned and paraded towards her castle with the bedraggled remains of her playing card army following behind her. Sherlock, meanwhile, was thanking the Bandersnatch for showing up and assisting when it did.

"No problem at all," The Bandersnatch replied. "I was happy to assist, but I really must return home to the wee ones or they will be plotting who knows what kind of garden mischief."

With that, the golden-green creature took off, and we were finally, all of us together with the Time Machine again in our possession.

At last we would able to go home, but would there be enough time left?

Chapter 15.

A Very Strange but Much Nicer Journey (And what incredibly beautiful music!)

As we all gathered around the Time Machine, I pointed out that we really had to leave, but I also asked Sherlock whether or not he thought the device could handle one more trip. It was already in rather poor condition when we had first arrived. We had overloaded its capabilities twice, and it been carted all over Wonderland by the Bandersnatch and the Jabberwocky.

Sherlock looked over the Time Machine. The rotating disc was warped and scorched. The varnished wood had been cracked in several places, and some of the brass railings were completely bent out of shape. "We have no choice, Watson. We must return to H. G. Wells' home and then to our flat on Baker Street if we are to succeed. Now, if we can all focus on the very SAME place, the home of H. G. Wells, let us try this again."

As Sherlock started to sit down in the passenger's chair of the Time Machine to try again, a soft ethereal music seemed to surround us all. It filled the area and sounded like it could have been a harp or a flute, or perhaps both of them together, or even something else entirely, totally unidentifiable but still incredibly beautiful. I had never heard anything quite like it before. It had a celestial, Celtic sound to it and was most enchanting and mystical, filling me with a great sense of peace. I had no idea what it could have been."

"What *is* that music?" I asked, "And where is it coming from?"

"In this place who knows," countered Sherlock looking all around.

The Unicorn held his head up high listening intently and answered, "I *know* who that is. That is Pixy Music. I would recognize that sound anywhere. She is the most musically gifted of all the Pixies and faire folk. Her music is quite beyond description. There is no one else like her. That is why they call her Pixy *Music*, because she literally *is* 'Pixy Music'. Isn't she just beautiful? There really is no comparison."

Sherlock closed his eyes, remained still and listened intently before he responded, "You know before today, I would have said that there are no such thing as Pixies, or Unicorns, or any of you really for that matter. But here we are, all together, and I have to say that is without question the most beautiful music I have ever heard in my life. My violin playing can never compare to that."

Under my breath I added, "Sherlock, your violin playing could never even *hope* to compare to that beautiful music. Your violin playing is more comparable to a cat being tortured on a rack."

Fortunately, he didn't hear me, but the Cheshire Cat did give me a particularly nasty look.

"Yes!" the Unicorn enthusiastically declared looking up in to the air in the direction of the music. "Yes, yes, and thank you sincerely. We are truly honored, Pixy Music. Thank you again."

The Unicorn turned to the rest of us with a smile and a warm glow emanating from him. "We are safe. Pixy Music will provide protection for our return journey to the home of Mr. Wells. She observed the condition of the Time Machine and knew that it would never survive the stress of one more journey. It would have completely failed, and we would have been lost forever. She wove a song of protection around it with her music. Now we can safely go home." And looking at Sherlock, the Unicorn added, "That is, to the home of H. G. Wells, of course."

Sherlock roused himself as if from a trance, placed his hand on the control lever of the Time Machine and began. "All right, one more time. Everyone think of H. G. Wells' home and touch the machine now!"

He carefully moved the lever forward, and this time it was as if we were surrounded by a celestial choir of harps and flutes. The rainbow lights and kaleidoscope were there almost the same as before, but it was not as chaotic or violent. It was a much smoother trip as we floated, more than raced, through the cosmos. The home of H. G. Wells seemed to be materializing all around us. We were once again back in his laboratory, and Sherlock slowly reversed the lever to the stop position for the last time. When Sherlock released the lever, and we all let go of it, the Time Machine collapsed into a pile of wood, brass and wires, while the spinning disc rolled off into a corner and fell to the ground with a loud metallic clang.

H. G. Wells looked at the ruined remains of his Time Machine and frowned, "You certainly are hard on your traveling accommodations. Remind me never to loan you my carriage in the future." He then broke in to a cheerful smile and exclaimed, "Welcome back everyone! I am glad you are all home and safe it seems. Is everyone all right?"

As we stepped away from the debris of the destroyed Time Machine, I thought I heard the last echoes of the enchanting music that had protected us on our journey home. I looked up, smiled, and turned to Wells. “Yes, we are all fine, but you would not believe where we have been to.”

The Hatter excitedly interjected, "I know I am usually never really certain or sure about anything, but this time, I am positive! We have been to MARS! Can you believe it? MARS! The Martians have giant mechanical walking tripods and heat rays and poison gas and maybe something even more terrible! They may even be planning an invasion!” At that point, with his eyes wide and shaking all over, he pulled his hat completely over his head, and the White Rabbit once again fainted. Wells, meanwhile, seemed deeply lost in thought while talking to himself, "Hmm, a Martian invasion with tripods and heat rays. What an interesting concept. I shall have to consider that as a possibility for a future novel: "The War of the Planets", or perhaps, “The War of the Worlds”, or something similar to that. I like it.”

We all returned to the tea room, much to the approval of the Unicorn and Jabberwocky. Sherlock and I apologized for the condition of Wells’ Time Machine and told him everything that had occurred while we were away.

“Amazing!” Wells replied. “Just amazing! I will never look at the planet Mars in the same way again. And Wonderland as well, that was incredible. Considering all that you told me, it is perhaps better that the Time Machine is destroyed. That way, it will never fall into the wrong hands. However, I am still reluctant to loan you my carriage.”

Holmes stood up and shaking the hand of his host, said goodbye. "Mr. Wells my dear sir, you have been most helpful, most helpful indeed. We must all take leave of you now and return to 221-B

Baker Street. It is there that the final portion of this journey will begin. Where it will end depends on what happens next. Time is indeed of the essence."

Chapter 16.

A Very Strange Brew (But really rather tasty.)

Hearing that Holmes had proclaimed the end of the gathering, The Unicorn proceeded to finish the rest of the tea, and the Jabberwocky emptied the last of the sandwich trays. The Hatter roused the White Rabbit, echoing, "Wake up Rabbit! It's time to go. Time is a-wasting. There's no time like the present. Let's be timely now. It really is about time," and other ill-timed comments.

Hearing that we were to travel again, the Rabbit threw himself at Holmes' feet pleading with him. "Please M-M-Mr. Holmes, no mm-more air travel!"

Sherlock assured him that it might not be necessary, and in fact, it did not seem quite possible without a carriage, unless they could procure a replacement.

The Unicorn then pointed its glowing horn at an empty table, nodded its head once and asked, "Would this help?"

Suddenly there appeared on the table, several small bottles with little labels that said, "Drink Me!" Recalling Carroll's novel, I pointed to them and asked, "What possible use would we have for a growth potion?"

To which the Unicorn corrected me stating, “The ‘Drink Me’ bottles that were described in Lewis Carroll’s novel were quite different than these ‘Drink Me’ bottles. If you recall, Dr. Watson, the bottles he described in his book had a red-colored liquid; whereas, the liquid in these bottles on the table is most distinctively lilac in color. I would think that even the most unobservant reader should be able to see that.”

"That's wonderful!" I exclaimed. "What does the color of the contents have to do with anything?"

The Cheshire Cat reappeared, sporting a red and lilac striped pattern, saying, "Well that is a rather 'off-color' remark. I'm surprised it did not stick to your palate. Is that what you call 'purple prose'? I have 'red' about that you know."

Ignoring the Cat, the Unicorn went on with his explanation, "Why everything! The color of the contents is quite significant. As illustrated in Lewis Carroll's novel, red is indeed a growth potion. Lilac, however, is a transportation potion. You just say where you want to go, drink it, and your there. It's really quite simple."

"Do you m-m-mean to say we could have completely avoided those last trips?" exclaimed the White Rabbit, jumping up and down in front of the Unicorn. "I nearly broke m-m-my watch bouncing around in that coach. M-my ears m-may never be the same again and those Time M-Machine trips, they were almost unbearable."

The Cheshire Cat of course added, "Well it's a good thing we did not see any 'bears' while we were 'bear rolling' along."

The Unicorn shook his head. "No, not exactly, my cute and cuddly traveling companion. This potion only works when there is absolutely no other possible option available. And as the only other option available now is the Jabberwocky flying all of you there without a carriage, I would say now is the appropriate time to use it. There are five bottles on this table. Jabberwocky and I would not need one as we can travel nearly as fast as the potion."

"Faster, if we avoid the scenic route!" interjected the Jabberwocky.

To which the Unicorn replied, "I have been there and back five times in the time it took you to say that."

Holmes then declared, "If you two would table your debate for just a moment, we could already be there and moving forward. Now, everyone, except Unicorn and Jabberwocky, take hold of a bottle and open it. Now repeat *exactly* after me, *'221-B Baker Street, London.'* Now drink."

In the moment that followed, a number of things seemed to happen. I heard five voices somewhat in unison recite the address to our flat, or something that sounded somewhat close to it. (I do recall wondering if that would affect the final result or destination.) The strange brew that we had drunk smelled sweet and fragrant, like a bouquet of roses. It tasted something like vanilla, and going down, it had seemed almost like I was swallowing the thorns from the roses. Once I had swallowed it, I felt briefly as if I were melting, when suddenly I was back in 221B Baker Street with the Cheshire Cat sitting on top of my head and commenting, "Well that was entirely better than being bashed about in the coach, and if I do say so, quite a quite bit quicker. Not as scenic though. It wouldn't sell nearly as many tour tickets."

The Jabberwocky, who was curled up in a corner, commented that the speed was due to not having to take the longer sightseeing route that Unicorn used, to which the Unicorn replied, that he had made the round trip seven times in the time it took us to arrive.

Holmes looked around to verify everyone was present, but he came up two travelers short. A loud knocking on the outside of the window indicated that the Hatter had ended up outside on the window sill, and he was quite relieved to climb inside when we opened it. "As we left, I was almost, but not quite certain or sure that I got that wording correct, but then you know that I am never really certain or sure about anything," he explained to Holmes. "And I may have added an additional word or two about being left out on a ledge."

"You're here Hatter", admonished Sherlock, "That's all that matters. Now where is the White Rabbit?"

The answer to that question was to be heard in the bakery across the street in the form of loud crashing sounds accompanied by someone yelling something about, "Get out of the carrot cake! Get out of the flour! Get out of this shop right now! This is NOT a pet shop, no matter how cute and cuddly you are!"

We looked out the window to see the White Rabbit running at top speed out the front door of the bakery, leaving a set of floury white footprints, a stream of cooking utensils flying behind him, and a fading voice screaming, "That does it. Tomorrow I am moving to France! No one in this country appreciates a good bakery."

The Unicorn seemed to blur for a second and then clarified again, this time with the White Rabbit on his back clinging tightly. With a proud but casual shake of his head, the Unicorn announced, "It seemed to me, he needed some assistance out there. I told you I am very quick."

The Rabbit slid off of the Unicorn's back, landed at Sherlock's feet, and looked up sheepishly saying, "Really sir, I was quite certain that I heard you say *Bakery* Street."

Holmes ignored the Rabbit's comments and asked me to fetch Mrs. Hudson, stating that she would be required to participate in the next step of the proceedings. I did not have to go far, as she was just entering the room with a tray of tea and sandwiches for us when she suddenly stopped in her tracks and gazed about the room at the odd collection of creatures.

"My goodness! How very curious! Sherlock, Dr. Watson, I was going to tell you both about the most wonderful and strangest thing that happened to me today. I was quite sure that I had seen the briefest glimpse of a Unicorn in the garden several times earlier this morning, but here he is right here in your study. Can you imagine that? There is a Unicorn in your study? And yet somehow it does not seem nearly as strange next to all the rest of your guests. Goodness! You have such a darling cat, a cute and cuddly rabbit, and a dragon in addition to the Unicorn! Sherlock, I really don't think the pet policy covers *any* of this."

Sherlock approached her and explained, "Yes, Mrs. Hudson, I am quite certain that you did see a Unicorn in the garden earlier. Later on, I can hopefully explain it all, introduce you, and you can formally say hello to him and all the rest of my guests. But right now, I need you to sit right here."

Sherlock took the food tray, set it on a table, sat her in a chair, and then arranged us into a circle with chairs for everyone except the Unicorn and the Jabberwocky. The right half of the circle consisted of the Hatter, Mrs. Hudson, and me; while the left half of the circle included the Cheshire Cat, the White Rabbit, and the

Jabberwocky. Sherlock had the Unicorn stand in the center of the circle while he slowly and contemplatively walked around the creature addressing us.

"Friends, I must ask you to maintain your position in this circle and not to say a word, or even move while I concentrate. If this works as I expect it to -- and I am not often wrong -- I may seem to vanish from your perspective, but do not be alarmed. It is imperative that you do not move, or you may disrupt the field that I create. Unicorn, with your permission, I will sit on your back while you stand in the center of the circle. If my deductions are correct, and I am certain they are, this arrangement will open the portal for me to travel to the reality outside of time."

We agreed, wishing Holmes the very best of luck in his endeavor. Naturally, he responded by saying, "Luck has nothing whatsoever to do with this. Even with all of the strange things we have experienced today this is still one hundred percent logic and deduction, of which I am the master."

"Well then, the very best of logic and deduction," the Hatter offered.

The Unicorn bowed low to allow Holmes to climb onto his back and returned to the standing position with Holmes sitting astride him. Sherlock looked around the circle at each of us, and with a long deep sigh, closed his eyes and whispered; "Now it begins."

Chapter 17.

A Very Strange Conflict (Just what exactly is going on here?)

I must confess that, at the time, I honestly did not expect much of anything to happen. I mean seriously, what could possibly have happened by having the group of us sitting around in a circle while Holmes sat there and concentrated? Yes, it is true that he was sitting on a real-live Unicorn, and it had been a somewhat unusual morning what with the talking cat and all, and there were those trips to both Wonderland and Mars, and we were in the physical presence of several imaginary creatures from a children's novel. A dragon had provided not one, but two, air trips between London and Guildford, and we had been somehow instantaneously transported to 221-B Baker Street by drinking a potion provided by a Unicorn. There was that incredible imaginary game of croquet, not to mention the Bandersnatch and the talking Snapdragons. Now that I think about it again as I write this, considering everything that had happened up to that point, I can't imagine why I had any real doubts.

But at the time, I did have doubts, many real doubts. What was Sherlock's plan? Why were we arranged in a circle? Why had he requested Mrs. Hudson to be a part of it? What did she have to do with the proceedings? Did any of this make any sense at all? Why don't I just get up, go out and have a nice relaxing breakfast and forget about all of this nonsense? It is probably just a bad dream or something. Yes, that's it. It is a very bad dream. I will just get up, walk out the door, go have a nice normal breakfast without talking cats and rabbits. And when I return, Sherlock will be sitting in his chair, puffing away on his pipe, or be at the table deeply involved in some arcane odd-smelling experiment. I will mention to him what a strange and curious dream I just had, and he will dismiss it completely, and we will laugh, move on, and never talk about it again. That was the right answer, to get up and just walk out the door.

As these and other questioning thoughts drifted through my mind, I suddenly felt a presence, as if another consciousness was in my mind along with me. A great sense of peace came over me similar to when the Unicorn had first laid its horn upon my shoulder. After that, I could have sworn that I heard its warm voice again, repeating its message to me: "Believe Watson, just *believe*!" I was also sure that once more I heard the enchanting and peaceful Pixy Music that I had heard when we took our final time-travel journey. It seemed to faintly fill the area with its ethereal hypnotic sound.

I redoubled my efforts and focused on the group, focused on the Unicorn, and focused on Holmes sitting on the Unicorn. I even focused on focusing. I cast aside all the questions and doubts and tried to truly see whatever it was that Holmes was seeing. As it turned out, I thought I was starting to see things when Holmes and the Unicorn suddenly became blurry and less focused. They somehow looked less solid, as if I was seeing them in a nebulous dreamlike environment.

They appeared to be standing in a river. A river was right there in our study in 221-B Baker Street! A RIVER! How could that be? As I watched them in their dreamlike state, they slowly stepped out of the river on to the shore, and the vision abruptly ended. I found myself staring at an empty space in the middle of the circle. We all looked at the empty space, and then each other, then back at the empty space. After that we waited. No one said a word. No one moved. We just waited.

We all knew that Holmes had said to remain in the circle until he completed his task and solved the logic puzzle, but how long would that take? When would he be back? Would he be able to return? Could he even solve the ultimate enigma of logic? What would happen if he failed? What would we do then?

Wait a minute! Of course, he would solve it. What was I thinking? This was Sherlock Holmes I was talking about. He is, without question, the master of perception, deduction and logic. I knew better than to think that he could fail. It was as if my mind was a battlefield of conflicting thoughts. A part of me had complete and total confidence in him, while another part of me wanted to run away and never look back. I felt like I was mentally under attack. In looking at the expressions of the others gathered in that circle, I saw similar mental conflicts going on in the rest of us as well. The White Rabbit was nervously glancing back and forth from his watch to the center of the circle while his ears twitched wildly. The Hatter was fidgety and looked like he wanted to shrink into his hat and hide. The Jabberwocky's long slender claws were tapping the floor impatiently as if it wanted to tear something into shreds. And the Cheshire cat seemed to be straining to stay solid and not just fade completely away.

Mrs. Hudson, however, seemed quite serene and as peaceful as if she were out for a stroll in the garden. She had a sparkle in her eyes and a soft, gentle smile on her lips that almost seemed to say, “Everything is just fine. I know Sherlock has it all under control. All we need to do is wait. When he returns, we will all have some tea and cakes. I must be sure and get some cream for that darling little cat and some carrots for that cute and cuddly rabbit. I wonder what Unicorns eat? He is such a handsome creature. And what on earth will I give to the large scaly beast over there?" Her peaceful demeanor, complete confidence and total acceptance of the odd situation gave me strength. I was able to push away the doubts and fight back against all the nagging questions. I breathed deeply and sat up straighter in my chair. I looked to my companions and tried to silently convey my renewed energy and belief in Sherlock's ability to resolve the situation. He was the master of logic and deduction. There was no mystery or puzzle on Earth, or Mars, in Wonderland, or anywhere else for that matter, that Sherlock could not solve, and anything the Time Guardians came up with would be mere child's play to him. I envisioned my confidence radiating out to the group and to Sherlock as well just to be safe.

As I did, I noticed the Rabbit seemed less nervous and not as concerned with his watch. The Cheshire Cat followed by growing more solid and less translucent. At that point, I would have sworn that I had heard the Unicorn's voice saying, "Yes, Watson, you are doing it. Don't give up now." The soft strains of the comforting Pixy Music grew stronger and clearer. Feeling more confident, I resolved to focus all of my strength on supporting Sherlock in whatever he was doing, wherever he was doing it. I could see by the posture of the rest of the group they were also feeling a renewed strength. It was as if in one mental voice we were saying together, "Sherlock, we are with you!"

At that very point, the room faded away as if I was waking up from a dream, and in its place as clear as day, was a river. Standing next to the river on a green and wooded shore were Sherlock and the Unicorn. In front of them, clothed in long flowing robes, stood the Guardians of Time.

Chapter 18.

A Very Strange Game of Logic (But my bet is still on Sherlock.)

The three Guardians were tall slender beings, each in a different color robe. One was in white, one was in grey, and one was in black. Their facial features were entirely hidden by hoods, and they appeared to be as motionless as statues. Standing nearby, frozen as if in a three-dimensional photograph, were Lewis Carroll and a young girl in a blue and white dress. I was certain that she must have been Alice. Off in the distance I could see the Walrus and other characters from Wonderland.

I was amazed! Holmes had really done it. He had actually reached the very moment in time that the Guardians had given life to Wonderland, Alice, and all the rest of its inhabitants. He had reached the lost beginning that Carroll had mentioned in his letter.

A cold, ethereal voice emanated from the direction of the Guardians, "Your terms are agreeable, Sherlock Holmes. If you can solve all of the logic puzzles we put forth, Wonderland and the lives of all of its inhabitants will be spared. But if you fail, Wonderland, as well as you, will vanish forever. It will be as if you never existed. Let the contest begin!"

I was shocked! Had I heard what I thought I had just heard? Sherlock had wagered his very life on his ability to solve the ultimate logic puzzle. Even Lewis Carroll had not been able to solve it. What would happen if he failed? What would we do then? My thoughts were interrupted as the first Guardian stepped forward and spoke.

“Sherlock Holmes, I am the first Guardian. You may call me Cryptic. Here is your question. What is greater than God, and more evil than the Devil? The poor have it in abundance while the rich need it, and if you eat it, you die?"

Holmes replied almost immediately, "Nothing. Nothing is greater than God or more evil than the devil. The poor generally have nothing, while the rich most certainly need nothing, as they typically have everything they want. And if we eat nothing, we will most definitely die."

The Guardian nodded his head and stepped back.

The second guardian stepped forward, stood for a moment, and spoke, "I am the second Guardian. You may call me Logic. Sherlock Holmes, your reputation as a great detective has reached us even here in the realm outside of time. You might say that your reputation is timeless. We have a crime for you to solve. A certain timepiece has gone missing and there are six suspects. Here are their statements. We know without question, that exactly four of the statements are lies and the rest are all true. Here is what they have said:

Suspect A said:
It wasn't B.
It wasn't D.
It wasn't E.

Suspect B said:
It wasn't A.
It wasn't C.
It wasn't E.

Suspect C said:
It wasn't B.
It wasn't F.
It wasn't E.

Suspect D said:
It wasn't A.
It wasn't F.
It wasn't C.

Suspect E said:
It wasn't C.
It wasn't D.
It wasn't F.

Suspect F said:
It wasn't C.
It wasn't D.
It wasn't A.

Who is the guilty suspect?"

Holmes tossed his head back, laughed and stated, "You gave me the answer yourself. It is suspect 'C'. If it were any other suspect, then there could not be exactly four false statements."

The second Guardian nodded and stepped back replying, "That is quite correct."

The third Guardian stepped forward and spoke, "I am the third Guardian. You may call me Rubic." He opened up his hand in which there appeared a small cube that consisted of many smaller cubes in a 4x4 array. That is, four squares long, by four squares high, by four squares deep. As he held it up for Sherlock to see, the stack of smaller cubes remained quite solid as if they were all glued together. Each of the six faces of the main cube was a different solid color, being red, yellow, blue, green, black, and white, so that on any given side, all of the smaller cube faces were of that one color.

"This is my cubic challenge. You will note that I am able to rotate the individual faces of the cube, while the cube as a whole, stays intact." He rotated one entire face of the cube 90 degrees so that the colors of the smaller squares had changed position, and the individual faces of the main cube were no longer all the same solid color. He proceeded to quickly rotate the rest of faces until all the smaller cube faces on each of the six main faces of the cube became a jumble of different colors. Handing the cube to Sherlock, he stated, "Your task is to return the cube to its original state of each of the six faces being a solid color. You have fifteen minutes. You may begin."

A large hour glass, which I know did not hold an hour's worth of time, suddenly appeared suspended in the air next to the guardian. Much to my frustration, Sherlock spent the first five minutes just staring at the cube. He examined it first from one side and then from the other. Sherlock turned the cube back to the first side, and once again on to a different face.

Why wasn't he doing something? I could see that he was mentally working out the nature and details of it, but time was flowing past with each gurgling splash of the river next to us and with each grain of sand that fell through the hour glass. When was he actually going to start returning it to its original state? Another five minutes of inaction went by, and I could almost stand it no more. I was about to break silence and yell at him to do something already, when he suddenly burst into action and started rotating the faces of the cube so rapidly I could not follow his movements. The colors of the cube became a rainbow blur as he rotated the faces first this way and then that way. I could see the intense focus in his eyes while the hour glass seemed to be emptying much faster than it should have been. It was a close race between the grains of sand and Sherlock. I was certain that he would solve it, but the question was, could he do it in time? Just as the final grains of sand were draining from the top of the hourglass, Holmes returned the final face of the cube to its original position, gave a long, deep sigh and held up the cube completely restored to its original state. With his wry smile he handed it back to the third Guardian saying, "That was actually quite exhilarating. You know, I believe there could be a future in marketing this thing as a toy or a puzzle. Of course, it would be just for fun and pleasure and not as a contest with one's life or the fate of a whole world at stake."

I almost detected a smile in the hidden face of the Guardian as it retrieved the cube from Sherlock, nodded and stepped back adding, "Indeed it does, Sherlock Holmes. The future does hold much greatness for this device when it finally appears in your world. You could even write an article on solving it. I imagine it would be called, *Using Logic Based Movement Patterns and Three-Dimensional Rational to Solve Rotational Color Grid Cube Puzzles."*

The first Guardian again stepped forward and spoke, "Long ago, a king was inspired by the concept of truthfulness. He decreed that everyone in his kingdom must always and without fail speak the truth. Anyone who did not speak the truth would be executed, and everyone who did speak the truth, no matter what he or she said, could not be executed. The proclamation was written out and posted at all of the gates to the kingdom. Guards were also posted to make sure everyone who entered the kingdom knew the rule and understood it under penalty of death. "One day a traveler approached the gates of the kingdom and the guards informed him of the proclamation and asked the traveler, 'Why have you come here?'

"His response was, 'Why, to be executed of course!'

"The guards apprehended the traveler and said, 'Oh, we have such a liar here. Let us take him to the king to be executed.'

"They brought the traveler to the king to be executed per the royal proclamation, but he was released. Why?"

Sherlock dismissively replied," It is obvious, of course. If he had been executed, then he would have been telling the truth, and per the proclamation, they could not execute him for telling the truth. They had to let him go."

The first Guardian again nodded and stepped back, as the second Guardian once more stepped forward.

"In addition to logic puzzles we also enjoy athletic competitions as well. We recently watched two foot races, a 100-meter race and a 200-meter race in which the same four contestants competed.

"Contestant 3 beat Contestant 4 in the 200-meter race.

"Contestant 1 came in 3rd in the 200-meter race.

"The 16-year-old won the 200-meter race.

"Contestant 3 came in second in the 100-meter race.

"The 15-year-old won the 100-meter race.

"Contestant 1 beat the 18-year old.

"The 19-year-old came in 3rd.

"Contestant 2 is 3 years younger than contestant 4.

"The contestant who came in last in the 200-meter race came in 3rd in the 100-meter race.

"Only one contestant finished in the same position in both races.

"Tell me the ages of each contestant and what position they finished in each race.

"You have five minutes."

Once again, the hourglass rotated while Holmes stood there silently staring at the Guardian. How was he supposed to solve the problem without a notebook or something to write on and put things in order? I could not even remember all of the statements much less determine who was who or how old they were and what position they finished in both of the races.

While I was starting to worry about the outcome, Sherlock seemed unconcerned. His eyes darted back and forth as he appeared to be mentally moving the various factors back and forth. The hourglass was not even halfway finished when he addressed the second Time Guardian. "Here is your answer. I believe you will find it completely correct as this is the only logical conclusion:

“Contestant 1 is 15 years old and finished 1st in the 100-meter race and 3rd in the 200-meter race.

“Contestant 2 is 16 years old and finished 4th in the 100-meter race and 1st in the 200-meter race.

“Contestant 3 is 18 years old and finished 2nd in both races.

“Contestant 4 is 19 years old and finished 3rd in the 100-meter race and 4th in the 200-meter race.”

The second Guardian bowed his head and responded, “Very good, Sherlock Holmes. Once again, you are correct.”

The third Guardian named Rubic again stepped forward. He raised his hand and made a curving downward sweeping motion. “Your logic skills are most excellent, Mr. Holmes. You have been appointed as the facilitator in a crucial peace negotiation between representatives of five warring tribes. Each tribe has sent two representatives to the meeting. It must succeed, or all is lost.

“Your task is to get all of them to the other side of a river to the meeting site for the negotiations. They have all previously agreed that once they are on the other side of the river, that they will not be hostile to one another. In addition, while in your presence as the facilitator, they will refrain from all violence. However, if they are left alone on this side of the river, violence most certainly will break out between them based on any and all of the following conditions:

1. The first tribe will attack members of the fourth tribe.

2. The second tribe will attack members of the first and fifth tribe, but only if both of the second tribe members are present.

3. The third tribe members will attack the first and fifth tribe member, but only if there is just one of them present.

4. The fourth tribe members will not get in the boat with the third tribe members.

5. The fifth tribe members are cannibals and will attack any one left alone.

6. The boat will only hold five people at a time, so you may presume that multiple trips will be required.

"Be careful whom you leave with whom, Mr. Holmes. This is no easy task. It is imperative that they all get across the river alive.

"My question is, how do you propose to get them all across the river safely so that the negotiations can be successfully completed? They arrive in two minutes."

Two minutes! How in the world was Sherlock supposed to accomplish this task? The fifth tribe members will kill anyone, so they would have to be taken first. Who should he put in the boat with them? He would have to take one of the second tribe members since they both need to present to attack anyone. Who would be the fourth person he would put in the boat? The conditions made it nearly impossible as far as I was concerned. There is no way he could transport them all across the river without someone getting killed. Could he wait until they are all asleep and then bring them over? But what if one of them wakes up while Sherlock was in the boat crossing the river? That would be disastrous. He could possibly tie them all up, but again, if even one of them managed to escape, it will be all over. How is he going to solve this? I watched in wonder as Holmes stood there in silence analyzing the information.

Sherlock raised a hand pensively and asked the Guardian if those were *all* the rules to this puzzle. I did not understand why he would have asked that particular question, as the rules already given seemed more than difficult enough to me. I would have considered it impossible as is.

Rubic tilted his head under the hood and replied, “Yes, those indeed are all the rules. What do you propose Mr. Holmes?”

Sherlock’s answer was simple. “Swim. That’s right, just *swim*. There is no *requirement* to use the boat. Every one of them swims across the river along with me at the same time. We don’t use the boat at all. No one is left alone with another tribe member. No one gets attacked. They all reach the other side at the same time alive and safe, and the meeting can begin. After we all dry off, that is.”

The three Guardians spoke in unison. "Well done, Sherlock Holmes. You have completed the basic logic riddles and have reached the final logic puzzle. This is the ultimate logic puzzle. It is the enigma. Your life depends on your ability to solve it. Do you wish to continue? You are aware that if you fail to solve it, you will forfeit your life. Or would you care to just go back home to your study on Baker Street with your Earthly friends who have been observing you and forget about Wonderland and all of its inhabitants? If you leave now, we will let you live, but Wonderland and everyone it, will vanish forever from the memories of your world. You will not remember it. It will be as if it never existed. This is your final chance."

Sherlock gazed around as if he could actually see us gathered in the invisible circle that surrounded him. He smiled and said simply, "I am ready for your ultimate logic puzzle."

Chapter 19.

The Ultimate Logic Puzzle (And of course a very strange one at that.)

The Guardians bowed their heads and then all three took a step forward together. There was a shimmering in the space next to them, and an open scroll entitled "The Rules" suddenly appeared suspended in the air as if it was hanging from some invisible post. Sherlock stepped up to the parchment and read it aloud.

"The Rules:

"The three of us, Cryptic, Logic, and Rubic, are from this point forward, and in no particular or predictable order, True, False, and Random. True will always speak truthfully, and False will always speak falsely. However, it is a completely random matter whether Random replies truthfully or falsely to any given question. Your task is to determine which of us is True, which of us is False and which of us is Random by asking only three Yes-No questions. Your questions may only be put to only one of us at any given time.

"As you are well aware, we do understand English, but for the purposes of this challenge, we choose to answer all questions in our own language in which the words, *yes* and no are *ney* and *niy* in some order, but not particularly that one. You must solve this puzzle in one hour."

The hourglass rotated so the sand was on the top again, and the three Time Guardians in one cold, calculating voice said, "You may begin."

What had Sherlock gotten himself into? This was no puzzle. This was shear madness! He was only given three yes-no questions. They wouldn't answer in English, he didn't know their language, and one of them couldn't even be relied on to give consistent or correct answers. This was insanity! How could he ever have been expected to solve this in the time period given?

Lewis Carroll was an absolute master in logic puzzles, and he had been working on it for years without having solved it before he passed away. How was Holmes supposed to solve this puzzle in less than an hour? I was not alone in my concern, for I observed the same uncertainty in the others seated around Holmes and the Unicorn.

The Cheshire Cat was again starting to look less solid, and, for the first time since it had appeared, was not grinning. The Hatter, meanwhile, was again fidgeting and seemed to be shrinking into his oversized hat. Looking towards the Jabberwocky, I was certain I saw smoke curling from his nostrils as he nervously tapped the ground with his razor like-claws as if he was thinking, "Let me at them! Just let me at them, and I can solve the puzzle in no time at all by simply tearing the Guardians into little, tiny pieces. No Guardians, no puzzles, no problem!"

I gave him a stern look that clearly said, "Don't you even think of moving! You heard what Sherlock said. We must hold our position. If we break the field that is maintaining his presence here, you know that all is lost, and all of this would have been for nothing. If anyone in the world can figure out the answer, I know that Sherlock Holmes is the one person who can solve it." I hoped I had convinced him, since I was still so uncertain myself. Looking in the direction of the White Rabbit, his ears and whiskers were drooping worse than ever. He had lost all interest in his watch and looked as if he might faint at any moment. I hoped he could hold himself together, as each and every one of us was needed to maintain the circle.

Of all of us, only the Unicorn and Mrs. Hudson seemed at ease. She sat there serene as could be, a picture of complete and total confidence in Sherlock Holmes, the incredibly talented, yet certainly odd, lodger she had come to know so well over the years. His eccentric behavior of shooting bullet holes in the wall, creating foul smelling experiments, smoking noxious pipe tobacco, seeing strange visitors at all hours, and playing his screeching violin at 3:00 A.M. had not unnerved her after all this time. So, in her mind, what was a simple, albeit incredibly complex and near unsolvable, question on which rested the entire fate of Wonderland and even Sherlock Homes himself? If anyone could solve it, Sherlock Holmes could. It was as simple as that!

The Unicorn was also the very essence of peace and serenity. Like a majestic ivory statue, it stood firm and resolute and a silver glow emanated from where it stood. I heard the gentle calming sound of the mysterious Pixy Music once more as well. There appeared to be a warmth about the whole area that enveloped us as Holmes stood lost in deep concentration. The ancient eyes of the Unicorn slowly glanced around the members of the circle, and I could see and feel each of us strengthened by its gaze as it passed over us. When it had finished looking upon us, it turned its gaze to Sherlock, looked at him with an intensity that defied description, and I would have sworn that Holmes himself was almost glowing.

As I gazed upon Sherlock who was lost in concentration and deduction, I could only wonder what was going on in his analytical mind. The puzzle was certainly beyond my deductive capabilities. So many times, before, Holmes had commented on how obtuse I was in matters that were as clear as daylight to him. He would explain his observations and conclusions and amazingly they would somehow seem quite simple and obvious. That was his way. That was Sherlock Holmes, but while I was sure that he could solve it, the question in my mind at that moment was could he solve it in time? The sand raced through the hourglass as Holmes stood there in complete silence staring at the scroll that hung suspended next to the Time Guardians. While there was no question that the sand was quickly disappearing, I saw a confident smile on his face that told me everything was going to be all right. With a smile, Sherlock started nodding his head, as if he was mentally working an equation, moving factors back and forth, this way and that way. Finally, Sherlock sighed, turned to the Guardian identified as Logic, and spoke with a voice that was as clear as a crystal and as deep as time itself.

"Here is my solution. I shall put forth my logical deductions and resulting conclusions for each possibility, and you will see that I have solved your puzzle:

Starting with you, Logic: if I asked you the question, 'Are you Random?' in your current mental state, would you say *niy?*

If you answer *niy*, you are indeed Random.

I would then ask Cryptic: If I asked you 'Are you True?', would you say *niy?*

If Cryptic answers *niy*, then Cryptic is True and Rubic is False.

If Cryptic answers *ney*, then *Cryptic is* False and Rubic is True. In both cases, the puzzle is solved.

However, if you, Logic, answer *ney,* then you are not Random. I would then ask you: If I asked you 'Are you True?', would you say *niy*?

If you answer *niy*, then you are True.

If, however you answer *ney,* then you are False.

I would then ask you: If I asked you 'Is Cryptic Random?', would you say *niy?*

If you answer *niy,* then Cryptic is Random, and Rubic is the opposite of you.

But if you answer *ney,* then Rubic is Random, and Cryptic is the opposite of you.

“Gentlemen, ladies, or whatever you may happen to be, that is my answer. If my deductions are correct, which I am certain they are, that is the only correct solution."

The silence was resounding as Holmes finished presenting his solution. The hourglass sand had first stopped mid-stream and then abruptly vanished along with the hourglass. The three Guardians stepped backwards one step, bowed as one and replied, "You have, indeed solved our ultimate logic puzzle, Sherlock Holmes. It is one which has never before been solved. To be completely honest, we were not even certain that it ever could be solved. However, in examining your deductions and conclusions, we see that they are correct. You have won the restoration of Wonderland and all of its inhabitants, as well as saved your own life. We shall now retire to our contemplations to create a new logic puzzle worthy of us. Congratulations to you and your associates. You may all leave."

With a grand sweep of their arms, the Guardians, the river and the wooded shore disappeared, and the in the next moment, we were back in our flat in 221-B Baker Street. Somehow, even Lewis Carroll and Alice were there along with us. I was about to congratulate him, when a tea cup went flying past my head, crashed into the wall, shattered into pieces, and the White Rabbit loudly exclaimed, "How wonderful! Even the M-M-March Hare is here!"

Sherlock looked closely at the pieces of the shattered tea cup on the floor and proudly exclaimed, “Hah! Exactly per my calculations in *Quantifying the Number of Pieces Tea Cups Will Break into When Thrown against a Wall Based on the Material Composition and Density of the Tea Cup.”*

Chapter 20.

Yet One More Very Strange Tea Party (And a most pleasant conclusion.)

Looking around and seeing that all of us had safely returned to our Baker Street parlor brought me an immense sense of relief which was unfortunately quickly shattered by a loud roar, crashes, and screaming coming from the bakery across the street. I looked out the window to see the baker and several patrons come racing out the front door of the bakery screaming something about the zoo keeper should be fired for not containing the animals and the baker was definitely leaving the country for anywhere that did not have zoos.

They were quickly followed by a golden-colored lion, wearing a tweed vest and spectacles and a walrus sporting a monocle. The Unicorn suddenly appeared on the sidewalk in front of 221-B gesturing with his horn towards our front door, to which the Lion and Walrus quickly made their way. The Unicorn reappeared in our flat, which was already somewhat crowded, what with the Jabberwocky and everyone else, when the door opened and in squeezed the Lion and Walrus, greeting everyone as they did. "Hello there," saluted the Walrus. "Good evening. It is nice to meet you. Whoops, sorry about your foot there, good fellow."

The Lion gave the Unicorn a friendly hug. "Unicorn, my old sparring partner, it is good to see you again. My, what a cute and cuddly rabbit you have here! Well, those are lovely looking tea cakes. Might you have any plum cake to go with them?"

"Gracious! What a large kitty cat!" exclaimed Mrs. Hudson, as the Lion paraded past her. "Would you like some milk? And perhaps some pickled herring sandwiches for your Walrus friend?"

The Jabberwocky quickly straightened his neck, picked up his head, nearly taking out a ceiling light fixture, and ventured, "Did I hear something about pickled herring sandwiches? What a lovely idea! Can I help you? I could go fetch a whole net full of fish from the wharf if you would like." He started to move forward, almost upsetting the coal scuttle and a stack of papers when Sherlock intervened, "Jabberwocky, why don't you just stay in one place for now until we get everyone settled. Things are just a bit crowded at the moment, but I am quite pleased to see all of you here. I can finally say that we were successful. Wonderland is saved."

At that point, the little girl in the blue and white dress stepped forward, curtsied and spoke, "Hello, my name is Alice. I was on my way to Wednesday-afternoon tea with Rabbit, Hatter and Cheshire Cat, when I somehow seemed to have gotten lost. I don't remember exactly where I was. Now I see that either I am found or everyone else is lost along with me. I can certainly tell that this is not Wonderland. In fact, this looks a great deal more like London, except that so many of my Wonderland friends are also here with me. I really don't understand it at all, but since we are all together, why don't we have the tea party right here? It would make it so much more fun. May I help with the tea in any way?"

"I'll help too!" cried the March Hare, flinging another tea cup across the room. This time, instead of crashing into the wall, the cup was expertly caught by Lewis Carroll, who snatched it out of the air and then handed it to Alice, who then went with Mrs. Hudson and the Hatter to get refreshments. Lewis Carroll smiled and exclaimed, "My dear friends, it is so wonderful to see you all again and to know that, thanks to Sherlock Homes, you won't disappear and be forgotten. You will live forever, not just in the hearts of readers around the world but in Wonderland itself! It is saved! Thank you, Mr. Holmes. Thank you ever so much! And thank you too, Dr. Watson, and the rest of you as well. I wonder though, how you managed to do it. How *did* you manage to step out of the river of time?"

"First things first!" cried the Hatter as he, along with Mrs. Hudson and Alice, reentered the room carrying trays with tea, sandwiches and cakes. "I am never really quite certain or sure about anything except tea time, so I am most pleased to say, it's TEA TIME!" Once everyone was settled in with their refreshments, although it was a mite crowded, we sat spellbound as Sherlock spoke.

"The first thing I want to say is that I discovered something most curious today. *Reality* really is relative. During my entire career as a consulting detective, I have focused on the consistency and importance of trifles that are invisible to most everyone else. I have relied on this unseen reality being both consistent and logical. I had mentioned to you earlier, Watson, that in this adventure, we were dealing with a whole different set of rules of reality. If you recall, it was about the time that the Unicorn walked into the room. That was the key to understanding what to do and how to do it. That is why I arranged you all in circle to gain access to the reality outside of time. But I am getting ahead of myself. And I will have no heady remarks from you sir," he added looking in the direction of the Cheshire Cat.

The Cat's grin widened as it replied, "Why I was not going to say anything about 'Heads' up! Here comes a good story because Sherlock Holmes used his 'head'." Then it winked at Sherlock, rotated its head completely upside down, and winked out, only to reappear sitting on the fireplace mantel, where it added, "Please do go ahead."

Shaking his head sideways, Sherlock went on, "As I was saying, by the end of the first two hours of the Cat's presence, I realized that the previous rules of logic and reality were no longer valid. As strange and improbable as it seemed, this was a whole new reality with a new set of rules. That was the only logical answer. From that point forward, it was a matter of adapting to the new reality. With each new event, regardless of how strange it was, deducing how to proceed became easier and easier, almost elementary."

The Cat grinned brightly and interjected, "Is that like a tree that only grows the twelfth, thirteenth, and fourteenth letters of the alphabet? I saw one of those once, a real L, M, N tree."

Sherlock paused for just a moment as if he were going to say something, raised his eyes to the ceiling, sighed, and then turned to Lewis Carroll. "I do want to say thank you, Lewis, for your clue regarding H.G. Wells. I knew that due to your agreement with the Time Guardians, you couldn't divulge more detailed information regarding the methodology for stepping out of the river of time, but Mr. Wells was able to provide exactly what I needed to know. That was an extremely clever clue. Even Watson, who has spent years observing me, did not notice it."

I looked at him and emphatically stated, "Sherlock, as you have said many times before, no one has better skills in observation and deduction than you. You should know that by now."

"That is true," he matter-a-factly acknowledged. "That is quite true, but while your deductive abilities may be sorely lacking, your insights and efforts in keeping the circle together and focused while I was in conflict with the Guardians was of immense help. We each have our own forte, Watson. I am truly glad you were there."

Sherlock turned back to the whole group to continue his story. "H. G. Wells was able to give me enough information about what I needed to do, so that I was able to devise a logic-based mental construct for stepping out of our reality. I do wish he was here, so I could thank him."

At that moment, the Unicorn blurred slightly, vanished, and then reappeared with a bewildered looking H.G. Wells astride him and clinging desperately on to his neck. "Well why didn't you say so?" asked the Unicorn, as Wells dismounted and slid down to the floor, still somewhat shaken by his near instantaneous ride. The Unicorn proudly stated, "There is room for one more, as long as we all don't inhale at once. What is it, Sherlock, that you want to say to Mr. Wells?"

Holmes put out his hand to Wells saying, "I want to thank you again for explaining the dimensional time travel process. As you can see, it worked, and we managed to save Wonderland. By arranging a circle with humans sitting on the right side and imaginary creatures sitting on the left side, I created a balance of logic and illogic. It was a balanced combination of fact and fantasy, so to speak. The Unicorn's ability to travel anywhere instantaneously gave me the ability to jump out of our reality. And those of you that comprised the circle provided the right balance of energy with which to do so and remain there. I really must write a paper on this someday. I think I will call it *Achieving Inter-Dimensional Travel Through the Balancing of Real and Non-Real*

Beings Based on their Logical Placement in a Circular Arrangement, Focusing on Travel outside of Time."

Sherlock turned and addressed Mrs. Hudson directly: "I knew there would be a great strain on all of us, which is why I wanted to include you, Mrs. Hudson. Your calm nature and complete confidence in me helped the others to maintain their courage."

Mrs. Hudson replied with a shy smile, "Why thank you Sherlock. That is most kind of you, but it still does not mean I approve of your violin playing at three A.M., your foul-smelling experiments, or the bullet holes in the wall."

Sherlock coughed twice and turned to the Unicorn, "And Unicorn, your strength and encouragement to all of them, as well as to me, was felt and very much appreciated."

Sherlock then paused for a moment with a far off look in his eyes and added, "That includes you as well, Pixy Music, wherever you are. You held the Time Machine together long enough for us to get home. We could not have done this without you." At that moment, an echoing musical laughter drifted through the room and touched us all, leaving a sense of peace and calm.

As the echo softly faded away Holmes resumed. "I am proud of all of you for not giving in to the mental attack that the Guardians launched against you. I know it was quite a struggle. You realize, of course, that had the strength of the circle failed, I would have failed, and we would have lost everything."

Humming loudly "*Will the Circle be Unbroken*", the Cheshire Cat, with an extra wide grin, stopped his tune and interjected, "Oh, I would not say that, most logical and victorious one. I am sure you would have gotten 'around' to it someday, perhaps when we are all more 'well rounded' on the subject. I will say this, however, the mental attack felt like a choir of out-of-tune accountants singing the multiplication tables backwards in Pig Latin. It just did not add up."

Sherlock looked squarely at the Cat, which vanished from the mantel and reappeared in the ceiling light fixture, adding, "Do go on, Mr. Holmes. Things are 'looking up' right now."

Resuming, Sherlock explained, "Once I reached the reality outside of time, I knew it was just a matter of observation, deduction, and rational thought to solve their puzzles. As long as the circle held, and I could remain there, I knew I could do it. Their initial puzzles were really quite elementary, but I will say, however, the final puzzle was certainly a challenge."

"But how did you solve that one Sherlock?" chimed in Lewis Carroll. "I was close to solving it, but I literally ran out of time."

Sherlock nodded his head, "I mentally created a 16 x 16 grid to map out all possible answers and variations. I reduced it to three logical connectives, or biconditional questions. It could have been solved in two questions if the first guardian had turned out to be 'Random'."

Looking intensely at Holmes, the Jabberwocky raised a claw and bowed its head saying, "If you don't mind, most deductive and victorious one, I will pass on that game of chess for now. Even without wings, you are at a level far above me."

Holmes bowed his head to the Jabberwocky answering, "That is fine with me, most scaly and aeronautically gifted one. Whenever you would like to have that game, it would be a pleasure and an honor to play a game of chess with you. Until then, you may want to take a look at my monograph on *Practical Applications of Deductive Logic and Rational Thought Process in Chess Openings Focusing on the First Three Moves."*

Lewis Carroll then stepped forward, offered his hand to Sherlock, and stated enthusiastically, "Holmes, that was brilliant, indisputably brilliant! I applaud you!"

"Me too!" cried Alice, clapping her hands. "I'm not sure I understood any of those big words, but it did sound most impressive, and best of all, we are not lost anymore."

Reaching for the curtains to blow his nose, the Hatter piped in, "That is so very touching. I think I am going to cry," but he was intercepted by Mrs. Hudson who handed him a tea towel and gave him a most stern look that said, "Now see here, I can deal with rabbits, cats, lions, walruses, Unicorns and even dragons in the tea room, but don't you even think about using my curtains as a handkerchief."

The Hatter accepted the tea towel from Mrs. Hudson and blew his nose, this time sounding something like a large frog croaking through a rusty, barnacle encrusted fog horn.

The gathering broke up into smaller groups as we each discussed our own parts in the incredible adventure, with many verbal jousts between the Unicorn and Jabberwocky regarding who was really the fastest. They eventually agreed that the Jabberwocky was the fastest winged creature in the room, while the Unicorn was, without question, the fasted four-legged creature.

Finally, Lewis Carroll stood and looking at the clock stated, "My time on earth, which as you all know has already passed once, is again coming to an end. I have to leave now, but this time I can go in peace knowing that Alice, Wonderland, and all of the rest of you are safe. Thank you. Thank ..." He never finished his sentence. He just faded away before our eyes. In a twinkling he was gone, and Alice buried her head in Mrs. Hudson's arms to hide her tears.

Sherlock stepped over to Alice, bent down, put his hand on her shoulder, and in the gentlest manner that I have ever seen displayed in him, Sherlock addressed her, "Don't cry, little one. Lewis Carroll will with be with you in every Wonderland adventure you have from this day forward. He is the father of Wonderland, so to speak, and he is never far away from you. His spirit will live on in Wonderland forever."

Alice looked up at Sherlock, and her tiny smile broke into a grin, and she replied, "Really? Really? Then let's all go play Wonderland croquet!" She jumped up, grabbing the hand of the Hatter and the paws of the White Rabbit and March Hare, laughing out loud, "Let's go Cheshire! I bet I can beat you this time!"

In an echo of laughter, she was out the door with her friends following her and the head of the Cheshire Cat floating along behind calling out, "Farewell all! It has been great fun and most curious. Do let me know if you are ever in the mood for some illogical musing or mewing, whichever you don't prefer least!" The Lion, followed by the Walrus, exited with many thanks and also saying, "See you soon Unicorn. Tomorrow we will continue our sparring match. Be sure and bring some plum cake. I will bring the brown bread."

And with that, the only ones that remained were Wells, Holmes, Mrs. Hudson and I plus the Jabberwocky and the Unicorn. They were discussing who should take H.G. Wells back to his home in Guildford and were about to get into another debate when Holmes interrupted, "Gentle creatures, Mr. Wells has already enjoyed the incredible privilege of riding upon a Unicorn, so it is only fair that Jabberwocky should be the one to provide him the return trip to Guildford. He has yet to experience the wonder of air travel. It really is quite amazing, you know. He may even find inspiration for another novel, Flying from the Earth to the Moon, or perhaps The First Men inside the Moon."

“I like the idea of men inside the Moon,” Wells commented. “I could really do something with that. I think that Jules Verne fellow has already written about a journey around the Moon and back. He imagined firing them out of a cannon of all things. And why would he put the launch site all the way over in Florida in the United States of America?”

"Wonderful!" exclaimed the Jabberwocky. "That sounds excellent! I think Mr. Wells will really enjoy the trip, as long we don’t have to follow the Unicorn."

While Wells and the Jabberwocky said their goodbyes and left, I saw Holmes talking quietly to the Unicorn and the Unicorn nodding its head in agreement, but I could not hear what they were saying. Holmes and the Unicorn together walked up to Mrs. Hudson and Sherlock addressed her. "Mrs. Hudson, earlier I promised you that if we survived this adventure, I would personally introduce you to this amazing creature. Well, Mrs. Hudson, it is my great pleasure to introduce you to the Unicorn. And Unicorn, this is my dear Mrs. Hudson."

The Unicorn then bowed low on his front legs and said, "Dear gentle lady, it is truly a pleasure to meet you. Have you ever wanted to ride upon a Unicorn?"

The biggest smile imaginable shone on Mrs. Hudson's face as she embraced the Unicorn and climbed onto its back. Glancing in my direction and seeing my concern, the Unicorn winked at me, "I do promise I will go much slower this time." Then as the Unicorn exited the room, I heard it call out. "Good bye, gentlemen. Always remember, I was the fastest."

We heard a faint echo that sounded like the Jabberwocky from somewhere outside and far above saying, "But I fly faster..." followed by another echo that sounded like the Unicorn saying, "But I'm still the fastest...."

Once they were gone, we returned to our chairs and sat in absolute silence for quite some time. I looked around the empty room and then at Sherlock and with a sigh stated, "Well, Holmes, I guess it is over. That was, without a doubt, the strangest most curious adventure we have ever had. I absolutely must record it, but as you mentioned earlier, I certainly cannot publish this right now. I must postpone its publication. Who would ever believe me? They would think I was crazy! Tell me Holmes, am I crazy? Did we really travel to Mars? Did we actually visit Lewis Carroll's Wonderland? Did any of this really happen? Or did we imagine all of it? I mean, what proof do we have that any of this ever occurred?"

Holmes looked at me intensely and pointed in the direction of the door replying, "Turn around Watson. Your answer is right behind you."

I quickly turned around only to see Mrs. Hudson come waltzing back through the doorway, flowers in her hair, and a childlike smile that was almost glowing. As she lightly danced passed us, she laughingly stated, “Sherlock, that was absolutely wonderful! You needn’t worry about the pet policy anymore. You can invite your friends over whenever you would like.”

In a twinkling she was gone, but I could not help but smile. “Well, Holmes, I guess I can see now that it really did happen. Amazing! I wonder, do you think we will ever experience another adventure as truly strange and curious as this one?” Before he could answer, there was a knock at the door and a tall bearded gentleman in some type of navy blue uniform entered and asked, “Is this the residence of Sherlock Holmes?”

Holmes looked the gentleman over, nodded his head and answered, “I am Sherlock Holmes. How may I help you?”

Removing his hat, the gentleman responded, “My name is Captain Nemo of the submersible vessel the *Nautilus*. I would like to engage your services to locate a missing person. His name is Jules Verne.”

The End

References:

1. Alice's Adventures in Wonderland, Lewis Carroll 1865

2. Through the Looking Glass, and What Alice Found There, Lewis Carroll 1871

3. Alice in Orchestrailia, Ernest La Prade 1926

4. Alice's Journey Beyond the Moon, R.J. Carter 2004

Book 2

Sherlock Holmes in The Nautilus Adventure

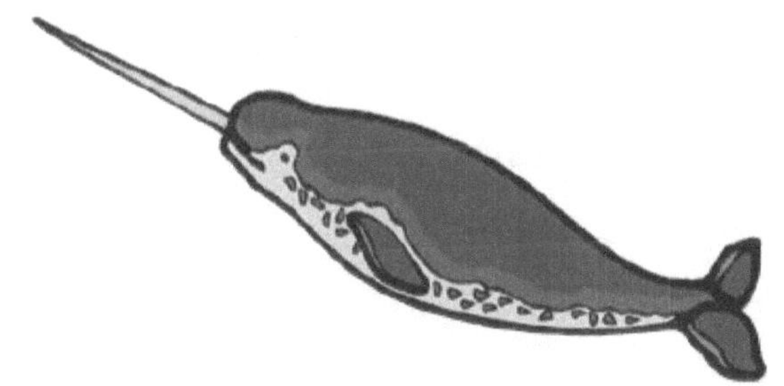

Sherlock Holmes in the Nautilus Adventure

Table of Contents:

A Note to Readers:

The following manuscript, Sherlock Holmes in the Nautilus Adventure, is part of a recently rediscovered collection of papers belonging to a Dr. John Watson, M.D. He was a noted surgeon and the biographer of Sherlock Holmes, a famous consulting detective who lived in Victorian England. Sherlock Holmes is the best-known detective in history, having solved the most baffling cases that confounded Scotland Yard. His skills in observation, perception, deduction and logic are beyond compare. His career was founded on seeing what no one else did and understanding its overall significance in the matters at hand. Dr. Watson recorded and published many of Holmes' more fascinating cases and adventures.

This particular tale, along with several other manuscripts found at the same time, had been requested by Dr. Watson to be set aside and not published for varying periods of time due to the unusual nature of the subject matter. I concur with him in that the content is indeed very unusual and at times difficult to accept. Sometime during the waiting period, the manuscripts were misplaced and forgotten until their recent discovery. As the requested waiting period has long since passed, they may be published without concern; however, the reader may be quite surprised by certain aspects of the stories due to the unique nature of these adventures, which are far different from the typical solving of a murder or locating a missing object. Be advised. In reading Sherlock Holmes in the Nautilus Adventure, you are in for a most unusual voyage literally and figuratively. Let it be said, "The game's afloat!"

Prologue
Memorandum:

To: Whom it may Concern From:
Dr. John Watson M.D.
Subject: *Sherlock Holmes in the Nautilus Adventure*
Date: February 1898

Everyone knows that Captain Nemo is the fictional main character of Jules Verne's novel, *Twenty Thousand Leagues Under the Sea*. That was my belief as well before we began the amazing journey that I recount in this manuscript. The reader will discover, as I did, there is much more to Captain Nemo than Jules Verne revealed. As I recall the adventure that unfolded, it is with great awe, and a certain sense of sorrow with which I write this. I find myself once again in admiration of Sherlock Holmes's abilities in logic and deduction and how he saved the world from a threat that few people alive today are aware of. But it is also with sadness that I remember a fond farewell that is still heavy in my heart.

While every word of this is true, it is too fantastic and unusual to be published during my life time. For the sake of my reputation as a doctor, the confidence of my patients, and the name of Sherlock Holmes, I ask that this manuscript not be published until seventy-five years after my passing. Your compliance in this request is greatly appreciated.

Dr. John H. Watson M.D.

Sherlock Holmes in the Nautilus Adventure

Chapter 1. A Most Unusual Visitor, (But not to be unexpected after the day's previous events.)

I looked at the gentleman standing there before us in Sherlock's parlor with utter disbelief. "You can't be serious!" I exclaimed. "Are you saying that YOU are Captain Nemo, the main character from Jules Verne's novel, *"Twenty Thousand Leagues under the Sea?"* Everyone knows that story is a fictional adventure novel. The next thing you will be saying is that you have the *Nautilus* docked right outside the front door of 221-B Baker Street!"

"Actually, it is currently submerged in London Harbor, waiting for a signal from me to surface and pick us up," he replied rather straightforwardly.

"Us?" Sherlock responded, raising one eyebrow with a quizzical look. "And who exactly is us?"

This was too much already! Sherlock Holmes and I no sooner had resolved The Adventure of the Grinning Cat, which I thought without question was certainly the strangest adventure of his career, and now this! As you recall, in the Grinning Cat adventure, the Cheshire Cat, White Rabbit, and Hatter from Lewis Carroll's *"Alice in Wonderland"*, had appeared at 221-B Baker Street seeking Sherlock's help in locating Alice who had disappeared from Wonderland, as well as Lewis Carroll himself whom they also could not locate. This visit resulted in us taking several aerial trips over London, visiting Alice's Wonderland, and eventually stepping outside of time itself. Between time travels into other realities, fictional characters coming to life, and meeting a Unicorn, as well as a dragon of sorts, it was one very illogical, strange, and curious adventure.

Now we had yet another visitor claiming to be a well-known fictional character, who was looking for his author who had gone missing. As unusual as it all seemed, I must say that the gentleman standing before us certainly did look the part of the person he was claiming to be. He was tall and well built, had a neatly trimmed dark beard, and a certain bearing about him that portrayed confidence, leadership, and an air of ageless wisdom. His eyes were wide set giving him a broad range of vision and were of the deepest blue that I had ever seen. I could not determine his nationality. His dark blue uniform was well used but meticulous, and his jacket bore the letter "N" in gold thread upon the breast pocket surrounded by the circular phrase, "Mobili e Mobilus". Now if you have read Jules Verne's novel, then you are aware that that the "N" stands for his vessel the *Nautilus*, while the phrase surrounding it is Latin for "Moving in the moving element." Yes, this stranger really did look like the fictional Captain Nemo brought to life. But how was it possible?

I turned to Holmes and asked, "What is your opinion on this, Sherlock? Have all boundaries between reality and literary fiction completely collapsed? What do you think is going on here? Do you believe this really is Captain Nemo of the *Nautilus*? How on earth would that be feasible?"

The tall stern-faced gentleman turned to me with a deep penetrating look and replied, "I understand your skepticism, Dr. Watson. You are a doctor, not a scientist." Then with a slow wave of his hand, as if pointing out the night sky, he stated, "This must seem as inconceivable as perhaps a trek through the stars. You do not know the full story behind Jules Verne's novel. Perhaps it would help if I explained. May I sit down?"

"Yes indeed," Sherlock responded, gesturing towards a chair. "May we offer you some tea?"

"No thank you, just some hot water." Captain Nemo replied, holding up a small tea tin. "I prefer my own seaweed-based blend. It's quite excellent you know, very healthy and beneficial for one's constitution. I drink it every day. You are welcome to try it, and I think it would be quite good for you as well as enjoyable." Looking at us both he asked, "Would you care for some?"

As a part of my medical practice, I had heard of the exceptional medicinal qualities of certain seaweeds, but somehow, I could not fathom a tea made from seaweed being enjoyable. Still, I did not think it would hurt, and Sherlock had quickly agreed, so Holmes indulged our guest, and he poured three cups of hot water into which Captain Nemo added his seaweed tea blend. The aroma was quite different and seemed to fill the room with a salt sea air that set the mood for the unusual tale that I thought was sure to follow. Little did I know where it was to lead.

We sipped our seaweed tea as Captain Nemo began to speak. His words issued forth as if an ocean fog had permeated the room; Nemo's voice being a distant fog horn, fading in and out. It was there and then gone, somewhere out in the distance. Even the room seemed as if it was moving, or perhaps "floating" would be the better word. I felt myself drifting away and losing consciousness. I tried to resist, but the pull of the tide was too strong. Darkness was enveloping me like a sea mist. In the strange twilight, it felt like tentacles of an octopus were grabbing hold of me and carrying me somewhere while odd voices whispered in the background. I heard the chime of a ship's bell tolling somewhere nearby. Then, all was silent.

The next thing I remember was waking up in a rather comfortable, velvet upholstered chair in a compact, but well-appointed room that was certainly not 221-B Baker Street. While the finish work of the salon was of the highest quality with red velvet furniture, varnished mahogany panels, polished brass, crystals and fine materials, the ceiling looked like it was made entirely of metal with pipes and gauges in place. The floors were covered with elegant Persian rugs. The walls contained fabulous works of art as well as shelves full of books and marine life specimens, and there was a large pipe organ against the far wall. Somewhere in the background, I could hear the rhythmic pulsing of some type of machinery, and there was coolness to the air. With rising fear and trepidation, I realized that somehow, as strange as it seemed, I was actually aboard Captain Nemo's submersible vessel the *Nautilus*.

Panicking, I glanced about and saw Holmes calmly sitting in a plush chair across from me holding a cup of tea and talking with our strange guest. "Sherlock!" I cried out, "The tea! It was drugged!"

Holmes raised the tea cup in his hand as if to salute me and calmly replied, "Yes, yes, Watson. I know it was. You don't expect something that simple to escape my astute perception and knowledge of all things related to narcotics, do you? I knew what it was as soon as he added it to the hot water. Don't you remember? Last year I wrote a monograph on *"The Therapeutic, Narcotic and Hallucinogenic Characteristics and Effects of Various Seaweeds of the Atlantic Ocean"*. As a result of my previous experimentations and test samples with seaweed (all in the name of forensic science, you know), the tea had no effect on me whatsoever."

He paused to make a wide sweep of his hand, to emphasize our surroundings and pointed out. "I am sure you can tell that we are indeed on board Captain Nemo's *Nautilus*. It's really quite remarkable. In fact, it is far more so than Verne's novel even began to indicate. Jules Verne is an excellent writer, but this! This vessel is beyond the power of description. It's too bad you were not awake. I had to help him carry you aboard myself. Did you know you were mumbling something about an octopus? Captain Nemo provided enough information after you passed out for me to determine that we really must assist him in this matter. He was just going into more details, when you came to. Perhaps he won't mind repeating a few of the finer points for you."

My mind was still foggy from the after effects of the tea, but if Sherlock said it was alright to trust this odd stranger, then I knew that I should, but still...

Captain Nemo stood up and held out his hand to me as he began speaking. "First I must apologize for the ruse with the tea. I could not be certain you would believe me when I told you my story, and the stakes are simply too high to fail. I thought that if I could just get you aboard the *Nautilus*, then you would see for yourselves and understand that it is all genuine. I truly am Captain Nemo of the *Nautilus*, and I must find Jules Verne. Sherlock Holmes is the only one in the world with the skills required to succeed in this task. So please do accept my apology and indulge yourself in some refreshments. I assure you these are perfectly safe, and quite delectable."

I cautiously shook Nemo's hand in acceptance of the apology, looked at the table, which appeared to offer a wide variety of the ocean's bounty, and then at Sherlock. Holmes responded by nodding his head and expounding. "Don't be afraid of the seafood, Watson. It is all quite good. And the fried squid is particularly excellent."

Nemo then added. "The squid is my own special recipe and I get a certain sense of satisfaction each time I serve it. You do understand of course, that the encounter with the giant squid in the novel was based on fact."

My head was still swimming, and it felt as if the rest of me had not yet caught up. I thought that perhaps a bite or two might help, and the aroma was exotic as well as appetizing, so, I did help myself to the seafood offerings as Captain Nemo began his unusual tale.

Chapter 2. A Most Unusual Tale, (And certainly a bit fishy.)

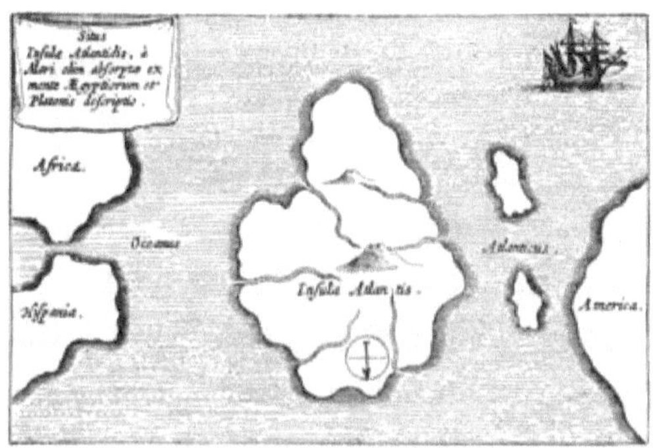

"Gentlemen, first of all, I want to say that what I am going to share with you is the truth. It may not agree with what you do or do not know about the world, history as it is taught, Jules Verne, his works, or for that matter, the representation of myself as a character in his novel, but it is true, every word of it.

There is a force, or should I say an organization, that exists behind the scenes and is invisible to the outside world. They have eyes almost everywhere… and more ears than eyes."

Hearing that, my own eyes grew wide with anticipation, and I inhaled deeply to express my concern, and almost as if he could read my mind, he continued.

"Don't be alarmed, Dr. Watson. They do not seek global domination or unlimited power. They have been monitoring this world since ancient times, observing its development and growth, giving it a nudge here or there as needed, or placing barriers when and where it is necessary. They are the Guardians of the world so to speak."

Recalling our dealings with the Guardians of Time in our last adventure earlier that day, I had to ask, "Are they any relation to the Time Guardians? I am sure your mysterious organization is aware of them if they are as all-knowing as you say, and I cannot say that I am very fond of the Time Guardians' activities."

Nemo looked at me with clear, piercing eyes and continued. "Yes, Dr. Watson, the two are, in fact, somewhat related. The Time Guardians are actually special entities, if I may call them that, whose task it is to keep time functioning in an orderly manner. They are extremely powerful in many ways. If there are too many random time travelers, things could get quite sticky, and you might end up with someone driving a Delorian automobile into the past and then back to the future and really messing things up."

Holmes raised his eyebrow and interjected. "But since we have not seen any 'Delorians' whatever they may happen to be, I deduct that things related to time are currently functioning properly and in a timely manner, so to speak."

Nemo nodded and agreed. "Yes, related to time, things are generally as they should be. The time wanderings of Lewis Carroll and H. G. Wells, or those of Jules Verne, have not adversely affected the order of things. On the contrary, they have helped keep things on track. As I said earlier, sometimes humanity needs a little nudge, and authors like H. G. Wells and Mr. Verne have provided it in a subtle yet effective manner."

Holmes leaned forward and asked. "Are you telling me that their works of fictional science or 'science fiction,' if I may call it that, are actually planting the seeds for the inventions and scientific achievements of the future?"

Captain Nemo smiled and relaxed a bit. "Yes, that's it precisely. By reading fictional accounts about the wondrous achievements and the terrifying horrors of the future, humanity can be gently guided in the right direction and eventually take its proper place in the grand scheme of things. That is why we are here, to ensure that it does happen at the right time. But there are those individuals and governments that would misuse the knowledge and the power that comes with such information, to gain control over the world. We also must be cautious and watchful to prevent that from happening."

"So, you are saying that you are one of this organization of guardians?" Holmes asked slowly.

Captain Nemo paused a moment, looked squarely at Sherlock, and replied, "Yes, I am. From my vessel the *Nautilus*, I have been observing humanity and its use of the ocean for centuries. I can tell you that more than one sea monster over the ages has been attributed to this ship. Cetus, Kraken, Devil Whale, Leviathan, Iku-Turso, the list is endless. All of them refer to the *Nautilus*. On many different occasions we have even been identified as a Giant Narwhale.

He paused and looked at Holmes and then me and went on. "Jules Verne's novel is a fictional version of my adventures with enough modifications that our real organization and its purpose remained a secret."

"So, is he a member of your group also?" I interjected.

"No, no! Not at all," The Captain replied. "Verne, Wells, and Carroll are all human enough, but they are also quite gifted so that they were able to see through the veil and learn how to travel in time and benefit from it, while we were able to use their fictional accounts and novels to our advantage."

Pointing directly at Holmes, he elaborated. "Mr. Holmes, now that you have broken through the veil and discovered time travel, you too will have an outstanding advantage in your line of work. Your powers of perception and deduction, which up to now have been rather good, in the future will seem absolutely uncanny. Your deductions and conclusions will seem next to impossible to the average intellect."

Then looking at me he added, "And you too have an impressive task in front of you, Dr. Watson. Not one word of this can be included in your chronologies of Mr. Holmes' adventures and cases. There must be no mention whatsoever of time travel anywhere in the adventures of Sherlock Holmes during your time period. Yes, you can record this adventure and the real truth, but it must remain unpublished for at least 75 years. By then it may be safe let the truth be known. Or it may have to wait longer. Only time will tell for sure."

Captain Nemo paused, took a sip of his tea, and after a waiting a moment for the impact of his story to sink in, he looked in Sherlock's direction and went on. "You really did do a remarkable job of resolving the Wonderland and Lewis Carroll problem. When you solved that final logic puzzle so quickly, we knew that you would be the one we could turn to regarding our current problem, but only if you could accept the reality of it all. As I stated earlier, that is why I had to get you both on board the *Nautilus*, so you can comprehend the truth of it all."

Holmes nodded his head in agreement and replied, "We understand that you and the *Nautilus* do exist, and you have related a fascinating story, but what is the nature of the Jules Verne problem at hand? And what per chance did you mean by "Verne, Wells and Carroll are human enough"? Are you saying that you are not human? And if you are not human, if you don't mind me asking, what exactly are you? I also note you allude to the fact you are centuries old. If that is the case, I must say you look rather well for your age. I shall have to rewrite my essay on *"Calculating a Person's Age Accurately to Within One Month Based on Readily Observable but Generally Overlooked Attributes and Characteristics."*

Captain Nemo set his tea cup down, sighed, clasped his hands together in front of himself, and stared at a point somewhere in the distance, as if he were trying to figure out where to begin answering Holmes' questions. The silence was heavy with anticipation, as we waited for his reply, while in the background the humming of some sort of machinery could faintly be heard. I again looked around the luxurious salon in which we sat, dumfounded that all of this was in a submersible vessel traveling underwater.

Captain Nemo finally broke the silence and continued. "So many questions. So very many questions... Yes, you need answers to all of them to fully grasp the situation. What exactly am I? You have heard of 'Atlantis the Lost Continent', I am sure. In fact, Jules Verne even mentioned it in his novel. But the sunken ruins he spoke of are just the surface of the story. Eons ago, the Earth was populated by a people that were put here by the Creator. Things went well enough for quite some time. Atlantis was truly magnificent beyond description. It was a wellspring of creativity, art, music, science, medicine, and knowledge such as humanity has never known. But perhaps their knowledge was too great, their thirst for more too demanding. Despite the objections from those of us that saw the danger, the leaders eventually lost their way and destroyed it all in a great cataclysm that sank Atlantis beneath the waves forever. But some of us escaped the destruction. In fact, it was the *Nautilus* that made it possible. Yes, the *Nautilus* was the pride of the Atlantean Navy. At one time, she was a research vessel. Now she is all that is left of our civilization.

"Eventually, humanity as you know it now was given its second chance on Earth. That's the current lot of you, by the way. We survivors of Atlantis vowed to watch over you and never let what happened to us happen to you as well. The Creator agreed and decided to let us remain here nearly invisible, behind the scenes, watching and guiding humanity until we can be certain they are not going to repeat our mistake. In order to do that, we were given greatly extended life spans. We have become the organization of watchers and guardians that I mentioned at the beginning of my story, subtly placed in key areas around the world monitoring and guiding your development.

"I know humanity has experienced its darker periods. The atrocities have at times been terrible over the centuries. But there has always been a light in the darkness, and you have pulled yourselves out of it. At times, it was with our help and at times you have done it on your own. We are proud of how far you have come."

Nemo hesitated a moment, took a deep breath, and exhaled. "We have been quite secretive about our presence, only accepting into our confidence those individuals such as yourselves and Mr. Verne, whom we were absolutely certain we could trust. However, someone or some group knows about us. Who it is or how much they know is uncertain, but they are the ones who have kidnapped Jules Verne. This much we do know."

Holmes interrupted the tale and asked, "How long has Mr. Verne been missing? Has his absence been noticed yet?"

"He has only been gone one day, and his absence has not yet been noticed, as he is supposedly off on a trip in his former auxiliary steam yacht the *Saint-Michel III.* He sold it several years ago, but just recently he received an unexpected invitation from the current owner to take a short cruise. The vessel happened to be in the area where Jules Verne was at the time, and it was to be a short cruise, "for old times' sake," as the new owner put it. Verne naturally accepted. We found the vessel adrift and abandoned in the middle of the English Channel. We now have some of my crew on board continuing the course that had been planned out in the log book, so nothing looks suspicious. There were signs of a struggle, and we found this. We have never seen anything like it before."

He held up a strange object that appeared to be a round metal disc or a medallion with a miniature star map, compass rose, and the stylized letter “M” superimposed upon it.

"As much as we have eyes everywhere and are masters at observing your world, we are not omnipotent, and sadly, we do not have all of the answers. That is why we need someone with your observational skills and deductive abilities, Mr. Holmes. We need you to locate Jules Verne before anything worse happens to him. His captors are most likely planning to gain from him his method of time travel and whatever scientific knowledge of the future he has. That would be a catastrophe. Can we count on your support, Mr. Holmes? I know you most recently have saved Wonderland, but now the fate of your entire world depends on you."

Chapter 3. A Most Unusual Journey, (And a great deal of seafood on the way.)

Sherlock examined the object carefully, looked at the back side of it, turned it over again, and commented, "I should like to examine Mr. Verne's sailing yacht for additional clues as soon as possible. If this object came from whom I think it did, Mr. Verne is in grave danger, and we must act quickly. But if your organization has access to the river of time and time travel as you allude to, why can you not just go back to the moment that he was abducted and intervene?"

Captain Nemo shook his head and replied. "An excellent question, Mr. Holmes, but over the course of the centuries, all of us Atlanteans remaining have reached the limits of our ability to time travel and no longer have access to that path. Yes, the Time Guardians are a part of our legacy, but they too must obey the rules that have been set forth. With Lewis Carroll deceased, H. G. Wells having reached his limit and being no longer able to time travel, and Jules Verne being kidnapped, the only potential time traveler left is you.

“But I must warn you: As astute in logic as you are, you too must play by "The Rules," so to speak. Your opportunities to time travel are not unlimited, and I caution you to use them wisely, so you will have that availability when you need it the most. You know your own skills, Mr. Holmes, and only you can determine when to play that card. And it will be a very tricky card to play, considering the method that you used to step outside of the River of Time. I believe it involved a Unicorn, a Dragon, and several other literary characters. I know enough of your reputation to trust your judgment in that matter. If you’ll excuse me for just a moment, I will have a course set to intercept the *Saint-Michel III*."

Captain Nemo turned a switch on a small control panel on a nearby pedestal and spoke into a device on the end of curved tube. He addressed his crew on the other end of the device, in a language unintelligible to me, and all at once in the background, there were sounds of the propulsion system increasing in power. I could feel a boost in speed. There was additional conversation between Nemo and his crew, and then he shut off the switch and turned to us.

"We will intercept the *Saint-Michel III* in less than a day. You seem to have an idea as to who might be behind this. Might I ask his name?"

Sherlock thought in silence for a moment and replied, "The initial “M” and graphics on the object lead me to believe it could possibly be a Professor James Moriority, but I will not say for certain until I see more evidence. He is a mathematical and astronomical genius and a mastermind of criminal activity and other evil doings, yet he has managed to keep his name spotlessly clean. The last I heard, he was controlling all of London's criminal activities from behind the scenes, but this sounds like something much farther than his reach. With all of the contacts he has, he could have found out about your presence, but the question is, how much does the kidnapper of Jules Verne know? Tell me about your network of Atlanteans. How many of you exist? Where are you posted? How do you communicate between yourselves? It is obvious there has been a compromise in your communication channels. We must find out where."

Captain Nemo nodded his head in concurrence and replied, "Well, we have one in the senior staff of the American President, Benjamin Harrison, and another is the in staff of the British Prime Minister, Robert Cecil. We have agents within and closely monitoring the governments of France, Germany, Poland, Russia, China, and Japan. We have twelve others positioned in the academic and scientific communities around the world, keeping an eye on developments. And there is myself and my crew. My crew members and I rarely leave the *Nautilus*, so I doubt it could have been any one of us. We believe that our Atlantean language is incomprehensible to humans, so we communicate relatively freely via post or telegraph and also using our wireless long distance communication devices."

Sherlock replied. "You mentioned you and your Atlantean companions have unnaturally long lives. How do your people prevent that from being noticed?"

"The crew of the *Nautilus* and I have no need to. As I mentioned, we are a rather closed group. Those Atlanteans who are outside of my crew quietly disappear and then reappear in a different country with a new identity and sometimes minor changes in appearance. A change of hair color or the addition or deletion of facial hair does wonders, as you would know. You are quite the master of disguise, as I understand. It is unlikely that any of them would be noticed."

Sherlock nodded as he answered, “Yes, I could see that. Returning to your Atlantean language that you believe is incomprehensible to us; may I see a written sample of it? Is it possible that your group has been too lax, and someone has deciphered and translated it? Last year, I wrote a paper on, *“Using Logic Based Perception and Mathematical Based Rational to Translate Ciphers, Codes and Unintelligible Languages with a Focus on Mythical Greek Writings”*. Now that I think of it, I did get a letter from someone identifying himself as a language scholar asking for clarification on an issue. I dismissed it at the time, but there may be a connection."

"I will see to it that you get some samples of Atlantean communications, Mr. Holmes. Right now, I have to attend to some ship’s business. If you will excuse me, I should be back in a moment.”

Captain Nemo again spoke in to the communication device, and then stepped out of the room.

"Well Holmes," I asked, “What do you think of all this? Honestly, this sound’s more farfetched than a talking cat telling us that Alice is missing from Wonderland and a Unicorn telling us that the H. G. Wells has the answer. And you know how that all turned out. It got stranger still."

"Yes, Watson, it is quite unusual. I will grant you that. But there is logic to it if you can accept the facts that are given. We are, in fact, on board the *Nautilus* traveling far beneath the ocean’s surface." And with that he pushed a lever in front of a circular metal iris, which then spun open to reveal a very large porthole. It was big enough to be called a window actually, and it showed us the expanse of the ocean floor as we journeyed on our way to intercept Jules Verne's former yacht. It was astonishing and hypnotizing to see the depths of sea unfold before us. A rainbow of marine life was displayed before my eyes. I saw several schools of multicolored fish arrayed in a wide assortment of different shades and hues. There were green sea turtles, grey and white sharks, and more. Off in the distance the aquamarine filament faded away into an inky azure darkness that concealed countless mysteries I was captivated until Sherlock pulled the lever and closed the iris.

"Tell me Watson, how can we be seeing all that if we are not on board the *Nautilus*?" It is the only logical conclusion. I believe what Captain Nemo says is true, and I also suspect that their language code has been broken. In fact, I may have inadvertently helped someone do it. That is all the more reason why I need to help them solve this disappearance."

At that moment, a crew member holding several letters written in Atlantean, entered the salon and handed them to Sherlock. "These are for you, Mr. Holmes. The Captain said if you need more samples to just ask, and I will get them for you." The crew member turned and left the salon and as he did, the door closed with a metallic echo that emphasized the unique strangeness of our surroundings.

Holmes was instantly lost in his examination and study of the Atlantean language. I was left to my own accord for some time. I wandered around the salon enjoying the bountiful selection of seafood that was available on the table, and I must say the sautéed squid was particularly excellent. I also examined the specimens of marine life and other items on display. In addition to the corals and sea shells, there were many priceless works of art. There were also volumes of literary works and scientific papers on the shelves. I even spotted one of Sherlock's works, *"An Analysis of Tea Consumption in Relation to One's Likelihood of Attending Violin Concerts"*. As I recall, that paper provided critical information in solving a significant mystery in the upper levels of London society.

We were quite a distance from London society now, however. Considering the previous day's adventure and where it had led us, I wondered where on earth we would end up next, if indeed it was still on earth. The way things were going we could end up in the belly of a whale or something even more unbelievable. That is not to say where we were at that moment was not truly astounding. The background hum of the machinery continued, and I again opened the iris to watch for quite some time in fascination as the *Nautilus* propelled its way through the never-ending mysteries of the undersea world.

Holmes was oblivious to me while he worked on deciphering the Atlantean language. He said nothing other than to request more tea, which was only an arm's length away from him, but that is Sherlock when he is immersed in resolving a problem. He also asked me to procure one additional Atlantean letter. I closed the metal iris and poured him another cup of tea. Since I did not know how their communication device worked, I had to knock on the door of the salon to get a crew member's attention to obtain one more sample letter. The metallic echo reverberated through our surroundings. With Sherlock having recently solved a nearly impossible logic puzzle, I imagined that this must have been much simpler for him, but he continued to work on it in silence, shuffling the letters back and forth and madly writing out lines of text on the note pad.

After some time had passed, Captain Nemo returned to let us know that we would be approaching Jules Verne's former yacht very soon and that as a precaution; he had started using a code in addition to their language. Holmes responded by handing Nemo complete translations of the sample letters and saying. "I understand your concern in wanting to use a code. I have just finished translating your Atlantean language. If I have done so that means someone else could have done so as well, even if they are not as talented as I. However, if we know someone is eavesdropping, we could use that in our favor and feed them misinformation. We could possibly even set up a trap."

Nemo stared at the translations and muttered, "So that is how it was done. All these years we believed our language was a safe communication method. Yes, I see your point. We wouldn't want to let on that we know that they know, whoever "they" may be. That is excellent logic, Mr. Holmes, but we don't know specifically where the messages are being intercepted."

"Understood," agreed Holmes, "which is why I suggest that we send our doctored message out to one Atlantean recipient at a time and watch for the result that tells us it has been read by someone outside of your group. It will be simple for me to come up with a message that will get their attention and cause them to react in a way that will be obvious to us. Just leave that to me."

Captain Nemo smiled and stated firmly, "Excellent, Mr. Holmes. I am pleased that we can count on you, but first your observational and deductive skills are needed topside. I can tell by our reduced speed that we are alongside the *Saint-Michel III*. We will be surfacing momentarily."

Chapter 4. A Most Unusual Clue, (And a very helpful dolphin.)

I had hardly noticed it, but the ship's speed had decreased while Captain Nemo was speaking. He indicated to us to follow him out of the salon and up a spiral metal staircase that led to a bridge/control room area that had two bulbous round view ports on the forward bulkheads. I could see that we had already surfaced while we were on our way to the bridge. There were several crew members present, with one of them at the wheel, while the remainders were positioned at various stations and other controls. What any of the controls might have been used for, I had no idea. I had never seen anything like it before.

A crew member spoke in English as we entered. "The *Nautilus* is matching her speed sir, and we have rigged a boarding plank and guy lines to get across to her."

Nemo nodded towards us as he left the bridge and stated, "Gentlemen, if you will follow me."

We followed Captain Nemo as he exited through an open doorway in the aft bulkhead of the control room. It felt good to be topside in the open air again. The brisk sea wind had a crisp, salty tang to it, and the sea spray felt good after being below. Looking forward, I could see the arched ramming spur of Captain Nemo's vessel. His submersible reminded me of a large metal shark slicing through the swells. She was the perfect coalescence of nature and technology. Cruising very close to the *Nautilus* was a beautiful white- hulled, auxiliary steam yacht of approximately one hundred feet in length. She was clipper bowed and schooner rigged with raked masts. Her lines were sleek, and she was moving along smartly. As I gazed at her bounding through the waves, she whispered softly of the romance and mystery of the sea. A plank had been run between them with guy lines stretched waist high on either side.

The Captain pointed to the yacht and stated, "That is Jules Verne's former yacht, the *Saint-Michel III*. She is quite beautiful, but we are not here to admire her lines. I am hoping you can find some additional clues that we may have overlooked, Mr. Holmes."

Holmes immediately replied, "I can see a vessel of this size would require a crew of at least ten, and you had mentioned there was the new owner that had invited him. Do you have any idea what happened to them at the time Jules Verne disappeared?"

"That's the strange part. The crew and new owner disappeared with Verne, but the ship's lifeboats are not missing. As I mentioned, there were some small signs of a struggle, some things knocked over on deck and in the cabin that appears to have been used by Jules Verne, but there was no trace of bloodshed. Our replacement crew was instructed to leave everything as it was found, as much as possible, when we discovered her. We had hoped that we could convince you to help us figure out just what had happened here and did not want to disturb any evidence beyond that odd token that I showed you earlier."

Holmes was already on the gangplank, walking between the two vessels as he called back, "A wise choice, Captain Nemo. I will investigate and let you know what I find. I am certain there may be clues on board that are invisible to the untrained eye."

Holmes quickly traveled the distance and was on board when he called out to me, "You come too, Watson. Your assistance is required here."

I looked at the narrow walkway that was strung between the two moving vessels in the rolling seas and was about to object when I recalled some of the journeys that I had taken earlier during the Grinning Cat adventure. Surely this could not be as bad as being inside a carriage being flown all over London by a Jabberwocky trying to follow a Unicorn at top speed. And those Time Machine journeys were something I would never want to experience again. With a firm resolve, I stepped onto the plank only to notice several fins in the water between the two vessels. My first thought was: Sharks! Needless to say, I nearly ran across the plank and made it to the other vessel even quicker than Sherlock.

As I stepped onto the deck of the *Saint-Michel III*, Holmes pointed at them and observed, "Look Watson! Those are common Atlantic Dolphins. *Delphinus Delphus* is the scientific name. Did you ever think you would see them so close in the wild? Rather exhilarating, isn't it?"

I looked back at them just in time to see one of them leap into the air and fall sideways back into the water with a large splash, completely soaking me with salt water. I was about to remark on the less than enjoyable "exhilarating" dolphin when Holmes commented, "We have no time to play with the dolphins, Watson. Start scrutinizing to see if you can find anything that seems out of place. You have been with me on enough investigations to know what I am looking for. It is the common place yet nearly invisible trifle, which will reveal what, has happened here."

Still dripping with salt water, I began to walk around the deck to get a good look at things. Having spent very little time at sea, I was not certain what in fact I was looking for on board a steam yacht that would be unseen to the common eye. The Atlantean crew welcomed us on board and reiterated that they had not touched anything other than what was required to run the vessel. I was certain that I could see them smirking as I left a trail of "playful dolphin" seawater behind me. Everything looked normal enough. The masts, the rigging, the steam funnel, and other ship's gear were as one would expect. The creak of the rigging and the hull all seemed natural. How was I supposed to see the invisible?

Of course, Sherlock came out of the cabin that had been Verne's almost immediately waving a sheet of paper in his hand saying, "Take a look at this, Watson. What do you make of it? I found it in Verne's cabin. It was on the desk but quite cleverly hidden under the desk pad. It was essentially invisible. It looks like the start of a poem, but I am quite certain there is more to it. Verne was very adept at ciphers and hidden messages."

He handed me a sheet on which had been written in French the start of a poem that translated, read as follows:

Salt Water

Salt water, salt water, the life blood of Earth.

Salt water, salt water, the source of our birth.

The answer you seek which is hidden from view,

is in the salt water that's all around you.

Fear not the creature that lives in the brine.

The life that she saves, it may be thine.

Salt water, salt water, the wide ocean blue

reveals the secret that's hidden from view.

As I held the paper, some of the salt water that was still dripping from my clothes ran across the paper and revealed additional writing that had been invisible just a moment before.

"Look at this Holmes!" I exclaimed. "The salt water is revealing a hidden message. You are right. There is more to this than just the start of a poem."

Holmes took the poem back, laid it flat on a cabin top, and asked me to wring my jacket sleeve over it, adding, "Good work, Watson. You should give your dolphin friend a treat for assisting us with this message."

I glanced back over the side, and the two dolphins were still keeping pace with the vessels. The nearer dolphin that had doused me did a spectacular leap that cleared the gangplank and guy lines before diving back into the water. As it leaped out of the water I noticed a white crescent shaped mark on the front of its head. I did ask one of the crew if there were any salted fish in the galley to give to the creature since it been so helpful. He laughed and went to see if he could find anything.

As the salt water moistened the remainder of the paper, additional writing came into view. Sherlock translated and read it aloud it as it appeared. *"I am in danger. The invitation to come on this cruise was a sham. The captain and crew are answering to somebody higher in command, and they intend on kidnapping me for reasons unbeknownst at this time. This vessel will be met by another shortly, so I have little time. I overheard a conversation that indicated their base is less than 75 nautical miles from this position. Latitude N. 50,111'2", Longitude W. 0,39'38". They appear to have great resources, so use caution. My life is in your hands, but Luna may be helpful. Trust her. Jules Verne."*

We both stood in silence for just a moment before Sherlock requested a nautical chart of the area adding, "We have to determine where they are headed. With the speed of the *Nautilus*, we should be able to intercept them rather swiftly, but we need to know where they are."

Taking the chart from a crew member who had hurriedly brought it to him from the cabin, Sherlock spread it out on the cabin top and looking at the coordinates given in the letter stated, "This can't be right." Then using a belaying pin as a straight distance measure from the scale on the chart, he drew a circle with a radius of 75 nautical miles around the point given by Verne. There was no land whatsoever within the circumference of the circle.

Captain Nemo had come over to the *Saint-Michel III* and was looking at the chart shaking his head. "Your position and circle are correctly placed, Mr. Holmes. But you are right, there is no land anywhere in that circle. Do you think that Jules Verne could have misheard the coordinates or misunderstood what they were talking about?"

Holmes considered a moment before replying, "I really don't know Jules Verne all that well. Only by reputation, actually. But he is noted for being very detail minded and quite specific in his writing. If he states that the base of this group is within 75 nautical miles of this position," and he pointed to a position on the chart, "then I believe that it is somewhere within this circle. We just need to know how to look for it. I am skilled in seeing the unseen. Give me a moment to reflect on this."

As Holmes deliberated the question, a crew member came out of the cabin with a small bucket of fish. "Here you go Dr. Watson. You can give the fish to the dolphins, as that one seems to have taken a liking to you."

I thought to myself, if drenching me with cold seawater is taking a liking, I would hate to see it upset with someone. I took the bucket of fish and moved closer to the railing to look over the side. The dolphins were still keeping pace with us, and the playful dolphin seemed to be watching the deck of the ship as it leaned its body to the left so that one eye was looking in our direction. I carefully picked up a few fish trying to avoid getting the smelly fish scales all over my hand and tossed them to the dolphins. The dolphin swimming furthest away caught a fish and swallowed it whole, while the nearer dolphin caught a fish and with a snap of its head tossed it right back at me. Without thinking, I reacted quickly and caught the fish, with a loud splat, ending up with a whole hand full of slimy fish scales. I am not sure who laughed more, the crew members snickering loudly, or the dolphin that was making a squeaking sound that sounded like a high-pitched laughter.

This was too much already. I dumped the remainder of the fish over the side, dropped the bucket on the deck, and turned to wash the scaly mess off my hands. Suddenly, fish started landing all around me. The playful dolphin was catching the fish and flipping them back on to the yacht. I had to duck several times to avoid being hit with them. I had no idea why it was behaving in this way, as I had no previous experience with dolphins. I turned back to the railing and out of frustration leaned over and shouted, "What's wrong with you? Don't you like fish?" As I was in the process of leaning over, the dolphin again made a spectacular leap, this time directly at me. As I lunged backward to avoid a collision, I lost my hat, and the dolphin grabbed it and swam away from the

Nautilus and *Saint-Michel III*. "My Hat!" I exclaimed. "That fish just stole my hat!"

Sherlock looked up from the chart he had been studying and pointed out, "Dolphins are technically not fish, Watson. They are mammals and very intelligent mammals at that. This particular one seems to be having great sport with you."

The dolphin had swum ahead and off to the left of our course and was sticking its head out of the water and waving my hat as if to say, "Here I am. Try and catch me if you want your hat back." It swam towards the two craft and then away to the left several times repeating the action. Holmes observed the behavior intently and stated, "Watson, that dolphin with the white marking is communicating with us. Its behavior conforms expressly to the examples I included in my recent study, *"An Annotated Guide to Non-Vocal Mammalian Communication Behavior, with an Emphasis on Indicating a Desired Direction of Travel"*. It wants us to turn to the left."

Captain Nemo had also been observing it and agreed. "It certainly does look that way, Mr. Holmes, but do we have the time go off on a wild dolphin chase? Who knows why it is acting this way? It could just be naturally playful."

Holmes shook his head. "I don't think so, Captain. It intentionally tried to maneuver Watson into a position where it could get a hold of his hat, something that we would need to retrieve and have to follow it to recover. I say that we should follow it. This may sound strange, but Jules Verne's letter did mention that an unidentified 'Luna', may be helpful. Unless you know of someone else that he knew named Luna, that dolphin clearly has a crescent moon shaped mark on it, and 'Luna' translates to 'moon'. It is my deduction, therefore, that this dolphin is the 'Luna' that Verne is referring to, and I say that we should follow it to where it is leading us."

Now I was really beside myself. By this time, I was soaking wet with my hand full of slimy, smelly, fish scales, and my hat, which by now was certainly ruined, was clutched in the teeth of an overly playful dolphin. First, we get kidnapped onto a fictional submarine that turned out to be real, then we were whisked off on a mission to save another missing author, and now we had to go chasing after a wild dolphin. What was next, a 'giant squid' attack?

Just then, one of the crew members pointed out over the starboard side of the vessel and called out, "Giant squid off the stern quarter, Captain! What are your orders?"

Captain Nemo, Holmes, and I all turned at once to see a massive cephalopod at the surface of the waves five hundred yards astern of us with its tentacles waving wildly. It was nearly the length of Verne's former vessel, and it looked like it could easily crush the ship in its large tentacles.

Holmes pointed out that, no matter what happened, we needed to follow that dolphin, and with Captain Nemo hurriedly ran across the gang plank to the *Nautilus* calling out, "Quick Watson, come over here. We can follow the dolphin easier from the *Nautilus*. Wave at it, or something, so it knows you're on this vessel and not the steam yacht."

Trying to keep one eye on the dolphin and one on the approaching giant squid, I raced across the gang plank to the *Nautilus*, where I stopped and waved at the dolphin who surprisingly flipped my ruined hat back to me. It seemed to know that we were going to follow it, so it no longer needed the hat. I quickly went below while the crew took down the guy lines and plank in preparation for submerging. I immediately went to the large circular window and pulled the lever to spin open the metal iris where I looked to see if could find Luna the dolphin. To my surprise, it was not far from the side of the *Nautilus*, repeating its action of swimming towards us and then away to the left.

Sherlock pointed out the window, saying, "There's that behavior again, we must follow it to the left." There was a rush of bubbles as the *Nautilus* descended beneath the surface of the waves and picked up speed turning to the direction the dolphin apparently wanted us to travel. Captain Nemo entered the salon and informed us that the *Saint-Michel III* was safely making good speed away from the squid in the other direction and that it did not appear that the monstrous creature was following us.

"I am sorry gentlemen, but following this dolphin is a higher priority, so you will have to wait until another time to try my outstanding recipe for Marinated Giant Squid Tentacles. It really is excellent. And giant squid are so hard to come by these days. Tis a pity."

Looking at the puddle of salt water at my feet, Captain Nemo added, "You may want to change your clothes, Dr. Watson. I will have a crew member bring you a set of dry clothing. You wouldn't want to catch cold. Not to mention, that is a 100-year old Persian rug you are standing on."

Sherlock tilted his head to the side looking at the carpet and added, "Looking at that rug and based on my research, *"A Comprehensive Report on the Manufacture of Persian Rugs from the Fourth Century Through Current Times"*, I believe it is actually 103 years, 2 months, and 22 days old. It was completed on a Wednesday during the waxing phase of the moon, and I can tell you the name of the weaver who made it, if you are interested, but it is 27 letters long and difficult to pronounce.

I shook my head and replied, "Just get me some dry clothes please."

Chapter 5. A Most Unusual Discovery, (And who would have ever imagined it?)

I had received a spare crew uniform and was finally warm and dry. A crew member offered me a cup of seaweed tea, stating that to appreciate its full flavor and get the most benefit from it, I may want to let it steep a bit more. I looked at the exceptionally thick, dark green beverage, and mentioned to him that from what it looked like, if it was any steeper, I would need mountain climbing gear to drink it, but he apparently did not find it amusing. "Suit yourself", he replied as he set it down rather roughly. It turned out my comment was fully justified in that when he set it down, the impact of the tea cup on the table split the china cup in two with the pieces falling away from the tea, while the tea retained its shape and form remaining quite solid almost as if it were a gel. Needless to say, I decided to forgo the tea.

With the unbelievable speed of the *Nautilus*, we had traveled quite some distance while I was changing clothes and getting dried off. During that time, Sherlock had created a message to send out to the Atlantean network, one person at a time, along with instructions to the communications officer how to determine where the compromise in their network had taken place. Our dolphin friend, Luna, had continued to indicate the direction of travel the entire time, but now she seemed to be circling. Captain Nemo gave the command to bring the *Nautilus* to a full stop, and we hung there suspended in the endless liquid environment, gazing out into the undersea world and wondering what was to be our next move.

Looking out one of the large circular viewing windows, Captain Nemo asked, "Now what do you propose? It appears that this is where the dolphin wants to take us, but I don't notice anything out of the ordinary. Let us initiate a slow circle of the vicinity to determine what it is Luna is trying to show us."

Captain Nemo issued a command into the speaking tube, and the vessel commenced a slow circular path as we peered out through the two viewing ports, not knowing what specifically we were looking for. The sea floor looked normal enough to me, not that I had ever seen it before that day. The colors faded from a deep azure blue, to purple, and then, to darkness. Sherlock stared intently out the viewing port and expounded, "What we are looking for is what should not be there, even if it is disguised as something that should be there. If only I had a copy of my paper, *"A Guide to Seeing the Unseen by Observing the Cleary Invisible yet Obviously Visible to the Trained Eye"*, you would clearly understand what I am talking about."

Sherlock turned his head as if a thought had suddenly struck him and asked, "How far have we traveled from the point mentioned in Verne's message? And how far were we from that point when we decoded the message?"

Captain Nemo checked a chart that was on one of the tables in the salon, performed several calculations and confirmed we were within the area identified by Verne as the possible location for the base of Verne's captors.

Sherlock continued staring out the viewing point while he answered, "I am certain that we will find something out there related to Jules Verne's disappearance. It is just a matter of seeing the unseen."

Captain Nemo suddenly pointed to a location outside the port viewing window and asked, "What about the clearly visible, yet completely out of place? Do you see that sperm whale there? The depth of this location is entirely too shallow for sperm whales. They are a deep-water species. You would never find one at this depth. And it seems as if it is just sitting on the ocean floor. That is very unnatural behavior. I have spent decades observing marine life in its natural habitat, and I have never seen anything like this before."

We gathered around the viewing port to see what Captain Nemo was referring to, and there sitting motionless on the ocean floor was a medium sized sperm whale. It was very bulky and long, and while it looked similar to the illustrations of sperm whales that I had seen in books in the past, there was something that seemed unnatural about it. It was almost too perfect.

"Look at it!", declared Holmes, "There are no scratch marks anywhere on its body. In every illustration of a sperm whale that I have ever seen, they are covered with scrapes and scratches from encounters with squid or other marine life. That creature hasn't a mark on its body. How would you explain that for a whale of this size, Captain Nemo?"

The Captain shook his head as he responded, "I can't. There is no natural explanation for that. The only possibility I can think of is that it is not a real whale. It's a fabrication. It is very realistic and natural looking, and from afar, it would fool most anyone. But seeing it this close and so clearly underwater, the perfection of it shatters the illusion."

"But why would anyone create an imitation sperm whale?" I asked. "What would be the purpose of such a creation? Do you think it could be a submersible vessel disguised as a whale? That there might be people inside that thing?"

The *Nautilus* was positioned directly across from it now with less than 100 yards between us and the mysterious creature. The skin was smooth and lifelike, but as Holmes had pointed out, it looked almost new, as if it had just been created. Suddenly there was a profusion of air bubbles around the whale, and it quickly bolted forward from its position with its tale rapidly flipping up and down in a movement that was more mechanical than natural. The eyes of the whale had a glow to them as if there was a light source behind them. In just a moment, it was out of the area covered by the viewing window, but the crew in the control room had a longer viewing range from the two forward-looking ports. They reported that the ship, or creature, or whatever it was, had executed a wide turn and was coming directly towards us at a very fast speed. Captain Nemo issued several commands into the speaking tube and told us to hold on to something. Just as the whale was nearing us and a collision seemed imminent, the *Nautilus* executed a very sharp turn that nearly pitched us on our sides. If the aquariums on the shelves had not been sealed, they certainly would have spilled their contents. Dishes and some of the food from the table were thrown to the floor as the artificial whale slid past us missing the *Nautilus* by the smallest margin.

Nemo issued another command, and the *Nautilus* surged forward at full speed away from the strange creation.

The captain looked at the ruined food and commented, "That was the last of our sautéed octopus that just landed on the floor of the salon. They are going to pay for that. Are they following us?" A crew member informed us that the whale had again made a turn and was indeed following us as fast as it could, but the *Nautilus* could easily outrun it, if the Captain so desired. Nemo informed the crewman that he wanted to stay just out of reach of it and issued a course heading, adding that if it worked out as he planned, we would be in for quite a sight.

As the *Nautilus* raced through the undersea world with the strange creature following us, Holmes having observed the creature the entire time stated, "Captain Nemo, in examining the motion and behavior of that 'whale' I can see that is most certainly a submersible vessel disguised as whale. What is your plan?"

The Captain had been briefly looking at a chart when he exclaimed, "It should be... right about... now!" As Captain Nemo finished his statement, he pointed out the viewing port to a spot up ahead and cried out, "There! That is what I was looking for, the giant squid that we saw earlier, I had hoped it would still be somewhere in the vicinity where we left it. Observe!"

The giant squid was indeed still in the area where he had expected it to be and it was even more terrifying to see its full length underwater. The tentacles were covered with hundreds of circular suction cups surrounded by tiny serrated teeth, and the parrot like beak was not something I would want to encounter first hand. Thankfully, the squid paid no attention to the *Nautilus* and maneuvered straight towards the artificial sperm whale. It is well known that the giant squid and sperm whale are natural enemies with the whales typically feeding on the squid, but my guess is that Captain Nemo hoped that, given the opportunity and its immense size, this particular squid would take the role of the aggressor and distract the whale submersible.

Sherlock pointed and interjected, "I see your plan, Captain. It appears to be working. The squid went right for the whale." Indeed, the cephalopod had wrapped its tentacles around the fabricated whale and had rendered the mechanical tale inoperable. Bits of artificial skin were being ripped off the whale in the struggle, revealing a metal structure beneath it. "But what about the people inside the craft?" Sherlock pointed out. "It is possible that Jules Verne may be held prisoner in there. We can't let the squid destroy the vessel."

Captain Nemo issued a command into the communication tube and responded, "That is true, Mr. Holmes. Please observe." The *Nautilus* closed the distance between ourselves, and the squid and whale submersible that were locked in terrible combat. The helmsman brought the hull of the *Nautilus* into contact with the body of the massive cephalopod. There was a bright blue flash as the exterior surface of the submersible delivered a strong electrical shock to the squid, which promptly released the whale and retreated from the area leaving a dark cloudy trail as cephalopods do when they wish to hide. The Captain watched as the giant squid vanished into the murky blue distance and commented, "That could have been an excellent meal of
marinated giant squid tentacles."

The tale flipper mechanism of the whale had been badly damaged during the battle with the squid, so the craft no longer posed a ramming threat, but we still had to find out who was inside it. A rush of air bubbles indicated that it was rising to the surface, and the *Nautilus* followed suit. As both vessels broke the surface, the *Nautilus*'s crew immediately secured lines to the mystery vessel and, armed with strange looking rifles, looked for some sort of access to the interior. There was a distinct mechanical sound from inside, and a section in the upper back portion of the whale's head opened up to reveal an entrance to the interior of the mysterious vessel.

Sherlock, Captain Nemo, and I climbed the stairs up to the deck of the *Nautilus* to observe the proceedings, and Holmes pointed out, "If you look closely, you can see where that hatch was designed to be nearly invisible when closed. My deduction is that this vessel is pneumatically powered by the use of compressed air cylinders. That would explain the mechanical motion of the tail propulsion, and the air bubbles. This is a very clever creation." Pointing towards the hatch, Sherlock drew our attention to several figures emerging with hands held up in surrender. "Look! They are exiting the craft. It appears that they are surrendering, but if they have any type of wireless communication device similar to that used by your Atlantean network and you take them aboard the *Nautilus*, that could be a way for their organization to track them and in doing so, track us. That would let their leaders know where we are. I suggest the prisoners be searched for any device that could be used in such a way, and if you are able to call your crew aboard Jules Verne's yacht; have them return to the area. The prisoners can be detained on board the *Saint-Michel III.*

Captain Nemo gave a command to his crew members guarding the individuals who had exited the craft. The three were all of medium build with dark hair and thin mustaches, wore dark colored uniforms and tall boots. They spoke accented English and explained that their submersible whale vessel had been severely damaged and would not stay afloat for long. They offered their surrender in exchange for safety.

Sherlock told Captain Nemo that he needed to see the interior of the vessel before it sank and entered the hatch calling for me to follow. Stepping through a hatchway into a vessel that one knows is about to sink is not something I would recommend to the claustrophobic or faint of heart or one who is overly concerned for their safety or, for that matter, anyone at all. Nevertheless, I followed Holmes into the dark recess below the hatch. Ignoring the creaks and groans of the foundering vessel, the rising water at his feet, and the sparks emitting from the control panels on the walls of the cramped interior, Sherlock stood in rapt fascination at the design and workmanship of the craft. "This is quite impressive, Watson! There is some very advanced design work here. I shall have to update my paper on *"Proposed Practical Applications and Logical Usage of Pneumatics in Transportation."*

Concerned with the water level and stability of the vessel, I hurriedly replied, "That's if we get out of here in time. What exactly are we looking for, Holmes?"

Sherlock quickly responded, "Anything that would tell us if Jules Verne has been aboard this vessel. Luna led us directly to this craft. There must have been some reason for that behavior. I believe we will find our next clue somewhere here if we can locate it before the vessel sinks."

Sherlock and I had experienced many short deadlines when looking for clues in the past. I can remember times when we had less than eight hours to find some clue or proof to prevent an innocent man from being executed. In this case, we had mere minutes to find some unknown bit of evidence before we lost our own lives. What could it be? The interior of the vessel was quite small and crowded with equipment, air tanks, and lines. There were assorted odds and ends everywhere, and the water was rising higher and higher by the second. Sherlock had gone into the forward compartment, and was I am sure, using his unequaled skill in perception, when suddenly, the amount of water coming from the stern of the whale shaped vessel increased dramatically and the back end began to tilt downward.

"Sherlock!" I cried. "We have got to get out of here!" I had hurried back up through the hatch and turned to be certain he was following me, when a rush of water burst out of the hatch and the vessel started to settle below the surface. The only things holding it up were the lines that held it to the *Nautilus*. Captain Nemo's crew was urging me to come back to the *Nautilus* before I would be pulled under by the suction of the sinking vessel. The interior of the craft was now completely full of water, and it seemed hopeless, but I was determined not lose my best friend and the world's most talented consulting detective. I was about to dive into the hatch to make one last attempt to find him, when the strangest creature began to climb out of the hatch. I stepped back, not knowing what it was, as it appeared to be some sort of giant sea shell with tubes and a mechanical valve mounted on it. As it continued to exit, I saw that it was not a 'creature', but it was Sherlock wearing some type of underwater breathing device over his head, air supply on his back, and holding a pocket watch in his hand. We quickly returned to the deck of the *Nautilus*, after which Nemo's crew cut the lines that supported the sperm whale vessel, and it returned to the depths for the last time.

As Sherlock removed the breathing device, I exclaimed, "Holmes, you gave me such a start! I thought you had drowned in there. How did you know what that contraption is much less what to do with it? And why did you risk your life just to retrieve a pocket watch?"

"If you look at this piece of equipment Watson, you will see it cannot be anything but a cleverly designed underwater breathing device. It uses a very large sea shell to hold the air and delivers it via hoses to the helmet. You do recall that paper I wrote *"On Determining the Functionality and Purpose of Unknown Objects in Less Than Three Seconds Using Rational Deductive Observation"*. Once you identify an object, it is quite simple to deduce how it works. I knew I would be able to use it to extend my time to search the forward cabin. While I did not find Jules Verne, I did find this."

As he spoke, Sherlock set the breathing apparatus and helmet down on the deck and held up the watch, so I could clearly see the initials engraved into the back of the watch case, "J.G.V."

Chapter 6. A Most Unusual Lead, (But certainly rather timely.)

Sherlock had found a watch with initials that matched those of Jules Gabriel Verne. It was a lead which quite possibly proved that Verne had been aboard the whale submersible, but now what were we to do, since the strange craft had sunk and taken with it any additional clues? As we spoke, a steam auxiliary was seen approaching from the West, and I commented, "That looks like Jules Verne's former steam yacht."

Captain Nemo confirmed my observation. "It is, Dr. Watson. We are going to deposit the captured crewmen on board the *Saint-Michel III*, so there is no chance of them in any way broadcasting our position to their leaders. According to them, they are just paid crew members on an experimental craft, and they were separated from the main vessel, which was observing the whale submersible's operation. They claim to know nothing at all about Jules Verne or his whereabouts."

Sherlock replied, "I don't need to talk to them to know that they are lying. This watch tells more than just time. It is also a message from Jules Verne himself. When your prisoners are removed from the *Nautilus*, please do meet me in the salon of your vessel, and I will explain. And by the way, do you happen to have a copy of Jules Verne's book, "*A Journey to the Center of the Earth*?"

Captain Nemo replied there was a first edition copy in the *Nautilus* library located in the salon and that he would be along momentarily. As we descended into the interior of Nemo's vessel, I wondered, how a simple pocket watch could be a 'message' from Jules Verne and why Holmes had asked about a copy of Verne's famous underground adventure. As soon as we reentered the luxurious room that contained Captain Nemo's library, Sherlock immediately went over to the bookshelves and retrieved a copy of Verne's novel. He then made his way to a table and set the watch and book down next to each other. "Now, I could use a writing implement, some ink, and some paper," he said aloud, to which I simply handed them to him, as he had left the items on the table where he had previously been working on the translation of the Atlantean language. Of course, since we were aboard the *Nautilus*, the ink was squid based, as one would expect.

"What are you doing Sherlock?" I asked quite bluntly. "What is so special about this watch?"

Sherlock clicked open the case of the pocket watch and pointed to the inside of the cover and simply replied, "This! It is a message from Jules Verne."

There were a number of very tiny marks scratched into the inside of the metal cover of the watch. They looked like no more than random scratching to me, more like a bird had been pecking on it, or perhaps the watch case had been left open while carried in a pocket full of sharp rocks or nails.

"And what is the significance of those markings?" I asked. "They don't look very important as far as I can see."

With his usual frankness, Sherlock replied, "That is because you don't see very far, Watson." Leafing through the copy of *"A Journey to the Center of the Earth"*, Sherlock continued, "You do remember that monograph I wrote a few years ago, *"Cryptology, Ciphers, Codes, and Secret Languages and How to Determine Their Hidden Meaning"*. I knew what this was as soon as I spotted it, but to read it, I needed a copy of this." He had opened Verne's book to the page that displayed the cipher that a character in the book, Arnie Saknusum, had used to hide a secret message. It had been written in Viking runic characters as well as in code and was a key point in the novel. Sherlock began copying the markings from the watch case and then used the runic cipher to translate the message. After only a moment, he set down the writing implement, and declared to Captain Nemo, who had just entered, "It's just as I suspected. Jules Verne was able to leave us a clue as to where they are taking him. This message contains the coordinates of the location they are headed to. We must alter our course immediately, Captain." Sherlock held out the paper that contained the course heading. Nemo took the information from Holmes and handed it to a crew member with instructions to adjust the course. Turning to Sherlock, he asked, "Did you find anything else of interest inside the vessel before it sank?"

Sherlock paused for a moment before answering, "Next to the *Nautilus*, that submersible was more advanced than anything any of the European nations have built to date. The French submersible *Piongeur* and the Spanish *Icentio II* were positively primitive compared to what I saw down there. The question is: Where did they get their technology? It is not at the level of your *Nautilus*, but it is still years ahead of the rest of the world. I am certain that the science of your *Nautilus* has been kept secret over the years, so that could not be the source."

Captain Nemo shook his head and affirmed Holmes' comment. "I assure you that the technology of the *Nautilus* has remained hidden from all except Jules Verne. That is why we need to rescue him as quickly as possible. Even in his novel, he did not explain the true nature and functionality of the power source of the *Nautilus*. He did an excellent job of telling an engaging story without giving away any important details. Where they acquired their science is beyond my grasp at this time."

"Where are we headed now?" I interrupted. "What is our next destination?"

Captain Nemo spread out the chart on which had been drawn the circle within which the home base of the mysterious group was located. "We are here," he stated, pointing towards two positions on the chart, "and we are headed here. It should not take us long. Again, there is nothing on the chart to indicate that there is an island or land of any kind in that location."

Sherlock, however, raised a question. "But what if they do not need dry land? What if their base is located on a seamount? An undersea mountain that never broke the surface of the ocean? Or perhaps an ancient volcano that has subsided to a depth below the surface of the ocean. If they have the technology to create that whale vessel, then it is only logical that they have also mastered the science of underwater living structures. They would be invisible to the rest of the world, much like you and your *Nautilus*. With their submersibles disguised as whales, they could go to and from their base without anyone noticing. And with that location, they could be a serious threat to shipping in the English Channel, especially if they have knowledge of advanced science and weapons from the future. How much does Jules Verne actually know of future technology at this time?"

The captain exhaled deeply. "Based on his writings, 100 years from now, Jules Verne will most likely be known as the man who predicted the future. He knows quite a bit, but in a more general way, as opposed to specific details. Still, he would not purposely divulge information to those who would misuse it. Nevertheless, I fear for his safety."

While they were talking, my gaze wandered toward the large circular viewing port, and I happened to spot Luna swimming alongside the *Nautilus*. As I watched her swim, the strangest thing occurred. I cannot say if it was an after effect of the seaweed tea I had tried earlier or a side effect of the air on board or perhaps something else entirely. I was not paying any attention to the dolphin. She was just in my peripheral vision outside of my main focal point when, for a moment, she appeared not as a dolphin but as a mermaid, swimming outside the viewing port. As impossible as it seems, for that brief second, she appeared to be a real mermaid with long, flowing dark hair, a strikingly beautiful face, the bluest eyes I had ever seen, and yes, a luminous green, scaly fish tail. She wore a metallic blue colored top that accentuated her lovely form. The vision lasted only a second, for when I focused more directly on Luna, I was looking at a dolphin again. Yet, I could not shake the picture of the mermaid I had seen, from my mind. I knew it was simply not possible. I would have dismissed it as just my imagination getting the better of me, but the crescent moon mark had been clearly visible on the nymph's forehead, and I would have sworn she had looked at me and smiled.

Now, Sherlock has stated many times that eye witnesses are the worst evidence for a case, as the human eye can be so easily deceived, and the human mind can so readily misinterpret what it thinks it sees. One client was positive his wife was a vampire. Another was certain his family was cursed and that a demon dog was after him. Sherlock was easily able to disprove these cases, yet the clients were absolutely positive of what they thought they had seen. This had to be a simple case of misreading what I saw and nothing more. I would certainly not mention it to Holmes.

Chapter 7. A Most Unusual Sight,
(So, there is some truth to that old tale.)

I had no sooner determined that what I had seen was an illusion resulting from, perhaps, fatigue, when again Luna briefly appeared to me as a mermaid. This time I was staring directly at her. One moment I was looking at Luna the dolphin, and the next moment, a mermaid was right outside the viewing port. This time there was no mistaking what I was seeing. She was extraordinary and beguiling as well! I quickly called to Holmes and Captain Nemo to look out the viewing port, and when they did, Sherlock commented, "Ah yes, it is Luna the dolphin. She is still out there, I see. That creature exhibits a strong intelligence. Eh, Watson? I wonder why it is that she continues to follow us."

Captain Nemo remained silent for a moment and stared at me before replying, "Why indeed? Yes, dolphins are quite intelligent. But then, the sea has many mysteries and things we cannot explain. I am sure you will experience more of these mysteries before our journey is over."

Now what did Captain Nemo mean by that? Did he know something about Luna that he was not saying? Was I really seeing a mermaid out there? But that could not be possible. Everyone knows mermaids are an old sailor's legend. I turned from the viewing port to focus my attention on the conversation between

Captain Nemo and Holmes, but my thoughts kept drifting back to Luna as Captain Nemo addressed Sherlock. "So, Mr. Holmes, if we do find an underwater base at this location what do you suggest?

Holmes thoughtfully replied, "Well, that depends a great deal on what we find. I would suggest that we approach the location with extreme caution and perhaps stop before we get to the destination. Is it possible to send an underwater scouting party to reconnoiter the vicinity? Jules Verne's novel described underwater breathing equipment and that whale submersible had the breathing device that I used to escape, so I deduce that you do have such equipment aboard the *Nautilus*. We do not know their weaponry or the extent of what they…"

Once again, my thoughts were drifting back to the mystery of Luna and the mermaid. What was I truthfully seeing out there? I had already experienced a considerable number of strange creatures and literary characters coming to life in our previous adventure, but there was a somewhat, sort of, possible logical explanation for it all. Perhaps Lewis Carroll's agreement and wager with the Time Guardians had somehow brought it all about. But mermaids? Impossible! They simply did not exist! That was it. Final! Finished! The end! No more discussion. If I looked out that viewing port again, I would see a dolphin named "Luna". No questions asked!

Of course, when I looked out the port I saw the alluring mermaid again, this time looking straight at me with the most dazzling, deepest eyes I had ever beheld. Her smile was radiant and mesmerizing. She was overwhelmingly captivating. This time I did not turn away. Truthfully, I could not turn away. She had enchanted me completely and unconditionally. I was hers forever. I continued to stare until, from what seemed like a faraway distance, I heard Holmes asking me a question. "Isn't that right Watson? What do you think?"

I blinked and once again there was Luna where the mermaid had been swimming. "What was that, Sherlock? I wasn't paying attention there for just a moment. Could you repeat the question? I don't think I am feeling quite well."

Sherlock looked at me curiously. "Indeed, Watson, pull yourself together. You look as if you have seen a mermaid or something. The captain was asking if you want to be part of the underwater scouting team, and I was saying, after all we went through in our previous adventure, nothing would bother you. But I am beginning to wonder about that. Are you feeling ill? Maybe you could use a cup of the medicinal seaweed tea."

"No thank you!" I replied rather abruptly. I was not in the mood for any more of a tea that one could cut with a knife, and most likely dull the knife in the process, if you did not break it out right. Yet what was he saying about going outside the *Nautilus* underwater? Maybe it would be an opportunity to see what was really going on with that dolphin or mermaid or whatever it was. I decided to accept the offer and replied, "Yes, thank you! That might be a fascinating experience. How exactly does the breathing apparatus work? What do I need to do?"

The captain escorted Sherlock and me to the airlock chamber of the vessel and gave us instructions on the use of his underwater breathing equipment. It was quite remarkable. The system was similar to the one that Sherlock had used to escape the whale submersible, but instead of a large sea shell to hold the air, it was comprised of a compressed air tank with hoses that were attached to a helmet that fastened to the collar of a suit that was made of a water-tight material. There was a belt with weights and metal shoes to prevent us from being too buoyant. He explained that with the air in the tank, we should have one hour of breathing time and to make sure we did not stray too far from the *Nautilus*. Attached to the wrist of the underwater suit was a watch that had been specially treated to be water-tight.

We had safely arrived at a place near our final destination but hidden from view behind a large rock outcropping covered with kelp and other seaweed. The Captain also gave Sherlock a special type of rifle of his own design that worked underwater and fired an electrically charged bolt. I hoped he would not have to use it. My thoughts were wholly on Luna and the mermaid. Was the dolphin actually a mermaid? How on earth could that be possible? Whatever the case turned out to be, I looked forward to receiving my answer soon.

The *Nautilus* had come to rest on the ocean floor out of sight of the seamount. Sherlock and I were to be accompanied by Captain Nemo and two of his crew members. He explained that we would be able to communicate with each other with the full helmets, which gave us not only air to breathe, but also a medium in which to speak. We would, however, need to be in close range to hear each other. Sherlock remarked that this experience would provide an excellent basis for the paper he was writing "*On Communication in Atmospheres and Mediums of Varying Densities and Determining Maximum Audible Range*". He cheerfully added, "This will be quite the experience, eh, Watson old boy! I imagine this underwater expedition will be even more exciting than our little jaunts courtesy of H. G. Wells' Time Machine."

"Exciting" was not the adjective I would have used for those trips, and I hoped that our underwater excursion would not be, in any way similar. We had barely escaped with our lives from that bit of madness. Referring to those "little jaunts" as "exciting" is like saying that being blindfolded and strapped to a wild horse as it gallops down the side of an erupting volcano is equivalent to an afternoon ride in the park. "Terrifying", "alarming", or "death defying" would be a more suitable description for that experience.

But now I was trying to focus on what I was about to do. I was going to step out of a perfectly safe and dry underwater vessel into a liquid environment that could kill me in a dozen different ways in seconds, using breathing equipment that I had never seen before, much less used. What was I thinking? Sherlock and Captain Nemo had already exited the vessel through a large hatch in the bottom of the floor of the air chamber room that opened into a pool of water. I was standing on the edge of the pool wondering what on earth I was doing, and why was I doing it, when one of the crewmen urged me forward and I stepped off the edge into the watery blue abyss. I was sure my life was over.

It was beyond belief! I slowly sunk to the sea bottom several feet below the open hatch in the *Nautilus*. I rapidly reached the ocean floor, raising a cloud of silt, and Sherlock grabbed my arm to move me out of the way of the remaining crew members who would be dropping from the hatch to accompany us. What an unbelievable experience! I was underwater and breathing! Even more miraculous, I was still alive. In spite of the water-tight suit, I felt chilled from the seawater that surrounded me with its frigid cold embrace. I gazed around me and noticed a wide variety of fish and other marine life, but I did not see Luna anywhere. I was still in the vicinity of Captain Nemo, Sherlock, and the crew members who had also descended to the ocean floor, so that could explain Luna's absence. Captain Nemo took the lead and indicated the direction we were to travel. While the equipment and weighted shoes had been cumbersome on board the *Nautilus*, it was easier to move about underwater due to the buoyancy. Still it was so foreign and strange to be walking on the ocean floor. It was almost intoxicating. We carefully made our way towards the seamount wondering what we would find there. As we made our way forward, I continued to look for signs of Luna, but without success. Captain Nemo abruptly held up his hand to stop our scouting group and then pointed to the seamount on the right. Upon the undersea plateau was a small underwater compound.

Several interconnected metal structures covered with a multitude of pipes and valves were located on the surface of the seamount. There were hatches on the sides of them which were most likely air locks similar to the chamber I had just used to exit the *Nautilus*. A docking platform was resting on pilings located on top of one of the structures. A second even larger platform seemed to be some type of elevator that could be raised to the ocean surface. This must be a base of operations. How could we possibly gain access to the interior without being noticed? I did not think it would be possible, when I heard Sherlock explain his plan to Captain Nemo. "It is really quite simple, Captain. They must have a power source to maintain their presence here and some type of apparatus to maintain their air supply. If you look over there, I would say that is the air system purifier for the entire base. Send your crew back to the *Nautilus* to get a concentrated quantity of the seaweed tea that you tried to drug us with and have them put it under pressure using one of your breathing cylinders. I can add it to their air supply and render the whole base unconscious. Then we can slip inside undetected to see what we can find."

As we waited for the crew to return, I was in awe at Holmes' deductive ability. He had just glanced at a complex structure based on science far beyond anything of our time and unquestionably known what to do. While we were waiting, I also took advantage of the opportunity to look around the vicinity to see if Luna was still nearby. I could not get the irresistible vision of her out of my mind and was determined to get an answer. The underwater visibility was somewhat limited, so I could not see very far. I decided to take a few steps away to see further into the murky blue depths when suddenly the mermaid appeared directly in front of me! She put one hand on my shoulder and one finger to her lip to indicate, “Don’t say a word.” She really did not need to caution me, as I was utterly speechless. I blinked my eyes several times, and she was still before me. This time, there was no question or doubting. The mermaid was real. How would I ever explain this to Holmes? It was not logical. But logical or not, she was there and pulling on my arm to move me further away from where Sherlock and Captain Nemo were waiting. With each motion of her scaly, green tail, the distance increased. Not knowing what to do, I gave in, and let her lead the way and she pointed to an underwater cave opening in the rock formation. With a flip of her tail she disappeared into the cave entrance and then immediately reappeared urging me to follow her.

As I entered the undersea cavern, I noticed that the sea floor sloped upward, and soon I was breaking the surface of the water inside the chamber which contained an air pocket. It was medium in size, and the ceiling which disappeared into darkness above me, was covered in sparkling crystalline cave formations, while the bottom consisted of a ledge that surrounded a small pool of water. I made my way over to the ledge to sit down, as I was overwhelmed by the complete strangeness of everything. In a moment, she had burst out of the pool and was sitting by my side with her tail still in the water and her hands clutching my arms as she pleaded with me to listen. I have to say that seeing her so close in her true mermaid appearance made it quite a challenge not to sit and dumbfoundedly stare at her. Any true English gentleman would tell you it is simply not proper. In spite of her intoxicating beauty, I did manage to avoid staring and listened intently to what she was urgently saying. She pleaded, "Sir, you must listen to me. Your life depends on it. If you are trying to save Monsieur Verne, you and your friends must not enter that structure. It is a trap! He was there, but they have taken him away in a flying machine. If anyone enters any one of those metal boxes, the air chamber doorways will be destroyed along with whoever is nearby. I heard them planning it. They know they are being followed and are willing to sacrifice their base to stop you. I will explain everything in more detail later, but you must stop your friends from going in there. Go! Go quickly!" And with that, she dove into the water pulling me with her and pushing me back out of the cave, when suddenly, the sound of a nearby explosion shook the area.

Chapter 8. A Most Unusual Turn of Events,
(But of course, Sherlock saw it coming.)

A feeling of dread and fear overwhelmed me. We were too late! While I was distracted by the mermaid, they had tried to enter the compound and had triggered the trap. Sherlock and the others were probably dead or seriously injured. Trying to see through the cloud of sediment that had been raised by the explosion, I hurried back to where I had left them and was relieved to see them still alive and well gathered behind the rock formation. How was it possible? I moved close enough to Sherlock to be able to communicate and asked him, "Holmes, how did you know about the explosives attached to the entry hatches?" To which he replied, "Watson, where have you been? And how did YOU know about the explosives attached to the entry hatches?

I was about to tell him when Captain Nemo motioned for Sherlock to move forward and asked him to check for any additional explosives. Holmes nodded and stated, "Don't be concerned. I will verify it is safe. This is unequivocally what I covered in my monograph, *"An Analytical Approach to Detecting Hidden Bombs, Booby traps, and Explosive Devices in All Situations with an Emphasis on Doorways"*. Give me just a moment."

Without waiting for my reply, Sherlock strode forward to the structures trailing behind him a thin rope line. Captain Nemo explained to me Sherlock had spotted the hidden explosives on the entry hatch while he was attaching the drugged gas to their air supply and that he had detonated the explosive using a trip line from behind the safety of the rock formation. He also asked me how I had known about the trap when I was not in the area when Holmes had discovered it. I turned to point out the mermaid, but she had again disappeared. I did not know what to think or what to say to the Captain. Fortunately, I did not have to answer as Sherlock returned to the shelter of the rocks trailing the line.

"It is as I expected. There was a second trap on the inner air chamber door. Brace yourselves!"

And with that, he pulled on the line, and there was a second explosion. When the turbulence ceased, Sherlock told us to wait while he investigated further. Nemo and his crew were looking in the direction of Sherlock as he trudged back to the structures, when I felt a hand on my shoulder and heard Luna's voice against the back of my breathing helmet. "Your friend is in danger. There is one more trap that he will not see. We must stop him!" And suddenly my arm was in the grasp of a dolphin that was quickly dragging me towards Sherlock with each flip of her powerful tail fin. Just as Sherlock was about to re-enter the structure, I grabbed his arm, pulling him into voice range and cautioning him, "Wait Holmes, don't go in. There is one more trap that you would not see!"

When I had pulled him away from the door, Luna, still in her dolphin appearance, quickly swam up to the chamber entrance carrying a piece of metal debris, which she flung into the chamber, and then swam quickly away. Just as she had reached a safe distance from the entrance, there was yet another explosion which blew open the entire chamber.

As the silt and turbulence from the detonation settled, Holmes went over to the remains of the structure and looked inside. I saw him reach in for a moment, and then he returned to where I was, leaned towards me and stated, "Let us return to the *Nautilus.* We are getting low on air and you need to explain what is going on with that dolphin and how you knew about the third explosive device without having entered the structure."

We had made our way back to the *Nautilus*, reentered the air chamber room, and were removing the underwater breathing gear when the pool of water at the entrance hatch in the bottom of the floor was broken by a large splash. First it looked as if a dolphin was jumping out of the water, but then the mermaid, burst through the surface of the pool. She gracefully sat on the edge of the pool with her iridescent scaly fish tail still hanging in the water, her long dark hair flowing over her shoulders, and a whimsical expression on her face. Her metallic blue top sparkled in the light of the airlock chamber. She smiled, looked at us, and simply stated, "Hello. My name is Luna. Yes, I really am a mermaid, and no, I am not a harbinger of storms, shipwrecks or death. I would imagine you have more than several questions. We 'shell sea', if I answer them." She then gave a playful swish of her luminous green tail.

The silence was at first overwhelming, then Captain Nemo and his crew started asking questions all at the same time, as they stared at her with wide eyes, and awestruck faces.

"How is it possible?" asked the Mate.

"Where did you come from?" the Bosun inquired.

"If you please, just where have you been hiding for the last several centuries?" The Captain politely asked.

"Are you married?" an unidentified crewman piped in, adding, “And if you are married, do you have any sisters?”

Sherlock, however, was much more practical in his approach, as he bowed slightly to her and said, "Greetings Miss Luna. Thank you so very much for your assistance. How is it that you knew of the explosive traps in the base? And what can you tell us about where they have taken Jules Verne?"

I shook my head in amazement. I have often stated that Sherlock Holmes is as unemotional as a calculating machine and as cold as a fish. Here, he had the closest thing to a talking fish sitting right in front of him, and he didn’t even blink an eye. An impossibly beautiful creature of legend, lies, and myth, a genuine mermaid, was sitting right in front of him, and he talks to her like a common London resident, no different than any other person he had ever questioned.

She nodded her head back to him and answered, "My existence is a very long story, which you do not have time for at the moment. I will go into greater detail on my history later. Regarding my knowledge of their traps, in my dolphin appearance, it was easy to overhear what they were planning. No one pays attention to dolphins no matter how smart they may seem. I do know that they have a flying machine similar to what Jules Verne described in one of his books. If you bring me a navigation chart, I can direct you to the location they have taken him. It is surrounded by water, so you should not have great difficulty in reaching that place."

Then looking directly at Sherlock, she added, "You have been very creative in discovering, understanding, and following

Monsieur Verne's clues as well as seeing and avoiding the enemy's hidden explosive traps."

As Captain Nemo sent a crew member to retrieve a nautical chart, Sherlock answered, "It is elementary, really. It is simply a matter of knowing correctly where to look, what specifically one should be looking for, and ignoring everything else in the vicinity. It is quite straightforward once one understands the process."

Shaking my head, I added, "And don't forget believing it when one sees it."

She turned to look at me, smiled, and replied, "That is where you have difficulty, good sir. I can tell that you have a very caring heart and a gentle soul, which is why I chose you, to communicate with. Yet still, it took me the longest time before you accepted that I was there and that I really am a mermaid. Even now you are overwhelmed by my presence. I actually find that very sweet. Returning to my dolphin appearance, people's lack of imagination and unwillingness to accept what they do not understand makes it very easy to hide in plain sight, since they do not see me as I truly appear. Sometimes, I enjoy confusing fishermen 'on porpoise'." She laughed brightly at her humor in a lilting, melodious voice and added, “But if I get nervous, I just ‘clam up’.” And she laughed again, this time echoing like wind chimes.

Then turning towards the chart that had been brought to her, she pointed at a spot and stated, "There! That is where they are taking him. It is a diminutive volcanic island off the coast of Iceland, deserted and rather remote. Your submersible craft can travel as nearly rapidly as their flying machine, so you can compensate for lost time, but you must be expedient."

Captain Nemo issued a command to his crew to set a course at full speed for the location Luna had indicated and commented, "If you do not mind my observation, your vocabulary is quite excellent for a mythical creature."

She gave a slight rustle of her tail and replied, "As is yours for a fictional, literary character. You are not the only one here that is older than their appearance. One can achieve an excellent vocabulary over decades of observing and listening to humans from the unnoticed vantage point of a dolphin."

Sherlock, however, interrupted the discussion to return to more practical matters. "When the current situation is resolved, you two can continue your debate on whose vocabulary is more prodigious, but for now, we must eschew that deliberation and lucubrate as much as possible on what will aid us in extricating Jules Verne. Luna, what more can you tell me about his captors? Based on what I saw at that base, I no longer believe that it was Professor Moriority. This is far beyond his capabilities. The science and technology of this organization is almost equal to that of you and your *Nautilus*, Captain Nemo. I would say that there is yet another group out there similar to the descendants of Atlantis."

Luna looked at Sherlock and stated, "It is as you observed, Mr. Holmes. The star map and initial "M" does not stand for your Professor Moriority. It stands for the survivors of the Lost City of Mu."

Sherlock pondered only a moment before replying, "The Lost City of Mu was proposed by Augustus Le Plongeon based upon his investigations of Mayan ruins in the Yucatan peninsula. He stated that the writings he had translated proved that they were much older than many other ancient civilizations. It is now a commonly-held belief that Le Plongeon actually got the name "Mu" from the French scholar and archeologist, Abbe Charles Étienne Brasseur de Bourbourg who in fact, had made a translation error while working with the Madrid Codex and a pre-

Columbian Mayan script. Brasseur was positive that a word he interpreted as Mu referred to an ancient land submerged beneath the ocean. Le Plongeon then misidentified this lost land as a continent which he conjectured had sunk into the Atlantic Ocean. The general consensus among most historians, however, is that it never existed."

Surprised to hear his detailed description of Mu, I observed, "Sherlock, when did you become the expert on lost civilizations?"

He dismissively replied, "Watson, you recall last year I had to do a bit of research to recover a collection of priceless artifacts that had mysteriously disappeared from inside a locked gallery in the London Museum of Natural History. In addition to locating and returning them, I also gathered enough information to pen a small monograph on "*A Logical, Deductive Approach to the Analysis of Lost Cities, Civilizations, and Continents to Determine Their Factual Status*."

Captain Nemo raised a pointed finger and interrupted Sherlock. "That was a detailed definition of the Lost City of Mu, Mr. Holmes, except for one small detail. It really did exist. Just as the Island of Atlantis actually existed and was destroyed, the City of Mu also existed and was destroyed. The pointed difference between Atlantis and Mu is that the one goal of the populace of Mu was world domination. They too, were technologically brilliant with advanced science, but they were entirely evil. When their island city was destroyed, we Atlanteans believed there were no survivors; that their threat to the world was over. Apparently, some did survive, and they have remained hidden until now."

Chapter 9. Another Most Unusual Turn of Events, (Who would have imagined yet another lost civilization?)

Captain Nemo sighed and continued, "The Atlanteans let the knowledge of the Lost City of Mu slip into myth, fable, and disbelief, so that it might be forgotten, and the dark influence of Mu would be removed from the world. But it seems a small group of them have survived over the eons, and their goals have not changed. They still seek world domination.

Luna acquiesced and agreed. "It is true. They slip in and out of the shadows collecting scientific information and knowledge that will help them recreate their reign of terror. I first came across them when they were creating the underwater structure we have just encountered. Being unaware of their past, I initially believed that they were scientists seeking to learn the secrets of the ocean first hand, by living underwater where they could observe the beauty of the sea and experience all the ocean offers. One member of their organization even seemed friendly at first, but later I realized their true nature, which is cruel and evil. They have no regard for life, human or otherwise.

"They believe that Monsieur Verne has knowledge of the future, as well as, time travel, and that they can extract that information from him to their benefit. That is why I chose to reveal my existence to you to aid in freeing him from their grasp. He is a good and kind man. He and I have had many conversations during the time he was voyaging on his yacht...."

Before Luna could continue, a crew member returned to the air lock chamber and informed us that two of the sperm whale submersibles had been sighted following us at a distance, and these two whales appeared to be somewhat larger than the one we had previously encountered.

Captain Nemo turned to her and said, "Luna, you have a greater familiarity with this group and their submersibles. Do those craft contain any offensive weapons that could be used against the *Nautilus*?"

She nodded affirmatively and replied, "They each carry two cylindrical explosive devices that can be launched towards other vessels. I have seen them do so. They have used them to sink unsuspecting ships. The explosions are small but powerful. The projectiles are not very fast though, and if they miss their target, they just continue on in the direction they are launched until they lose momentum and fall to the ocean floor. They only seem to explode when the forward end of the projectile strikes a solid surface."

Sherlock, who had been staring off into the distance while Luna spoke, suddenly interjected. "Captain, unless Jules Verne's novel left out some details on offensive weapons aboard the *Nautilus*, I deduce that you only have the ramming spur and the electrical charge to the hull: is that correct?" The Captain shook his head affirmatively, and Sherlock continued, "Luna, can you tell me the distance from which they can effectively fire their weapon? And do you know of any unexploded projectiles-- I believe they are called torpedoes-- that may have come to rest on the ocean floor in our current vicinity? I have a plan that will stop the two craft pursuing us."

Luna thought for just a moment before answering. "I would say that the effective distance of their weapon is only five times the length of the *Nautilus*. Regarding any unexploded torpedoes, Captain can you show me on the chart where we are now. I have seen several of them near the area we just left."

Captain Nemo pointed out on the chart the seamount where we had started from and where we currently were at the moment. Luna examined the chart briefly and pointed out a position. "There! There are two of them resting on a rise right in this area here. I am sure I could locate them again. What did you have in mind, Mr. Holmes?"

"Well as I see it, the torpedo hitting a solid surface should be no different than a solid surface impacting the front of the torpedo. We lead their submersibles in a wide circle that takes them back over their torpedoes sitting on the ocean floor and then detonate them from a distance. That should immobilize the two vessels."

“And how do you propose that we detonate them?” asked Captain Nemo.

“Just after we pass over the devices, we drop two divers with your underwater rifles at a safe enough distance from the intended explosion. The impact of the rifle projectile on the front of the torpedo should be sufficient to set it off. The question is, what is the range of your underwater rifle, and is it far enough to set off the explosion without harm to the divers?"

Captain Nemo thoughtfully replied, "I designed and built those rifles. I am an expert in their use, and I would stake my life on my ability to hit those torpedoes from a safe distance, but I don't believe that any of my crew would be accurate enough at that interval. Your plan is sound, but will it require my skill to be able to hit the exact point that will set off those torpedoes. I will only be able to fire at and detonate one of them."

"Not necessarily," added Sherlock. "There is another way to detonate the torpedo. Luna, if she is agreeable to this plan, can place a metal bowl attached to long enough lines over the curved front of the second torpedo, and when the whale submersibles are directly over them, we provide a strong enough force to pull the bowl against the front of the torpedo, and that will provide the necessary impact to set off the explosive. All you need to do is put holes near the rim of a solid metal bowl and attach lines to it. She can lead the lines back to a safe place from where your divers can provide the brute force."

While it was an interesting approach, and it could work, I was concerned for her safety and expressed my thoughts. "Luna that would be a dangerous task and you could get injured."

She looked at me with a surprised expression and responded. "I thank you for your concern, Dr. Watson. That is very kind of you, but I have lived my entire life underwater in an environment full of predators, dangers, and worse. I have even survived several marriage proposals from overly amorous sailors. If Captain Nemo's crew can create the device, then I can safely place it in position."

The Captain gave his crew orders to prepare the items we would need and to adjust the course to allow us to slowly circle back to the position which Luna had indicated. We monitored the position of the two whale submersibles as we made ready everything we needed. The captain and two of his crew donned their underwater breathing suits and equipment, and Luna carefully gathered the bowl and lines. To my surprise, she handed them to me to hold on to while she stated that she had to go swim ahead to find the exact location of the torpedoes, and that she would be back to take the detonation device from me after she had located them and set the *Nautilus* on the right track. She cautioned me to be careful and that as soon as she retrieved the bowl and lines, to drop the two divers that would provide the pulling force. Then when we had passed them to a safe distance, Captain Nemo would exit to his position forward of the torpedoes.

I must say that Sherlock had come up with some clever and complicated plans in the past, but this was by far the most unusual. Luna smiled at me and dove into the pool of water in the air chamber room while the crew, stationed at the viewing ports, reported on her progress as well as the status of the two craft that were pursuing us. I waited and wondered if she would locate the devices where she expected them to be and if they would be oriented correctly and if they were even still functional. What if the plan failed? Would I ever see her again? There was so much I wanted to ask her. It all seemed so strange, yet I felt somehow connected to her.

My thoughts were broken by a crew member exclaiming, "She has found the torpedoes and indicated our course. Be ready to hand off the detonator." My hands were trembling as I stood ready and waiting for her to reappear. Just as she broke the surface of the water in the entry pool, I thrust the device into her hands and almost fell in after her. I fortunately recovered my balance, so the two divers were able to depart. Just as they did, one of the other crew members announced, "Captain, it looks like the whale submersibles are preparing to fire their weapons. The forward mouth section of the whales has opened."

Captain Nemo resolutely answered, "We must go through with this!" and he exited with his underwater rifle, as we had reached the point where he could safely fire from. I could see nothing from where I was, but the crew at the aft facing viewing ports stated that it appeared that everything was in position and we just had to wait until the Mu craft were over the torpedoes and hope they did not fire at us before then. Sherlock instructed the crew to be ready to drop all ballast immediately if the whale craft did fire, which was fortunate, for the first submersible launched a torpedo at us just as it passed over our trap.

"Torpedo launched!" Cried one of the crew. "Drop all ballast!" Then I heard two distant explosions over the rush of water being released from the *Nautilus* and felt the turbulence of the two torpedoes detonating while the *Nautilus* quickly ascended out of the path of the weapon that had been fired at us. As the turbulent water and silt cleared, the crew reported Sherlock's plan had worked perfectly, as both craft were disabled, and he could see Captain Nemo waving to indicate that he was unharmed.

"What about Luna?" I asked. "Do you see her anywhere? Is she okay? And how did your divers fare?"

As we were safe from the torpedo that had been fired at us and missed, the helmsman reduced the speed of the *Nautilus*, and turned back to retrieve Captain Nemo, Luna, and the two divers. The crew at the portholes reported both submersibles had released their water ballast and ascended to the surface where they were apparently powerless. The *Nautilus* crew contacted their fellow crewmen on board Verne's yacht to let them know of the two disabled vessels, as we would need to continue on our course after we had everyone back on board. We first picked up Captain Nemo, who, as soon as he had removed his breathing helmet, congratulated Sherlock on his plan. Sherlock responded by complimenting the Captain on his marksmanship. The captain replied, "I was able to detonate the one torpedo, but it was your makeshift device that set off the second one. What do we know of Luna and my divers?"

"We are coming up to our divers now," a crew member replied. "But there is no sign of the mermaid."

I worriedly wondered what could have happened to her. She must have reached a point of safety with the lines, if the divers were able to detonate the second torpedo. Perhaps they could provide some information when they came aboard.

Chapter 10. A Most Unusual Dilemma,
(And a new plan of action.)

As soon as the crewmen, who had been assigned the task of pulling the detonation lines, reentered the air lock chamber and removed their breathing equipment, Captain Nemo questioned them as to what had happened and if they had seen Luna anywhere.

"We saw her swim towards the torpedo with the bowl device, but she never brought the lines back to us. We don't know if she detonated the device or if the explosion from the torpedo that you fired at caused it to explode, but it was not us. We did not see any trace of her after the turbulence and sediment cleared. Should we go back out and search for her?"

I was about to say yes, of course, they must go back and look for her, but the Captain replied, "This is a most unusual and difficult dilemma. Every second we wait, could put Jules Verne's life in greater danger and give the enemy an advantage, if they gain any information from him. We have already lost considerable time in stopping the two vessels that were pursuing us. We cannot lose any more time."

"We would not even be here if she had not gone out there to stop them!" I exclaimed. "How can you think of going on without her?" In my mind I saw her injured and left behind, helpless. I longed to have told her my feelings for her before she had departed.

Captain Nemo solemnly replied, "I appreciate your concern, Dr. Watson, I was out there as well, we both understood the risks. This is not an easy decision. What is your opinion, Mr. Holmes?"

Sherlock looked from me to the Captain and answered, "It should be quite obvious. If you did not see her anywhere in front of the torpedoes up to where you were stationed, and your divers did not see her anywhere behind the torpedoes up to the location where they were waiting, then for some reason, she swam either to the left or to the right. My conclusion is that one of the torpedoes had somehow been shifted in its orientation to our course on the sea floor, and she could not lead the lines back to where the divers were waiting. She had to lead the lines sideways, or the plan would not have worked. There was always a fifty percent possibility of that happening. I am quite sure she is out there and will be along any moment."

I was staring intently into the entry pool, wondering where she could be, wishing she would return, and very concerned for her safety, when much to my surprise and relief, the surface of the water in the entry pool burst forth as Luna suddenly emerged from the water, completely drenching me for the second time that day. She once again, sat on the edge of the pool with a playful smile as she commented, "My dear Dr. Watson, you are completely soaked. You will catch a terrible cold if you are not careful. You do understand that I did not do that on 'porpoise'. I can make you some wonderful seaweed tea. It would be quite good for you." Then looking at the Captain, she inquired, "What are we still doing here? The pursuing craft have been neutralized. We should be heading to that island as quickly as possible."

As the captain gave the command to resume the previous heading at full speed, I answered her. "We were concerned about you! I was concerned about you. You never brought the lines back to the divers, and they did not see you after the explosions. What happened?"

Her answer echoed Sherlock's deduction to a T. "The second torpedo had changed position 90 degrees, and the divers were not in the correct location to provide the proper pulling force. I had to lead the lines off to the left to make the detonation device properly function. You know there was always a fifty percent probability of that happening. Fortunately, I have the strength of a dolphin when I need it. It has come in quite handy on many occasions."

I did not know what to say. She sounded just as logical as Sherlock but was entirely more attractive and most delightful to gaze upon. I must confess, in spite of being completely soaked in sea water again, I could not take my eyes away from her. I was so pleased that she had not been injured or worse. And did she call me "dear"? As we continued on our course, she asked what our plan was when we arrived at their base.

Sherlock took the lead and answered, "Well, that would again depend on what we find. You say they have an airship of some type. That gives them a certain advantage. It also depends on if Jules Verne is still there. So far, we have found evidence of his presence in each location that we have been to, but he has not been there. Yet, in each situation, he managed to leave a hidden clue to help us follow him. That last structure was no different."
"But Holmes!" I interrupted, "We never went into the underwater base. You just looked inside what was left of the entry hatch for only a moment or two, and then we returned to

the *Nautilus*. How could you have found anything in that short time?"

Sherlock smiled with that look of his when he knows something that he and he alone is aware of. In times like those, he is the master of suspense. Just when we could wait no longer, he explained, "I knew that Jules Verne would leave us another clue, just as I knew that his captors would be careless regarding him, since they were rigging the entryway with explosives. They did not believe that anyone would get in there alive, so they paid no attention to what Verne was doing before they removed him from the facility. Knowing that there were traps, he had to leave his clue somewhere near the entrance, yet safe from the effect of the explosives. I only needed a second to retrieve this."

He held up a small watertight metal box that had the image of a mermaid engraved on its cover.

Luna cried out, "I know that box! I recovered it from a shipwreck and gave it to Monsieur Verne several years ago! It was for his birthday as a thank you for all the pleasant talks we had. He was like a father to me in explaining the ways of the surface world. I wanted him to have something to remember me by after he sold his yacht and would no longer be sailing."

I must confess that when I heard Luna refer to Jules Verne as a father figure, I was so very relieved, as my feelings for her were growing quite strong. I imagined her giving me some small token of affection. I would treasure it always.

But what could I possibly offer to her, a mermaid? I pictured us together in a moonlit sea, whispering to each other. Perhaps I could write her poem…"

Sherlock interrupted my thoughts as he continued, "And he knew that we would recognize this box as another clue from him. Let us open it and see what he has to say."

Sherlock opened the mermaid box and removed a folded sheet of paper. Carefully unfolding it, he commented, "This time it is not in any type of code. He must have had little time to write. Here is what he says: *'Being taken to island base off coast of Iceland. They seek my method of time travel to gain weapons of the future. They cannot know this, even if it costs my life. Base must be destroyed. Volcano is their power source. Use it against them. Make it erupt!'*"

Luna's eyes grew wide with concern as she responded, "The location they are going to is a volcanic island. If the volcano were to erupt, that would certainly destroy their base, but we must save him first." With a questioning look, she added, "Is it even possible for humans to cause a volcano to erupt?"

Captain Nemo cleared his throat and interjected, "It is not as difficult as one might imagine. The catastrophic explosion of Krakatau several years ago was caused by the last decedents of Lemuria when they tried to harness the energy of that volcano. They were working in hidden caverns beneath the mountain, and they lost control of their experiment. The results were devastating. That eruption claimed 36,000 lives and altered the world climate for years."

Sherlock nodded and added, "The Dutch authorities reported 36,417 to be exact, but some experts put the number at 120,000 lives lost, and the explosion was heard over 3,000 miles away. I do not think Jules Verne is suggesting anything at all of that magnitude. If we can just initiate something more localized, it could disable their communication and transportation systems as well as their weapons and construction facilities. That would trap them on their island until the proper authorities could be notified and sent to apprehend them. If this island location is their main base, then that should capture the majority of the group. They have already abandoned the underwater base that we just left. Their two large submersibles are disabled and under the control of your crew on Verne's former yacht. Luna, do you know if they have any other bases located anywhere else?"

Luna stared in the distance before replying. "I have heard mention of only one other place they sometimes travel to. It is another small volcanic island in the Atlantic Ocean, far off the coast of Portugal."

Captain Nemo replied. "That will be near the Azores. It must be a very small and well-hidden facility, or our Atlantean network would have surely known about it."

Holmes responded retrospectively, "That may not be true if you are not looking for it. You and the *Nautilus* have managed to remain hidden from civilization all these years, not counting a few sea monster sightings. You stated earlier you thought all the inhabitants of Mu had perished. You have not been looking for them, so therefore, you have not seen them. We must continue to their island base near Iceland and rescue Jules Verne as well disable their main facility. Then we can investigate their final base in the Azores to finish this once and for all.

Chapter 11. Another Most Unusual Journey,
(And a very quick one at that.)

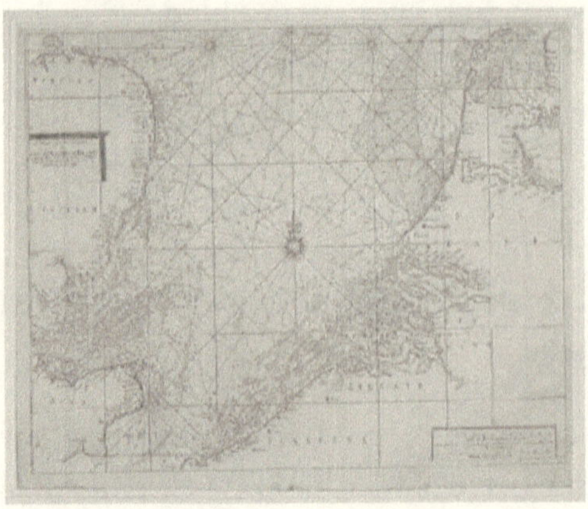

The top speed of the *Nautilus*, as described by Jules Verne in his novel, was 50 knots or nautical miles per hour. Captain Nemo confirmed Verne's claim and proudly stated there was no faster vessel above or below the surface of the ocean. We would easily reach their island base in less than ten hours. What type of power source could maintain that kind of speed was beyond my comprehension, but Sherlock seemed to have a solid grasp on the subject. He asked if Captain Nemo had read his paper entitled "*A Speculation on Hypothetical Power Sources and the Speeds Capable of Being Attained in Their Utilization*". The Captain replied that he had indeed read Sherlock's paper and, while it was interesting and creative, it had only touched the surface of a fascinating subject. If Sherlock was interested, the Captain could show him the propulsion room, to which Holmes readily agreed.

The crew had already returned to their duties, so when Sherlock and Captain Nemo left the air lock chamber, both of them deep in conversation regarding the power source of the *Nautilus*, I was at last left alone with Luna. Of course, I was still dripping wet, shivering, and at a complete loss at what to say to the most attractive female I had ever laid eyes upon, even if she did happen to be a half human, half fish, mythical creature that may have been four times older than I and at times looked just like a dolphin. What does one say in that kind of situation? "Hello. Do you know that you are the most beautiful creature in the world? What are your plans for dinner next week?"

I could not believe I had just said that! What was I thinking? I felt ridiculous, but Luna just smiled and laughed in an enchanting, melodious voice that was like crystals in the wind.

"And just what did you have in mind, my dear Dr. Watson? Afternoon tea, with scones and jam and maybe some pickled herring sandwiches, perhaps?"

I clumsily replied, "Please do call me John. Yes, afternoon tea would be lovely. That is, as long as the tea is not seaweed based."

What was I thinking??? In all the strange and unusual circumstances that I had ever experienced while accompanying Sherlock, I had never found myself at such a total loss of composure. Her eyes twinkled as she again laughed. "My dear, sweet John. You are so humorous. I do understand that seaweed tea does take some getting used to. You needn't worry about that. But I do wonder where we would go for tea. The sandwiches could get rather soggy you know."

To emphasize her point as she replied, with a grand flourish, she swirled her tail and again doused me with sea water from the pool. I slowly came to my senses about the shear impossibility of the situation as she gently took my hand and stated, "You are very sweet and a true gentleman, but you are also soaking wet, shivering, and you need to get into dry clothes before you do catch cold. Do not worry, John Watson. I will not disappear. We have a task to complete in rescuing Monsieur Verne."

Still in a bit of a daze, I agreed and left the air lock chamber to go back to the cabin that was mine and change into dry clothes. When I arrived there, I discovered my own clothes had been dried and were left folded on the table. It felt good to be back in my original attire. I somehow felt more grounded in reality. I was myself again and not some love-struck school boy. Yet still, I could not shake my thoughts and feelings about Luna. I knew the sheer impossibility of the situation, but it did not stop me from wondering. To help me sort things out, I tried putting my thoughts down on paper but only ended up writing a poem to Luna. I had to face the fact. I was head over heels drowning in my feelings for her, and logical or not, she was a mermaid. She was not only ravishing, but intelligent and charming as well. But I was, quite exhausted from the previous day's adventure that had led right into this journey without a moment's rest, and I soon found myself sound asleep and dreaming that I was drowning. I dreamt the ocean was swallowing me and I could not breathe! I was helplessly being pulled out to sea as Luna sat on rock singing and calling to me like a mythical siren. I was about to go under for the last time, when thank goodness, Sherlock showed up at my door to wake me. Leave it to Sherlock Holmes to provide a life preserver in the form of his cold logic regarding our task of rescuing Jules Verne. Not to mention stopping the organization that had kidnapped him.

"Watson, you need to get a grip on yourself," he flatly stated as he walked into the cabin with a large book in his hand. "We will need everyone focused when we reach their island base. We have to rescue Mr. Verne, disable the entire facility, and prevent anyone from escaping in their air ship. It is rather straight forward actually, but it will require your participation and full attention."

"Straight forward?" I questioned. "Just what did you have in mind? It does not sound very straight forward to me. You have never even seen the base. You have no idea what we will find there, and yet you make it sound overwhelmingly simple."

With a loud thump, Sherlock placed the large book that he had brought with him on the table and opened it to a page with a detailed map and stated, "Yes, quite simple. Good fortune is with us, Watson. It turned out, that when Luna gave us the coordinates of the island base, something about them sounded vaguely familiar to Captain Nemo. He returned to his library and searched until he found this; a set of detailed charts and maps of the caverns of this island. It appears that Captain Nemo and his crew had scouted out the entire island some time ago to determine its feasibility as a possible supply base. They are always looking for well-hidden locations to use as safe havens. They determined the volcano has made the island too unstable to safely use. Apparently, the descendants of Mu thought otherwise, and according to Verne's message, they have developed some way of tapping into the magma of the volcano to power their base. If you look here, you see there is a direct path into a hidden lagoon that is close to the magma chamber. All we have to do is place a timed charge near the magma, set to go off after we exit, and it should cause a small enough eruption to disable the entire facility."

"And how do we prevent an explosive charge from going off after we place it next to pool of magma that is who knows how hot?" I asked.

Sherlock stared at the ceiling of the room as he casually replied, "Actually volcanic magma ranges between 1,300 and 2,400 degrees Fahrenheit. Considering the air temperature of Iceland this time of year, I estimate the magma will be 1,973 degrees Fahrenheit. I wrote a paper once on "*Calculating the Distance to Heat Sources at Which Explosives Will Detonate Based on Temperature of Heat Source and Quantity and Type of*

Explosives". I never thought I would have the opportunity to perform a field trial on my calculations. It should be quite informative. I hope I will have the opportunity to take notes. We will place the charge in a sealed metal box with sea ice in the box to keep it cool enough to prevent it from detonating prematurely."

"And what about the airship? How will we prevent it from taking off and escaping?" I queried.

With a dismissive wave, Sherlock explained, "That is the easiest part. At this time of year, there are significant amounts of sea ice on the surface of the ocean near the island. Using the electrical charge of *Nautilus*'s hull, we will rapidly melt a sufficient quantity of ice into the water to create a massive fog bank that will blanket the whole island. Using the fog as a cover, we can get someone close enough to the airship to disable it with a small charge.

"But Sherlock!" I exclaimed. "If the island is covered with fog, how would anyone be able to find their way to the airship or know where to place a charge to prevent it from flying? None of us have ever seen it before. And they are sure to have guards on board. Somehow their crew would need to be neutralized to be able to get near enough with the explosives. You will need someone with first hand skill in that kind of operation. It is much like some of our previous exploits."

Sherlock grabbed my hand and shook it, responding, "Good point, Watson. I am so glad that I spoke with you. Thank you for volunteering for the task. Now how do you propose to do that? Luna has seen the craft, and she can tell you how it functions, so you can determine its weak points. You will not have a great deal of time once we put our plan in motion."

I looked at him with disbelief. "How did I get shanghaied into disabling the airship?" I asked. "Sherlock, that is more underhanded than drugging sailors to get them aboard a ship."

Sherlock gave a sly look and quickly replied, "Why Watson, that is brilliant! What a clever idea! It is exactly like drugging sailors to get them aboard a ship, except you will be drugging them to keep them from getting off the ship. The *Nautilus* crew can make a very effective knockout gas out of a concentrated form of that seaweed tea. All you will have to do is get it aboard the airship to neutralize the guards, so you can plant the small explosives to disable the ship. As I stated, Luna can help you determine the best approach, since she has seen it before. I am sure you won't mind talking to her again. I have seen the way you look at her."

I started to object, when he interrupted me with a wave of his hand. "Watson don't even try to object, or explain your way out of it. I could tell your feelings for her if I was blindfolded, sound asleep, in another room, in a completely different building."

I looked at Sherlock a bit embarrassed and asked, "Is it that obvious?"

He looked at me, disdainfully, and replied, "Yes, absolutely! Even if I were in another country it would be obvious. And Watson, I do understand your situation. I still have the song of Pixy Music from our previous adventure floating about my head. I have not been able to shake it. That music has been positively haunting me since we returned from our adventure in Wonderland, so I do know what you are feeling now to some extent. Just abide to stay focused."

I nodded my head and left the cabin to learn what I could from Luna about the airship. As I walked back to the air lock chamber, it dawned on me that Sherlock had not gone into detail on how we would locate and free Jules Verne. I wondered what he had in mind. Captain Nemo and his crew had been there previously, but, it was before the descendants of Mu had adapted it as their base. Who knew what modifications had been made there? Of course, I was certain that Sherlock had a plan in mind. Sherlock always has a plan.

Chapter 12. A Most Unusual Plan, (As well as a good deal of ice.)

I returned to the air lock chamber to find Luna inside the entrance pool resting her arms on the edge of it, while her silky black hair floated upon the azure blue water. There was no question about it. Just to gaze upon her, was complete surrender. She was astonishingly enthralling, and I felt myself loosing grip and drifting out to sea never to return. Her warm embrace was all I could think of, but I reminded myself, I was there to discuss how to disable the crew of their airship. I composed myself and approached her.

"Hello Luna, it is wonderful to see you again. Sherlock tells me that you are familiar with the airship on the island. I need to determine a way to disable its crew with the use of a knockout gas that Captain Nemo's crew is preparing and then place a small explosive charge to prevent it from flying.

What can you tell me about the airship and any entry or access points?"

She turned and smiled when she saw me and replied, "Hello John Watson. You are dry once more. I can take care of that if you would like." Then as playful as a dolphin, she laughed and gave only a slight swish of her tail, which fortunately did not get me wet. But out of instinct, I backed away from the splashing water, to which she added, "What's wrong? You don't want to get wet again? If you plan to spend any time at all with me, you will have to get used to that, you know. Or would you prefer I toss some fish at you? It was so humorous to watch you try and dodge the fish on Jules Verne's yacht. You are so sweet and funny." She then gave a powerful flip of her tail and emerged fully from the pool, to sit on the edge of it.

"Yes, I have seen their airship," she stated, "It is quite similar to the one Jules Verne described in his novel *Robar the Conqueror* except it is smaller. It does have propellers on both ends and a great many that face upwards. The hull structure is similar to Monsieur Verne's former yacht, but not nearly as grand. There are large hatches on deck and several opening ports along the sides of the hull. There are no funnels that I have seen, so I do not know what powers the propellers. If you intend to disable the crew, then you will need to get the substance into the interior where the humans will be."

I thought for a moment and conjectured, "That would involve going through the deck hatches or the hull ports. Are they typically closed and secured or are they open?"

She considered my question and said, "That depends. The deck hatches are closed when they are flying but usually open when they are on the ground. I have seen long cables lead from points on the large moveable platform on the base, to something inside those hatches. It seems as if they connect them every time the airship is on the platform. The hull ports may be for weapons, because I have never seen them fully closed or secured. They are not far from ground level when airship has landed."

"That is it!" I replied. "I can drop the knockout gas canisters in through the hull ports. If Sherlock's plan to create a fog bank works, I should be able to get close enough to do that without being seen. From what you have described, I will need to damage several of the vertical lift propellers to prevent it from taking off. Do you remember how many of those there are?"

She raised her eyebrows as she concentrated a moment before answering. "There are two rows of them, perhaps five or more in each row. I have only seen the craft twice, and from the surface level of the ocean. The platform they landed on was raised above the water's surface each time it was there." Then, as if the thought had just occurred to her, she changed the subject and asked, "Do you know how they plan to locate and rescue Monsieur Verne?"

I shook my head negatively. "Sherlock did not mention that part to me, but I am sure he has something worked out. He is extremely skilled in that sort of thing. You would be impressed at all that he has accomplished."

Luna smiled softly and responded, "I see you think very highly of him. It is understandable. He is most logical. That is why the echoes of the Pixy Music he heard previously, are so troubling to him. It is because that music is so illogical. But you need not worry, he will come to understand it."

I was taken aback. "But how could you know about Pixy Music? That episode occurred when we were in Wonderland. You were here in the ocean, nowhere near where it happened. How is it possible?"

To my dismay, I did not receive an answer, as we were interrupted by Captain Nemo entering the airlock chamber.

"There you are," stated Nemo. "It is imperative we go over the timing of this plan. When we arrive at the island, you will have less than 10 minutes to disable their airship, while I place the explosive charge near the magma, and Sherlock frees Jules Verne. My crew has prepared your small explosive charges as well as your knockout gas canisters. In examining the maps of the island from our previous visit, we have determined there is only one location their airship can safely land. You will exit the *Nautilus* off shore from that point. Luna will guide you to the beach and then back to the point where we will recover you both."

I looked at Luna with an expression of surprise, and she smiled and stated, "Why John, surely you know that mermaids have a perfect sense of direction. It is like an internal compass. If I have been in a place once, I can find my way back to it with my eyes closed, swimming through a cloud of octopus ink. It is part of my nature."

We continued to converse as we went over the details of the plan. Then, as we drew near the island, the *Nautilus* began to use the hull's electrical charge on large amounts of sea ice to create the fog bank. In truth, I had found myself wondering if that part of Sherlock's plan would really work, since our success in this whole endeavor depended on using the shroud of fog as a cover to hide our movements. I needn't have worried, though, for just as Sherlock had said it would, the massive cloud of fog welled up out of the sea like a murky, nebulous monster that swallowed the entire island. Soon it would be time for us to exit the *Nautilus* and find Jules Verne.

Chapter 13. A Most Unusual Sequence of Events, (And a glowing success.)

Sherlock's idea had worked brilliantly. A heavy, dripping, grey mist covered everything in sight. The fog was denser than anything I had ever encountered in London. It was perfect. It was almost too perfect. How was I supposed to see Luna to follow her? And how would I find the airship once we had landed? We had reached the point where I departed the *Nautilus* in a small launch that was rowed by four of Nemo's crew. Luna swam in front of us, pointing to the right or left as required. I strained to see her through the misty grey mantel that hung over the sea and repeated her directions to the oarsmen through hand signals. The oars and oarlocks had been covered with cloth to prevent them from making any noise, and the fog seemed to absorb what few sounds we did make. So far everything was going according to Holmes' plan.

We reached the shore safely, and as I stepped into the shallow water near the beach, Luna gave me the compass direction to follow, embraced me, and whispered to me, "Please do be careful." She had instinctively known unerringly where we were on the beach in relation to the map we had studied. She also knew the direction to where Captain Nemo had calculated the airship would be located. He had given me the distance in paces to where it should be anchored, so with my compass in one hand and the first of my tranquilizer canisters in the other, I stepped forward into a dense, grey blanket of icy fog that surrounded me completely. I was stepping into oblivion.

I counted to myself the paces towards my destination. '*One, two, three.*' I could not see anything. I was relying completely on the compass and the calculations. I could only hope they were correct. '*Four, five six.*' I almost stumbled on a loose rock. I stopped to listen if anyone had heard the noise, but all was still quiet. '*Seven, eight, nine, ten.*' I was half way to where it should be, and I still could not see beyond my out stretched hand. *Eleven, twelve, thirteen.*' Wait, what was that? There were voices somewhere ahead. I could not understand them or be certain where they were coming from. I proceeded more cautiously.
'*Fourteen..., fifteen...*' Now I heard them again, but to the left. '*Sixteen..., seventeen...*'There it was again. Would I be discovered? If so, what would I do? I found the answer to that more quickly than I would have liked, as a guard suddenly appeared out of the fog directly before me. He was clearly more surprised than I and before he could make a sound, I instinctively knocked him unconscious with a swift right hook to the jaw. The unfortunate thing, however, is that was the hand in which I had held my compass. I had silenced the guard but destroyed my only method of navigation and determining direction. If I somehow managed to survive this, how was I to return to the beach? How would I get back to the *Nautilus*?

I was only three paces from where the airship was calculated to be, so I counted out the last steps hoping that it would be there and that I was still going in the right direction. '*Eighteen..., nineteen..., twent...* I abruptly came to a halt mid-count as a large dark shape loomed out of the heavy grey mist right in front of me.

It was definitely where the Captain had said I would find it. I decided to worry about the return trip after I had disabled the airship and proceeded to work my way along the hull looking for the gun ports. I had only taken four steps to the right when I came across the first one. I quickly activated the first tranquilizer canister and dropped it in the port and moved on. After another eight steps I discovered the second port and repeated my action with the next canister. I again followed the hull, but it started to taper inward, so I retraced my steps in the opposite direction. I had passed both of the gun ports I had already taken care of and located the next one. I could hear a commotion inside, as the crew was reacting to the tranquilizer gas. I heard the sounds of yelling, coughing, and guards falling to the floor as they lost consciousness and collapsed. "Have a cup of seaweed tea!" I said to myself, as I thrust the next canister into the open port. I worked my way down the hull, dropping a tranquilizer canister in each port, until I had used the last one.

Captain Nemo had said that the gas would be immediately effective on the crew but would dissipate very quickly. I was to wait four minutes from the time I set off the last canister, before I ventured on board the ship to place the charges. While I was working my way down the hull, I had found what had appeared to be an entry hatch, so I retraced my steps back to it as I anxiously waited for the air to clear. After what seemed like an eternity, I was able to enter the craft to work my way up to the propeller deck. I stepped inside and saw several of the ship's crew lying unconscious. The seaweed-based gas had been most effective.

I found a staircase that led to the upper deck and worked my up to the forest of masts which supported the horizontal propellers providing the lift to the airship. Shivering from the cold fog that enveloped me and a nervous perspiration that I am sure comes with handling explosives, I began to activate and place the charges on the masts. Luna had said that they were in two rows, so once I had found the first mast I was able to work my way down the row to find additional masts and place the explosives. I had finished one row without incident, when suddenly, a crewman wearing a breathing apparatus similar to the one Sherlock had used to escape the whale submersible, came blundering towards me with a small ax. The visibility was next to naught, and his vision was also restricted by the underwater gear, so I had a distinct advantage. He was swinging wildly as he came at me, but I was able to duck behind a mast to avoid him. As he passed, I pushed him toward an open hatch which he fell into with a loud crash followed by silence. That took care of him.

I finished my task, and somehow was able to work my way out through the exit without tripping over anything. The charges were all placed. All I had to do now was find a way to return to the beach without the aid of a compass. But how was I supposed to accomplish this? I decided anywhere else was better than standing next to the airship, as quite soon the explosives attached to the propeller masts would start detonating and I could get injured by flying debris. So, with a deep breath, I took several steps away and immediately could not see anything. Even the vessel had been swallowed up by the dismal grey darkness. I looked all around me wondering, which direction should I head? I was lost! I didn't know what to do next, when I happened to notice a glowing spot in the sand. What could it be?

I moved towards it and immediately noticed another spot slightly further away and then another and yet another, all of them leading me in what seemed like the direction I needed to go to get back to the shore. How fortunate was that? I followed the glowing marks until I reached the shoreline and saw Luna next to the launch, waving at me from the water. Somehow, her hands seemed to be glowing in the same fashion as the marks I had been following.

As I sloshed through the shallow water to climb into the small vessel, she embraced me and exclaimed, "I knew the phosphorescent trail would lead you back to me." She then removed a device that had been somehow placed on the back of my belt, and explained, "That is why I attached this to your belt when I embraced you before you left. It released drops of glowing marine algae as you walked towards the airship, to help you find your way back. Hurry! We must move quickly. We have no time left."

As she had spoken, the first explosive charges on the airship's propeller masts started detonating. We departed as quickly as possible. With Luna leading us and the oarsmen rowing double speed, we made our way back to the rendezvous location where we would meet the *Nautilus*. It was only then I realized, against all odds, stumbling about in the sheer darkness of the fog bank, without a compass, I had actually succeeded. The airship was disabled, and I was somehow still alive. I only hoped that Sherlock and the Captain had been equally as successful and would be waiting for us when we returned.

Chapter 14. A Most Unusual Volcanic Eruption, (And a very pleasant reunion.)

Luna had stopped swimming and held up her hand to indicate we had arrived at the proper place when there was a great disturbance in the water from air bubbles ascending to the surface, followed by the topsides of the *Nautilus* rising out of the sea. I uttered a huge sigh of relief. They were here! Or at least the *Nautilus* was. I was certain they would not have left without Sherlock or Jules Verne. I looked forward to seeing them. Luna dove underwater to reenter the vessel via the airlock, I climbed aboard the deck, and the crewmen secured the launch to its location near the stern of the vessel. I was making my way back towards the hatch when the muffled sound of a series of loud explosions came from within the volcanic peak that dominated the view, as it protruded out of the fog bank that covered the island. The explosions all seemed to be on the seaward side of the mountain. One large blast obliterated the upper portion of the volcano and started lava flowing down the mountain side into the sea of fog, and in the direction of the base. I was astonished and transfixed at the destructive force of the eruption and the river of lava that burned its way down the slope illuminating the grey haze. We had to leave the area immediately.

I started to enter the hatch but was taken aback by the appearance in the doorway of a medium-built man with dark hair and a thin mustache. He was wearing black clothing and tall boots and looked to be one of the crew we had captured from the first submersible.

What could have happened in my absence? How did the enemy crew get on board? I was about to act against him when to my surprise, he spoke to me with Sherlock's voice. "Welcome back, Watson. I am glad to see you have survived your little jaunt. You succeeded, I presume. We accomplished our mission as well. We rescued Jules Verne."

Hearing Holmes' voice emitting from this strange interloper stopped me in my tracks. In absolute disbelief, I stared at him. I leaned in closer, looked him straight in the eyes, and whispered, "Sherlock, is that you?"

With a smile and a snicker, he removed the fake mustache and replied, "Of course it is, Watson. Who did you think it was? If I fooled you, then it is no surprise that nobody in the base questioned me. This is how I freed Jules Verne. Please do forgive my theatrics. Come down below, and I will tell you all about it as we head to the Azores."

I was amazed; Sherlock had come up with a perfect disguise that had given him access to the enemy's base, so he could free Jules Verne. But why did he choose that particular appearance, and how could he possibly have known where in the base he would find Jules Verne? As I returned to the airlock chamber, my thoughts were swimming. Surely there is nothing in the world that is impossible for Sherlock Holmes. I anxiously looked forward to hearing how he had done it.

When I arrived in the airlock chamber with Holmes at my side, Captain Nemo, Jules Verne, and Luna were already there. Seeing Jules Verne for the first time, revealed a quiet, smiling gentleman, of enigmatic appearance. He was tall and slender, with grey hair, and a graying full beard. His smile conveyed a certain sense of peace and awareness of things beyond the norm. He did not speak English, but Sherlock, Captain Nemo, and Luna spoke French. I discovered later it was Verne whom had taught Luna to speak French during their many conversations while he was cruising on his yacht. I introduced myself to Mr. Verne with Luna translating for me, and he thanked me for my efforts in disabling the airship, with Luna translating for him. "My deepest thanks and appreciation to all of you, but how did you know where, they would be holding me?"

Sherlock smiled and began speaking in English for our benefit, with Luna translating into French for Jules Verne. "Let me explain. In examining the map of the island Captain Nemo and his crew made less than a year ago, I realized that the new occupants would have specific requirements and needs for their nefarious activities. Certain sized cave rooms would be needed for specific purposes; storage, sleeping quarters, work areas, laboratories, and so forth. They could only have made a minimum of modifications in the time since the *Nautilus* was last there with most of their work going towards tapping into the volcanic magma chamber as a power source. In studying the map of all the preexisting rooms within the cave system and with my knowledge of how the criminal mind works, I determined there was only one logical, possible place a prisoner would be held. I determined I had to access that location without being discovered. "I recalled that the crewmen of the whale submersible we sank earlier all shared the same physical features of dark hair and thin mustaches, which is not surprising if they all trace back to one heritage, that of the island City of Mu. If you remember, all of them wore a specific uniform of black clothing and tall boots. Just to be certain, I had verified with Luna that many of the occupants of the underwater base she had seen shared the similar physical features and attire. This made it very easy for me to create a disguise that would allow me to blend in perfectly with them. The dark hair and fake mustache even fooled you, Watson. You should have seen your face when you heard my voice. Please forgive me for having a bit of sport with you, but I could not resist. By knowing without a doubt where Mr. Verne would be held and being able to blend in to their populace perfectly, I had solved half the problem. The task was as good as complete.

"At that point, I only needed a way to open the cell and return Mr. Verne to the *Nautilus* without being noticed. Since a significant amount of their activity on this island involves divers, it would not be unusual to see men walking about with diving equipment or in underwater suits. I attired myself in their standard uniform of dark clothes and tall boots, courtesy of the *Nautilus*' clothing supply. I then brought with me one of their dive helmets. It was the one I had retrieved from the Mu submersible along with some dark clothes and boots for Mr. Verne. The prison cell was clearly where I had determined it to be, and I walked right up to the cell location without anyone questioning me.

"I was quietly able to render the guard outside the cell unconscious using venom derived from a cone shell specimen Captain Nemo had supplied me with from one of his aquariums. I had recalled my recent paper on "*Gastropod and Cone Shell Based Toxins, Venoms, and Tranquilizers, and Their Practical Applications*", and quite fortunately, he had a living example of the Magician Cone Snail, *Conus Magus*, on board. Its venom is one thousand times more powerful than morphine, and the effect is near instantaneous. I was able to extract the amount I needed to make a very effective tranquilizer. After the guard was incapacitated, I had access to his cell keys, so I had no problem opening and entering it. Once inside, the diver attire and the helmet provided an acceptable disguise for Mr. Verne. He did an excellent job of looking quite casual and normal wearing the dive mask to hide his beard while we returned to the rendezvous location to meet the Captain.

"By the time I had returned with Jules Verne, Captain Nemo had placed the charges in the magma chamber, and we were able to escape in the *Nautilus*. As I told Dr. Watson earlier, it was quite straight forward. I did hear the smaller explosions, which, if I am correct, would be the blasts disabling their airship. I assume that your task, Watson, was a glowing success?"

I looked at Luna and smiled at the thought of her and replied, “Yes it was, Sherlock, literally a glowing success.”

“Excellent!” voiced Captain Nemo. “And the explosive charges we placed near the magma worked perfectly to cause the volcano to erupt without blowing the island as well as ourselves completely out of existence.”

“Monsieur Verne says, that is good to know,” Luna translated for Jules Verne. “But he wonders how you were able to get near enough to the magma chamber. When he first arrived at their island base, their mechanism that drew power from the heat of the molten material was located directly adjacent to the magma, and there were always men nearby working with it.”

“That is a good question,” replied Captain Nemo. “The answer lies in our previous visit to the island. The main underwater entrance to the hidden lagoon is quite visible to any submersible craft, and that is, indeed, where they entered, and the lagoon that it leads to is where they connected their power source to the magma chamber. That would be the obvious choice for their access point."

"But there was another less obvious entrance to a cavern on the other side of the magma chamber. When we left a year ago, we made certain that the second entrance was well hidden, so if we ever needed to return, we would be able to do so unnoticed. I was able to set the charges on the magma chamber without any of the Mu descendants realizing what I had done."

"That is why the initial explosions were all on the seaward side of the peak," I remarked.

"You are correct, Dr. Watson," he replied. "The secret lagoon and hidden access are both on the seaward side. We were able to control both the direction and magnitude of the eruption. It worked very well. With their airship disabled and their last submersible destroyed in the eruption, they will be stranded on the island until European authorities can be notified to send a force to apprehend them."

Sherlock turned to Jules Verne and, speaking in French asked if he could describe anything more about the group. Verne answered with Luna translating his response. "When they kidnapped me from the *Saint-Michel III*, I did not know why or who they were. They seem to be very confident in their actions, as if they are not concerned about possible repercussions. They transported me via a small whale-shaped submersible to their underwater base, and then via the airship to this island. I must say, it was rather like being in one of my *Voyages Extraordinaire*. The technology was fascinating. I am sure I would have enjoyed it more if I were not being held prisoner. I tried to leave coded, hidden clues behind in each location, hoping the right person would find them. I know that Captain Nemo had been watching after me, and I am glad he contacted you, Mr. Holmes, when I went missing. Thank goodness for your perceptiveness and skills in observation. You were able to discover and correctly decipher each of my hidden, coded messages."

"Of course," Sherlock answered, "but Luna was most helpful in directing us and providing information."

Luna smiled and blushed somewhat as she translated Verne's response to Sherlock. "Ah, yes, Luna. I was not sure how to explain her. How does one tell an unknown benefactor, or even you, Captain Nemo who I have known for so long, that you should look to a mermaid for assistance? You would not have believed me. And I must think of Luna as well. The only way to keep her safe is to keep her existence secret. The world cannot know about her. Perhaps many years in the future her story can be fully told, but I digress. I was talking about my captors.

"The members of this group, while they all share the same background, speak several different languages, and they seem to have a main contact somewhere in Europe with whom they are working. It is someone who is providing for their financial resources. Who it is, I never discovered. I did overhear, that as soon as they have learned the secret to time travel, they intend to use it to gain access to the weapons of the future. Consequently, the empire will be unstoppable.

They laughed at the word "empire". I believe they intend to betray their benefactor once they achieve their goal. I am afraid this is all I can tell you. I was kept locked away most of the time.

They had planned to interrogate me in depth at their main base, which you destroyed just in time. I tried to tell them my stories are based only on extensive research of existing inventions, that I know nothing of the future, but they did not believe it. I assure you they learned nothing from me while I was in their captivity, but somehow, they did already know about the existence of time travel, and their technology seemed quite advanced. How is that possible?"

Captain Nemo nodded affirmatively, and replied, "Yes, that is the question. We hope to discover that when we get a response from our communications operator regarding the doctored message you composed, Sherlock. So far nothing has been noticed, but I will let you know as soon as we discover something.

"But right now, let us celebrate our success. We have freed Jules Verne from his captors, prevented them from gaining knowledge of the future, and struck a sound blow against them by rendering their airship inoperable and stranding them on the island. Thank you, Sherlock Holmes and Dr. Watson for your invaluable assistance. And Luna, thank you for all that you have done."

Luna smiled, flourished her tail, and laughingly said, "I only did what I 'cod', even if it was a bit 'fishy' at times." At which she laughed at her word play even more.

Chapter 15. Yet, Another Most Unusual Journey, (And Sherlock plays the violin!)

At the speed the *Nautilus* was traveling, it would take us thirty-two hours to travel to the Azores, the location of the final base of the Mu descendants. What would be waiting for us there we had no idea. The Captain had contacted his Atlantean compatriot posted in Great Britain, to inform him of the group that we had left stranded on the Icelandic island. The agent would know how to inform the proper authorities about them with a suitable reason for them to be arrested and contained.

Now it was just a matter of waiting until we arrived in the Azores. We had been working almost non-stop in locating and rescuing Jules Verne, so Captain Nemo suggested we rest a while, and he provided another magnificent seafood dinner for us with sincere apologies for the lack of marinated giant squid tentacles, but a strong recommendation for the sautéed sea cucumber. He even provided a comfortable accommodation for Luna that allowed her to be in the salon and yet still be in contact with sea water. A large container filled with salt water and a chair made it possible for her to join us, but to my dismay, she spent a good deal of time conversing in French with Jules Verne. I knew she had been very concerned about him, but I still felt somewhat disappointed.

Sherlock sat down beside me. "Feeling at a loss, Watson old boy? Don't worry, she has feelings for you. I can see that clearly, but you must realize there would be more than just a small amount of difficulty in getting serious with someone, so water bound as she is. At least when this adventure is over, you will be able to go back to 221-B Baker Street and forget all about this. I wish I could do the same with the Pixy Music we heard on our prior adventure in Wonderland. I have not been able to get her melody out of my head no matter what I do. I have even considered taking some of that cone shell anesthetic that I used on the guard to help me escape from it."

I looked at him intensely and asked, "Sherlock, is it really that terrible?"

He emphatically shook his head back and forth and replied, "No, no. It is not at all bad. Don't even think that, Watson. It is the most beautiful sound I have ever heard. But I cannot escape from it. It seems it is always there, an echo in the background, calling to me from a distance. It is a captivating and enchanting melody I can't quite hear. This song! This is unlike anything I have previously experienced."

I thought for a moment before answering. "You know you are trying to approach this with logic, keeping it at a proper distance. Have you considered embracing it?"

"What are you talking about, Watson?" He replied.

"You can't seem to escape it, Sherlock. Why don't you just embrace the music? Play along with it. I am sure the Captain has a violin here somewhere. He always seems to have whatever we may happen to need tucked away in the hold of the *Nautilus*. In fact, I would not at all be surprised to learn that he has a Stradivarius on board."

Just then, Captain Nemo approached us with a violin case in his hand and addressed Sherlock. "Mr. Holmes, since we have some time before we get to the Azores, and we are celebrating, may I ask you to indulge us with some violin music? I have heard you are quite the virtuoso on the strings. I have an excellent quality Stradivarius in perfect condition here that is just longing to be played."

Holmes looked at me intensely, raised his eyes to the ceiling, inhaled deeply and let out a long breath. I shrugged my shoulders and stated I did not have a thing to do with the Captain's suggestion. Sherlock accepted the violin case from Nemo and, with great care, set it on the table and opened it. He stared at it for some time before gently removing it and placing it at his shoulder. He picked up the bow, hesitating, almost trembling for a moment, and then began to play.

I cannot say if it was the quality of the violin or the mystical music that had been playing continuously in his head, but I had never heard Sherlock play so magnificently in all my life. The music was unlike anything he had played previously, and it is well known he himself owns a Stradivarius he acquired from a broker for a mere 55 shillings. How he managed it is anyone's guess. At last estimate, it was stated to be worth 500 guineas. At that moment, traveling through the undersea world, Sherlock's music was truly magnificent.

He did not have any sheet notes in front of him, and I must confess that what I heard closely resembled the ethereal music I recall from our previous adventure in Wonderland. I know this may sound strange, but it is almost as if he were playing a duet with the entrancing Pixy Music playing one side and Sherlock playing the other. There were clearly two exquisite and distinctive lines of music being played, each interweaving with the other, floating back and forth and creating an ethereal harmony. It was infinitely enchanting.

When Sherlock finished playing and set the violin back in its case, there was not a sound in the salon beyond the background humming of the machinery of the *Nautilus*. We sat there in silence not knowing what to say. Sherlock slowly closed the violin case, and as he walked past me to leave the salon, he leaned over and whispered so that I alone could hear him say, “She spoke to me.” And he left the room.

All of us had been mesmerized by the music, but after he exited, the conversation picked up again.

Luna began by mirthfully expressing, “That was most enjoyable and also rather familiar. He is really quite the musician, isn’t he?”

I nodded and replied with a smile, “Yes, but I have also heard that mermaids are very gifted in music as well.”

She laughed and replied, “Do not believe everything you hear about mermaids, John Watson. After all, how many people do you know have actually seen one?”

She translated what she had said for Jules Verne, who just nodded and smiled. I replied, “Now that you mention it, I do believe I can truthfully say that everyone in this room has seen a mermaid, and a most beguiling one, at that.”

Like a playful dolphin, she splashed the water in her container and responded, “You are so funny, my dear John Watson.”

I would have liked to respond to her, but one of Captain Nemo's crew entered the salon with a concerned expression and handed the Captain a message. He read it with a scowl on his face and said, "If you will all excuse me, I must go find Sherlock Holmes. He needs to see this."

Chapter 16. Yet Another Most Unusual Discovery, (And I am certain Sherlock suspects something.)

We were taken aback by the abrupt change in Captain Nemo after he had read the message. What could it have been that had affected him so severely? We silently wondered and imagined, until he returned to the salon with Sherlock following closely behind him.

Holding up the message, Captain Nemo began speaking as Luna again translated into French for Jules Verne. "We have determined the location of the leak in our communication network. It is somewhere in London, England. We had been transmitting Sherlock's fabricated message to determine the source of the compromise, to only one of our agents at a time, so we can watch for an indication it has been intercepted, and as of yet, we have not seen the expected response. We had not sent the fake message to our operative in Great Britain. But it appears the genuine message I sent to our agent in the British government regarding the group of hostiles we left on the volcanic island has been intercepted. He reports that a ship has suddenly been chartered for a very "urgent" trip to a small island off the coast of Iceland. The party chartering the vessel said that price is no object. They will pay whatever the ship owner requested. Their only concern is speed. They have already left for the island." Captain Nemo looked at us and went on. "Friends, we now know that the communication break is within the British government. It will take some time to determine a more exact location and the individuals involved. I must request that, as soon as we complete our business in the Azores, we head directly back to England to find the party responsible."

I raised a question, "Yes that makes perfect sense, but what of the group of hostiles we left stranded on the island? If their people get to the island first, then they will be set loose. That would be a major blow to us. The party that set out to free them has to be stopped. However, you cannot have your agent call for the military to sink a privately chartered vessel. The owner and his crew are innocent people who just happen to be on board. It is not done in the civilized world."

Nemo looked directly at me and replied, "I am sure that if the Mu descendants reach the island and free the group stranded there, they will kill the owner and crew of the chartered vessel, as they will have no further use for them. These people do not respect the laws of civilization, and accordingly, they do not deserve the consideration of those same laws. I do not look to the military to intervene. I will stop them. The *Nautilus* and my crew have existed outside of the awareness and laws of your society for years, so I will deal with the Mu descendants. But you need not worry, Dr. Watson. I am not going to sink the chartered vessel or harm its crew. My only intent is to damage the vessel and render it incapable of reaching Iceland, so they cannot free the group we left there. The military can then rescue the ship owner and his crew, and tow them back to London as well as arrest their passengers. This will cause a slight detour and delay in our trip to the Azores, as well as some inconvenience to the ship owner, well worth the cost of saving his life and that of his crew even if he never knows it. Now if you will please excuse me, I must get an accurate description of the chartered vessel and plot an intercept course. From this point on, all communications will be double coded."

As Captain Nemo left the salon, Sherlock looked up and commented. "It is pleasing to see that my idea to send a fabricated message to determine the location of the communication breach worked, even if it was Captains Nemo's genuine message that achieved the same goal. But it is very concerning to me that the intercept location is in London, England. That makes me wonder about the exact nature and source of the compromise. I must deliberate on this."

With that, Sherlock turned to the library shelves as if we did not exist, began scanning the books, occasionally pulling one or more out and throwing them onto the table. I would have wondered about his actions, but the library held a great many reference books in addition to fictional novels. After completing his search of the book shelves, he sat down and started examining them while looking at the chart that depicted England in the greatest detail. As far as Sherlock was concerned, we could have been in a different ocean.

I turned to Luna and asked her what she thought of the Captain's plan. She shrugged her shoulders looking quite graceful in the process, and very straightforwardly replied, "His plan is almost sound, but I think you will need to launch some more of the seaweed tea knockout gas canisters at them just to be safe. They may be rather 'crabby' when their vessel is damaged."

I looked at her with a surprised expression and was about to say something when she laughed and stated, "You did not think I was serious did you?" And then she gave a slight flourish of her tail to splash some water in my direction.

"Well of course not, Luna," I replied. "But do be cautious about splashing salt water on Captain Nemo's Persian rugs, they are quite old."

With a coy smile she responded, "But not as old as I am. I met the gentleman that wove that rug. It was completed on a Wednesday during a waxing moon. I could tell you his name, but it is 27 characters long and not easy to pronounce."

Jules Verne excused himself to return to his cabin to rest, as he had been through a great ordeal with the kidnapping and the rescue. While he was leaving, he thanked us again and gave Luna a kiss on her forehead.

We were finally alone, or somewhat alone as Sherlock was still there, but he was so engrossed in his deliberating that I could have paraded a forty-foot cephalopod, a Narwhale, which is the Unicorn of the sea, and Poseidon himself right past Sherlock, and he would never have noticed. I asked Luna what she had meant when she had said that the violin music sounded familiar. She responded with a dreamy smile as if she was remembering something pleasant from a long time ago, and answered, "The haunting ethereal songs of Pixy Music are not easily forgotten. Your friend, Sherlock Holmes, has made that realization, and is having a difficult time understanding it. They do not fit into his framework of logic and rational thinking."

"But who or what is Pixy Music?" I asked her. "The Unicorn from Wonderland appeared to be acquainted with her and explained to us she wove a "sphere of protection" around the time machine with her music to protect us during our return trip, but she never actually appeared. None of us ever saw her. And how is it that you are aware of her. To my knowledge, she is from Wonderland, and you are from the seas here in our world."

Our conversation was loudly interrupted as Sherlock pounded a fist on the table and exclaimed, "It cannot be! It just cannot be!"

I glanced in his direction with concern and asked, "What is it Sherlock? What's wrong? Did you discover where the communication was intercepted?"

He looked up as if he had suddenly noticed we were there, and then dismissively replied, "No, no, I think I just misread something. Everything is fine. Go on with your conversation about forty-foot cephalopods, Narwhales, and Poseidon, or whatever it was you two were talking about."

We were about to continue, when Captain Nemo returned to the salon and stated, "I have the course and descriptive information on the chartered vessel. They will not be far from the track we are currently following. It should be easy to recognize their ship when we come across it. We will damage their craft just enough to make certain they cannot get to that island, and then we can return to our original course to the Azores. The fact they chartered a vessel tells me they did not have any more of their submersibles available. That is excellent news. That means we are making progress."

Looking at the profusion of books and papers scattered about the table, Captain Nemo asked Sherlock, "And what about you, Mr. Holmes? Have you made any progress on the calculations you have been working on? If you don't mind my asking, what exactly have you been working on?"

Sherlock answered that he was investigating where, specifically the communication breech in England had occurred, but so far, he had not discovered anything conclusive. His previous sudden outburst and something in the tone of his voice told me that he knew more than he had disclosed, but he had his reasons for not sharing what he had learned at that time. I did not question his reply, but I stared at him and wondered.

The Captain then turned to Luna and said, “We will soon be approaching the vessel that we will be taking action against. We must return your portable accommodation to the airlock chamber. If anything happens, you will have quicker access back to the ocean.”

She looked at him and answered, “If anything happens to the *Nautilus*, it would most likely fill with sea water, which as you are well aware, I have lived in for all my life. Your logic is ‘all wet’. But if you insist, I will return to the water pool chamber. How do you endeavor to disable their ship?”

Captain Nemo replied the ship in question had a pair of side paddle wheels and a stern propeller. He would first pass a safe distance under the craft and release two very small explosives attached to cork flotation devices directly under the vessel on both sides, so they would be drawn up into the side paddle wheels, rendering them inoperable. Nothing too large, so as not to damage the hull, just enough to ascertain their paddle wheels are out of operation, and he would then incapacitate their main propeller with his ramming spur. That will make certain they do not get to their base near Iceland, but on the other hand will not sink them.

“But how can you be certain that the explosives will damage the paddle wheels? What if they miss their mark?” asked Sherlock. “Any number of things could cause them to go astray. I can list five possibilities, three probabilities, and one absolute certainty, without even trying. Not to mention random chance.”

Luna chimed in saying, “I could attach them to the paddles. That will make sure they reach the right location. I could exit the *Nautilus* underwater and wait for them. When they pass by, I can swim up and place the charges on the paddle wheels. You could pick me up before you disable their propeller."

Sherlock answered her, "Luna, I admire your courage, and your idea has merit, but it is simply too dangerous for you to try to get that close to the vessel and the turning paddle wheels traveling at such a high speed. The vortex of the turning wheels could create a suction that could trap you near them. Might I suggest you attach your explosive charge to the cork float, using a long enough line, you can remain a safe distance away from the vessel as it goes past. Position the float in the path of the side wheel. The turning wheel will capture the float, drawing it upward, wrapping the tether around the paddle, which will bring the explosive up to the wheel box.

"It does sound like a safer approach," I said, "but how much time would Luna have to get out of the range of the blast, and is there any chance that the turning paddle wheel could dislodge the charge from the line that is attached to the cork float? If that happens, then the explosive would be falling directly down towards Luna.

Captain Nemo responded confidently, "The blast will be small and localized, just enough to destroy the paddle wheel without damaging the hull. I am sure my crew and I can construct a device that will work perfectly without any danger of breaking the tether. And it will allow enough time for Luna to safely retreat from the area. We will begin working on it immediately."

Chapter 17. A Most Unusual Revelation, (And who would question it considering the source?)

The Captain left to begin work on his explosive device, and Sherlock was immediately again lost in his examination of the communication breach. The intensity and concerned look I saw in the expression on his face still told me that he had found something of grave consideration but did not want to reveal it just yet. Several of Nemo's crew arrived to transport Luna and her salt water chair back to the airlock chamber.

"Do be cautious with that, gentlemen," Luna teased. "You would not want to spill salt water on Captain Nemo's Persian rugs, not to mention you would not want to spill me. Who knows the storms, shipwrecks, and disasters an angry mermaid could cause? Why the great flood that wiped out all the dinosaurs would be like a summer shower compared to what I can provoke."

Luna laughed at the look of fear in the crewmen's faces and then cheerfully told them, "Do not worry. I would not let anything happen to the *Nautilus*. The seven seas are my friends. I know that because they always ‘wave’ at me.” Then looking at their confusion she added, “Really, it is okay, it is a ‘shore’ thing.”

Luna’s playful humor and bewitching smile had me again lost in my thoughts about what would happen when this adventure was concluded. I accompanied them back to the air lock chamber, where Luna dove into the entry pool. I looked at her and saw myself someday having to say goodbye to her for the last time. I did not know what to say.

Luna, however, sloshed water at me with her tail, and said, “You look sad, John Watson. What is it that bothers you? Have you sat on a porcupine fish? That is not the ‘point’ of them you know.”

I smiled at her playful humor, as I sat on the edge of the entry pool rim, and not wanting to tell her my true feelings yet, I answered, “I am concerned for your safety. It will be dangerous when you go out to disable that ship.”

With a thrust of her tail she propelled herself out of the pool to sit on the edge next to me. “Oh, dear sweet John, you are so caring. You must realize that living in the ocean, my entire life has been filled with danger. It is almost like spending one’s life searching for hidden clues, solving mysteries, and chasing after dangerous villains. Can you even imagine what that must be like?”

I questioningly looked at her and with a twinkling in her eyes, and the sweetest laugh, she gave me a kiss on my cheek and dove back into the pool.

She is such a conundrum. I was completely enamored by her charm, beauty, playfulness, and intelligence, and yet I found myself at a loss for words when I was around her. Sherlock had made it clear there was no logical way the two of us could ever be together. Her existence itself is illogical, and yet there she was, right before my eyes. I sat in silence as she cavorted in the entry pool bursting with laughter as she occasionally splashed water in my direction. Finally, I recalled a question unanswered from our previous conversation. I asked her, "You never mentioned to me; how is it that you are familiar with Pixy Music from Wonderland."

With a splash, she again emerged from the pool to sit by my side and replied, "Oh, yes, I remember. We were interrupted. Something about a communication break in England causing the end of civilization as you know it. There was some truth to your comment about mermaids being gifted in music. We are very attuned and sensitive to all different types of music from all different realms. We can hear and sing across dimensions, if you understand what I mean. Pixies are mystical beings who have that same ability. They generate music that transcends distance and space for those that are attuned to it. Your friend, Sherlock Holmes, is now very attuned to the song of Pixy Music since he heard it so clearly in your previous journey and truly embraced it moments ago when he played the violin. She will now be with him forever. From this day forth, whenever you hear Sherlock Holmes playing the violin, you are hearing him speak to Pixy Music, as she is speaking to him though her song. She will be a part of him forever, even if they never see each other or meet in person.

At a loss for words I said nothing. Luna continued. "There is an author who lives in your country, somewhere in London I believe, who is much attuned to Pixies, Faeries, and the mystical spirit world as well. He too, clearly hears their song. I would not at all be surprised if, in the future, he writes books on the subject. His name is Arthur Conan Doyle. Have you heard of him?"

I did not know what to say. The ethereal, enchanting music Sherlock had played earlier, was beyond anything I had heard from him previously, but this talk of Pixies was difficult to accept.

Of course, I was hearing it directly from a mermaid, so it did lend a good deal of credibility to the idea of a spirit world.

At that moment Captain Nemo entered the chamber to inform us we were approaching the area where the ship would be intercepted. He wanted to impart to Luna the details on how the plan would unfold.

With a pang in my heart, I said goodbye to Luna and the Captain, and I left the airlock chamber to join Sherlock in his "pondering" on the communication break. I entered the salon and found him eating spoonsful of seaweed tea directly from the tea pot and saying aloud, "No! No! No! It just cannot be!"

He looked up and offered me a spoonful of the odd smelling, mushy green substance commenting, "Hello Watson. Did you know that, in addition to making outstanding tranquilizers and knockout gas, there are types of seaweed that make excellent beverages to improve mental focus and clarity of thought? Not to mention the outstanding energy boost you get from it. I discovered if I just eat the seaweed directly, it works even better. It does not taste like much, though. I believe that someday someone will sell these beverages as a mental boost drink. I can see it now. *Dr. Watson's Miracle, Monster, Seaweed Mind Elixir, guaranteed to improve your focus or your money back!* What do say old boy?"

I looked at him incredulously and asked, "So you have determined the source of the communication breech? You cannot hide it from me, Holmes, I know you too well."

He set the spoon down and looked at me intensely and replied, "Yes, you do know me very well. I have an idea, but I am not one hundred percent certain. It is too unlikely and too inconceivable, Watson. It is simply too impossible to believe just yet. When I have eliminated all of the other possibilities, every single one of them, then I will know for certain, however improbable it may be. Then I will let you know."

Chapter 18. A Most Unusual Way to Stop an Auxiliary Steam Ship, (But it went quite well, all things considered.)

Captain Nemo entered the salon to inform us that the chartered vessel had finally been sighted, and we were ready to intercept them. He had been cruising at the surface level of the ocean with the control bridge viewing ports above water to be able to search in all directions for them, while still keeping the *Nautilus* in a low profile. When the vessel had been sighted, the *Nautilus* immediately submerged to remain hidden from view. The Captain had determined their heading and was following the same course they were, except underwater. The Nautilus pulled ahead of the vessel to provide the distance required, adjusted the depth, and Luna exited the airlock chamber with the cork-tethered explosive charges. We were able to watch her from the aft facing windows in the steering room. Everything seemed to be going well. The first float had been released and was nearing the surface as the vessel quickly churned its way towards us. Luna adjusted her location to the port side, released the second float, and immediately dove deeper to get away from the forthcoming explosions no matter how small they were to be. We could hear the rhythmic pulsing of the paddle wheels as it approached the proximity of the tethered explosive charges. The visibility in the clear water was exceptional, but the float was so small, it was hard to see just what was happening. Sherlock, looking at his watch and counting, stated, "Based on the length of the tethers and the speed of the ship, we should hear the first charge… detonate… right about…" As he said the word "Now!" we heard a muffled explosion as the first charge detonated, and we saw the starboard paddle wheel disintegrate. The entire vessel shook slightly and lurched as it lost the driving force of the wheel. A moment later, the port paddle wheel shattered into splinters as the second charge went off.

Sherlock clasped his hands together, sighed, and stated, "Yes. Precisely as I calculated. The paddle wheels caught the floats and pulled the charges right up to the paddles with no harm to the hull. That is sterling."

The twin paddle wheels had been destroyed, and there was a rain of wood and debris that drifted down from the vessel as it continued on its course using only the stern propeller. Their speed was significantly reduced, but it was still making progress. We could only wonder what their reaction was on board, as they realized the loss of both side wheels. The *Nautilus* was suspended motionless in the depths, while we waited for Luna to return to the airlock chamber. The vessel passed directly overhead, with remnants of the paddle wheels still drifting downward. Along with the slowly sinking debris, we noticed projectiles streaking past at high speeds. They acted like rifle bullets that had been fired into the water. Apparently, the crew of the vessel was along the railing firing in to the depths. The clarity of the water was relatively decent in that part of the ocean, and they may have seen the mass of the *Nautilus*'s hull and thought it to be a sea monster of some sort. They would certainly have a whale of a tale to tell when they returned.

Their rifle bullets could not harm the *Nautilus*. However, Luna was still somewhere out in the surrounding seas, and she could possibly be injured. The Captain increased the depth of the ship to take us out of their range and provide more protection to Luna as she returned to the vessel. The hull of the *Nautilus* would provide an excellent shield. I left the bridge and hurried to the airlock chamber, so I would know the moment she had safely returned.

With growing concern, I paced back and forth along the side of the pool as I waited for her. I wondered if she had been injured by the concussion from the charges, or perhaps she had been struck by a stray bullet. Finally, I sat down on the rim and stared intently into the entry pool. To my great relief, she came bursting out of the pool literally into my arms, of course soaking me with sea water for the third time.

"Why John, you were worried about me again. That is so sweet of you." Much to my surprise and no small pleasure, she then kissed me on the cheek and slid back into the pool, saying "I am fine. Now quickly go tell the Captain I am back on board the *Nautilus*, so he can go after the steam ship. We must 'seas' the day. We cannot let them escape." Once again, I was dripping with salt water as I worked my way back to the bridge to let Captain Nemo and Sherlock know Luna was safely aboard the *Nautilus*.

Captain Nemo thanked me and stated that we would now continue after the vessel to disable the stern propeller. Looking me up and down, Sherlock appraised me and asked, "What did you do, Watson, jump in after her to go swim along with her? You know, if you two continue to go on meeting like this, you will need to lay in a good supply of towels and cold medicine. You had better stay away from the Captain's Persian rugs."

I looked at him, asked if he had any messages with invisible ink writing to be revealed, wrung the salt water out of my sleeve onto the floor in front of him, and left to change into dry clothing.

I returned to my cabin to change clothes yet again, while Captain Nemo commenced his pursuit of the vessel. Constantly adjusting speed, course and depth, while avoiding rifle and small cannon fire, the Captain and his crew were flawless in their maneuvering of the *Nautilus*. With a doctor's precision, he used the ramming spur to damage their rudder and propeller without harming the hull whatsoever. We retreated a distance from the vicinity to observe them and verify that, while they had lost propulsion, they were still safe and seaworthy. We had thought that, without use of their paddle wheels and propeller, they would be stranded, but they immediately commenced to put out a jury-rigged rudder and set all the sail they could. It seemed as if they were determined to reach that island.

Since the vessel was a steam auxiliary, she carried sail in addition to their steam engine, and they were hoisting all the canvas they could. Captain Nemo observed that while the *Nautilus* was very effective against paddle wheels and propellers, and if we wanted to sink it outright, against the hull itself, he could do very little against the sails.

Sherlock observed the vessel under sail and replied to Captain Nemo's observation, "That may not be the case. It just so happens that I have recently written a paper "*Practical Applications for Catapults, Trebuchets, Mangonels, and Other Non-Explosive Powered Ballistic Devices*". We could use a catapult to launch small explosive charges into their sails and rigging. Nothing too powerful, just enough to destroy their masts. I could design something quite quickly, and your crew could assemble it with what you have on board. We will have to wait until dark to deploy it since we must be close enough to reach them, which, by the way, will put us in range of their gun fire."

Captain Nemo sighed and with an incredulous smile asked, "With all of the modern technology on board the Nautilus at our disposal, you are suggesting we employ a device that dates back to ancient history?"

Sherlock nodded and replied, "It dates back to 339 BC to be exact, and it has been quite effective over the centuries. Of course, the trebuchet is the most effective type of catapult. In the 1304 siege of Sterling Castle, they deployed a massive trebuchet called *Warwolf*, which, with a single 300-pound shot, leveled an entire section of the castle wall, effectively ending the siege. In fact, when the castle defenders saw it being assembled, they were so intimidated, they tried to surrender, but Edward I of England refused their surrender because he wanted to witness for himself the destructive power of the weapon. Of course, we do not require anything that large. It took thirty wagons just to transport the materials to build the machine, and three months to assemble it. I only need something simple that can launch the explosive devices from the deck of the *Nautilus* into their rigging to bring down the masts."

"That is a paramount concept," Captain Nemo replied, "The *Nautilus* is at your disposal."

Within a short while, Holmes had come up with a workable catapult that could launch small charges at their sails. They lashed spare parts together to make the frame and mounted a metal bowl to the end of a pole for the launching arm. When I informed Luna of the plan, she laughingly commented that, at the rate Sherlock was using up the Captains metal bowls from the galley, there would be none left for cooking, and she was quite 'bowled' over.

Per Sherlock's direction, we would mount the catapult on the deck, aft of the raised steering and observation bridge, to provide as much protection as possible for him and the crew members who would be assisting him.

The Captain informed us there had been only enough material left to make four charges, since we had previously used the same materials for the explosives that had damaged the paddle wheels. The catapult would have to be accurate.

Sherlock confidently replied, "Using navigation instruments on board, I have calculated the distance between the *Nautilus* and the other ship, the relative speed of both vessels, the height of the masts, the angle of the firing arm when the charge is released, the force with which it will hit the cross bar, the weight of the charge, the wind speed and direction, the wave height, and the current. I assure you, my calculations are altogether accurate, and I will only need two of them; one for each mast."

I looked at him with a smile and said, "Sherlock, I am impressed, but did you check air temperature and relative humidity?'

Sherlock looked at me and answered, "Indeed. They are both factored into the calculation, as is the barometric pressure and the salinity of the ocean."

With darkness as our ally and all interior lighting extinguished, the *Nautilus* quietly drew up a stern of the sailing vessel. All of us held our breath to avoid any noise as Sherlock prepared the catapult. He signaled he was ready to launch the explosive charge from the bowl at the end of the firing arm. He waited for the exact moment, gave the command to release, and the charge made a perfect ark into the mizzen topsail, where it detonated and brought down the mizzen mast. While Sherlock and the *Nautilus* crew rewound the strap that provided the tension and reloaded the bowl, the crew of the vessel we were pursuing assembled at the stern rail with rifles and began firing at us. In the dark, they could not see well, and their shots went astray or bounced harmlessly off the *Nautilus*'s hull. Again, Sherlock gave the command, and the second charge was launched, this time destroying the main mast. As the wreckage of the masts and rigging collapsed to the deck, the vessel lost all forward momentum and came to a halt. They had finally been stopped and we could resume our course to the Azores.

Before we did, however, Captain Nemo produced a small iron chest, and per his request, Sherlock launched it at the vessel, dropping it squarely on to the deck. "That should cover the damage to their vessel." The Captain stated with satisfaction. "It is not their fault they took on the passengers they did."

Sherlock nodded and asserted, "I would think so. The gold coins in that chest can most certainly purchase a brand-new vessel, and more."

"And I also included a note to the owner of the vessel," said the Captain, "to subdue and restrain his passengers until authorities arrive to tow them back to port and safely relieve them of their dangerous guests."

Chapter 19. A Most Unusual Solution,
(And it's amazing what a good cup of tea can do.)

The makeshift catapult had been disassembled and stowed, the *Nautilus* had submerged, and we were back on course to the Azores. We had all gathered again in the salon, and Luna was once more in her water chair, translating as needed. Jules Verne complimented Sherlock on his clever idea and reiterated that not all solutions need be based on futuristic technology. He asked what the plan would be when we arrived at their final base, since we did not know what to expect or what resources they might have available.

Against the background noise of the *Nautilus* engines running at full speed, Captain Nemo responded, "That is true, we are taking a risk in going there, but I feel it is worth it if we can strand a large portion of their group and incapacitate them. Success at their final base, along with our Iceland victory would eliminate the majority of their organization. The only question remaining is the source of the communication breech in England." Then turning to Holmes, he asked, "Have you made any more progress on that Sherlock?"

Holmes distractedly looked up from the papers and material he was working with and mumbled, "Eliminating possibilities, Captain Nemo, eliminating possibilities. It is really quite elementary, but at the same time most demanding and time consuming."

Luna looked askance and asked, “But how can it be easy and difficult at the same time? Is that not like saying it won’t take long at all, only as long as it takes?”

“That’s it precisely!” exclaimed Sherlock. “You are quite perceptive. The deductive process itself is very straight forward and simple, but it is time consuming to do a proper and thorough job of it. I must look at every single possibility.”

I thought to myself, "Yes, Sherlock, and even the ones you don’t want to see." Something in his behavior and attitude had changed since he had begun working on that problem. Normally, Sherlock worked with a cold, emotionless determination that was dedicated but detached. This particular problem seemed to have touched a nerve with him, as if he had found the answer but would not accept it. It was as if he had to keep working at it to find an alternative solution that was more agreeable. I wondered what it was that he could not accept.

Captain Nemo, returning the discussion to what we would do when we arrived, turned to Luna and said, “You have overheard them talk about this last base. It is located somewhere in the Azores. There are nine major islands in the group, divided into three smaller groups. If I showed you a chart of the Azores, do you think you could determine which one of them it might be? That would be most helpful.”

With a smile and laugh, she answered, “Well Captain, ‘eel’ see what I can do. I did hear something about the odd shape of the island and the excellent wine found there.”

Jules Verne looked up and stated, “That would be the island of Sao Jorge, or Saint George. It is very long and slender with many steep cliffs along its coast. It was once noted for its fine quality wine. I had an opportunity to try some at the 1867 World

Exposition in Paris. It was quite excellent. It is sad that a grape disease has struck the island. The wine making enterprise there was devastated. It is all but gone."

"My question is," stated the Captain, "where can they be hiding their base? I know those islands are very remote, but there is a small population there. How can they avoid being seen? Do you think it is another underwater base? I cannot imagine that they have too many more submersibles. We have already eliminated four of them. I would think that their airship would be noticeable, even in a place as remote as that."

Sherlock set down his writing implement, looked up, and sharply stated, "It is senseless to speculate. We must wait and see what turns up when we arrive. Only when we have gathered all the facts, can we determine what it is the facts tell us, and whether or not it is true or false. The information we currently have is: 1. They have a base there. 2. Following the example of their other bases, it is most likely well hidden. 3. The island is small, remote, and features tall cliffs. 4. There is a native population on the island. 5. Not that it has any bearing at all on the subject, they make good wine. Tell me, what conclusion can we draw from that without further information? Now, if you will excuse me, I will be in my quarters. And Captain, if I may borrow your violin." With that, Holmes stood up, collected the violin case, and left the salon.

It is known, Holmes has a reputation for being odd, eccentric, and at times arrogant, but this was unusual even for him.

Luna watched him as he left and commented, "His mood is worse than a school of tuna that has been stranded on the beach after a high tide and left in the sun to bake for a week. Is he unhappy or upset about something? Perhaps the Captain could prepare a nice sautéed sea urchin and pickled herring casserole to cheer him up."

We cringed at the thought of Luna's suggestion, but before anyone could answer, the sound of violin music began to echo through the *Nautilus* -- a sad, haunting melody.

I commented to Luna, "He has been working on locating the communication breech in the Atlantean network, and something about it has been bothering him. He can get very involved in his calculations and deductions, and at times he may get too tense."

Luna smiled brightly and asked, "What kind of tents, wigwams or tepees?" and then she laughed at her word play, and added, "What he needs is a good cup of the right kind of seaweed tea."

Just then the violin music stopped abruptly, and Sherlock came rushing back into the salon with a very satisfied look on his face and cheerfully stated. "I have figured it out. What I need right now is a good cup of the right kind of seaweed tea. Captain, may I have access to your dried seaweed stores and one of the laboratories on board?"

I thought to myself, "Now, is that the ultimate in irony, or am I as soggy as Luna's ocean metaphors?"

Pleased to see the positive change in him the Captain readily agreed, and Sherlock exited the salon whistling the tune *Tea for Two*. I was at a complete loss as to what had just happened, but I was glad to see he had resolved his concern.

We continued on course, uncertain of what we would find, while Sherlock spent all of his time in the *Nautilus*'s laboratory working with the dried seaweed. I checked in on him once, to see how he was doing, and he considered me and asked, "Who are you? Do I know you?"

I looked at him in surprise and replied, "Sherlock, It's me John Watson! Of course, you know me."

He looked closer at me and responded, "Oh yes, yes, I do, don't I? This is excellent. Just excellent! Perfect timing, Watson, old boy. Carry on." He returned to his work so engrossed he did not even know I was there.

I left the laboratory with several more questions than what I had when I entered. I found Luna back in the entry pool chamber and asked if she had any idea as to what was going on with Sherlock.

She laughed and said it seemed 'fishy' to her, but she did not want to be 'shellfish', so she explained, "His mood is like the tide: It went out and left him stranded. He was left high and dry so to speak, with no place to turn. But then the tide came back in and refloated him, so now all is well. He is back on course."

I looked at her luminous face with outright confusion and asked if she could please explain without using ocean metaphors. Luna laughed and said, "I of course I 'cod' do that. He has come to a realization about what is troubling him and accepted it. And in doing so, he has come up with a solution to the problem. That is what he is working on in the laboratory. You will see. Everything will be fine. He will be as happy as a wet clam. And I do know firsthand how happy clams are when they are wet.

"Luna," I commented, "I am pleased to see you seem much happier now than when we first met. Your humorous, lighthearted nature is delightful."

"That is because Monsieur Verne has been rescued and is now safe. I was so concerned for him. He is not in good health, and those people are terribly cruel. When you and I first met, my only concern was freeing him. It was like a dark cloud of octopus ink hanging over me. But now my ocean is full of sunfish, and of course star fish, and moon snails, and rainbow guppies, and…"

I just smiled and listened as she continued listing a multitude of different sea creatures, while in the background the haunting organ music of Captain Nemo filled the *Nautilus*.

Chapter 20. A Most Unusual Situation, (And some excellent wine.)

We had arrived at Sao Jorge Island, surfaced, and observed it from a distance. Tall cliffs protruded out of the sea, as waves crashed against them relentlessly. The verdant green vegetation of the island stood in contrast to the vibrant azure blue of the ocean. A flock of sea birds cavorted and soared near the shore. Nothing seemed out of the ordinary. We commenced a circumnavigation of the island, looking for something that did not seem right. We had almost completed rounding Sao Jorge, when Sherlock pointed out a large building near the water located in proximity to a small harbor. It had two smoke stacks on the landward side, and the seaward side came close to the water where two large doors could be opened to allow objects to slide into the harbor. It looked like a facility for constructing vessels of some kind. Captain Nemo pointed out that the last time he had been near this island, it had not been there.

As we observed the building, we noticed two men in dark uniforms and tall boots patrolling the shore. The low profile of the *Nautilus* in the water prevented them from seeing us, but we quickly retreated out of sight and submerged. The enemy was there and blatantly out in the open. That made for an interesting situation. Captain Nemo stated that before proceeding any further, he wanted to scout the perimeter of the island underwater. The Azores are known to be of volcanic origin with many caves and caverns. There might be an underwater entrance to a hidden lagoon.

We cautiously followed the shoreline and the cliffs, being wary of the surging tide near the rocks and shallows. On several occasions, the *Nautilus* started to enter a cave only to discover it to be a dead end and had to retreat back out in reverse. The Captain's skills in helmsmanship and navigation were impressive. On and on we went until we had completed our search of the island's perimeter. We found no underwater access or entrance to the interior. We decided to wait for nightfall to investigate the large building we had discovered near the shore.

Darkness fell, and the *Nautilus* was positioned not far from land in a deserted area of the coast, yet as close to the large building as we dared. Using a variety of items found aboard the ship, Sherlock, who is a master in the art of altering one's appearance, created disguises that would allow us to blend in with the local islanders. The Captain spoke Portuguese and French, while Sherlock understood French and German, so we hoped to find out what in fact was going on there. We utilized the launch from the *Nautilus* to make our way to the beach and then hid the craft and ourselves from view.

From our hidden location, we observed the islanders for a period and noticed a sadness and fear in them, as if their lives had been drained of all hope. We continued to watch, until we spied an older gentleman who appeared to be a farmer, walking along the path. We casually walked out into the pathway as well, and the Captain pleasantly greeted him. He looked up at Captain Nemo, appraised him, and replied, “Hello, my friend. In spite of your native attire, I see that you are not from this island.” Then staring intently into Captain Nemo’s eyes, he continued. “Forgive me if I stare at you. You remind me of my son whom I recently lost. I do not sense danger from you. But this is a dangerous place. What brings you and your companions to Sao Jorge?”

The Captain bowed his head and said he was sorry to hear of the gentleman's loss, and we were curious regarding the very large building near the harbor, as it had certainly not been here on his previous visit to this pleasant island.

The man looked at the building, sighed, and said it was both a blessing and a curse. Sherlock assured him that we meant no harm and asked if there was somewhere safe we could talk. And perhaps we could help him.

He looked at us as if to determine if we could be trusted, glanced to the right and the left, nodded his head, and asked us to follow him. His home was only a short distance away, and we could see that, at one time his property had been a vineyard, but the surrounding vines were all withered and dead. The home while simple, indicated that the owner had been well off in earlier times when the vineyard was prosperous. Now there was a sparseness to it that conveyed a sense of loss.

Seated inside his home, at a rustic wooden table, he offered each of us a glass of the island’s wine. He stated that, once the wine was gone there would be no more, as the grapes had all been killed by a disease. He was obviously happy to share the last of his wine with us. He said he could see goodness in us, as compared to those who ran the factory in the large building. “Have you seen what they build in there?” The Captain asked.

The old man shook his head, "I have not been inside myself, as I am too old to work in there, but those who have say they build boats that look like whales, and they swim underwater like whales. That sounds unbelievable, but it is true. You must believe me. And the factory owners treat the workers like slaves. The conditions are truly terrible. When they first arrived and said they were bringing work to the island, everyone welcomed them. We are very remote here, and there was no other work after the grapes started dying. The island men were happy to get jobs, but then we realized how cruel these people are. My son tried to stand up to them, but he was killed. They said it was an accident, but I know better. I believe they killed him to set an example. No one has dared to question them since he died. We are like prisoners on our own island. Is there anything you can do to help us?"

Captain Nemo shook the man's hand and assured him saying, "That is why we are here, to stop this organization and free you from their grasp. How many people of that group are on the island? Can you tell me where they are at this time?"

Sherlock then added, "Sir, it is most important. Can you tell me how many of these whale vessels they have built?"

We learned from the farmer, that there were only ten members of the organization still remaining on the island, and the islanders provide all the labor in the factory and work under the cruelest of conditions. Four of the whale vessels had been built and had left the island, while a fifth was nearing completion. He did not know where they went when they left. He did know, at night, the members of the organization all stayed together in a smaller structure behind the main work building, except for those who patrolled the area. Usually two guards were on patrol around the factory building all night long.

We learned what else we could, thanked him for his help, and told him that we would be back momentarily to deal with the factory owners. We returned to the *Nautilus* to collect the two remaining explosive charges, more of the seaweed knockout gas, several of Nemo's crewmen, and my service revolver just in case. Our plan was to surprise the exterior guards, render them unconscious, and then use the knockout gas on the remainder of the group in the small building so they could be locked up, and removed from the island permanently. The factory and submersible were to be destroyed.

We made our way toward the factory area, found the first guard, and with Sherlock in his disguise providing a distraction, I was able to surprise and disarm the guard with a solid right hook. Captain Nemo and his crewman had dispatched the second guard, and soon, we had them both tied up. Sherlock discretely peered through the dust-covered windows of the smaller building that contained the remainder of the foe to determine our best approach based on the location of members of the group inside. It turned out that simply opening the front door, throwing both canisters inside, and closing the door was the indeed the most logical approach. As we waited for the seaweed knockout gas to take effect, Sherlock grinned and said, "Well Watson, once again, the simplest approach is the best. That seaweed based knockout gas has proven to be most effective. I shall have to update my paper on the subject when we return.

It did indeed prove to be most effective. When we entered the building, every one of the descendants of Mu were unconscious. With the help of the *Nautilus* crew, as well as several men from the island who came to assist us once they realized what had occurred, the entire group of Mu descendants were restrained and transported to the island jail. We explained to the islanders that foreign authorities would later arrive to take the prisoners away. The islanders were most grateful and thanked us profusely.

The only task now remaining was the destruction of the factory building and final submersible. Captain Nemo and Sherlock first examined the workings of the factory and its machinery and were very impressed. The Captain made mental notes on various subjects pertaining to their technology. The sophistication of it all was far beyond anything existing in London. Captain Nemo noted the world, as it is, was not yet ready for such futuristic science. We placed the explosive charges, retreated to a safe location, detonated the devices, and eliminated the last remnant of the Mu technology. The island men who had helped us, cheered as the factory was destroyed but then looked at each other as if wondering what to do next.

Realizing the islanders were once again at a loss for work, since their grapes had succumbed to disease, Captain Nemo assigned two of his crew, a biologist and a botanist, to help the islanders develop a new crop they could grow and harvest there. He had a feeling that oranges would do quite well in this climate and provided them with what they needed to get started. He assured them he would be back to see how they succeeded and to pick up his two crewmen. They thanked us again for coming to their rescue and insisted we accept several bottles of their excellent wine. Now we were bound for England, and, at last, the mysterious source of the Atlantean communication breech would be revealed.

Chapter 21. Another Most Unusual Plan,
(And I think Sherlock is still being vague.)

Once we were back on board the *Nautilus*, we gathered again in the salon with Luna in her water chair, and we related to Jules Verne, and Luna, who had stayed behind, the events that had transpired on the island. We explained how the Mu descendants had utilized their advanced technology to build the submersibles using the forced labor of the remote and isolated islanders. Jules Verne thought about it and commented, "That would be an intriguing subject for a novel, but I think I would place the events in a *City in the Sahara* far out in the desert. It is even more remote out there."

Luna frowned and asked how he would explain the whale submersibles out in the desert. "Is that not like a fish out of the water?" she laughingly asked.

He just waved his hand and said, "Submersible vessels in the shape of whales? No one would accept that. It is too strange even for fiction. I will have them use helicopter-planes." Then with a wink he added, "Whale submersibles are almost as impossible to believe in as mermaids."

Luna laughed and whisked her tail to splash a small amount of water at him and said, "'Whale' see about that." Then changing the subject, she added, "So what is our plan when we get to London? Without a proper plan, we really will be like a fish out of water, and you know what that smells like after several days."

Sherlock cleared his throat, paused a moment to get our attention, and answered. "Friends, things are not always as they seem. Several of the facts that we thought we knew before we arrived at Sao Jorge turned out to be not quite as we believed. We knew there was a Mu base there, but it was much more than just a base. It was a fully operational factory. We believed it would be well hidden. It was not in the least bit hidden; it was out in plain sight. And the wine, or lack of it, did actually have something to do with the situation. What that tells us is that what we think we know is not always what we really know. You do know what I mean, don't you?"

We all stared at him in silence, except for Luna who brightly asked, "Is that like the wisdom of the sealed oyster that reveals no pearl? I have always believed that it is quite obvious, as clear as a cod fish on a kelp bed."

Not even attempting to translate or answer Luna's sea life metaphor, Sherlock went on, "What I am trying to say is I believe I know precisely where the breech in communication is, but I am not one hundred percent certain. If it is as I suspect, I already have a plan in place on how to effectively treat it. If it is not as I suspect, I will not be overly saddened, but then we shall have to keep looking, which will be a challenge. To make the final determination, I shall need your help to execute my plan.

"When we arrive in London, Watson, you, Jules Verne, and Luna shall come with me…"

When she heard this, Luna conspicuously sloshed water with her tail and asked, “Excuse me, and how indeed are we to do that? It is not as if I can swim down the boulevard, unless you are planning to flood all of London. That would be more exciting than playing croquet with puffer fish for croquet balls and hammer head sharks for mallets.”

Sherlock answered, “Why it is most elementary. We humans have special suits made of waterproof fabric that holds the water out to keep us dry when we are breathing underwater. That same material can be made into a flexible, comfortable skirt to hold water in around Luna’s tail as she sits in a wheeled chair with a blanket over the lower half of her body. It will look quite normal to anyone; just a lady in a wheelchair with a blanket over her legs.”

Luna flashed a radiant smile and exclaimed, “What a delightful idea! I will get to see the surface world up close without even having to flood London. I thought that idea was all wet! Maybe someday I could even use the chair to come and visit John Watson for afternoon tea." Then with a coy grin, she added, "but Mr. Holmes, why do you call it "elementary?" I don’t understand at all what it has to do with a tree that grows the twelfth, thirteenth and fourteenth letters of the alphabet.”

Confused, Captain Nemo looked at Luna oddly, and she answered with the brightest smile, “An “L”,”M”,”N” tree!”

Sherlock shook his head and asked her, “Have you by any chance met the Cheshire Cat from Wonderland?”

She thought a moment and replied, “No, I can’t say that I have. But I have met several catfish, a few dog fish, and even a cowardly lion fish, but none of them went by the name of 'Cheshire'.”

Holmes ignored her humor and went on. “Now as I was saying: Watson, Jules Verne, and Luna will come with me to a certain government building at 10:45 AM. Captain Nemo, at precisely 11:00 AM, you will send a message to your fellow Atlantean who is positioned in the British government. I will provide you the message. If the breech is where I believe it is, we shall see the results first hand. I will respond accordingly, and if my new tea formula works as expected, our problem shall be resolved. Any questions?”

I immediately asked him why he felt it necessary for Luna to be there and if she would be in any great danger.

He casually replied, “Of course not, Watson. I would not ask her to come along, if there was any more danger than disabling hostile submersibles, airships, or steam auxiliary ships.”

Luna replied cheerfully, “That is wonderful. I am skilled in all of those tasks. I am as ready to assist as an octopus is to arm wrestle.”

“We will not need your skills in those activities, Luna," Sherlock answered, “but I will need you to translate for Jules Verne and possibly to emphasize a point in a way that only you could do.”

Captain Nemo looked at Sherlock and asked, “If this plan of yours works, then the communication breech in our Atlantean network shall be sealed, correct?”

Sherlock replied, “Not only the breech, but if I am correct, the resources that have been supplying the descendants of Mu. After we had determined the location of the communication leak was in London, it was wise that you contacted your agents in other governments to apprehend the Mu criminals that we left in Iceland and the Azores, as well as those on the disabled chartered vessel.

They will be incarcerated and will no longer be a threat to the world. Now we have only one person left to deal with."

While Sherlock was speaking, I noticed that he had been holding what looked like a coin in his hand and moving it back and forth. When he finished his statement, he flipped it in the air, caught it, and put it in his pocket. It was then I noticed it was the round disk that Captain Nemo had found aboard the *Saint-Michel III* when Jules Verne had gone missing. It was the one with the star map, compass, and stylized letter "M".

The remainder of the voyage to London was rather sad for me. I was pleased that we had rescued Jules Verne and stopped the descendants of Mu in their plans for world domination. And I was happy that Sherlock seemed quite satisfied with his plans to resolve the breech in the Atlanteans communication network. But once this adventure was concluded and we were back in our flat in London, that meant I would probably never see Luna again. As disappointing as that was, I did not want to express my feelings, as she seemed so very happy and excited about the prospect of seeing the surface world in a new way from the special wheeled chair and water containment skirt that the *Nautilus* crew was fabricating. I told myself not to worry about it now and to be satisfied with what time we still had together and make the most of it. And so, I gazed at her endless beauty and enjoyed her playful wit and charm in silence.

Chapter 22. A Most Unusual Confrontation, (And it turns out a good cup of tea is the answer.)

The time to commence our final plan had at last arrived. We had returned to London, and using an empty, abandoned pier in a remote section of the waterfront, secretly disembarked from the *Nautilus* under the cover of darkness. We made our way to the home of Captain Nemo's Atlantean counterpart in London and waited for daylight. Sherlock and I were dressed in Mu uniforms and boots, which he had taken from the factory before it was destroyed, and we darkened our hair and wore thin mustaches. He explained it was all a part of his plan, and that at the right moment, we would bring Jules Verne and Luna into a particular government office, and the answer would be revealed. Many times, in the past, without explaining anything in advance, Sherlock had planned out grandiose and elaborate ruses with great flair to expose a villain, and I assumed this again was one of his grand theatrical masterpieces.

As we traveled to the government buildings, I pushed the wheeled chair that held Luna and her water skirt, which was safely concealed under a thick woolen blanket. She expressed surprise and amazement at the wonders of the surface world. As two large clusters of people crossed a busy thoroughfare trying to avoid the horse-drawn hansoms and growlers, she commented it was like watching two schools of herring trying to avoid a pod of dolphins at feeding time. Jules Verne, who was walking next to her, laughed when she translated her comment, and he explained some of the various things they saw along the way. Sherlock checked his pocket watch and said it was time to execute his plan.

While I was still at a loss as to where we were going, Sherlock knew the way unerringly. The government buildings are a large complex crowded with people coming and going, but Holmes guided us through it and eventually led us down a long corridor to an unmarked door and had us stop. People looked at us in our uniforms, with the elderly Jules Verne and Luna in her wheeled chair, but no one said anything. Sherlock checked his watch again, looked at us and stated, "Captain Nemo's message has been delivered to his government counterpart. Now we wait."

The British Government routinely employs numerous messengers to relay communications and documents between agencies and offices, and it was typically done with the usual stoic manner and sluggish steady pace of that level of employee. The halls had been filled with delivery boys slowly and resolutely carrying their notes from one office to the next.

We had not waited long, however, when an uncharacteristic and out of breath messenger came rushing up to the office where we had been waiting. His entire nature was different from the other couriers. There was an air of urgency about him and his task. He was about to enter the office, when Sherlock stepped directly in front of him, quickly glanced at the message in the boy's hand, and said, "Excuse me, my good fellow. We are going in to see Mycroft Holmes right this minute. I can take that in for you. Your note actually pertains to my companions and me. Now I am sure you are quite busy and have many other messages to deliver. Here is a thank you, for your efforts." Sherlock then handed the messenger two shillings, deftly removed the note from the boy's hand and urged him on his way.

I could not believe it! Mycroft Holmes was the source of the communication breech! It was no wonder Sherlock was so upset after he had determined who it was. That must have been a devastating realization. From what he had told me about his brother, Mycroft Holmes was an integral part of the British government. At times, he *was* the British government. Why would he be involved in something like this? What was going on here? Where was this unusual adventure heading next?

Sherlock, with the note in his hand, opened the door and with a brusque attitude ushered us into the office. It was large, elegant, and cluttered with books, papers, and maps. A tea service stood on a small table off in the corner. The walls were lined with book shelves, and there was a large walnut desk in the center of the room. Behind the desk sat an equally large, heavily built man whose brow was raised and showed signs of great intellect. His suit, while of excellent quality, was unkempt as if he simply could not be bothered to spend the effort required to maintain his appearance. This was Mycroft Holmes, Sherlock's brother.

Taking the lead and in a disguised voice, Sherlock handed Mycroft the note, casually threw the medallion with the star map, compass, and stylized "M" on the desk, and said, "Here is your latest message. Your delivery boy seems to be a bit lax and slow today. This message tells you to expect two envoys from Mu, that we have the code medallion for identification, and that we are bringing Jules Verne and his lady interpreter to your office for a visit. He only speaks French you know. But we are already here. Imagine that! We have finally convinced Jules Verne to share with you the secret of how he travels in time. Now at last, the weapons of the future will be available for the good of The Empire."

Mycroft shifted in his chair and replied, "That is excellent news. It will be of immense help to Great Britain and to the descendants of Mu as well, but why did you chance bringing him here to my office? That is taking an unnecessary risk. I have kept this association between the descendants of Mu and myself secret for a reason. I agreed to fund the rebuilding of Mu culture as well as the reestablishment of your science and technology. Your people agreed to use it for the good of the British Empire, and to gain the secret of time travel from Jules Verne. With that ability we can obtain weapons from the future, but the agreement was to be kept a secret. No one else in the government knows what I am doing here. Not even my own brother knows."

Sherlock quickly pulled off his fake mustache, and in his own voice stated, "I would not say that, dear brother. But my question is, Why? Why are you doing this?"

Mycroft's eyes grew wide with astonishment as he realized it was his brother who stood before him, and he exclaimed, "Sherlock, what on earth are you doing here? And how did you find out about this? Do you have any idea what you have done? You have interrupted an important plan to bring power and security to the British Empire. The world is heading towards a great war. With my knowledge and insight, I can see the inevitable results as clear as day. Not this decade, nor the next, but eventually the whole world will be at war. It will be devastating. The weapons of the future would have protected Great Britain. Why would you, of all people, want to prevent that?"

Sherlock looked at his brother and shook his head. "Mycroft, you have more knowledge, facts, information, and insight than anyone in the world, but you have been so blind. The organization that you have foolishly associated yourself with has no intention of sharing the weapons of the future with anyone. I do not know how you met or came to be working together, but the populace of the lost city of Mu has been striving towards only one goal since ancient times, and that is world domination. We have seen the result of their activities in the Azores. They enslaved the islanders to build their ships. They have no regard for human life whatsoever."

Taking the initiative, Luna leaned forward and addressed Mycroft. "It is true what your brother says. These people are evil and without remorse. They have cruelly used their submersible vessels to sink countless ships with hundreds of innocent lives lost. I have seen it with my own eyes more times than I care to remember."

Mycroft looked at Luna with scorn and asked, "And who are you that I should believe you? How could you have seen them sink all those ships you say they have destroyed? You are sitting there in that chair and telling me that you have witnessed them sinking countless ships? The next thing you will be telling me is that you are a mermaid who swims the seven seas, and you saw it firsthand."

Luna let her blanket fall to the floor and pushing up against the arms of the wheeled chair, she lifted her lower body from the water skirt, to fully reveal her luminescent scaly green tail.

"I assure you sir, I have seen it with my own eyes. And yes, I am a mermaid! For emphasis, she flourished her tail and drenched Mycroft with saltwater.

Sherlock's brother was completely stunned. As well as soaking wet, Mycroft was speechless. It was not surprising really, as Luna does have that effect on people. I would actually say, he was more shocked discovering she was a mermaid, than when he realized it was his brother Sherlock, who was standing in front of him moments ago.

"She...she's a mermaid! Sherlock where did you find her? How did you find her? It's impossible! I have had people searching the world over for creatures like her. You remember our childhood wager? That if mermaids really exist, I would find one before you did." He stared intently at Luna and exclaimed, "Who are you? What are you doing here?"

While slowly moving her tail back and forth in her water skirt, she glared back at him and exclaimed, "Why you barnacle encrusted, slimy, sea slug! I am helping your brother stop a threat to your world as well as mine. The pack you are running with has killed hundreds of people. Don't you see that? Or as Sherlock said, are you too blinded by your facts and information?" She then undulated her tail and splashed him again.

Holmes replied, "Yes, Mycroft, she is a mermaid, and not one to argue with. Our age-old bet is unimportant now. That is not the question. I want to know how you intercepted the Atlanteans communications."

He dismissively waved his hand and said, "Sherlock, you know that all information in the government comes to me and goes through my office. I am privy to everything. Nothing happens in this administration that I am not aware of. Your Atlantean friends have a highly placed official in our government, but I am sure you knew that. I noticed some odd messages coming through to him in an incomprehensible language. It got my attention. I usually do not like to expend any more effort than is absolutely required, but this was intriguing. Actually, it was you who helped me decode it, brother. Your paper on deciphering ancient languages was most useful. Although I did have to write you a letter for clarification on one point. Of course, it came from an ancient language scholar, and not me.

"This gave me insight regarding the Atlanteans who have been monitoring us, as well as to what Jules Verne was doing with time travel. About the same time, I was contacted by the survivors of Mu. They had access to advanced technology and science, but they needed funds to develop it. They assured me that once they had completed their work, the British Empire would benefit greatly from it. It seemed like a reasonable idea. A rather serendipitous coincidence, if you please. Discovering the possibility of genuine time travel and those who promised they could acquire it seemed to be perfect timing. We could benefit from working together, and no one else needed to know. I have enough influence in the government to request funds without question. It was all going very smoothly, until you stepped in. But from what you and your fishy lady friend are telling me, it is apparently a good thing you did. A point for you, brother."

Luna doused him again and replied, "Fishy lady friend indeed! Your reasoning smells worse than a two-week-old beached blue whale!"

Sherlock looked at Mycroft askance and flatly stated, "They never told you which empire would benefit from their actions, dear brother. You failed to see their true purpose. But they have been stopped. We have destroyed their bases, their ships, and their submersible factory. They are all in custody, even the ones that set off to free their associates near Iceland. They are all locked up, contained, and this is over. It is done. And so, it seems even the great Mycroft Holmes is entitled to a human error now and then. But let there not be hard feelings between us. Let us share a cup of tea. You look as if you could use one."

While he was speaking, Luna had replaced the blanket over her tail, and Sherlock had poured two cups of hot water from the tea kettle in the corner of the office. He removed a small tin from his pocket and poured a greenish mixture into Mycroft's cup and handed it to his brother. “It was an interesting and worthy idea, Mycroft, but this time, you did not think it all the way though. You let the information get in the way of your judgment. I am sure you won’t let it happen again.”

He raised his cup and held it up for a moment, they saluted one another with their tea cups and drank their tea. “Do drink up, Mycroft. This tea will do wonders for you. It is seaweed based you know.”

Mycroft finished his cup of seaweed tea, set it down, and immediately started blinking his eyes. He looked rather confused for a moment, turning his head first to the left and then to the right. Finally, he rubbed his eyes, opened them wide, and looked with surprise at his brother. “Sherlock, when did you arrive? I did not notice you entering. Why does your hair look darker? And what is that odd uniform you are wearing? Are you and Watson working undercover on a case? Your disguise would never fool anyone, you know. I knew it was you as soon as I noticed you were here. I must have been in a very deep concentration. I find it hard to believe I never saw you enter. When *did* you arrive? Do you, by any chance, know why I am completely soaked in salt water? And who is this lovely lady with you? A client?”

Turning to Luna, he addressed her, “Good day, madam, I hope you are well. Pardon my sogginess at the moment. I must have been out in the rain, or something. I assure you that whatever your problem is, you can count on my brother to assist you. And if I am not mistaken, this is the famous author, Jules Verne. What brings you to England and in the company of my renowned brother, no less? Has someone made off with the *Nautilus*? You will forgive my humor. I really am an admirer of your work. You have such a clear vision of technology. Submarines, airships, rockets to the moon. It is almost as if you have seen the future."

Luna translated Mycroft's comments, and Jules Verne smiled and answered, "Thank you sir, but I assure you, it is research, pure and simple research. Nothing more."

He then turned and winked at us.

Sherlock set his cup down and thanked Mycroft for his assistance. Mycroft stated he did not know what, if anything, he had done, and he was still wondering why he was soaking wet. Sherlock bid goodbye to his brother, and we left the office.

Chapter 23. A Most Unusual Conclusion, (And a sad farewell, but an encouraging promise.)

With a sense of satisfaction at the conclusion of the day's events, we made our way back to the deserted pier, to once again, join the *Nautilus*. I did, however, make a quick detour to a lady's fashions shop and purchase a stylish hat for Luna to wear on our return journey back to the ship. I gave it to her and fondly said, "When we first met, you swam off with my hat. Here is one that will look much better on you, and you can keep it."

Luna giggled with delight and answered, "Why dearest John, that is so very sweet of you. You are right, though, this hat does look much better on me than it would on you."

We continued our way back to the pier in silence, each lost in our own thoughts on the extraordinary adventure we had just concluded. We were nearly there when Luna expressed that she was not feeling well. Her tail was very sore and hurting, unlike anything she had ever previously experienced.

Back inside the *Nautilus*, we discovered the material we had used to make her water skirt had caused a reaction with the scales of her tail, and that was the cause of the pain and discomfort. We moved our final gathering to the airlock chamber, so Luna could be immersed directly in the sea water entry pool. She immediately felt much better. While the chair and water skirt had worked this time, it would not be healthy for her for any future usage. My heart sank when I heard the news.

We informed Captain Nemo of all that had occurred and assured him that the communication breech was closed, but he would have to continue using code instead of the Atlantean language for contacting his agent in the British government, since Mycroft Holmes still saw all communications of interesting or unusual nature.

Sherlock explained to us he knew had discovered the source of the leak but was concerned until he had determined a way to properly address it. “I was actually testing the tea that time you looked in on me Watson, and I did not recognize you. I had to make sure I gave Mycroft the exact dose that would cause him to forget this whole episode, without affecting the rest of his prodigious memory and mental faculties. He is an extraordinary person, and important to the country.”

“Yes," I replied, “and you bested him. And then you erased his memory of your doing so. That was kind of you, Sherlock.”

“I did not do it out of kindness for him. I did it to protect the Atlanteans and Jules Verne, as well as Luna.” Looking at Captain Nemo, he went on, “As you had mentioned when we first met, Captain, your group of Atlanteans must remain invisible to the rest of the world, so you may continue your task. And as H. G. Wells expressed in our previous adventure, the government cannot know of the existence of time travel. It is best kept a secret for now.”

Jules Verne nodded with an all-knowing smile, and said, "I agree completely. That is why, although I have quite often traveled in time, I have never written about time travel. I will never bring up the subject. I will leave it to H. G. Wells. I wonder though, where does he get his ideas? Invisibility serums and human animal hybrids? That is real fictional science."

Sherlock agreed and said, "Yes, but I think the term 'science fiction' sounds better."

As Sherlock and I prepared to leave the *Nautilus* and return to our flat, Captain Nemo stated that after we left, he would return Jules Verne to his former yacht, now under the command of Nemo's men, and that Verne would continue his short cruise on the yacht. No one would ever know what had happened. The world could not know what had happened. "You saved the world today, my friends. Thank you for your assistance in this effort. It could not have been done without you Mr. Holmes, Dr. Watson, nor without you, Luna." He turned to Sherlock and me, and continued, "I must apologize one more time for the tea ruse that I used to bring you aboard."

Sherlock grinned and said. "I understand completely, Captain Nemo. You needed to get us on board the *Nautilus*, so we could see for ourselves what you were saying was true. I bear no hard feelings."

I agreed and added, "But you must understand, that after this adventure, I will never touch another cup of seaweed tea as long as I live."

We laughed, and Sherlock remarked, "I have enough information from this journey to write a new paper on *"The Multiple Applications, Usages, and Possibilities Derived from Seaweed Tea, With an Emphasis on Knockout Gas and Memory Inhibitors"*. And it has already been successfully field tested!"

Sherlock exited the airlock chamber, along with Jules Verne and Captain Nemo, to gather some items before we left. Luna had spent her time during the group discussion swimming in the salt water, and she was feeling back to her aquatic self. She gave a quick thrust of her tail and again was sitting next to me on the edge of the pool. Of course, I was once more drenched in sea water, but I did not mind in the least. I was happy to be near her one last time. It saddened me deeply to say good bye to her and know I would most likely never see her again. She looked at me and said, "My dearest sweet John Watson. You have been so kind and caring. You are beyond compare, and I give you this gift from my heart." She placed in my hand a golden seashell that had been strung on a strand of her long dark hair. On the shell she had written, 'Luna'. I thanked her profusely for it and removed from my pocket the poem I written for her earlier. I gave it to her, and she clutched it as if it were gold. With her lilting musical voice, she slowly read it aloud:

"The Mystic Magic Sea"

The sea is calling, hear its voice,
a mystic magic song.
Its spell, enchanting leaves no choice.
Its echo lingers long.

It weaves a web of salt sea air,
and tides that ebb and flow,
to lure you with a song so fair
that it seems to glow.

A sea of diamonds in the sun
glitters far and wide,
sparkling till the day is done,
drifting on the tide.

Now a mist is softly creeping
gently o'er the sea.
Soon the ocean will be sleeping,
quiet as can be.

The silver moon is now ascending
o'er the misty grey bank of fog,
that's never ending,
drifting on its way.

Dolphins dance and mermaids hide
in the waters deep
where their secrets can abide
always for to keep.

The sea is calling, hear it sing,
a mystic magic tune,
that timeless will forever ring
beneath the silver moon."

She held it close to her and exclaimed, "John this is truly beautiful! I will treasure and remember it always! I will remember you always. I promise you, John Watson, we will meet again. Someday…" Then Luna embraced me with a kiss that I shall never forget, dove back into the water, and she was gone.

I sat in silence for some time staring at the golden seashell in my hand and wondered if I ever would meet her again. I placed her precious gift in my pocket and left the airlock chamber to go find Sherlock.

We said goodbye to Jules Verne and Captain Nemo, stepped out on to the deserted dock, and watched as the *Nautilus* silently submerged beneath the waves and vanished into the endless mystery that is the sea.

Sherlock looked at me and commented, "Watson, you are soaking wet. You know, you are going to catch cold. You should take something for it. "

I turned to him and replied, "That may be, but don't you even think of suggesting seaweed tea."

He grinned and said, "No, I would not dream of it, but how about some nice hot seaweed soup?"

Post Script: Again?
(Yes, it can get even more strange and unusual.)

Three days later, I was still sick with a cold. Nevertheless, I had managed to record the two fascinating adventures we had so recently experienced, while the facts were still fresh in my mind. Sherlock and I were enjoying a cup of tea, and I can assure you it was most definitely not seaweed. I was eternally grateful to once again be savoring Earl Grey, and we agreed that nothing could possibly compare to the recent episodes. We were certain we would never again experience anything so strange or unusual, when there was an odd clattering sound in the hallway outside of our door. It sounded almost like a horse's hooves, but more musical.

We were wondering what it might be, when the door burst open to reveal a knight in chain mail armor. He boldly stepped inside the room, and announced, "I am Sir Percival, knight of the Round Table of Camelot. In the name of King Arthur, High King of England, I seek to engage the services of one Sherlock Holmes in locating a missing person. That person being the Right Honorable, Alfred Lord Tennyson.

Book 3

Sherlock Holmes and The Round Table Adventure

Table of Contents

A Note to Readers:

The following story, *Sherlock Holmes and the Round Table Adventure*, which I refer to as book three of the Sherlock Holmes and the Missing Authors Trilogy, is one of the most odd and unusual Sherlock Holmes adventures ever written by his trusted friend and biographer, Dr. John Watson. They have shared many an adventure together over the years, and I would say Sherlock Holmes' fame is due in equal parts to Sherlock's uncanny skills in logic, perception and deduction, and Dr. Watson's outstanding skill as a scribe in collecting and recording their adventures. This manuscript was discovered at the same time as the first two books of the trilogy, and the reader may notice that it seems to contradict much of what Sherlock Holmes had many times previously stated about the absolute impossibility of magic, yet I assure you that it is presented here word-for-word just as Dr. Watson had recorded it so many years ago.

As in the previous two manuscripts, *Sherlock Holmes and the "Adventure of the Grinning Cat,"* (Book One) and "*Sherlock Holmes in the Nautilus Adventure,"* (Book Two of the Missing Authors Trilogy), Dr. Watson had requested that this story not be published until seventy-five years after his passing. Again, as this document was lost for many years and has been just recently rediscovered, the requested amount of time has more than passed, so this story may be published, and presented for your consideration.

Be prepared for a very odd, yet thoroughly enchanting and magical adventure.

Prologue

Memorandum:

To: Whom it may Concern

From: Dr. John Watson M.D.

Subject: *Sherlock Holmes and the Round Table Adventure*

Date: February 1898

I stand (figuratively speaking that is) before you, the reader, with yet another incredible tale of Sherlock Holmes and a missing author. This is the third in a series of similar adventures involving vanished literary leviathans happening in such quick succession that I am still overwhelmed by the entire experience. The first two cases involved Sherlock Holmes, searching for Lewis Carroll and Jules Verne respectively, with famous characters coming to life right from the pages of their novels and appearing in our lodgings at 221-B Baker Street. From that point, the tales grew more strange and unusual as they unfolded.

This final tale is without question the oddest of the trilogy, yet the outcome is also without question, the most satisfying. Yes, it is true that history itself was slightly altered as a result of this adventure, but in reality, Sherlock actually helped to bring about events that had already taken place. They had already happened and had been recorded, so our little foray into the past was simply the catalyst that brought them to fruition.

And without question, this is also a love story. It chronicles Sherlock's journey to meet an ethereal musical pixy whom he had previously encountered twice before in our last two adventures. He was utterly mesmerized and captivated by her hauntingly magnificent music, and he simply could not rest until he found her. Her enchanting song would not be denied.

That being said, for the sake of Sherlock's reputation as a consulting detective and his standing with Scotland Yard, and my own practice as a doctor, I must still request that this manuscript not be published until seventy-five years after my passing. Your compliance in honoring my request is appreciated.

Dr. John H. Watson M. D.

Sherlock Holmes and the Round Table Adventure

Chapter 1.

A Very Odd Visitor, (And a knight to remember.)

Sherlock Holmes and I looked at one another in utter disbelief. Yet another fictional character from literature was standing before us in the doorway of our lodgings at 221 B Baker Street asking for Sherlock's help in locating a missing author. We had just, days ago, concluded adventures involving the Cheshire Cat, White Rabbit, and Mad Hatter, searching for Alice of Wonderland, as well as Lewis Carroll himself, whom had both disappeared. Then Captain Nemo of the "*Nautilus*" arrived seeking to engage Sherlock in locating Jules Verne, who was missing. Now we had a Knight of the Round Table at our door seeking Alfred Lord Tennyson? This was more than I could accept.

Our most recent adventures had left me with a terrible cold, and Sherlock in a rather forlorn and despondent state regarding an ethereal musical Pixy whom we had crossed paths with. He had heard her enchanting music on several occasions and was positively mesmerized by her. The way he described it, he was sweetly haunted by the silver toned echoes of her captivating music and could not escape from it. Her melody was ringing in his thoughts constantly. It was akin to catching a fleeting glimpse of the most beautiful woman you have ever seen, hearing her lilting voice, as you share a brief, but unforgettable conversation with her knowing that she is that special one you have longed for eternally, but then she vanishes! The emptiness you are left with is overwhelming. There is simply nothing to fill the endless void.

Over the last several days, Sherlock, with a starry-eyed distant look had said that when he played his violin, he was somehow communicating with her, which was wonderful, but it left him longing for more. It made the ache worse. He was at a loss as to what to do. Strangely enough, when he played, I could hear echoes of her melodies playing counter point and harmony. It was beautiful and melancholy at the same time. Perhaps this odd new adventure would take Sherlock's mind off his winsome Pixy Music.

The brown haired, grey-eyed gentleman of muscular build standing before us did look convincingly like a medieval knight with well used chain mail armor over which he wore a tunic. The sword which hung from his belt also looked quite authentic. He had burst into our flat claiming to be Sir Percival of Camelot and was requesting Sherlock's help in locating Alfred Lord Tennyson, England's former Poet Laureate and author of *"The Idylls of the King*," the well-known series of poems that tell the timeless tale of King Arthur and the Knights of the Round Table.

"You do know that Sir Alfred Lord Tennyson has been dead for six years," Sherlock pointed out to the armor-clad stranger standing in the doorway. "He passed away on October 6, 1892 and was buried in the Poet's Corner of Westminster Abbey near the graves of Chaucer and Robert Browning. His family was present at the time of his death. It would have been quite difficult to have contrived that, as he was one of the three most well-known individuals in the country at the time. He was a personal friend of Queen Victoria, herself."

Then with a wry grin he asked, "Can I assist you in finding some other equally inaccessible person of literature, perhaps the famous poet and playwright William Shakespeare or possibly Merlin the magician?"

The stranger, however, not deterred by Sherlock's response, persisted. "Pray tell, I am not familiar with this 'shaking spear' person you mention. From his name, it sounds like he would strike fear and dread into the hearts of his readers."

I thought to myself how true his statement was when it came to many students of English literature, but the knight went on speaking. "And it was Merlin the Enchanter himself who made it possible for me to be here. I know it may sound odd to you, but Alfred Lord Tennyson did not actually pass away in 1892. He just passed out of your world, or if you will, your *time period,* and into ours, and now he truly has gone missing. He has vanished! We must locate him, and Merlin made it very clear that you are the only one with the requisite skills to find him."

With a distinct note of skepticism in his voice, Sherlock responded, "Did you hear that, Watson? I am apparently quite well known before I am even born."

"But you don't exist!" I exclaimed in frustration while pointing directly at the stranger. "King Arthur and the Knights of the Round Table, Camelot, Excalibur, that entire story is just that, a *story* based on legends and myth. *"The Idylls of the King"* is just the most recent retelling of it by our former Poet Laureate, Tennyson. It is based on Thomas Malory's "*Le Morte D'Arthur,*" which itself is based on earlier versions by Robert de Boron and

Geoffrey of Monmouth's "*History of the Kings of Britain*". They are all just stories, nothing more!"

"Merlin predicted that you would say that." He nodded, going on. "He also said to tell you that you have been very sick for the last two days with a cold."

"I am sure anyone could guess that just by looking at me!" I interrupted him.

"Caused by repeated soakings in cold seawater during your dalliances with a mermaid named Luna aboard a vessel named the "*Nautilus,*" which somehow travels underwater. He did not explain the details of the underwater ship. Do such things truly exist in this time?"

How on earth could this stranger have known that? Sherlock and I had not told anyone about Luna or the "*Nautilus*". We had not even left the flat since we returned from our last adventure.

Turning to Holmes, he continued. "Merlin also said to tell you, Sherlock Holmes, that you store your pipe tobacco, whatever that may be, in an old Persian shoe. You acquired your Stradivarius, which I believe is a musical instrument, for a mere 55 shillings, and when you play it, you are, in truth speaking to an ethereal musical Pixy for whom you have a heartfelt longing and wish to meet once again. Merlin did mention that as this quest may take us into the Realm of the Faerie, it could quite possibly lead you to her and be the answer to your wistfulness."

For the second time that day, Sherlock and I looked at one another in disbelief. How could he have known any of these things? Maybe there was something genuine to this odd stranger.

With a glimmer of hope in Sherlock's eyes for the first time in days, he gestured towards a chair and said, "Maybe you had better take a chair and tell us your entire story."

With a deep sigh, the knight walked over to the chair, picked it up, and asked, "Where would you like me to take it to, good sir? We have limited time before we must begin our journey."

Sherlock shook his head negatively and replied, "What I meant was, please sit down and make yourself comfortable while you tell us how you came to be here and what it is you want me to do."

He set the chair down, sat in it, sighed impatiently, and replied, "I came here through a portal in an ancient formation of standing stones, and I want you to come with me to Camelot and locate Alfred Lord Tennyson. It is really most simple. Now, may we be on our way? The gateway is only open for a limited amount of time."

With an enthusiasm in his voice, most likely because of the possibility of reaching the true source of the music that was endlessly calling to him, Sherlock asked, "Can you explain this portal you speak of? Where is it located? How does it function? How did you get from the portal to Baker Street?"

I looked at Sherlock and said, "Holmes, you don't really believe him, do you? Yes, he inexplicably knows more than a few highly personal facts about us that no one could possibly guess, much less know, but there has to be a logical, rational explanation, other than he just walked out of a poem or somehow traveled through time. There always is. Just the other day you were able to look at the map of a cavern you had never seen before and know exactly which room, out of dozens, a prisoner would be held in. And before that, you knew that I was not going to invest in a South American gold mine just from the chalk on my finger. You should be able to see right through this fraud."

Sherlock looked at me and replied straight forwardly, "What I see Watson, is that he does know several facts which would be impossible for anyone outside of the "*Nautilus*" crew and ourselves to know. And based on my monograph "*Determining a Persons Occupation Through Observation of Obvious but Typically Overlooked Characteristics,*" I see that he also is wearing clothes of a weave and fabric that have not been used for centuries. The scar on his forearm was clearly caused by a broad sword, while the scar on his cheek is the result of a glancing blow from a chain mace wielded by a left-handed person. His gait, when he crossed the room to pick up the chair, indicates he is an accomplished equestrian, spending one and a half hours per day in the saddle. The way he holds his left arm is indicative of one used to holding a shield. He has abrasions on his ears from a helmet rubbing against them. Everything I see tells me that he is truly a medieval knight with knowledge of us that is not readily explainable."

The stranger's eyes widened, and he exclaimed, "Forsooth! You must be a great wizard also to know such things about me. Merlin stated that your skills in observation and deduction are beyond compare. That is why you must come with me. The standing stones that contain the portal are in the vicinity of a village called Wiltshire. The passage way only opens for a limited time and then it closes. It is invisible to anyone who is unaware of it."

"You say it is near Wiltshire. You must mean Stonehenge, the ancient circle of megaliths that is thought to be a burial site and an astronomical calendar," stated Sherlock. "It is said that standing in the exact center of the circle one can see the sunrise directly over the heel stone on the summer solstice."

The knight's smile broadened, and he replied with great enthusiasm, "You *do* know the location I refer to! It is indeed a place of great power. Besides being a portal from our time into yours, it can also be an entrance into the Faerie Realm. We fear that Alfred Lord Tennyson may have unknowingly wandered into, or has been lured into, that mystical land. Its call is difficult to resist, much like the ethereal Pixy Music that enchants your thoughts. We know not where he has gone. Merlin predicted that your far-seeing ability will be able to find him, but the nature of your skills demand that you examine his lodgings to do so. We must be off to the standing stones."

I pointed out, "But Wiltshire is ninety miles from London. It would take us several days at least to get there," then with a wink towards Sherlock, I added, "unless we travel via Unicorn, and I am certainly not looking forward to another high-speed Unicorn journey any time soon. Our Wonderland adventure had more than enough of those."

Just as I said that, there was a loud clattering of hooves in the hallway, and a majestic white Unicorn paraded into the parlor. With a proud toss of its head, it asked, "Did someone call me? Is it finally time to depart? It certainly took you long enough to convince them. I can't wait to return home to Camelot. This is the strangest quest we have ever been on, Sir Percival. While you were conversing with the wizard and his apprentice, I perused the vicinity of their village. They have great smoke-belching metal beasts harnessed to whole lines of carriages. And they feed the beasts black rocks. I have never encountered anything like it."

"That would be a train pulled by a steam locomotive, also called an "iron horse". And I am not a wizard's apprentice; I am a practicing doctor," I replied.

The Unicorn nodded his head towards me with his spiral ivory horn emitting a silvery glow, and answered, "When you are done practicing, will you be a fully-fledged doctor? How soon will that happen? Why do you call that beast an "iron horse" when it does not, in any way, resemble a horse? It looks more like a large furnace encased in a suit of armor with wheels attached to it. And it makes the most horrible screeching sound. How do you stand it?"

I tried to explain, “The name would be a reference to the *horsepower* of the machine, or the equivalent number of horses it would take to do the work of it not actual horses. And “practicing” is the term we use today for doctors that are actually working in the field doing medical work.”

“The Unicorn tossed his head again, replying, “But you are not out in a field, you are here in this rather comfortable interior accommodation.”

Sherlock interrupted, “We do not have time for discussions on how the English language has changed over the centuries. Sir Percival how exactly did Alfred Lord Tennyson travel to your world or time period, and what can you tell me about his disappearance?”

The knight turned his head at an angle as if looking for a way to answer Sherlock’s question. “Merlin understands it better than I do, but he did give me information that I can share to try and explain. I do not fully comprehend it, but I will do my best.

“The story of King Arthur and Camelot is genuinely true but dates back to a time before history was written. It was remembered and told and retold, sung by bards, troubadours, and minstrels. It was, or I should say is, the history of our life. It is going on right now as we speak. Merlin the Enchanter was born of a human mother and a supernatural father, and due to the nature of his birth, he has great abilities, including the gift of seeing into the future. That is how he discovered you, Sir Wizard. He only uses his powers for good and as a counselor to guide the King. He saw that history would go through a very dark time, and much of what has occurred in the past will be forgotten or be considered to be mere legend and myth. Our entire existence would be considered merely stories. Can you possibly imagine what it is like to know that your whole life will be just a collection of stories and fables to be told as an entertainment?”

Sherlock looked at me and commented, "Imagine that Watson. If the future had to rely only on your overly exaggerated and romantically fancified versions of our exploits, they would imagine me to be some type of super detective rather than the plain and simple practitioner of the highest level of logical observation and rational deduction that I am."

The knight ignored Sherlock's comment and continued, "But there have been those rare individuals whose perception is such that they see beyond your visible world. They can actually see the Faerie Realm. It is somewhat similar to the way that you are hearing the echoes of Pixy Music. You have become attuned to that realm. In your own time, there is another who is very much connected to the Faerie world. His name is Arthur Conan Doyle. Do you know of him?"

When the knight had mentioned Pixy Music, I noticed a subtle change in Sherlock's demeanor, as if pangs of joy and sorrow enveloped him simultaneously. Although he said nothing, I could sense his longing desire to be with her.

"These gifted ones can sense the real truth of the past. Merlin has been able to reach out and touch those individuals and impress upon them the histories of Arthur and Camelot, so they can be recorded for the benefit of your civilization. That is why the stories of Arthur and the Knights of the Round Table have been told and retold over the years by different authors in your world. As you said, Alfred Lord Tennyson is just the most recent of those with the vision of Camelot and King Arthur. He was the one chosen to record it for your generation."

"So, what exactly happened when it was presumed that he had passed away?" Sherlock asked.

"Merlin said to say that it was exactly like the method you used in the Grinning Cat Adventure to pass from your realm to the reality outside of time, except that it did not require a circle comprised of real and imaginary creatures and beings, only the Unicorn. And he did not pass outside of time, just to an earlier time. And there were no questions from the Time Guardians. And it was permanent and not just a temporary state. But beyond that, it was entirely identical. Regarding Sir Tennyson, I believe that you are aware of the Unicorn's healing powers."

At that moment, the Unicorn interrupted, pointing his spiral horn at me and said, "If you would like a demonstration, I could take care of that cold for you very quickly. You will feel entirely better."

I was about to accept his offer, but Sherlock interrupted, "When Alfred Lord Tennyson passed on, his entire family was with him at his bedside. How could they not have noticed anything unusual?"

"Yes, that is true, but as you are aware, and as your scribe has recorded in your previous adventures, the swiftness of the Unicorn is almost beyond perception. When Sir Tennyson's time for passing was imminent, with just a minor distraction, the Unicorn was able to replace him with an identical looking fabrication created by Merlin, and at the same time, Alfred Lord Tennyson was healed by the Unicorn's spiral horn. No one noticed a thing"

The Unicorn once again pointed his horn at me. "The *proper* term for my horn is '*Alicorn*,' and I *really* could help you with that cold."

I was again about to accept, when the knight carried on with his story: "With a minor disturbance outside the room and the swiftness of the Unicorn, it all occurred so instantaneously that no one was able to realize a replacement had been made. It is not the first time that people have been switched. I believe the French author, Alexander Dumas, is going to write a tale about a man in an iron mask which involves something of that nature. I can't imagine why anyone would wear an iron mask. Do you have any idea what my helmet weighs?"

Not waiting for a response, he went on, "You are aware that Alfred Lord Tennyson was very melancholy. He is remembered as being one of the saddest poets in history. That is because his true desire was Camelot. "*The Idylls of the King*" was written based on his personal observations during his visits there, except for the conclusion of course. That was fabricated just to provide a moralistic end to the story for the readers of your time. All of the conclusions that have been written are made up. That is why there are variations in all of the different versions written over the years. Arthur is still alive in the time that I come from. Our lives have not yet come to an end. Sir Tennyson visited Camelot on many occasions, and he was his happiest during those times. That is why he was so melancholy when he was back here in your own time."

The knight paused and, with a sad look in his eyes, explained, "As he lay dying, he whispered a wish to visit Camelot one last time. Merlin granted him that wish, and as a result, he was also healed by the Unicorn. Sir Tennyson was brought through the portal, so he could visit Camelot in appreciation for his efforts in keeping us alive in your memory. That is how he came to be in our time period."

"But what about the Time Guardians?" I asked. "How was he able to avoid them when he traveled into the past? If you have traveled through time to get here, then you know all of time travel is controlled by them. We met the Guardians during the Grinning Cat Adventure and would not choose to cross paths with them again."

The knight hesitated a moment, glanced down at the floor, and then looked up, almost as if embarrassed, and replied, "Merlin predicted that you would ask that question. The portal in the Standing Stones is a shortcut that bypasses the Time Guardians.

He did not have to answer their riddles. But it only works when traveling to or from Camelot, so it does not create a great many problems.

"Alfred Lord Tennyson, having written twelve epic poems about King Arthur, was well suited to live in our time. When he arrived in Camelot, he sighed, and said that at last he was home. He prospered and was happy, which is why we are concerned for him. We do not believe he would have willingly left Camelot of his own accord. That is why I was sent to seek you out, Sir Wizard. You have the ability and far seeing vision to find him."

Before anyone could say anything else, the Unicorn added, "And I have the ability and the Alicorn that can cure you, Dr. Watson."

To which I quickly replied, "Yes! Please, before any one says another word!"

Chapter 2.

A Very Odd Journey, (And without question, the absolute best cure for a cold.)

The Unicorn gently lowered his spiral horn and touched my forehead, and in a glowing instant, my cold was gone. In truth, every ache, pain, soreness, and even fatigue had vanished. I had never in my life felt better than I did at that moment. It was as if a wave of healing, silver light passed over me, and when I emerged from it, I felt more alive than ever before. Every fiber of my being longed to bask in that feeling forever.

The Unicorn tossed his head back letting his flowing main flutter as if in a soft breeze. "Yes, I am aware I would make a most excellent doctor. I have heard that sentiment many times before. But just as you are a doctor, not a wizard's apprentice, I am a Unicorn and not a doctor. It is my nature." Turning to Sherlock the Unicorn added, "But I am sorry to say that, as powerful as my Alicorn may be, it cannot relieve what ails you Sir Wizard. There is but one cure, and should you accompany us, Merlin believes that your destiny is to meet the one whose music dances endlessly in your dreams and haunts your days."

"Either way, I thank you sincerely..." I started to say, but before I could continue, Sherlock interrupted. "Yes, yes, now that your cold is out of the way, let us return to the matter at hand. If Merlin can see into the future well enough to have located me, and knows what awaits me and what I am longing for, why can he not locate Alfred Lord Tennyson? Considering his powers that you have alluded to, it should be simple for him, unless some force is blocking his abilities, or Sir Tennyson has passed into a realm not visible to Merlin."

The knight's eyes grew wide in amazement, and he replied, "Your perception is astounding, Sir Wizard. That is exactly why Merlin cannot find him. Normally Merlin can sense the presence of Lord Tennyson, but something is blocking his vision."

Sherlock pondered a moment and answered, "Yes, that would also be a possibility. You are correct, Sir Percival. It appears that we do need to visit your time period to determine what happened to Alfred Lord Tennyson. However, if we are going to accompany you into the past, we will require suitable attire. I believe we would be rather conspicuous wearing 1890's clothing."

"Thank you, Sir Wizard. I have brought robes for you both in my traveling pack. You can wear them over your current clothes if you desire. But I must ask you, is your attire actually comfortable? It appears you are being strangled by those silken cords around your necks."

Not waiting for a reply, the knight reached into a leather rucksack and produced two brown woolen robes with rope cords to secure them. Sherlock and I donned them, but not before Holmes performed a quick navigation of the room picking up various items from the shelves and tables and then depositing them into his coat pockets. Standing in front of me, with a contemplative look on his face he addressed me: "My dear Watson, you look like a character out of "*The Legend of Robin Hood*." My instincts tell me that your service revolver could prove very useful in this adventure, but we cannot risk bringing a modern weapon into the past without the danger of altering history. That is the one thing we *must* avoid, so we will have to make do with these."

He handed me a sturdy walking stick that looked old fashioned enough, and for himself, held up an antique sword he had produced from some hidden corner of the room. After adjusting his robe, setting the sword belt securely on his hip, and gazing sadly in the direction of his pipe, he commented, "We must also leave this behind, Watson. It is another contrivance of our time that would be out of place in Camelot."

The Unicorn replied, "In my perusal of the area surrounding your domicile, I saw several men partaking of those odd devices, and they were spouting more smoke than those iron horses that eat the black rocks. It cannot imagine that it is at all healthy. Why would they do that?"

Ignoring the Unicorn's question, Sir Percival proceeded to explain the plan. "Unicorn will first take me to the portal and then return for the two of you. Merlin mentioned that you are both experienced in the wonder of travel via Unicorn…"

I must admit, upon hearing that, I was nearly sick at the thought of another high-speed Unicorn journey dodging trees at blinding velocities, but I did not interrupt Sir Percival.

"…and how it is near instantaneous. However, I do have to ask if either of you are prone to sea sickness or nausea. It has been mentioned that riding a Unicorn at high speed is comparable to being at sea in a great storm, in small boat, with the wind blowing from all directions all at once."

At that point, the Unicorn did interrupt the knight with a proud look. "I assure you I am not at all comparable to a small boat. I am merely the fastest creature on four legs and much faster than most any winged creature."

Ignoring the Unicorn Sir Percival carried on, "And then I will lead all of us through the portal. As I mentioned, it is invisible to those who do not know of its existence. Shall we be off to Camelot?"

At that point, the Unicorn then Sir Percival blurred and vanished from the room. Realizing that it might be quite some time until my next cup of tea, I leaned forward towards my tea cup on the table, only to find the Unicorn suddenly materializing beneath me.

I abandoned all hope of any tea and desperately wrapped my arms around the Unicorn's neck and closed my eyes in fear. After a good deal of wind rushing by I chanced to open my eyes, to see one very close call with a large stone monolith. Soon I found myself standing in field next to Sir Percival. Sherlock was examining one of the standing stones with his magnifying glass and commenting, "This is extraordinary, Watson! For all practical purposes this megalith appears no different than any of the others, yet it is a doorway to the past. That is unfathomable, yet it must be so. Shall we be on our way? The game is most definitely afoot, as we will certainly not find any trains where we are headed."

The Unicorn snorted and replied, "If you mean those rock-eating, smoke-belching, metal behemoths, I say good riddance. I would rather face a real fire-breathing dragon any day."

My eyes grew wide as I looked at Sherlock and asked, "Did that Unicorn just say there are real *fire-breathing dragons* where we are going?" Sherlock gave me a push through the portal and answered, "I am sure it was just a metaphor, Watson, just a metaphor."

It was as if reality turned inside out. I felt like my body was being stretched until it snapped, and suddenly I was again standing next to the stone beneath a full moon. Holmes was commenting, "You know, Watson, with these most recent adventures, I have enough material to pen a monograph on *"A Study of Phase Transitional, Chronological, Temporal Transportation, and its Practical Applications"*. What do you say, old boy?"

I was too utterly terrified to answer, as I was looking directly at a bright red dragon less than two feet away from me!

I was, of course, quite relieved when I realized it was only a realistic painting of a dragon on a shield that happened to be in directly front of me. The knight, whose shield had given me such a fright, was talking to Sir Percival.

"You have returned, Sir Percival, and in truth, you have brought visitors. Pray tell, is this the Wizard and his apprentice that Merlin predicted would find Sir Tennyson?"

I recovered my composure and interjected, "That would be Consulting Detective and Doctor, if you do not mind. I am Doctor John Watson, and this is the famous and apparently timeless, Consulting Detective, Sherlock Holmes."

The Unicorn interrupted saying, "If you think their speech is strange, their attire is even stranger, and they have the strangest mechanical dragons in their time period."

The knight looked aghast, and he exclaimed, "Mechanical dragons? Forsooth, Sir Wizard, why would one create such a creature? Knowing real dragons as I do, I would imagine that it would be near impossible to control."

Sherlock looked at me and under his breath responded, "Considering how poorly trains adhere to the published schedules, he is not far off in his concerns."

He turned to the knight who been waiting for us and said, "It is a pleasure to meet you, sir knight. You need not worry about combating mechanical dragons. We did not bring any with us. I see by your attire that you have already recently encountered white tailed deer, brown bear, wolverine, and wild boar." Turning and addressing our guide, he continued without even taking a breath. "Now Sir Percival, shall we proceed directly to the lodgings of Alfred Lord Tennyson, or are we to meet first Merlin the Enchanter?"

Chapter 3.

A Very Odd Encounter, (And a clever rhyme as well.)

"By Faith!" cried the new knight. "Indeed, I have. Pray tell, how is it possible for you to have known all this when you have just arrived? Do you possess the far sight or is it the evil eye?"

He looked at Sherlock suspiciously, and he placed his hand on the hilt of his sword, slowly backing away from him until Sir Percival stepped in. "Fear not, Sir Bedivere. This wizard possesses skills in observation and deduction that are far beyond compare. He and his apprentice doctor friend have come hither to help us."

"But Sir Percival," stated the Unicorn, "Doctor Watson is no longer an apprentice as he is now here in this field and not residing in his comfortable domicile."

I thought about trying to explain the difference, but decided against it, as it would have been futile. In truth, I was astonished by the environment we found ourselves in. The standing stones which surrounded us seemed to be almost alive. They looked much younger and less worn than I remembered them to be, which made sense, as we had somehow traveled centuries into the past. The fragrance of the area had a natural, musky earthiness to it, much like an autumn forest after a rainfall. It was as if the entire surroundings were alive in a primordial way. Most noticeably, the stillness of the night was profound. The noisy clatter of London and all of its bustle and activity were gone. There were no sounds around us other than crickets and the occasional frog.

Sherlock broke the silence by explaining to the knight how he had known what he did. "Sir Knight, my skills are neither magic nor sorcery: they are acute observation, plain and simple. I was able to tell the last four creatures you encountered by looking at you and your surroundings. It is quite obvious that you have strands of white tail deer hair on your sleeve; there is a recent tear on the shoulder of your tunic that could only have been caused by a bear claw. The wolverine gives off a distinct odor which is still on your person, and there is a roast of wild boar cooking on your campfire over there. As I stated, it is all observation."

"Indeed, it must be, Sir Wizard," the knight said as he relaxed his sword hand. "You are as gifted in seeing as Merlin. And as of late, he has only been speaking in riddles and prophecies."

"But if I am correct," Sherlock replied, "he has predicted that I will locate Lord Tennyson and also meet the one whose music is haunting my dreams. Let us be on our way to see him. Which direction are we going?"

"Which direction indeed?" A deep voice suddenly echoed from out of nowhere and continued:

“Follow your feet,

and you shall meet,

the person you seek,

but do not be weak.

East is the least,

West is not best.

North will not lead forth,

and South is uncouth.

So, what do you

say upon this day?

Do you know

wherefore to go?”

Sherlock looked up into the night sky, and replied, “Merlin, you are here with us now. If we need not travel in any direction, then I deduce you are already here. Based on the direction of the echoes and the audible volume of your voice, I believe you are behind *that* stone.”

Sherlock spun on his heels and pointed directly at one of the medium sized standing monoliths to the left of us. From behind it stepped an aged wizard with long grey hair and an even longer grey beard. He was wearing a deep blue robe tied with a gold cord, and he carried a gnarled wooden staff that appeared to be an old tree branch, which had the appearance of a dragon's head on the top of it. His most striking feature, however, were his eyes. They were the deepest, clearest, and brightest blue that I had ever seen. They looked as if they could see into eternity or into one's soul.

"Well done, Sir Wizard.

By my gizzard,

you have detected well.

Come sit for spell.

I will tell you why

beneath the night sky,

you are here;

because mystery is near."

"I do understand that," replied Sherlock. "This entire adventure is a mystery, but we are here, so tell us what has happened. Sir Percival has explained how Alfred Lord Tennyson was healed and came to be here in Camelot. Apparently, I am to discover where he has gone, and what has become of him. Tell me. What occurred over the last six years between his arrival and his disappearance? Did he have any enemies in Camelot? In what condition was his health? Was he inclined at all to wander far away? Who were his companions? How did he spend his time?"

From within his robe, Merlin produced a glass vial, held it up and swirled its contents, as he spoke. "Memories of time gone past, fleeting things that still do last witness here, the poet's life, you will see there was no strife.

Memories of time now flown

Captured as the years have grown

Look and listen, and you will see,

where the poet perchance may be."

As he finished speaking, with a wide sweep of his arm, he turned the vial upside down and poured the contents out of it. Much to my surprise, the liquid did not just spill to the ground; it formed a cloud, or a mist that hung in the air before us. Upon the cloud were images of Alfred Lord Tennyson living in Camelot. It was as if daguerreotypes of Tennyson were printed directly on the misty cloud. We saw him walking among the people of Camelot, having meals with them, telling them stories, writing poems, and more. Merlin was somehow showing us scenes from the life of Sir Tennyson since he had left our world. We had observed his peaceful and harmonious new life for quite some time when the image showed Sir Tennyson standing in front of a doorway with his hand on the door knob. The next image showed him looking back towards the direction from which he came, as if he knew he was being watched, and wanted the watcher to see him entering the room. The next image showed him turning back to the door and entering the room, followed by a picture of a completely empty room. As the mist faded and cleared, Merlin again spoke.

“He passed through that door’

and then was no more.

The room you can see

Is quite empty.

Wherefore did he go?

You must learn and know.

By the great dragon’s bones,

Tell us Sherlock Holmes.”

As Sherlock contemplated, I stared at the empty space where the images had somehow been displayed. How on earth had Merlin been able to do that, I wondered.

Sherlock finally responded, addressing Merlin, “How soon can I inspect that room? Has anyone been in there since he disappeared? How is it that you capture and display the images we just watched?”

Merlin smiled softly and answered.

“What you see,

comes from me

What I view,

I show you.

That very room,

Is like a tomb.

No one would dare

Go in there.

For you to see,

Follow me.

Let us now go,

And you shall know."

As he finished speaking, he turned and strode away from the circle of stones using his dragon staff as a walking stick. Sherlock and I followed, accompanied by the Unicorn and the two knights. I asked Merlin how long it would take us to get to our destination, and his response, while detailed, left me less informed than before he answered. In his simple rhyme he had responded,

"How long indeed?

What is your speed?

How fast you go

Tells what you want to know.

The distance traveled

Can be unraveled

Look to the sky.

Do not ask why.

When the sun eats the moon

We will be there soon.

When the time is right,

Thus, ends our flight."

Sir Percival chimed in, "Now you see what I mean about talking to Merlin. Pray tell, how does King Arthur make any sense out of Merlin's advice? I would have gone daft ages ago." Sir Bedivere then nudged him and interrupted, "Gadzooks! This is being stated by one who travels in the company of not just a Unicorn, but one with the gift of speech?"

Percival responded, "You may gad about my questing companion, but we have been to the future and seen their mechanical dragons. And we have brought hither the Wizard and his apprentice doctor. It is said that he can see the invisible!"

I was about to comment, when the Unicorn waved his Alicorn and said, "You are all aware that we could already be there if you allowed me to provide the transportation."

Merlin abruptly halted, turned to face the group, and stated,

"Verily indeed

we require speed.

The beast is right.

He will aid our flight."

Then turning directly to the Unicorn, he went on.

"If thou please,

the moment seize.

To make haste there,

we are in thy care."

And with that, first the Unicorn, then Merlin blurred and disappeared, followed by Sherlock and Sir Percival.

"And I shall keep watch over the horses and meet you there," sighed Sir Bedivere.

Meanwhile, I closed my eyes and braced myself for yet another high-speed Unicorn ride dodging trees, stone monoliths, and in this time period, who knew what else. The Unicorn materialized beneath me, and fearing the worst, I wrapped my arms around its neck and held on for dear life. There was a sudden, brief rush of wind, and then I heard the Unicorn's voice announcing, "If you please, you can stop strangling me now, Dr. Watson. We have safely arrived. Your Wizard friend is already examining the premises. Based upon your reaction to the incredibly unique and most honored experience of riding upon a Unicorn, one would perceive that you do not enjoy it. Pray tell why is that?"

"It is because, on several occasions, I *have* experienced breathtaking Unicorn rides at speeds beyond my imagination. I still wake up at night from nightmares of near collisions with trees that are trying to jump in front of us."

"Well, yes, that would explain it," the Unicorn answered. "There are those of our species that relish the experience of traveling faster than the wind, even if it does involve an occasional near miss with a tree or two or, in *very* seldom instances, having to pry one's horn from the trunk of a tree. We try not to mention those occasions when that does happen."

My eyes grew wide when I heard its last comment, but Sherlock was already voicing his observations on the last location of Alfred Lord Tennyson. "Yes, he was at the entrance to this room. Based on the images of him that you showed me, I can deduce his height, weight, shoe size, the length of his stride, and a slight limp, and there are matching footprints going up to the door. But if you look closely, you will see they do not enter the room. There is a clear indication here of when he stopped and turned to look back. It is as if he wanted to give the impression of going into this room and make sure that your observation of him showed him doing that, but I assure you, if you look closely, you will not see any footprints entering this room. It is as if it never happened. I penned a monograph on "*Determining Direction and Misdirection in Footprints Based on Readily Observable but Typically Invisible Attributes*." This is a classic example of misdirection in footprints."

"But how could he just disappear from here?" I asked. "Could a Unicorn have whisked him away? I have no familiarity with the workings of this time period."

I looked to Sir Percival and Merlin for answers, but Sherlock continued to examine the ground in front of the doorway using a magnifying glass he had taken out of one his pockets and answered. "As nebulous, transitory and quick as Unicorns have proven to be, they do leave evidence of their prior presence no matter how brief it is."

The Unicorn lifted his head with a puzzled expression, turned towards Sherlock, and remarked, "Is that true? I had no idea. Pray tell what evidence would you be referring to? Would it by any chance, be the radiant silver glow of my Alicorn that remains after

I have graced an area? Or, could it be the unmistakable aura of magic that follows me where ever I go?"

Sherlock pointed to the doorway with one hand and to where Merlin was standing with the other and explained: "It is much simpler. You see where you deposited Merlin, there are very slight traces of Unicorn hair, and the ground is slightly disturbed from your hooves. The same holds true for where Sir Percival is standing. But in the last location where Sir Tennyson was seen, there are no indications of a Unicorn's presence."

Sherlock entered the room to continue his examination. While he did, I looked through the doorway myself to see what might be in there. It was a simple accommodation with a bed and small table along one wall. There was a writing desk and chair near the adjacent wall, which also held several shelves full of scrolls. The third wall had a fireplace and what looked like a basic kitchen facility of that era. A slightly larger table with chairs around it filled the center of the room. Sherlock stood just inside the doorway, turning his head slowly, looking around the room and taking it all in, when he suddenly stopped and turned back to one of the shelves. He walked over to it and examined a glass vial very carefully with his magnifying glass. After a moment, he gestured for Merlin to come into the room and inspect it.

"Merlin, does this vial contain the same substance that you used to show us images of Sir Tennyson? The residue is the same color and thickness as the contents of the vial that you used."

The aged enchanter ambled over to where Sherlock was standing and replied:

"Far you see,

Farther than me

Yes indeed,

The answer is freed.

It was not him

That did not go in.

Only a shade,

of him was made."

"Astonishing!" I exclaimed. "But who would have the same skills as Merlin to be able to create such an illusion? And why would they do such a thing? It was obviously intentional to prevent anyone from seeing where Lord Tennyson actually went. But, who would do such a thing?"

Sherlock bent down to the floor in front of the shelf. He picked up something that was invisible to my eyes from where I was standing, studied it, and the ground in front of the shelf, stood up again and answered, "The last person to hold this vial before we arrived was female, tall, slight in stature, and had long copper colored hair. Can any of you tell me who that might be?"

With a look of concern and wonderment in their faces, Merlin, Sir Percival, and the Unicorn all answered in unison, "Morgan la Fey!"

Chapter 4.

A Very Odd Realization, (And the discovery that one plus one does not necessarily equal two.)

I thought for a moment and realized his conclusion was not at all logical. I asked Sherlock, “But how could it only be an image when you discovered his footprints going right up to the doorway. If he was not really there, then where did the footprints come from? And where did they go from here? How could there be both real footprints and an illusionary image? It does not make sense.”

Sherlock looked at me and nodded. “That is an excellent question, Watson. That is the point! You are getting more observant. That is exemplary, but you miss what is behind the obvious. Two different clues clearly tell us that he did not enter the room; the image vial and the footprints that stop at the doorway. They both say the same thing, but they contradict each other. Either one by itself would provide the required proof that he did not enter the room, but both of them together, irrefutably prove he really did enter this room.

“Whoever left the clues wanted to be certain that one would be found but did not count on both of them being discovered. Look at that ceiling beam. Its position provides the perfect anchor for one to use a rope to swing from the doorway to directly in front of this bookshelf without leaving any footprints. If you look closely at the beam, you will see there are rope fibers caught in the grain of the wood. Sir Tennyson's footprints appear again right here alongside the female's foot prints. And from this point, both sets actually do disappear completely. Now that I have explained what happened here, can any of you tell me who is Morgan la Fey, and why she invokes such concern?"

Before anyone could answer, Sir Percival exclaimed, "But pray tell, you did not explain what happened, Sir Wizard. You clearly illustrated how he could have moved from the doorway to the book shelf without leaving footprints and that Morgan la Fey was standing next to him here, but where did they go? In truth, how could they both have vanished?"

Sherlock paused and enjoyed another of his immensely favored theatrics, those moments when he, with great flair, unveils the hidden secret that only he knows. He casually asked, "Is it not obvious? This bookshelf is actually a doorway to a hidden chamber behind it. They passed through the secret entrance which is why their footprints seem to have vanished."

He then slowly ran his finger over the top edge of the shelf until he reached a particular spot, at which he stopped, exerted a slight effort which produced a clicking sound, and the shelf swung back into a dark recess that revealed a stairway leading down to who knew where?

Indicating caution, Sherlock held up his hand, and again reiterated, "However, before we descend into the dark, forbidding, unknown abyss before us, I would like to know more about the owner of this domain. What can you tell me about Morgan la Fey?"

The Unicorn, who was still standing outside the room, stamped his hoof and responded, "Well, that would depend upon whom you ask. Even though she is Arthur's half-sister, and at one time was a gifted student of Merlin, there are those who view her as a villain and an enemy of King Arthur and Camelot. Others see her as the heroic protector of the Faerie Realm. She is fighting to prevent magic from disappearing. Arthur, however, is a harbinger of change. In his poems of Camelot, Lord Tennyson often quoted King Arthur's very words, '*One age passes to make way for the next.*' He feels that change is inevitable. Morgan la Fey is using her powers to prevent the age of the Faerie Folk from vanishing into myth and legend, just as Arthur is striving to keep the vision of Camelot alive as history devours the present. It is indeed a paradox." Tilting his horn in my direction, the Unicorn looked at me and added, "Although what '*two* doctors' have to do with the problem at hand, is beyond my powers of comprehension."

"Fie!" exclaimed Sir Percival, "It matters not how many doctors are involved! Morgan la Fey is a powerful enchantress who has used her abilities to vex Arthur many times. In truth, she is an enemy of the kingdom!

"But how can that be?" I asked. "As the Unicorn stated, and according to the stories I have read, Morgan La Fey is Arthur's half-sister. But he has no magic. So how can she be a powerful enchantress? And why would she be against Arthur, and why would Arthur be against the Faerie Realm when he has Merlin himself, the most well-known wizard of literature, at his side, and one of his own Knights of the Round Table travels in the company of a Unicorn."

Merlin laughed and voiced,

“Why indeed?
The forces are freed.
You must see
beyond her and me.

She and I
are like the sky.
Dark in the night,
but in the day light.

Yet still the same
in nature and name.
Look and you’ll find,
we are ever entwined.”

Sherlock responded in frustration, “Mysteries and rhymes are all we are getting out here, Watson. I suggest we simply go and see where this passage leads. It cannot be any more unusual than what we have already experienced in this odd adventure. And I am certain the answers to Lord Tennyson’s disappearance, as well as where I might find Pixy Music, are through this door.” With great apprehension and recollections of similar predictive statements that proved considerably otherwise, I entered the room and prepared to follow Sherlock into the secret chamber and wherever it would lead to.

As he passed through the doorway, I heard him call back to me, "Cheer up, Watson old boy, this is no different than the monograph I wrote on, *'Determining the Correct Direction of Travel at an Ambiguous Crossroads by Eliminating the Obviously Incorrect Directions Through the Use of Rational Logic and Deduction'."*

Then Sherlock Holmes vanished before my eyes!

Chapter 5.

A Very Odd Set of Rules, (And an even odder resolution.)

What on earth had just happened? Sherlock was there and then suddenly he was gone. We all looked at each other in disbelief. Was this another portal? I was about to ask Merlin when much to my surprise, Sherlock reappeared in the doorway, saying, "Are you coming along, Watson? You really have to see this. It is quite remarkable."

And then he disappeared again. Relieved to see Sherlock, and trusting in his judgment, I made up my mind to follow him. Without hesitation, I entered the doorway and somehow found myself standing in a wooded glen. Sherlock was standing nearby examining the ground and commenting. "It is as I suspected, Watson, the two sets of footprints came through the doorway, out of the portal, and they head off in this direction. And if my senses do not deceive me, which they rarely do, I believe we are in the Faerie Realm. Let us be after them."

The hidden doorway had been a portal of some kind, and I gazed in amazement at where it had taken us. We were in a clearing within a small circle of moderately sized standing stones that was surrounded by a wide variety of trees and shrubs. The trees soared up to the sky, casting a soft shadow over the entire area, except for the sunlight that filtered through their branches in fluttering rays blinking in and out as a slight breeze played in the limbs. A rainbow kaleidoscope of flowers in every color and type grew in abundance, many of which I was certain I had never seen before. It was a botanical paradise. If this was the Faerie Realm, I could understand why Morgan was trying to keep it alive, but I did not see any of the danger that Sir Percival had warned us of. It appeared to be the most peaceful and entrancing place I had ever visited.

My thoughts were broken by the arrival of Merlin, followed by the Unicorn who announced as he appeared, "Sir Percival will wait on the other side of the portal. He stated that he will prevent any unwanted intruders from following us, but I believe he is hesitant to set foot into the Faerie Realm. It is said that few who enter ever return. In looking around I understand. Why would anyone want to leave? It is most inviting here."

In an impatient tone, Sherlock pointed upward through a slight break in the branches and voiced his opinion: "I could provide a dozen reasons without even mentioning the large dragon-like creature that is circling above. We are here to find Alfred Lord Tennyson, and I feel in my heart that Pixy Music is somehow connected to this place. I cannot explain it but I know she is here somewhere. For the first time in days I feel alive again. My only regret is that I did not bring my violin. How will I be able to speak to her?"

"I am sure you will find a way." I optimistically answered.

"Yes, I am certain I will. I know with all my heart that I must." and he pointed towards a pathway. "The footprints lead off in this direction."

Glancing up into the sky, I followed him and inquired, "Don't you mean the *metaphor* that is circling above?"

Merlin ambled towards the path, saying to no one in particular.

"Dragons fly,

while pathways lie.

Secrets to know,

so, let us now go!"

The Unicorn followed Merlin, gazing to the left and to the right, commenting on the beauty that surrounded us. Sherlock, at home in his element of following a trail of clues, no matter how impossible or improbable the environment, walked along the pathway stopping to examine trifles that would have been invisible to anyone else.

"The two of them passed by here only days ago with the female leading the way," he called back to us. From several feet down the trail, he called out again, "They stopped here to rest and were joined by a multitude of very diminutive beings. The creatures, while sporting human-shaped feet, were impossibly smaller than any I have ever encountered in the past. Their visitors apparently vanished without leaving any discernible footprints leading away that I can detect, another oddity in this adventure, and then the two of them continued on in this direction. A different breed of creature with larger and less human looking footprints followed them for a time but wandered off in that direction." Then with a shortness of breath and an excitement in his voice, he whispered to me, "And even more promising, Watson, is that I *hear* her. I can feel the echoes of Pixy Music more clearly than ever before. Every one of my senses tells me she is somewhere in this land. Her music is imbued in the earth, floating in the air, ringing in the trees, and surrounding me like a golden glowing cloud. I know I will find her. It is only a matter of time…"

With a nod, the Unicorn commented, "Your sorcerer friend sees very well. Most humans would never notice the Faerie Folk if they were right in front of them, much less seeing evidence of their previous presence."

My mind reeled as I tried to grasp the implications of what the Unicorn was saying. Based on Sherlock's observations, this place was populated by beings known only in fairy tales and myth. Who knew *what* we would encounter next?

The answer came in a deep booming voice that emanated from somewhere up ahead on the path, "None shall pass!"

A heavily armored dwarf sporting a beard reaching all the way down to the ground was sitting upon a large rock alongside the pathway. His armor looked well-seasoned, and in addition to the large axe he held up to bar the way, he must have had at least a half a dozen additional weapons hanging from belts and chest straps. I would not say that he was unsightly, but I will say he strongly resembled a large furry dog that had been stuffed into a miniature suit of armor. He repeated more adamantly, "None shall pass!"

Sherlock, not in the least bit concerned, walked right up to the imposing figure and addressed him. "Those are the rules, Sir Dwarf, none shall pass?

The dwarf shook his axe threateningly and responded in an even louder voice, "NONE SHALL PASS!"

Sherlock simply replied, “Then do your duty and let us pass, my good dwarf. My companions and I are all called ‘*None*’.”

The dwarf laughed heartily and responded, “A most clever ruse, you trickster. If you are all called ‘None’, then what be your surnames?”

Without hesitating, Sherlock answered boldly, pointing at Merlin, “This is the Wizard, None Too Tricky.” Then pointing in my direction, he continued, “Here is my associate, None of Your Concern; the Unicorn, None Too Modest; and allow me to introduce myself. I am None of Your Business.”

I nearly choked when I heard his response, but the dwarf was apparently pleased, and with one hand, he casually swung his axe and buried the blade in a nearby log saying, “I give way to ‘None’. You may all pass! Give my regards to the Lady in Green.”

"I shall give her your regards and let her know that you are doing an admirable job. Most passable indeed!”

The dwarf retrieved his ax from the log and called out, “There are none that sneak past me!”

I caught up to Sherlock and whispered, “That was very clever, Holmes. How did you come up with that idea so quickly?” He answered with a grin. “It was ‘none too challenging,’ Watson, quite elementary, actually. It is only a matter of observing and assessing the situation and taking the most logical approach.”

“Logical?” I replied incredulously, “There is nothing at all logical about this adventure. The next thing you know a knight in shining white armor will be blocking the road and challenging all who want to pass, to a duel.”

Sherlock nonchalantly dismissed my comment. “Don’t be foolish, Watson, you should know that all knights blocking paths and demanding a duel are attired in black armor.”

Of course, as soon as we rounded a bend in the road, there was a tall knight in pitch black armor, blocking the road and demanding a duel.

Chapter 6.

A Very Odd Duel, (With just a bit of trickery on Sherlock's part.)

"I challenge ye to a duel!" the knight declared as he threw a gauntlet to the ground, "Declare your choice of dueling implements!" At that moment, the tall fearsome figure pointed to a weapons rack containing numerous different swords, axes, maces, flails, spears, halberds, and other even nastier looking implements of death and dismemberment. The situation looked most assuredly bleak. While Sherlock was skilled in fencing with foil and saber, the weapons the knight offered were of a completely different nature.

Holmes, however, walked past the weapons rack and pointed at the small repast of mead and biscuits that the knight had sitting on a large flat stone and replied, "I choose mead and biscuit dueling."

"What?" the knight incredulously responded. "That is my noon meal, not a dueling weapon. What trickery are you trying to accomplish here?"

Sherlock held his ground and pointed at the meal replying, "I am following your directions and choosing my dueling implement as you demanded. You pointed in this direction and said 'choose'. I choose mead and biscuit dueling. Of course, where we come from, it is typically *tea* and biscuit dueling, but the most civilized beverage ever to grace this country has not yet arrived in England, so mead will have to suffice. Do you accept my choice of dueling implement, or do you forfeit the duel?"

The Black Knight stood silent like a great statue in obvious disbelief before he replied, "I have never before engaged in a duel with mead and biscuits. I typically just eat my biscuits and then drown them in ale. They don't fight back. You will have to explain the rules of this odd duel."

He then removed his helmet, set it on a log, and with great powerful steps, strode over to where Sherlock was standing. "I am Sir Bruin, the Black Knight. Any party who wishes to pass must engage me in a duel, but I do not comprehend how biscuits and mead may be used as dueling implements."

I gazed at the knight as he stood awaiting a reply. He was massive in stature and looked as if he could snap a tree branch in two without even trying. His hair was black and straggly, and his eyes were deep and dark. There was a base primal air about him. I wondered if the array of weapons were his trophies from previous contests.

Sherlock, undaunted by the imposing presence of the knight, sat down on a log near the mead and biscuits and pointed to an empty space across from him. "Move a rock here and sit down. It is cool under the trees here. I will explain the rules. Dr. Watson, you will officiate"

The knight picked up a large stone, and with a loud thud that shook the ground, placed it opposite Sherlock. In truth, he looked as if he could have crushed the rock into pieces if he had wanted to. Sherlock pointed at the mead and biscuits. "It is quite simple really; we will each have a cup of mead in front of us. Dr. Watson if you please."

I found an extra flagon and set it in front of Sherlock, as the knight had already had one for himself. I set the plate of biscuits in between them. I filled each of their vessels to the brim and set the mead down to see what Sherlock had in mind, as I myself, had never heard of tea dueling or, in this instance, mead dueling.

"It is quite straight forward, actually," Sherlock explained. "We each take a biscuit and dunk it into the mead while Dr. Watson counts to ten out loud. At the count of ten, we each remove our biscuit and hold it as long as possible before eating it. If it falls apart prior to being eaten, then the opposing contestant is awarded a point. The first one to attain five points wins. As I stated, it is most simple. You try to postpone eating your biscuit as long as you can without it falling apart. Do you have any questions?"

The knight looked at Sherlock with a disappointed expression and exclaimed! "That's it? Just ale and soggy biscuits? No swords, daggers, axes, flails, or maces? Not even spear throwing? What kind of duel is this? Upon my honor as a knight, I demand something more challenging!"

Sherlock stood up and removed a dagger from his belt and held it up. "All right, something more challenging it is. Take a biscuit and throw it up into the air."

The knight looked confused and asked, "What kind of challenge is that?"

Sherlock made an exaggerated gesture pointing upwards towards the trees with one hand, while he held his dagger at his side with the other and replied, "Just throw a biscuit up there; that is if you are able."

Upon hearing his ability questioned, the knight harrumphed and grabbed a biscuit from the plate and heaved it upward. With an incredible swiftness, Sherlock hurled his dagger upward also, and in an instant, his dagger fell back to the earth with the biscuit impaled on its blade.

Sherlock pointed at the skewered biscuit, picked up a new one, prepared to throw it into the air, and stated, "Now it is your turn. Is that challenging enough for you, Sir Bruin?"

The Black Knight's eyes grew wide with amazement, and he exclaimed, "Forsooth! I have never before seen such speed and skill with a dagger. I yield to you, sir. You and your companions may pass."

Sherlock picked up his dagger, removed the biscuit, and casually tossed it up into the tree saying, "Well then, we will be on our way. Enjoy your biscuits and mead. The highest I have been able to count before eating a dunked biscuit is up to sixty. Do give it a try and see if you can match that. We may pass this way on our return trip."

And with that, we made our way past the knight who was busy dunking his biscuit into his mug of ale and counting out loud while glancing up into the tree wondering why nothing had fallen back to the ground.

If it is possible for an equestrian creature to snicker, then I would say the Unicorn was most assuredly doing so as we continued on the path. When we were far enough along the path not to be heard, it addressed Sherlock, "You are not only a master of observation and deduction, Sir Wizard; you are also marvelously adept at sleight of hand. I saw what you did there. You distracted the black knight by pointing up into the trees, while you impaled a biscuit on your dagger *before* you threw it. That was most clever of you. But how did you know the biscuit he threw would not come back down along with your dagger?"

Sherlock smiled and replied, "Ah ha! Now that was the truly clever part. I positioned us beneath the trees, because I knew the creatures hiding up there would grab the biscuit he threw into the branches but would certainly avoid one with a dagger impaled on it.

The Unicorn nodded, "Oh yes the Brownies that were hidden in the leaves watching. I am surprised you noticed them. They are all but invisible to humans."

"I see everything. Of course, I noticed them. And according to folklore, they do like biscuits. I convinced the knight to toss his to them, and they did not bother mine while it was impaled. That is why I tossed the biscuit back up into the tree after I removed it from the dagger. The brownies were quite cooperative, and it all worked out very well."

Merlin then chimed in.

"Very well,

time will tell.

You won the day

with your play

of sleight of hand

and a band

of creatures rare

in the air."

"That was brilliant, Sherlock." I stated. "The magicians at the hippodrome can't hold a card to you, but telling him that you have held a dunked biscuit for sixty seconds? Don't you think that was going too far?"

Sherlock looked at me with a wry grin and replied, "All right, so I neglected to mention that it was a week-old stale biscuit. It will keep him busy trying."

Chapter 7.

A Very Odd Creature, (And without question, the most outstanding music I have ever heard.)

While Sherlock was following the footprints, I wondered what would be in store for him if he did actually encounter the source of the enthralling music that that filled his thoughts and desires. He had certainly not been himself over the last several days. He would play his violin for hours listening intently to her echoing reply, and then gaze silently out the window. I knew where his thoughts were. They were off somewhere in a far distant realm, longing to be close to her. But now in this strange and enchanting land, she was closer, but still no nearer than before. The anticipation must have been unbearable for him. Who knew what we would encounter next?

We had been traveling for some time down the path under the shade of the trees when Sherlock came to a sudden halt. The forest had thinned out, and we were about to pass into an open area.

"Why have we stopped?" I asked. "Is it another Black Knight or a dwarf blocking the path? I don't see anything."

"That is because you are not looking in the correct direction," he offhandedly replied pointing upwards. "You may want to look up there, although that is not to say things are looking up."

I could not believe my eyes! Through the clearing that had opened in the trees, I spotted a large, scaly green, winged creature circling above. It had sharp pointed claws on both its front and hind legs, large leathery wings, and a long lizard like tale. The face had a look of ancient wisdom and cunning cleverness and was almost handsome if you ignored the teeth and horns. The eyes were a deep gold and seemed to burn with an intense fire. There was no question about it. I was looking at a genuine, real dragon!

"What was that you were saying about metaphors?" I turned and asked Sherlock. "Now what do we do?"

The Unicorn however, seemed not to be afraid and boldly walked into the clearing, raising his head and calling out, "Greetings, Malachite the Musical!"

The dragon turned its head towards us and swooped down to land in the path very lightly considering its size. In the sky, it had been impressive, but upon the ground standing before us, it was positively fearsome!

In a booming voice that sounded somewhat like a harpsichord, which as you know has often been described as a keyboard instrument that creates musical notes with a mechanical twang on the end of them, the great beast bowed his head and replied, "Unicorn! It is pleasant to see you again. And you bring visitors as well. This must be the time of year for guests. Morgan La Fey passed through here only days ago. It was fortunate she had a poet with an excellent singing voice along with her. You do remember the rules for passage through my domain in the Faerie Realm."

As I heard that, I whispered to Sherlock, "Not another challenge to travel down this path! And I thought the toll roads in our time were outrageous. This beats them all hands down."

The dragon slowly turned its head towards me and, with a smile that was more frightening than friendly, laughed, "Apparently your traveling companion is not aware of how sensitive a dragon's hearing truly is."

The Unicorn quickly responded, "Indeed, Malachite, they have just arrived in our land. They are not familiar with the customs and have never met a real dragon before, not to mention, one as musically gifted as you."

The dragon responded by playfully blowing a puff of flame into the sky and singing up and back down again the notes of the musical scale. "Well, in that case, I can excuse them, but that still does not change the rules."

Sherlock stepped forward and with a flourishing bow addressed the beast. "We thank you for your consideration, green and great maestro. If you would explain these rules you allude to, we would appreciate it. I deduce by what has already been stated they pertain to, us providing some type of musical challenge or an amusement. I myself have some small musical skill and may surprise you."

The dragon's smile was, I imagine, clearly meant to be friendly and, I am sure meant to display some degree of happiness, but it was like looking into the teeth of a half a dozen buzz saws.

"Outstanding!" He declared. "It is verily quite simple. For your group to pass by, one of you must provide some type of musical performance that is new, novel and unfamiliar to me. The poet accompanying Morgan La Fey sang an impressive epic song about a charge of a cavalry light brigade. It was stirring but sad. I am only 100 years old, so I am certain that there are still a few songs or types of musical entertainment that I have not yet heard. Since you have not brought any instruments with you, you may enter my cave over yonder and choose one that is suitable. I do have an outstanding selection. Yes, I know, most dragons tend to hoard gold and jewels, but to me, music is so much more valuable than gold or any of those precious rings you hear about. Truthfully, as gold must be first smelted and poured and then polished to attain its brilliance, it does not hold a natural beauty to me. Music on the other hand…"

Malachite did not finish his sentence but instead seemed to be lost in profound contemplation on the wonder and beauty of music. Indeed, he seemed to be conducting an imaginary orchestra with one of his fore claws. This was assuredly not what I had expected in a dragon; however as certain as I was regarding Sherlock's musical skill, we were somewhere in the sixth century, and the violin had not yet been invented! How was he going to resolve this challenge?

Merlin and the Unicorn waited with Malachite while I accompanied Sherlock into the dragon's cave. I expressed my concern regarding what he would use since there were no violins in this time period. The instrument, as we know it, would not appear for another thousand years.

"Fear not, Watson," he replied. "While the violin of our era may not be present, I am certain that we will find a bowed stringed instrument that is close enough to suffice. You may not be aware, but I recently penned a monograph on "*The Evolution of Stringed, Bowed Musical Instruments, and Their Effect on Civilization, With a Focus on Their Involvement in Criminal Activities.*" In gazing around, I am confident that I will find what I am looking for."

The dragon's cave was astonishing! Musical instruments of every kind filled the cavern. There were many types of lyres, harps, lutes, horns, trumpets, bagpipes flutes, tanburs, and more.

Many types of instruments I had never even seen before were present and some simply defied description. The collection that surrounded us would easily put any museum in London to shame.

Sherlock stood perfectly still gazing about the space and taking it all in. His eyes darted from left to right as he analyzed the available choices and considered his options. Music had evolved considerably since the sixth century; would he be able to find something that worked? The dragon had not been clear, or for that matter, even mentioned the consequences of not producing an acceptable musical performance. Recalling his toothy smile and claws, I chose not to consider that possibility.

Sherlock, however, seemed quite pleased with himself. He had found a bow and an unusual odd-shaped stringed instrument that seemed to somewhat resemble a violin, even if the body shape was totally wrong. "Ah, yes," he said aloud. "This will do just fine." And he exited the cave.

The dragon turned his head at an angle as he considered what Sherlock had retrieved from the cavern. "What have we here? You selected a bow from an ancient Greek lyre and a smaller early four-stringed fretless lute known as the barbat. That is an interesting combination. I am intrigued. This may be quite fascinating."

Sherlock proceeded to tune the instrument he had selected, and the dragon twisted his neck to observe the process even closer.

"Hmm… G, D, A, and E. That is an interesting tuning. I have never heard that particular combination before. Where did you come across it?"

Sherlock stared longingly into the distance and wistfully replied. "It comes from a musical instrument that does not yet exist in this time, the violin. But the melody that I am going to play is timeless and will remain close to my heart always. It is, both simple and profound; deep, yet unfathomable. It is beyond words or description, yet it speaks volumes. It is enchanting me endlessly."

Malachite nodded his head in acceptance and sighed, "Ah, a love song. Those are always pleasing. You may begin when you are ready."

While the diminutive lute was not at all shaped like a violin, it was small enough for him to tuck under his chin. I must say, it was certainly an odd-looking contrivance. But the sound that came out of it when Sherlock drew the bow across the strings was once again magnificent. I instantly recognized the haunting and mystical melody of Pixy Music that I had first heard on our way back from Wonderland and again aboard the Nautilus when Sherlock had played Captain Nemo's Stradivarius. Through the beguiling tune, he had somehow connected to the ethereal creature, Pixy Music. It had been echoing endlessly in his mind since he had heard it, and now he was embracing it. The melody he played was moving, like a playful breeze that dances in the trees, drawing you ever onward. It teased and whispered softly, then called loudly. It was bold and shy, bright and gentle. It was captivating beyond description.

Once more it sounded as if a duet was being performed, with Holmes playing the melody and Pixy Music playing the harmony. Impossible as it was, we heard two distinct and separate musical lines dancing playfully together even though there was no one but Holmes playing. She was reaching out and touching Sherlock with her song, and he was responding with all his being. The melody was truly alive with warmth and passion and energy.

Merlin and the Unicorn closed their eyes to let their senses flow with the ethereal, enchanting music to wherever it would take them. Their heads were swaying and nodding gently to the enrapturing song. The dragon, however, stood as still as a statue, his eyes opened wider than it seemed possible, glowing as brightly as if they were on fire. His entire being seemed to be consumed in the song. I noticed a slight fluttering in his claws as if he too, was accompanying them in the mesmerizing tune. Entrancing and hypnotizing, the music continued until it softly came to a halt echoing briefly. And then all was still.

It was not until that moment that I noticed a tear in the dragon's eye. Malachite twisted his neck downward so that he was level with Sherlock's eyes. He stared intently at him for just a moment, bowed his great head, and finally spoke. "That was more than a mere love song. It was pure rhapsody, a love duet that transcends time, distance, and worlds. You have gently touched the mystical Pixy Music, and she has in turn, sweetly caressed you. I will remember this day forever. You may go forward. Your destiny is waiting."

Chapter 8.

A Very Odd Development, (And a clarification on swords, which of course, Sherlock had already written a paper on.)

Sherlock was about to set down the odd instrument and bow when the dragon added, "I am honored to have heard and experienced such ecstasy. Please, keep the lute and bow with my sincerest thanks. They are my gift to you. No one could ever bring them to life in the way you have, and I foresee you will need them again before your journey in the Faerie Realm is concluded."

Holmes bowed his head in acknowledgement and replied, "Thank you, Malachite. It has been an honor, but we must be on our way."

As we started towards the path again, I glanced in the direction we were heading, and I would have sworn that there were a multitude of fantastic mythical creatures gathered there in rapt attention. I blinked and looked again, and they were gone. I turned to the Unicorn, who was walking next to me, and asked, "Did you see that? What were those creatures?"

The Unicorn slowly nodded and replied, "Yes, I did, and I am not surprised. Your friend has clearly announced his presence in the Faerie Realm. His duet with Pixy Music was heard by not just Malachite and ourselves. Music resonates in ways humans have not yet begun to understand. I am sure that now all of the Faerie Realm is aware of Sherlock Holmes' connection to Pixy Music.

"But what does that mean?" I asked. "How will that affect our effort to find Alfred Lord Tennyson? Does that help or hinder us?"

Merlin, who had been silent up until this time, chimed in.

"What indeed?

Meaning is freed.

Their songs proclaim

with great fame.

Sherlock is here,

Pixy Music is near.

Go forth now

and somehow,

time will tell

all is well.

You will see

what will be."

I turned to Sherlock and asked, "And *what* exactly is that supposed to mean? If Merlin is Arthur's counselor, it is no wonder he was unaware of what is happening here."

Sherlock responded with a sigh, "Do you not see it, Watson? It is obvious. As illogical and improbable as all of this seems, you must examine it for what it is and deduce the implications. Like Wonderland from our Grinning Cat adventure, this is a realm beyond our normal rules of science. When I play the melody that I first heard in Wonderland, and Pixy Music accompanies me, we are communicating. Her music resonates beyond normal physical limits. The other faerie creatures of this time can also hear it. I imagine Morgan le Fay is also well aware of our presence by now. Yet somehow Merlin sees that in the end, it will work out well."

"And so, it shall," a soft female voice replied from somewhere nearby. We turned to look, and there we saw a white-haired maiden in a shear light-blue satin gown bound lightly by a silver chain. A circlet of fine silver held back her long hair. If it is possible, her eyes were even deeper and bluer than Merlin's. She was not overly tall, and while she did not appear to be old, there was a gentle look of wisdom in her gaze and smile. A necklace of sea shells adorned her graceful neck. I thought to myself, could this be the legendary Lady of the Lake?

Merlin's eyes brightened when he saw her. With his arms outstretched he quickly strode over to where she had appeared, and exclaimed,

"Nimue, my child,

come to me!

Here in the wild

How can it be?

Did you forsake

your watery home,

and leave the lake

all alone?"

They embraced warmly, and she replied, "You have taught me well, dear Merlin. My form can briefly be here, while my spirit is still in the lake, but I must not tarry. I do long to see you again." Looking in the direction of Sherlock, she added, "Your Wizard friend exquisitely announced his presence and his connection to the aerial musical Pixy, so I knew you were near. Bring your traveling companions with you. I have news of the poet he is seeking. When you reach the lake, we shall once again enjoy a moment together. Until then, my dearest Merlin…"

The maiden held out one hand as if to say farewell and then faded away into a nebulous mist. "That was astonishing!" was all I could say. Merlin meanwhile stared into the mist and replied,

"Goodbye my dear.

Return to thy lake.

Do not fear,

I will not forsake

the love we share,

timeless and true,

endless and rare

ancient and new."

The Unicorn, with a nod of his horn in the direction of the road asked, "Did you hear that? The Lady of the Lake has information on the whereabouts of the poet. That is promising. Shall we be on our way?"

We all continued down the path, and I asked, "So where exactly is the body of water that is her home? I have heard of her in the stories of Camelot. I believe she is the one that gave Arthur his legendary sword, Excalibur. But I thought he withdrew it from a stone."

Sherlock cleared his throat and whispered to me, "Watson, if you had read my little monograph, "*A Brief Synopsis of All Formally Named, Historically Important Swords and Their Influence on History,*" you would know the answer to that question."

Since I had not read his paper, the Unicorn filled me in on the details, and with the air of a lecturer, he held his head high, and responded, "Well, first, 'the lake' is known as Dozmary Pool. It is down the road a short distance. The sword that Arthur removed from the stone to claim his kingship has often been confused with Excalibur, but they are two separate and unique weapons. The first sword was placed in the stone ages ago with the prophecy *'Whoso Pulleth Out This Sword of this Stone and Anvil is Rightwise King Born of all England.'* Arthur achieved the throne by doing so and then uniting the warring minor kings.

"He received Excalibur, also called Calibourne, from the Lady of the Lake early during his rule. While the sword is mighty, even the scabbard has great power. It can heal wounds and prevent blood loss. It is almost as powerful as I am. I sometimes wonder if an Alicorn was used to make the scabbard, but I know the Lady of the Lake would never do such a thing."

I nodded and inquired, "If I may ask. What is the relationship between Merlin and Nimue? They seem quite close."

The Unicorn turned his head towards Merlin who was spiritedly walking along the path with a pleasant smile on his face then looked back to me. "Yes, they are more than close. They are soul mates. She is one of the Queens of Avalon and the Guardian of the Lake. She watches over the watery realm, similar to the way that Morgan La Fay watches over the Faerie Realm but without Morgan's animosity. Merlin has been teaching her all of his enchantments and has grown quite fond of her. I have heard him say that he will be hers forever. He is completely enamored.

"Morgan la Fey is terribly jealous of them and was furious when she found out. For many years, Morgan had also been a student of Merlin, excelling in all of the arcane talents, nearly equaling him. She had, at one time, fancied herself as being close to him, but it was not to be. In her anger, she cast an enchantment on Merlin that prevented him from speaking, so he could not communicate with Nimue. But Merlin found a way around the spell by speaking in rhyme. The heart of a poet is one of true love and always finds a way."

I smiled and replied, "It sounds very romantic, but what do think she meant by she has news of the poet we are seeking? Do think she had anything to do with his disappearance?"

The Unicorn shook his head negatively and responded, "No, of course not. That is less likely than the scabbard of Excalibur being made of Alicorn. While Arthur is working to move England forward, he does respect the land and waterways. The Lady of the Lake gave him Excalibur to aid in his task. She knows the poet is important to Arthur and Camelot. She would never harm Lord Tennyson."

Merlin, meanwhile with an energy and nimbleness that defied his age, made his way towards the lake home of Nimue all the while reciting a love poem.

"Nimue, my dear…

Every road it leads to you no matter where it goes

This is certain. This is true. My deepest heart it knows.

To the mountains frosty air to walk in snowy fields

amidst the ancient beauty where my heart to you it yields.

To the timeless ocean blue and the salt sea air.

My heart it longs to be with you, and my love you're there.

Within the emerald forest tall, the silence and the peace,

I hear but one true endless call. My love will never cease.

Though I travel far and wide to places nigh and near,

I long to feel you by side to hold you close my dear.

Like a beacon burning bright a loadstone sure and true,

your love it is an endless light, leading me to you.

You're ever in my fondest dreams. You're all my heart's desire.

Every path and way it seems it longs to lead me higher.

Higher, deeper, farther too, I know that it is so.

Every road it leads to you. This my love I know."

As he finished reciting the poem, a body of water loomed in the distance not far ahead. Merlin stopped abruptly and starred as if he sensed something was wrong. I was about to ask him, when he suddenly pointed and exclaimed,

"Unicorn, to the lake!

For Nimue's sake.

We must make haste!

No time to waste!"

First the Unicorn, and then Merlin, blurred and disappeared, reappearing near the shore in the distance. Sherlock then vanished and reappeared standing next to him. I closed my eyes and prepared myself for another terrifying ride at speeds beyond comprehension being thankful there were no trees or stone monoliths along the way. I felt the Unicorn materialize beneath me and wrapped my arms around its neck. The next thing I knew I was standing in a foot of water near the shore while Merlin and Sherlock were standing on dry land only a short distance away from me.

I looked first at the Unicorn and then down into the water, and with a toss of his head, he stated, "You do realize, that near instantaneous travel is not an exact science. At least there were no trees or stone monoliths here to get in the way."

Sherlock meanwhile was already closely examining the area and flatly stated. “It is as I suspected. Morgan La Fey and Alfred Lord Tennyson were here earlier. Their footprints are clearly visible.”

Merlin with a look of great sadness, turned and responded,

“It is worse than that.

Where she is at

I cannot say.

Morgan’s taken Nimue.

Chapter 9.

Another Very Odd Realization, (And an even odder explanation from Sherlock.)

Sherlock, while still looking down at the ground, declared, “Morgan was here with Sir Tennyson two days earlier. They continued off in that direction,” and he pointed to the north, “but then she returned by herself only moments ago. There was a struggle near the shore, and then she vanished from the area somehow taking a portion of the lake and shoreline with her. My deduction is that some type of sphere of containment was cast around Nimue also capturing a segment of the shore and the lake. Morgan apparently transported the sphere to another location. However, we are in luck. Prior to being taken captive by Morgan la Fay, Nimue was able to leave us a message.”

Taking several steps away from the shoreline, Sherlock pointed at a random grouping of shells and rocks and commented, “If you look closely, you will notice that the sea shells over here are arranged in very specific way. The shells that are right side up spell out a message. ‘Look under Round Table.’ It is obvious that

Nimue discovered some bit of information, and she was able to communicate that to us in time."

I looked at him and asked, "So now what do we do, continue on the trail of Morgan and Lord Tennyson or follow this new lead regarding Nimue? I imagine that the Round Table she is referring to is back in Camelot."

"Indeed, it is," interjected the Unicorn. "It is located in Arthur's grand hall. I cannot imagine how there could be a clue, or a message hidden beneath it. The Round Table has been a central part of Arthur's rule since he assumed the kingship. It conveys the message that all the knights who sit there are viewed equally. All discussions regarding what goes on in Camelot occur there.

"But if I understand correctly, Morgan La Fey was not included in those discussions, and that is why she is resisting Arthur and why she has taken Tennyson," Sherlock replied.

The Unicorn replied, "Truthfully, we do not even know if she has '*taken*' him. He may have gone with her willingly. She can be very persuasive."

"But I believe that is unlikely," answered Sherlock. "From what I have learned so far, Alfred Lord Tennyson was devoted to Arthur and Camelot."

Merlin, who had remained silent since discovering Nimue was gone suddenly spoke,

"Enough of this talk.

Let us now walk.

If four becomes two

we will find what is true.

Two paths remain.

We have much to gain.

It must be so.

Let us now go."

Sherlock looked up and replied, "He is correct. We could make more progress if we split up. Merlin and the Unicorn could go the court of Camelot and search underneath the round table while Dr. Watson and I continue along the trail. With the speed of the Unicorn, they could be there and back in almost no time."

The Unicorn held up his head proudly and answered before Merlin could reply, "At last there is someone who truly appreciates the speed of a Unicorn. I will have Merlin there and back most expediently!"

First the Unicorn and then Merlin blurred and vanished, leaving Sherlock and I utterly alone in a very odd land. With them gone, it was as if our safe connection to the place had disappeared, and the strangeness seemed to intensify a hundredfold. It felt like dozens of hidden eyes were watching us from the mists. It was as if we were surrounded by unseen beings that whispered and pointed at us. I was certain I could hear strange voices chattering somewhere nearby. I was frozen in my tracks and was about to say something when Sherlock tapped me lightly on the shoulder saying, "Well Watson, let us be on our way or they will be back before we have even moved. We do need to make some sort of progress while they are gone, if we are to live up to my reputation here."

Hearing Sherlock undaunted by the situation brought me back to my senses and broke the spell that had seemed to have come over me. I looked around and nothing was out of the ordinary. The placid waters of the lake looked like any other body of water and the surrounding area once again appeared quite normal. I passed it off as only a side effect of my imagination getting the best of me and began walking behind Sherlock as he strode off along the pathway that followed the misty shoreline.

"Their footprints are as easy to follow as if they were leaving sign posts!" I heard him call out as he hurried down the road, stopping here and there to examine some near invisible trifle that caught his eye. I quickened my pace to catch up to him, and was nearly there when he turned to me and asked, "So Watson, did you happen to notice the odd little creatures that were watching us whispering and pointing when the Unicorn and Merlin left? I think they may have been some of the same beings that had gathered to listen to the musical interlude that I played for the dragon."

I stopped in my tracks and stared at him. "What did you say? Are you saying that there really were a multitude of mythical beings there, that it wasn't just my imagination?"

He glanced at me with an incredulous look and replied, "You would need a good deal of imagination to conjure up some of the inhabitants of this place, Watson. Faeries, Pixies, Brownies, Gnomes, Goblins, Silkies, and those are just the ones that are relatively friendly."

I shook my head in disbelief. "Sherlock, I cannot believe that is you talking. Are you not the one who said that your detective service is firmly grounded in reality? No ghosts need apply! Prior to these most recent adventures, you would have dismissed all of this as shear fantasy and nonsense. You would not have even considered it. Yet here we are wandering around 'Faerie Land' with a fictional wizard and a talking Unicorn on a mission for King Arthur to locate a poet who actually died six years ago. And you are more than hoping you are going to encounter the nebulous, ethereal Pixy whose music is haunting you!"

"Yes, Watson, perhaps that realization is more than a bit odd. I will grant you that. But as I have explained many times earlier, sometimes even the most improbable situation can turn out to be the truth when you eliminate everything else. I am sure when this is all over and we are back in our flat, you will remind me of this adventure when we are faced with some other equally minor perplexing conundrum."

"Good sir pray tell, we are dealing with not only the disappearance of Alfred Lord Tennyson and the Lady of the Lake, but the revelation of a secret chamber hidden beneath the Round Table of Camelot! A secret listening chamber in the King's own meeting hall! I assure you, this is not a minor concern, if that maketh what a conundrum translates to in your time."

Sherlock and I quickly turned to look to where the deep, baritone voice had come from. There standing next to the Unicorn, who had returned without our noticing, stood a tall, well-built, dark-haired knight who radiated confidence, success, and ability. His very posture spoke of skill and victory in all knightly endeavors. He was proud and somewhat arrogant, yet there was a sadness to his countenance as if all of his success meant nothing.

"I am Sir Lancelot, the Right Hand of King Arthur and champion of his Queen Guinevere and the victor of countless tournaments," the knight proclaimed. "When Merlin and the Unicorn returned to Camelot and urgently instructed us to look beneath the Round Table, we thought he was jesting. 'Merlin,' the King declared, 'What are you saying? Are you making joke? We already have a court jester. Why would you have us look under the table?' but he was most insistent. When we discovered the hidden chamber, the King sent me to inform you."

Sherlock looked up as he pondered Lancelot's words and quickly responded. "Tell me about the listening chamber. Have you found the passageway from some other nearby location that leads into it? If I am correct, there are small female footprints and strands of long copper colored hair present, possibly the fragrance of certain herbs and forest plants."

Lancelot's jaw dropped, and his eyes grew wide. "Yes, yea, and yea verily! Pray tell, how is it possible for you to know such things when I just arrived and have not yet told you? The room was somehow hidden even from Merlin's sight."

The Unicorn nudged Lancelot and whispered, "I told you he would know everything you were going to say before you stated it. He is truly a great wizard."

Sherlock shook his head negatively and answered, "There is no magic in my abilities. It is merely the highest possible level of observation and deduction. Based on the obvious, I believe that Morgan La Fey has been listening to all of Arthur's plans and decisions as they are being made. She is possibly even influencing matters subtlety using herbal means. There are certain herbs and botanical compounds which if diffused into Arthur's meeting chamber, would cause a myriad of unexpected effects. That could explain her advantage and how she was able to lead Lord Tennyson away."

"By the Sword of Arthur, and my reputation as the greatest knight of Camelot, she shall pay for this!" thundered Lancelot. "None shall stand before me…"

"I did say *possibly* influencing matters, Sir Lancelot," interrupted Sherlock. "While I am quite certain she has been listening, I am not absolutely positive that she has been using means to adversely affect Arthur and his knights. From what I understand, she is only trying to keep the Faerie Realm from vanishing, just as you are striving to protect Camelot."

Lancelot was about to reply when a puzzled look came across his face, and he paused briefly, looking to the left and right as if trying to determine what to say in response. After a moment, he firmly gripped the hilt of his sword and continued in a loud voice, "But I am Sir Lancelot, the Right Hand of King Arthur, the champion of Queen Guinevere, the victor of countless tournaments, and the defender of Camelot. I cannot abide by Morgan La Fey's interference. Something must be done!"

Sherlock quietly held up his hand to calm Lancelot "And I assure you something is being done, Sir Knight. Did you per chance discover where the passage leading from the chamber went to? That will possibly tell us something useful."

"That is the strangest thing, Sir Wizard. The passage from the chamber under the table led to a dungeon cell, the very one she somehow escaped from many months past."

When I heard that, I could not restrain myself and exclaimed, "Arthur had his own half-sister put in a dungeon? What on earth for?"

Lancelot turned to me and responded, "She had burst into the Round Table chamber and boldly threatened to kill the King and Guinevere in front his entire court. Arthur tried to reason with her, but she was insistent, she said the only way to stop her was to imprison her. By faith, of course she was imprisoned to protect the King and Queen. Arthur made certain her cell was quite comfortable, but after only five days, she had disappeared from the prison cell. It was still securely locked, but empty. She had somehow vanished. The chamber we discovered beneath the round table led directly back to that cell. The entrance from the cell to the passage was cleverly hidden, and not discovered until moments ago."

I looked at Sherlock and asked, "What do you say Holmes, do you think the threat to kill the King and Queen was just a ruse to gain access to that room in the dungeon, so she could create a passage to the round table?"

Nodding affirmatively, Sherlock replied, "Indeed Watson, your perception is increasing. But the question is how did she then escape from a locked cell? My conclusion is that she was hiding in the listening chamber, and it only appeared completely empty, so it was left unlocked. She was then able to return to the cell and leave in disguise. After that, she could come and go dressed as one of the workers. No one would pay attention to her, so she had unlimited access to the cell and the chamber beneath the round table. Or she may even have a servant working for her. It was quite clever actually."

"But what are we to do, Sir Wizard? Arthur has posted guards at the cell and in the Round Table meeting chamber. What do we do next? By the Towers of Camelot, we must do something! You have the Sword of Lancelot, Champion of the Queen, and the Right Hand of Arthur at your command!"

Sherlock quickly responded, "Then return at once, and remove the guards. Leave the cell unlocked. Return the Round Table to its original position and instruct Arthur to call a meeting of all his knights."

If it were at all possible, Lancelot looked even more surprised by these directions than by Sherlock's previous revelation, and he interrupted, "By faith! You would have us leave the cell and access to chamber unguarded? Forsooth why?"

With a wry smirk, Sherlock elaborated, "Instruct Arthur to use this meeting to read the provisioning list, the laundry list, the tax records, anything that will keep the gathering going as long as possible."

Turning to the Unicorn, he asked, "Unicorn, after you have brought Lancelot back to Arthur's court, can you return here, and convey me to Camelot? Then, I must request that you return here to Dr. Watson."

Turning in my direction he addressed me. "Watson, when the Unicorn returns, I want you both to continue following the trail left by Morgan. You have accompanied me long enough to know what I am looking for. It is the near invisible, undetermined '*something*' that no one else would see, and if they did, they would pay no attention to. It is quite elementary, actually. If I had a copy of my paper on "*Seeing the Unseen by Looking for the Obviously Invisible with a Focus on the Hidden Trifles,*" you would understand. If do you find anything significant, send the Unicorn back for me. Meanwhile, I have a Round Table meeting to attend."

Chapter 10.

A Very Odd Predicament, (And an even odder bridge, if you can call it that.).

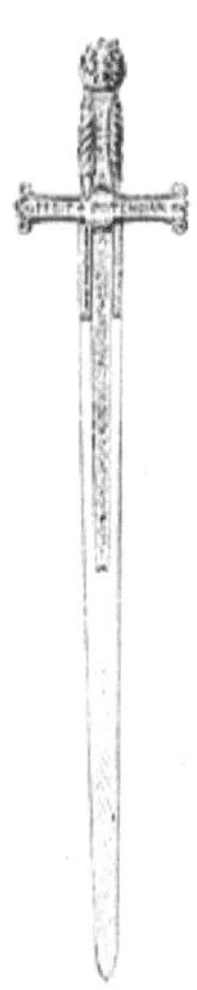

The Unicorn and Lancelot returned to Camelot while Sherlock was assuring me that I would be just fine. He was certain I would find *something*, although he could not say exactly what, but I would know it when I saw it, and then a moment later, he was gone. Once again, the odd feeling of utter alienation returned.

I stood transfixed in silence for a moment, listening and looking for strange creatures or unexplainable beings peering at me through the haze. I was straining to see through a swirling undulating mist that seemed to rise up from the lake towards the land like a giant nebulous octopus, when the Unicorn suddenly appeared in back of me commenting, “We should probably be on our way, you know. During the foggy season, the visibility along the shoreline can be exceptionally limited at this time of day.”

I nearly jumped out of my shoes at the suddenness of his return, but I managed to retain my composure and replied, “Yes, that is probably a very good idea. Just out of curiosity, when exactly is the foggy season?”

The Unicorn looked up for a moment pondering and then turned and answered, “I would say all year long or at least for the last several hundred years, as far as I am aware. It could be even longer than that. Either way we should be off.”

I cringed at the thought of a foggy season lasting more than several hundred years and began studying the footprints that meandered along the lakeside trail. Having worked on cases with Sherlock countless times in the past, I had some degree of confidence that I would be able to successfully follow them to wherever they led. My assurance quickly faded, however, as the path transitioned from a soft sand to a harder rocky surface.

“What’s this?” I asked out loud as the footprints faded away. “All right, now what do we do?” I stopped and studied the ground looking for some type of clue that would indicate the passage of Morgan la Fay and Lord Tennyson. It was then that the words of Sherlock echoed in my mind: “*Look for the invisible trifle. See what no one else does.*”

“Yes, the unseen invisible…” I muttered.

"Would that be the slight scuff marks on the ground?” I heard the Unicorn ask. “If you look closely, you can see a slight scrape mark there and then again further along. It matches the pace of Lord Tennyson’s stride.”

I examined the areas the Unicorn had indicated and realized that he was correct. Sherlock had previously mentioned that he had noticed a slight limp in Alfred Lord Tennyson’s footprints, and the scuff marks clearly fit the spacing of his stride.

“An excellent observation!” I commented. “You are quite good at this.”

“Yes, it is true. Unicorns do have a close connection to the land. I could tell you if even a rabbit passed this way, but your Wizard friend has observational powers that are beyond anything I have ever witnessed.”

“Indeed, Sherlock is quite talented.” I replied and continued to follow the all-but-invisible trail. As we walked, I asked the Unicorn, “What would Morgan la Fey want with Alfred Lord Tennyson? Did she kidnap him just to vex Arthur? Do you believe she intends any harm to him? Considering his age when he arrived in Camelot, he would be eighty-nine years old by now.”

The Unicorn pondered briefly and replied, “Morgan la Fey is passionate about keeping the Faerie Realm from fading away, and she is quite angry with Arthur, but I do not believe she would harm the poet. She admired his works. She is also furious with Merlin, which may explain why she acted against Nimue. But with Morgan, it is hard to understand or say anything. She is quite unpredictable.”

After a while, the rocky ground gave way to a softer earth, and the two sets of footprints were once again clearly visible.

"Ah, this is much better." I mentioned aloud, as I pointed to the now clearly discernible trail. “I wonder where this will take us.”

By now, you may be thinking that I should have known better than to vocalize such a question, considering where my previous pondering vocalizations had led to on our most recent adventures. But at the time, I was feeling confident and rather sure of myself in following the footprints, and I was clearly not considering what the answer to my question might actually be. Whatever it was, I was certainly not expecting a *sword bridge*!

I have previously read of how Sir Lancelot overcame the near impossible task of crossing a mystical sword bridge in several of the literary retellings of Camelot, but I never imagined such a thing could actually exist. Yet there it was right before us, spanning a deep chasm across a turbulent, raging river. It was an impossibly large sword set lengthwise vertically on end with the sharp edge facing upwards. Although the path led directly up to it and the trail continued on the opposite side, how could it even be called a bridge? No one could cross that and survive. What were we to do?

The Unicorn looked at me and asked, “You aren’t expecting me to cross that, are you? Even as swift and nimble as I am, I still require some sort of footing. And you can see the river at the bottom is far too dangerous to attempt a crossing.”

I looked to either side of the bridge and saw no other crossings as far as one could see. The gap only grew wider as the distance away from the sword bridge increased, so this was the narrowest crossing point, but how to achieve it? It seemed all but impossible. I looked closer to see how it was supported, and that is when I saw that the hilt of the sword was being supported not by rocks but by a pair of greyish colored knobby hands. Looking even closer, it was then I saw a diminutive creature residing in a depression in the rocks and holding the sword in place.

“Hello! Who are you? What are you doing in there?” I asked.

A sharp gravelly voice replied, “I am a Kobold. And I am also the bridge keeper. What does it look like I am doing? I am holding up the sword bridge. It should not take a wizard to see that.”

The Unicorn stepped forward and replied, “But he is not a wizard; he is either an apprentice or a doctor, depending on where he is standing at any given moment. It’s rather complicated actually. I don’t fully understand it myself.”

Ignoring the Unicorn's comment, I asked the creature, "Why are you holding it with the sharp edge up? How is one to cross the bridge when the sharp edge provides no footing?"

The creature grumbled with sound of rocks scraping against each other and answered, "That is none of my concern. My task is to hold up the bridge, and that is exactly what I do. Not that it is very interesting."

It was then that an idea came to mind. I whispered to the Unicorn to get ready to quickly take us across when the opportunity presented itself, and then I bent down to look at the creature. It was old and gnarled and did not seem to be very happy with its task.

"I imagine that is so," I said. "It must be extremely difficult. When do you even get a chance to have your meals? You must get very hungry holding up that bridge all day. Are you allowed to set the hilt down at all to eat?"

It looked at me with a surprised expression. "Of course, I can set it down when I eat. How else would I be able to otherwise?"

I removed from my pocket, some of the biscuits that I had brought with me from Sherlock's mead-dueling contest and offered them to the Kobold. "That may be, but would you care for some of my biscuits? They are most delicious, and I would be happy to share them with you."

The creature's expression brightened somewhat as it started to move, and its voice changed from gravely to something more akin to a rusty gate hinge. "Well that is the best thing I have heard you say since you arrived. That is most kind of you."

He set the handle down which caused the sword to rotate ninety degrees so that the flat edge was now facing upwards creating a narrow surface that one could just barely walk upon. Then he stretched and flexed his fingers with a distinct popping and cracking sound. “Some fresh biscuits sound most welcome right about now, perhaps with a good flagon of ale.”

I glanced at the Unicorn to get ready, and then set the food on a flat rock near the trail. “Here you go, good sir. Enjoy!”

As the Kobold moved towards the food, I quickly nodded to the Unicorn, and in an instant, he blurred, materialized beneath me, and then took off like a race horse with my arms franticly wrapped around his neck. I tried not to think about the impossibly narrow surface of the sword we were going to traverse, or the consequences of not making it across. However, in less than a moment, we made it across the sword bridge and were making excellent progress down the path on the other side of the ravine, and for once, I truly appreciated the speed of a Unicorn.

Chapter 11.

A Very Odd *Something*. (I would not have expected it but knew it when I saw it.)

The Unicorn eventually slowed down, stopped, and I dismounted to examine the ground for clues. As I did, the creature observed, "That was a rather creative approach, even if you did give away your evening repast. But I must say that it was certainly more expedient to cross the sword bridge when it was horizontal than if it had been vertical."

"I am curious,' I replied, "I wonder how Morgan and Lord Tennyson crossed the bridge. Their footprints are clearly on this side of the ravine and they keep going along this trail. How did they manage it?"

We continued following them until *it* happened. It was at that point that the unknown *something* that Sherlock had stated I would find suddenly appeared. Or actually disappeared, so to speak. The two sets of footprints had been clearly visible for quite some distance when they veered towards an exceptionally large oak tree, went right up to it, and totally vanished.

"What's this?" I asked aloud. "Could this be the mysterious *something* that Sherlock was talking about? I *do* wish he were here right about now."

I looked around both sides of tree and tried to see if they continued further down the trail, but I could not see a thing. I looked up towards the branches, but the lowest limbs were a considerable distance up into the tree, and it did not seem likely that a man of Tennyson's age could have made his way up there and safely taken an aerial route through the forest. What could have happened to them? Was this tree another type of portal? This was certainly an unexpected *something*, even if it was just a mysterious vanishing of the footprints.

I tried knocking on the tree in several different locations to see if it was hollow or if it was a portal that just happened to look like a tree. I had not noticed that the Unicorn had vanished until he reappeared with Sherlock who immediately offered a comment, "You won't get anywhere like that, you know. Haven't you learned anything from observing me in the field, Watson? The Unicorn said you requested my presence."

I quickly turned to find Sherlock standing next to the Unicorn gazing at the tree with a confident look on his face.

The Unicorn came to my aid by replying, "Don't be too hard on him, Sir Wizard, you would have been most proud of the way he outwitted the bridge keeper and secured our passage across the ravine.

Sherlock walked towards the tree, and gave me a light pat on the back, while answering. "Well, that is good to hear. There is still hope for you Watson. Now if you will excuse me, I will open the hidden door, and we can continue following their trail."

I looked at him with relief and surprise, as well as bit of incredulousness. “But how could you know where the hidden door is? You just got here. There is nothing obvious that I can see.”

“That is because you have not read my monograph on “*Detecting and Revealing Hidden Doorways, Entrances, Passages, and Access Points with an Emphasis on the Unseen but Obvious Locking Mechanisms.*” It is quite straight forward actually. In fact, I would say it is elementary.”

And with that Sherlock walked up to the tree and pushed a small round spot in the bark on the trunk, at which point there was a clicking noise and surprisingly, a large section of it swung open like a door revealing a set of stairs heading down into the ground. Even more surprising was the appearance of a small white-bearded gnome at the top of stairs. He was wearing a tall, red pointed hat, blue trousers, and heavy black boots. I have to say he looked just like one of the garden gnome statues that have been appearing in front lawns and gardens around London since Sir Charles Isham brought back twenty-one of them from Germany. They have become quite the fashion. But I must say, back home they are just statues yet here, I had one standing before me that was very much alive.

The creature looked at both of us and crossly stated, “First of all, it’s not polite to open someone’s door unless you have been invited in, and second of all this is an oak tree, not an “L” “M” “N” Tree. That should be obvious to anyone. Those trees grow in the woods behind the old school house. They are very handy for making alphabet soup you know. I suppose you are following Morgan le Fay and the poet. They passed by here not too long ago and took the underground passage. She said that if anyone came following, I should point them to the wrong direction.”

With that, the white-bearded Gnome pointed towards the East saying, “Over that way is the wrong direction. All right, now that

I have pointed out the wrong direction, I suppose you are going to want to continue to follow them through my tree house in the correct direction. Do wipe your feet and try not to break anything on your way through. If you would like to stop in for a cup of hot spiced mead, I am sure the Missus would be delighted. We don't get many visitors. In fact, other than Morgan and her poet friend, you're the only visitors we have had in ages. Creatures walk past our tree day and night, but no one ever stops in."

"Maybe it is because your home looks just like a normal tree, and they do not realize that it is someone's dwelling," Sherlock suggested, adding, "How did Morgan le Fay know to pass through your home? And if you do not mind my asking, where does the underground passage lead to?"

The Gnome laughed in a voice that sounded like someone crumpling a sheet of paper and responded. "Lady Morgan knows everything about the Faerie Realm. She is its Guardian. Why she would point you off to the East is beyond me. Everyone knows the Dark Forest lies in that direction. It's not a pleasant place to visit. It just so happens that the back door of our home leads directly to the underground passage that bypasses the Dark Forest. It can be rather confusing though. It is quite a labyrinth. Are you sure you would not like a spot of nice hot spiced mead?" Sherlock shook his head negatively and answered, "Thank you very much, but not at this time. We really must catch up to them. You mentioned that the underground passage is a labyrinth. Do you know the way through it?"

The Gnome's eyes brightened, and he beamed with pride. "Do I know the way through it? I should hope so. I created it. I dug it out myself. I needed to find a way around the Dark Forest. The trees in there are not very friendly, and their beastly obnoxious branches kept stealing my hats. They had taken so many, I would have renamed it the 'Red Hat Forest,' but the Missus said it would only attract a group of ladies in red and purple hats, so I left it as is. I decided that I would dig a path under the forest to get around them. My sense of direction at first was not very accurate, which is why it turned out to be a bit of a maze. I eventually sorted it out and completed the passage. And now I don't have to worry about losing any more hats."

"That sounds excellent!" I commented, thinking the trail would finally get easier. But then the gnome elaborated and dashed all hopes of that.

"Of course, the roots of the trees have a nasty sense of humor and like to trip travelers as they walk through the passages. In fact, if you stand in some sections too long, they will tie your boot strings together."

"Well then we will just have keep stop walking until we get to the exit," replied Sherlock. Please lead the way good sir. Time is of the essence."

"Follow me," the gnome replied and turned to enter the tree, "but do watch your step."

As we followed the gnome into the tree, I asked Sherlock what he had found out in the round table hall of Camelot. It turned out that Morgan herself was not using the secret chamber, but she had a devoted servant listening in and reporting to her. Sherlock had deduced exactly when the spy was present and had previously instructed King Arthur to make a statement of such urgency, that the spy would need to immediately report to Morgan. Merlin and Sir Lancelot were following the servant while Sherlock returned to me.

The entry into the tree and the passageway were just large enough for the Unicorn to accompany us, and the glow of its horn emitted a soft silvery light which illuminated our way.

"I must say," The gnome commented, "this is the first time I have had visitors in my tunnel, besides Lady Morgan and the old gentleman, I mean. She did not stop for refreshments either. Why are you surface folk always in a hurry, with no time to appreciate the journey? Do you know how long it took me to make this passageway?"

Sherlock looked at the intricately carved wooden panels lining the walls of the tunnel and replied. "Well, to answer that question, I would need to know the distance we will travel before we get to the exit. I can see that you put great effort into the finish work. Tell me how long it took you to carve each one of the panels, and how long the passage is, and I will tell you how long it took you to make the passage way."

The gnome's expression brightened, as he replied, "Verily? You can do that? Actually, the wall panels come already decorated. As long as I needed wall support panels, me thinks they should be attractive to behold. The view down here would be sorely lacking otherwise. Wouldn't you agree? I am curious. How long do you say it took me to make this? It is 800 paces in length, not counting the 400 paces in wrong turns I originally took."

Sherlock considered a moment and asked him, "Is the soil density the same throughout the entire passage? By 'pace,' do you mean the standard measurement that is equivalent to five feet, or do you mean paces of your stride that would be a tad smaller?"

The gnome frowned and kicked at a tree root that was trying to grab at his boots. "Like I said, the tree roots can be tricky down here, but they are nowhere near as bad as the branches. I always say, you need to get to the root of problem." He then laughed at his humor and went on, "I do mean standard surface folk paces, and the soil is indeed the same throughout the whole passage, soft earth with many pesky tree roots."

Sherlock paused a moment and then answered, "Well in that case, considering the density and composition of the ground, your height, the span of your arms, the length of your stride, the quantity of material that would have to be removed, and the wall support panels that would have to be brought down here, the placement of support beams, the occasional retrieving of your tools from the tree roots, lunch breaks, and holidays, I would say it took you three years, two months, and twenty two days."

The gnome stopped in his tracks, turned, and exclaimed, "How could you possibly know that? I did not even know that. The Missus told me how long the task had taken when I was finally finished. I was surprised. I had no idea it had taken that long, but she was keeping track."

Sherlock replied, "It is all simply a matter of observation and noting the finer details, just like before you take another step you should probably take care of your boots, which have been tied together by the tree roots while you were standing talking. You did caution us not to stop for very long."

"What?" the gnome exclaimed while looking downward to his feet. "Pesky tree roots!" he muttered as he untied his boot laces. "We should keep moving. I still don't see how you could have known that. Were you spying on me?"

The Unicorn piped in, "He has no need to do that, Sir Gnome. He can tell you everything about yourself from a brief glance and even more if he looks really closely at you. Why, he can even tell you what you had for dinner yesterday."

Again, the gnome stopped in his tracks and exclaimed, "No! Truly and verily? I am not even sure what it was. The Missus said it was a surprise, and after I tasted it, I understood that it really was a surprise. I did not *want* to know, if you know what I mean. I did not tell her that though. I said it was creative and left it at that."

Sherlock smirked, turned to me, and commented. "It is probably a good thing he left it at that. I don't think he would want to have known."

Then he turned to the gnome and pointed out, "You need to untie your boot laces again. Have you considered boots without laces?"

The gnome exclaimed, "Vexing troublesome tree roots!" and again untied the laces and continued down the path. The remainder of the underground journey was mostly silent except for occasional grumblings from the gnome of "How could he have known that?" "How does he do that?" and more than one time, "Pesky tree roots!"

We had reached the end of the tunnel, and were exiting into daylight, when a woman's voice coldly stated, "Well gnome, what is this? I thought I told you to send them off in the wrong direction. Perhaps, I should turn you into a lawn statue. I understand they are very popular in the England your wizard friend comes from."

We looked up, and there before us was Morgan le Fay.

Chapter 12.

A Very Odd Metamorphosis, (But it did not affect Sherlock one bit.)

We all froze at the sound of the voice, and even the tree roots seemed to recoil back into the ground. The silence was profound and terrifying as we waited to see what was going to happen next. Finally, the gnome turned to me and whispered, "What exactly is a lawn statue?"

Morgan le Fay merely smiled and stared at us. She was very attractive; being slight of build with long, copper colored hair. She wore a forest green gown with a lighter cape the color of jade. Her emerald eyes were clear and cold and seemed to hide another more bewitching side of her beyond what was visible. She had dried flowers sewn into the edges of her cape, and the belt she wore was, in fact, a willow vine woven around her waist.

Several crystals and small pouches hung from the belt and contained who knows what type of potion or magic.

The gnome turned to her, and exclaimed in a nervous and trembling voice, "I did exactly as you requested, oh great Lady in Green. I pointed them in the direction of the Dark Forest. Did you mean for them to actually go *into* the forest? No one goes in there anymore. If you had said to send them into the Dark Forest I most assuredly would have done so, but you specifically said to *point* them in the wrong direction."

"And I can assure you he truly did his best to point us in that direction, Lady le Fay," commented Sherlock, "but it was more than obvious that your footprints did not go any further into the forest. I would have seen them if they had. The only possible way you could have gone is through the underground passage. You do realize, of course, that I have been able to successfully track you all the way from Lord Tennyson's chambers. It is only a matter of time before we catch up to you."

Upon hearing what he had said, I turned to Holmes and asked, "What are you talking about, Sherlock? What do you mean before we catch up to her? She is standing there right outside the tunnel."

Sherlock pointed at the ground and replied, "What you heard, and saw was simply a projected image of some type. If you look closely, you will see she is not casting a shadow."

I looked closer and saw that Sherlock was indeed correct. Morgan le Fay was not casting a shadow! She was an image similar to the scenes we had seen of Lord Tennyson, except when she spoke, we could hear her cold calculating voice.

"So, you have, Sherlock Holmes, so you have. Your skills in observation and deduction are outstanding, and you have successfully met all of the challenges I have left for you. Let's see how well you can follow me when I do this!"

And as she finished speaking, she waved her hands in a peculiar manner and uttered a phrase in an arcane unintelligible tongue, and before our eyes, the lady in the image began to shrink and change form, her body condensing while at the same time, sprouting gossamer wings and delicate antenna. I could not believe what I was seeing. It was terrifying yet transfixing. I could not avert my eyes. When her transformation was complete, she had become a very large bee!

"Did you see that Holmes?" I exclaimed. "I am going daft, or has she turned into a bee!"

"A *Megachilidea Pluto*, in fact. It is the largest species of Leaf Cutter bees, to be exact. Knowing their habits and nature as I do, she will be considerably easier to follow. You know I have actually written several monographs on "*Analyzing the Behavior and Travel Patterns of Bees, with a Focus on Large Cleptoparasites and their Nesting Traits Primarily Looking at the Queens.*" I never imagined they would be useful here."

The Unicorn responded, "You truly do speak another form of English in the time you are from, but I believe what you mean is that you can still follow her in that form. You are aware that she can change forms and metamorphose as she chooses. Merlin also has that ability. They had a duel once that involved transformations into so many different creatures, it was like a visit to the Zoological Gardens back in your London, except the creatures kept changing right before your eyes, and your Zoological Garden does not have any manticores, griffins, chimeras, or trolls. It wasn't something you want to watch right after eating lunch."

Sherlock nodded and watched as the large bee that had been Morgan le Fay flew off and the image grew nebulous and finally faded away.

"That is nice to know," he muttered as he dashed off from the tunnel entrance into the woods, stopping here and there to closely examine various leaves, branches, crevices in tree trunks, and fallen limbs. With the air of a lecturer, he commented, "Each one of these signs tells a detailed story, Watson. Bees are elementary to follow, if you know how to read them."

The Unicorn replied, "I understand what you are saying. It is simple for me to read the signs of magic in or having passed through an area. When Morgan le Fey is not in her human form, she leaves a certain aura or disturbance in the air. I can assure you, Sir Wizard, you are on the correct path. Only certain creatures like myself can sense magic, but you are without question the only one I have ever met that can follow a specific insect."

At that point, the gnome stopped and held up his hand saying, "Verily, it has been most pleasant meeting you all, but I do not want to be around when you do catch up to her. She can be quite formidable, and it is time I returned to my home."

Sherlock and I replied that it was pleasant meeting him, thanked him for the directions through the underground passage, and wished him well. In a moment, he had disappeared back into the labyrinth, and the Unicorn and I were following Sherlock as he examined cut marks in leaves and observed aloud, "Did you know, Watson, that fossil record of the Megachilidea Bees date back to the Middle Eocene era? They are truly fascinating creatures. In fact, I am thinking about taking up bee keeping when I retire. Not that I am planning to any time soon."

The Unicorn stopped in its tracks and, looking off to the left replied. "If by 'retire,' you mean ceasing your present occupation to pursue more enjoyable but less profitable activities, you may not get that opportunity. Look over there!"

Not far in the distance were several small, hairy, and odd-looking creatures with sly expressions on their faces. They looked rather mischievous and unpredictable. They were uniformly dressed in grey tunics, brown trousers, and black boots.

“Those are Hobgoblins!” stated the Unicorn. “They are the less friendly, distant relatives of Brownies and are most fond of practical jokes when they not doing something even more unpleasant. They appear to be planning something devious.”

The creatures were grinning, muttering and pointing at us while looking from where we stood towards a location several yards down the path.

“Those are certainly an unpleasant lot of blighters. What do you think they intend to do, Sherlock?” I asked.

"Based on their behavior and actions, I would say nothing. They have already set a trap, and they are waiting for us to blunder into it. We do not have time to play their games, so I suggest we deal with them quickly.”

With that Sherlock removed from his pocket several of the biscuits left over from his mead dueling contest, took a bite out of one them commenting on how delicious it was, waved them in the direction of the hobgoblins, and then threw them further down the path in front of us. The creatures as one leaped forward on to the path to grab the food and were at once caught in large wooden cage that suddenly fell from the tree above.

Holmes turned to us and asked, “Shall we proceed? As I stated, we do not have time to waste.” And with that he threw one more biscuit into the cage, nodded in their direction, and proceeded to continue down the path.

The Unicorn looked at me and observed; “Now I see from where you get your cleverness and indifference towards food. If we run into any more obstacles, we will not have any provisions left. Still that was handled rather well.”

Chapter 13.

A Very Odd Meadow, (But most inviting indeed.)

We left the area with the hobgoblins happily devouring the biscuits and seemingly oblivious to the fact that they were the ones trapped in the cage. One of them even muttered a thank you for the food and offered an invitation to return if we had any more. He assured us they would most likely be there waiting for us.

Holmes offhandedly replied, "I would imagine you will be, since I am quite certain that you have not read my monograph on, "*A Basic Guide to Escaping from Traps, Cages, Pens, and Prisons, With an Emphasis on Makeshift Methodologies Due to Lack of Proper Tools*." It could have been quite useful." And then he went on his way, once more making minute observations on the behavior of the Leaf Cutter Bee and the ease of following Morgan le Fey while she was in the form of a bee.

As we followed Sherlock down the path, I heard in the distance behind us one hobgoblin ask the other two if they had understood exactly what the wizard was saying. One of the others answered, in between bites on his biscuit, "I think the wizard said he doesn't believe we have any libraries here." Surprised by his answer, I turned to look back and saw the hobgoblin removing a scroll from his tunic. He opened it up, and shrugged his shoulders, saying, "I cannot imagine what he is talking about. It says right here, "*A Basic Guide to Escaping from Traps, Cages, Pens…*" and his voice faded off into the distance.

The terrain gradually transformed from a forest into a wide rolling meadow that was bursting with multicolored flowers as well as buzzing with a multitude of bees. I looked at the scene and my hopes crashed as resoundingly as a knight in a full suit of armor falling off his horse. How was Sherlock going to be able to find one bee amongst hundreds? I looked at the Unicorn and asked, "Can you tell with your ability to sense magic which one might be her or which way she went?" He shook his head and said that she had certainly passed through the area but had apparently returned several times and then left again several more times going in a multitude of different directions. Sherlock stopped at the edge of the meadow and studied it intently for some time. I took advantage of the opportunity and observed the area myself.

I must say that in spite of our urgent task to find Lord Tennyson, this attractive meadow was truly a paradise, and I enjoyed the moment to take it all in. The blossoms were colorful, fragrant, and bright, with an abundance of different blooms. I felt myself relaxing and not being as concerned with which insect might be Morgan le Fey. There was an overpowering scent of lilac and tea rose in the air, which was very soothing. There were low hills and hedges leading off in many directions with narrow pathways alongside the hedgerows. It looked very much like a meticulously cared for garden and as if it was purposefully laid out. After a moment of gazing at it all, I began to notice what looked like minute structures that blended perfectly into the surrounding vegetation and grounds. If one did not look closely, they could easily have been missed, as they were so naturally camouflaged. Although they were constructed of twigs, branches, bark, moss, leaves, and other natural materials, they were most certainly miniature houses.

I was about to exclaim, when Sherlock held up one finger to his lips to request silence. I did not know what to expect, so I said not a word and remained motionless. My eyes darted about in all directions, wondering what it was he anticipated, when a number of tiny, winged but human looking creatures began emerging from behind the flowers and shrubs as well as from within the Lilliputian dwellings. The tallest of them was less than ten inches in height. Their wings were varicolored, iridescent, and gossamer, and they were the most delicate and perfectly formed beings I had ever seen. They were the very picture of gentleness and beauty. I thought to myself they must be faeries or perhaps pixies. I certainly had never seen anything quite like them before.

Very slowly, so as not to frighten them, Sherlock removed from his pack the musical instrument and bow that he had received as a gift from the dragon earlier. He set it against his shoulder and began to play. The creatures were immediately drawn to him. It seemed as if they were glowing as they fluttered around us bobbing and drifting to the exquisite melody. Their dance was a hypnotic combination of music and motion unlike anything I had ever witnessed. Once again, in addition to Sherlock's music, I heard a haunting second melody that played harmony and counter-point to his. The ethereal song of Pixy Music was once more accompanying him. The two lines of their duet wove around each other playfully cavorting as if in a folk dance, then slowly and gently caressing as two partners in a waltz. I could hear pure ecstasy in their music, and the result was captivating. I found myself wishing it would go on forever. I thought perhaps, here in this mystical meadow, Sherlock would finally meet Pixy Music, but sadly she did not appear.

After an interlude, Sherlock stopped playing and with one hand, made a wide sweeping gesture in a circle. He shrugged his shoulders while holding up his hands to indicate a question. It was then I realized what he was doing. He had gained their confidence by playing the mystical music, and in sign language, he asked them which way we should travel. How they could possibly know what direction we wanted to go or even that we were following Morgan le Fey was quite beyond me, but I knew better than to question the deductions of Sherlock Holmes.

The faeries must have understood him, however, because they fluttered in one direction heading towards the east and paused. They returned to him and repeated the motion. He bowed his head to the group in acknowledgement and replaced his makeshift violin and bow in his pack, then turned back towards me the Unicorn and gave a quick tilt of his head in the direction they had shown to indicate that we should again be on our way. He straightforwardly added, "We really must be off, Watson. There is no time to spare. We are not far behind Morgan le Fey and Lord Tennyson, and as I played, I felt the presence of Pixy Music. It was exquisite. I know she is not far away."

I must say I was reluctant to leave the charming meadow. I felt I could lie down and bask in the peace and serenity forever, but I knew we had to keep moving to find Lord Tennyson. Holmes was already leaving, so with considerable effort, I forced myself to keep going.

While Holmes was as observant and diligent as usual, he was somewhat quieter while he followed the trail, keeping his perceptions and deductions to himself. I am sure that he was reliving the delight of his musical interlude, as well as wishing Pixy Music had actually appeared. The Unicorn, however, was more vocal in its observations. "I must say, Dr. Watson, you did a champion job of resisting the temptations of the Faerie meadow. You are aware, of course, there have been many travelers to this mystical vale who have come here and never had the strength to leave."

I looked at the creature and suddenly realized how tempting the urge had been and I was very thankful that Sherlock had been so insistent.

The Unicorn nodded in Holmes' direction and added, "Should your wizard friend ever grow tired of following clues or bees, he would indeed make an excellent court musician. Of course, he will first have to successfully resolve his encounter with the enchanted Mirror that stands in our path."

Chapter 14.

A Very Odd Mirror, (And Sherlock proves there is most certainly more than one way to look at things.)

I looked up and saw not far along our path a large oval mirror mounted in a carved wooden frame set in the middle of the road. The wood work surrounding it was very ornate, detailed, and of the finest quality. It looked more like something that one would find in a palace, not sitting in the middle of a remote path in the wilderness. But then in this place one never knew what to expect.

Sherlock approached the mirror slowly while commenting, "Hmm, what have we here? It appears to be a fairly standard looking full-length, glass mirror, mercury backed, with beveled edges set in a carved mahogany frame with images of Camelot, King Arthur, and his knights on one side, while the other side featured Morgan le Fey and various faerie creatures. Most intriguing…

"The image is somewhat odd though. I can see myself, but the background appears to be rather blurred. It is almost as if the reflection is not certain or exact. How strange… Did you know, Watson, that there is a great deal of superstition and fear connected with mirrors? They are said to be able to capture one's soul, which is why household mirrors are typically covered with drapes at the time of a death in the family to prevent the soul of the dearly departed from being trapped inside it. Breaking a mirror is thought to bring seven years of misfortune, and some believe that mirrors can be a portal or doorway to other realms. I am sure Lewis Carroll could have told us a great deal about that.

"Alfred Lord Tennyson himself wrote a poem, "*The Lady of Chalot*", in which the lady in question was cursed to view the world only through the reflections in a mirror. When she did dare to look directly at Camelot, the mirror cracked, and she fell dead. Rather sad actually. If you had read my monograph, "*A Complete History and Analysis of Mirrors as They Relate to Problem Resolution, Clue Detection, and Crime Solving with an Emphasis on Determining the Unknown*," you would certainly understand what I am referring to."

Just then a profound, crystal clear feminine voice resonated in the still air, seeming to come from nowhere and everywhere all at once. It surrounded us with a deepness that echoed like a bottomless pit, with tendrils that pulled you deeper and deeper into it no matter how much you resisted.

"That is an interesting and reflective, if somewhat superficial, discussion of mirrors, Sherlock Holmes; not surprising considering your purely observational and analytical approach to subjects. You have really only scratched the surface, if I say so myself, which, based on my personal experience as a mirror for the last 150 years, I do feel qualified to say so. You neglect to mention that mirrors can also show the past and the future, what has been, what may be, and what will be."

As the voice spoke, the image in the mirror began to change and no longer showed Sherlock's reflection, even though he was clearly standing in front of it. First the mirror showed Sherlock sitting in his chair across from the Cheshire Cat, followed by the Hatter and White Rabbit entering 221-B Baker Street. Then a hazy blur of images from the Grinning Cat Adventure appeared, followed by Captain Nemo of the "*Nautilus*" coming through our doorway and then a number of reflections from the "*Nautilus*" Adventure.

The image then grew dark and cloudy and showed a struggle between two men on cliff overlooking a waterfall. They each seemed very skilled and evenly matched with neither gaining the upper hand, when suddenly one of the two made a move that forced them both over the cliff and down into the falls. I felt a grip of terror overcome me when I saw the expression of one and realized that it was Sherlock Holmes himself. After that, the mirror grew black reflecting nothing at all, and the crystalline voice went on: "Mirrors can show your greatest desires, or your worst fears. They can show what you long to see more than anything in the world or what you would close your eyes forever not to behold. The greatest question, Sherlock Holmes, is what truly lies behind the mirror? Are you prepared to answer that question?"

I was still trembling in fear from what I had seen the Mirror foretelling of the future when Holmes replied, "What lies behind the mirror depends on the perspective of who is standing before the mirror. It depends on what they bring and what they seek to take away. It also depends very much on the inclination of the mirror itself. You should understand that better than anyone, Mirror. How many other false images have you reflected before today?"

"That is an astute observation, Sherlock Holmes. All of the false images that I have ever revealed were no more than what the person seeing it wanted to see or what they despaired more than anything, the very thought of seeing. It is not my fault that after seeing the image, they themselves caused it to happen."

Sherlock edged closer to the surface of the Mirror and responded, "Is it the fault of the arrow, the bow, the string, or the hand that releases the arrow from the bow which causes a death?" he asked. "Or could it be the fault of the creature that happens to be standing where the arrow strikes? When you reflect a death, are you drawing that person to its exact location at that time and therefore causing it to happen? Are you spinning a web of deceit? What is your perspective, Mirror?"

The Mirror's image changed from darkness to swirling grey clouds, and the voice grew angry. "No one dares to question the reflection in the Mirror! I can show you the very moment of your death, if I desire. And it will haunt you the rest of your life."

Sherlock calmly stood his ground and replied, "You can show me anything you desire, but if I do not accept it as reality, it means nothing to me."

The grey and black clouds in the Mirror's surface swirled more violently than ever. Lightning bolts flashed and illuminated the image. The entire surface of the Mirror seemed to be trembling and shaking in the frame.

"Nothing? Nothing you say? Behold this!"

The clouds in the Mirror parted, and the image returned to the scene of the waterfall that I had chanced a glimpse of earlier. "*NO'* I thought to myself, not that! But Sherlock did not seem to be concerned in the least.

"Each of us creates our own destiny," he proclaimed to the Mirror. "Each of us is in control of every situation in which we place ourselves."

At that point, the image in the Mirror seemed to flutter and change. There was a ray of sunlight that pierced the clouds, and in that light, I saw only one of the two figures fall to his doom. I could not see the face of either, but Sherlock was smiling as he stood defiantly before the Mirror.

"I do not choose to see what *you* would desire to show me but only what *I* would choose to see. Now show me what is behind the Mirror, what is beyond the Mirror. Show me where I will find Morgan le Fey and Alfred Lord Tennyson. Show me what she has done with Nimue, the Lady of the Lake!"

The Mirror was shuddering even more violently than before as the image showed Morgan and Lord Tennyson sitting calmly in front of the entrance to a cave located in a peaceful vale surrounded by lilacs and roses. In a nearby pool, which seemed to have some type of energy dome over it, Nimue, the Lady of the Lake, was trying to break the enclosure that held her prisoner. The lightning bolts in the Mirror again began flashing around the perimeter of the image clouding the picture. It seemed as if lightning was crackling on the very surface of the mirror itself. Sherlock, sensing that something was about to occur, reached beneath his robe. As a bolt of lightning arced from the Mirror directly towards him, he quickly removed and held up a small pocket mirror which reflected the lightening straight back towards the enchanted Mirror. All at once, there was a brilliant flash, accompanied by a deafening crash of thunder, and then all was silent. The surface of the Mirror was once again normal, if there is such a thing in that odd land. It simply reflected the image of Sherlock standing before the Mirror with the wooded background behind him. It looked no different than any other reflection.

Holmes turned towards us, sighed, and addressed the Unicorn asking, "Good creature, would you happen to know where in this uncanny land the cave near a pool surrounded by roses and lilacs might be found? We must be on our way to rescue not only Lord Tennyson but Nimue as well."

Chapter 15.

A Very Odd Discussion, (And Sherlock actually sees the invisible.)

The Unicorn replied, “We are going in the correct direction.” And it returned to the pathway with Sherlock walking along next to the creature, observing the rocks, vegetation, and trees. I quickened my pace to catch up to him. Not knowing quite what to say, I commented, “Well, that was rather unusual, wouldn’t you say, Holmes old boy?”

He turned to me and answered, “Watson, for all of the sensational exaggerations and over-romanticizing in your accounts of my adventures, you sometimes have the most incredible gift of understatement imaginable. Seeing various possibilities of one’s death portrayed by a vindictive enchanted Mirror is more than what I would call “unusual.” It’s somewhat like going for a Sunday stroll and seeing your gravestone, except without the friendly spirits of Christmas Past and Present and the happy ending that that Dickens fellow was writing about. It took all of my strength to reject her influence and create my own destiny. However, I will be a bit more cautious when it comes to waterfalls though and possibly in the bath as well.”

"How can you be so cavalier about it all?" I asked adding, "But you did succeed, Holmes! You not only rejected her manipulations and suggestions, but now you know where Lord Tennyson and Nimue might be."

"What attitude should I take, Watson? I am not going to avoid any running water I come across. That might end up inadvertently causing my own downfall, which in effect would end up fulfilling her prophesy of a waterfall being my downfall, either literally or figuratively."

The Unicorn then interrupted, "Dr. Watson, in observing your Wizard friend all this time, I am certain he would never fall for that. He is much too clever. I am more curious to know as to how we are going to find and get to the Island of Avalon where the cave is located."

"What did you say?" Sherlock and I both turned and asked at the same time. "Are you saying the cave is on an island? Where?" We asked in unison.

The Unicorn answered affirmatively, "What I said was, the cave that was shown in the mirror's image is on the Island of Avalon. Yes, it most definitely is an island and being a mystical island, no one knows exactly where it is except the three Faerie Queens: Morgan le Fe, the Guardian of the Faerie Realm, Nimue, the Lady of the Lake: and the other one."

"The other one?" I asked. "Who is the other one?"

The Unicorn turned its head to an angle, thought for a moment, and answered, "That is an interesting question. She is more mysterious, and less is known about her than the island itself. It has always been said that there are three Guardian Queens of Avalon, and we know she really does exist, but she has become such a recluse that no one really knows anymore who she is or where she can be found."

"What about Merlin?" I asked. "I would think he would know the answer or at least be able to figure it out. He is almost all knowing. After all, he found Sherlock Holmes centuries in the future. What is a simple mystical queen who wishes to remain hidden? How difficult could that be?"

"An excellent question, Watson", Sherlock answered. "That is, indeed, the question. And deducing the answer after careful observation is a job for the consulting detective, and fortunately for us, I happen to be the best one in this time period or any other. Unicorn, you recognized the image of the cave as being on the island of Avalon, yet you say that its location is unknown. How is that possible?"

The Unicorn stopped walking, looked up into the sky for a moment, and replied, "It was long before Arthur's time. It is said that the three Queens were Guardians of the mystical Island of Avalon. It was a place of healing and peace. When people were seriously sick or injured, they were taken there to be healed. Once they had recovered, they were returned to Faerie Land, or wherever it was they came from. Many of them described the beauty, magic, and enchantment of the place. They longed to return, but the island remained hidden. That is how I came to hear of it and how I recognized the description. The location in the Mirror's image was unmistakable.

"When Arthur came, there was a difference of opinion between Morgan and Nimue. As you already know, Nimue supported Arthur and what he was doing, while Morgan stood against him. The third queen, I believe her name may have been Aoleous, but no one knows for sure; she chose to remain neutral and simply vanished."

Sherlock seemed deep in thought as he nodded his head, "Yes! Of course, she did. What else could she do? She needed to remain aware and accessible to the island but not in an obvious or open way, so she changed her identity and became someone else able to traverse multiple realms, to listen to and communicate with all of them, yet still be able to observe the Faerie Realm and Avalon, unseen and unknown. It all makes perfect sense. She has been hiding in plain sight, so to speak."

I stood dumbfounded not knowing what on earth he was talking about. "Holmes, I know you can see minute details of situations that no one else does and that you can put two and two together in ways that would equal any number you might need to fit your equation, but I have no idea what you are getting at. Could you please explain yourself?"

Sherlock was actually smiling as he whispered, "No, Watson, you would not, nor could you ever, but it is so obvious."

And with that he walked over to a medium-sized rock, sat down, took out his improvised violin and bow, set it to his chin, and began playing it.

The Unicorn looked at me with a puzzled expression and asked, "Does he do this kind of thing often? I mean make obscure and cryptic statements about a subject and then just sit down and start playing music?"

"You have no idea." I answered, adding, "Actually, yes, quite often. This is rather normal behavior for Sherlock Holmes." Sherlock, however, was oblivious to our discussion. He was lost in his music, which was, once again, exquisitely beautiful. It was a haunting melody, which danced and played on the wind echoing, during brief moments of profound silence. I was certain I could hear the accompanying strains of Pixy Music's melody as well. They were interweaving and harmonizing, in addition to calling and answering each other musically. Sherlock would play a line of a deep tonal chords followed by Pixy Music answering with a light and delicate refrain. The result was multilayered and resonating with a musical depth and beauty beyond imagination.

I had stood for quite some time overwhelmed with fascination and mesmerized by what I was hearing when I noticed that there seemed to be a radiant glow hovering in the air near where he was seated and playing his unworldly melody. The accompanying song that was Pixy Music's seemed to be emanating directly from within the glowing cloud. There appeared to be a form of some type inside the hazy aura, but I could not make it out. Could that be her, I wondered. Was she finally here? I was certain that this time he might actually meet her and realize his longing desire. The intensity of the music grew in energy and passion, reaching a quavering crescendo, but sadly that was all.

The glowing radiance gently faded away as the captivating music came to a halt and the last echoes evaporated into the air. I was waiting quietly for Holmes to say something, when the Unicorn broke the silence stating rather straight forwardly, "So it turns out that the missing third Queen of Avalon is Pixy Music. That explains where she disappeared to. As you said earlier, Wizard Holmes, it really does make perfect sense."

With his eyes closed, savoring the interlude they had shared, Sherlock sighed and responded, "I saw her, Watson. This time, I actually saw her."

Chapter 16.

A Very Odd Game of Chess, (And Sherlock clears the board, literally.)

With a far-off expression, Sherlock sighed again, "This time, I really, truly saw her! Watson, she is beauty beyond description. She is incomparable! While her haunting music is unimaginably enchanting and captivating, it is a mere reflection of her physical grace and charm. If you were to gather all the delicate, majestic loveliness in the entire universe and all of creation and combine it into one form, it could not hold a candle to her. I shall never find another woman this attractive for the rest of my life. Perhaps someday, there may be a woman… one woman, that can possibly match me in knowledge, wits, or trickery and she will be known as "*the woman,*" but there will never be another for me."

I looked at him and asked, "Holmes, are you feeling alright? Not once before today have I ever heard you speak like this."

The Unicorn gazed at Holmes and stated, "It was said that the third Queen of Avalon was most stunning in appearance, but few beings are around who remember. Perhaps, like your wizard friend, they were so star struck, bewitched, and overwhelmed that they have forgotten the entire experience."

Holmes sighed again, shook himself all over, and went on, "Yes, I do understand. My heart longs to remain here communing with her forever but our task is calling. We need to continue on the trail. She did tell me where Avalon is located. And she also cautioned me that the situation may not be what it seems and to be careful in how I interpret things."

Turning to look at me, he shared, "She also said that you, Watson, have a considerable role to play in this game, and it will become more obvious before it is finished. Just do not jump to conclusions."

I looked at him with a puzzled expression wondering what exactly she meant by that. "What do you think she was saying, Holmes? After all, you are the detective and the one following the clues. That is your specialty. You are the one Merlin specifically requested. How would I make a difference? All I do is gather the details and record the adventure when it is all over. Anyway, you have successfully tracked Morgan le Fey and Lord Tennyson this far. Where do we go from here?"

With a stamp of one hoof, the Unicorn echoed my question, "Yes, where are we headed? With my swiftness, we could be there already."

"But forsooth, you cannot go anywhere, Sir Wizard," an elderly female voice creaked. "Your assistance is desperately needed here. Alas, my son is trapped. You are the only one that can save him. Will you help a poor old woman?"

We turned and looked in the direction of the voice and saw an aged woman, leaning on a walking stick. She was dressed in typical peasant garb for the time period. Her wrinkled skin gave the appearance of considerable age. The long grey hair flowing down her shoulders still showed signs of once being reddish in color, but her green eyes were bright and alive looking. Sherlock addressed her asking, "What do mean he is trapped, gentle woman? Where might he be and who or what is trapping him? And why do you call me a wizard? I am only a mere traveler passing through these lands."

The old lady threw her head back and laughed. She raised her walking stick and pointed at me and the Unicorn answering, "One who travels in the company of a Unicorn and has an apprentice, and who can summon pixies with enchanted music. You may be very modest good wizard, but you are still a sorcerer. My son is trapped in a game."

"A game?" I blurted out. "How can he be trapped in a game?"

"My son was captured by Sir Robert, and he will not be released until his captor is beaten in a game of chess. Sir Robert commands his captives to be the playing pieces on a large chess board. He feeds them and provides shelter for them, but they cannot leave until he has been defeated. I am an old woman and have no one to take care of me without my son. Can you please help, good sir? Can you free him? It is not far out of your way."

I looked at Sherlock, and asked, "What do you make of this Holmes? Do you trust her?"

"Can we trust anything in this place?" he answered looking off into the distance. "It should not take me more than four moves to defeat Sir Robert. Let us take care of this, return the lady's son to her, and get back to our task."

Then turning to the woman, he asked, "How far away is this Sir Robert, dear lady?"

"Oh, thank you, Sir Wizard. Thank you! I will be eternally grateful to you. He is just over the hill. You will see the large chess board in the center of his garden. He commands his captive pieces to stand at attention all day, ready to begin a game at the drop of feather. He also keeps several geese on hand, so he has feathers to drop whenever he begins a game. He is a strange one, Sir Robert is. But forsooth, please do not tell him I said that, or I shall end up on the chess board as well."

"You need not worry, dear lady. I will not say a word," Holmes replied. "Please lead the way."

We began following the old woman, and I asked Sherlock if any part of her story seemed odd, and he answered that everything about the whole place was more than odd. It defied rational thought and logic, but it was still the way things were here, and he would apply his skills in observation, deduction, and rational thought to see where it takes us. He stated that he planned to write a monograph on the subject when we concluded this business. He was thinking on calling it *"A Logical Step-by-Step Guide to Finding the Reality in Unreal and Non-Logical Situations Using Observational, Rational, and Deductive Thought Process*."

I nodded and stated that it could be handy considering our current situation.

We quickly reached the estate of Sir Robert, the odd chess master, and it was as the old woman had said: A stone manor house stood on a low hill. There was a large chess board constructed of black and white stone tiles in the center of a beautiful enclosed formal garden. Brightly colored blossoms adorned the pathway leading into the playing area. The chess pieces were various people of different ages each wearing a tunic with the symbol of the piece that they represented.

Sir Robert, attired all in black, sat in an ornate chair that resembled a throne on the far side of the board, and the pieces that he commanded wore black tunics, while the people on the near side all wore white tunics. To either side of Sir Robert stood a number of men-at-arms dressed in black chain mail and holding pole axes and cross bows. I would presume this was to prevent his captives from trying to escape.

Sir Robert, himself was of medium build and rather slender. He sported dark hair, somewhat unkempt, and he had an intense, wild look about him. His eyes darted back and forth trying to take in everything at once. When he saw our odd group approach, he stood and addressed us.

"Ah, is this a challenger perhaps? And one who travels in the company of a Unicorn, an apprentice, and a crone. I am impressed. Do you seek to try your skill in chess against me? To be the one who frees all of my captives? You do understand, I have never lost a match, and anyone who loses the game becomes a captive to be part of my reserve playing pieces."

The old woman, looking somewhat embarrassed, coughed and whispered, "Oh yes, I may have forgotten to mention that little condition. But I am certain that you need not be concerned. I listened as you communicated with the musical pixy that haunts your thoughts, and you are most gifted in many ways, Sir Wizard."

Sherlock ignored her and stepped up to the platform that overlooked his side of the board. Looking first to the left and then to the right, he began speaking to his opponent in a loud formal voice. "I do challenge you to a game of chess, Sir Robert. I am Sherlock Holmes, a great Wizard who has traveled from the future to free your captives. I am a master of logic and deduction and have never been defeated. I see beyond the visible, and I know your deepest inner thoughts. Even now you grow anxious. Let the game begin!"

And with that, Holmes called out, "King's pawn, two spaces forward," adding, "You are doomed Sir Robert. You should surrender now to avoid the defeat which is inevitable."

The person representing the King's pawn moved forward two squares and stopped.

Sir Robert sat down and said nothing beyond, "King's pawn two spaces forward," with his pawn repeating the movement. Sir Robert's eyes were darting in every direction, and he looked uncertain.

Sherlock immediately responded with, "King's Bishop to Queen's Bishop four, if you please."

The gentleman representing the bishop moved to the space indicated by Sherlock, as Holmes continued to address his opponent. "It is not too late, Sir Robert, to avoid the disgrace of losing so quickly. Look around you; do you want to lose in front of all of these people, your guards, and the famous scribe, Dr. Watson of Londonderry? Your defeat will be immortalized for all of history."

Realizing what Holmes was up to. I quickly spoke up to add to the distraction and confusion. "Yes, I am the famous scribe and bard who records the Wizard Sherlock's victories and exploits and tells them for all to hear. They are known throughout the land."

Sir Robert, looking nervous and uncertain, was somewhat reserved and called out, "Queen's pawn one space forward," And his Queen's pawn took one step forward into the next square.

Sherlock replied, "It is just as I expected; your end is near. Queen to King's Rook five. Watch the left side of the board, Sir Robert. Watch for what is invisible."

The tall lady wearing the white Queen's tunic crossed the board diagonally to the space indicated by Holmes.

With just a quick glance at the chessboard, his opponent jumped out of his chair and called out, "I know what you are doing, but it will not work. I see your Queen hiding there. King's Knight to King's Bishop three! Your Queen is in danger!"

The Knight walked to where he had been directed and stopped, shaking his head the entire time, as if he knew what was going to happen next.

Sherlock laughed, and replied, "Queen to King's Bishop Seven. Queen takes Pawn. Your King is in Checkmate! The game is over."

The White Queen gracefully crossed to King's Bishop Seven, tapped the pawn on the shoulder and took his place, and the young lad left the board.

Raising his arms, Holmes addressed the stunned people who had been the playing pieces, and said, "The game is over for good. You may all go home now. You are free."

In one motion, all the captives who had been the playing pieces began to tear off their tunics and throw them to the ground cheering Sherlock. As they left the chess board, Sir Robert stood silently starring at the scene in disbelief. He had lost and in the four moves that Holmes had predicted. It was brilliant.

I looked over to where the Unicorn and the old lady had been standing expecting to see the old woman reunited with her son, but she was nowhere to be seen. Where had she gone? I gazed into the crowd of people, but they were dispersing quickly, and soon the chess board was empty. As Holmes stepped down from the player's platform, I told him about the old lady disappearing and asked him if he had seen where she had gone off to.

He said that he had not, but he was not surprised. He had had his suspicions about her from the very beginning.

"Then why did you go along with her and this whole chess game challenge?" I replied. "What if your distraction ploy had failed and you had lost? What would we have done then?"

The Unicorn tilted its horn forward and piped in, "I could have spirited us away from here in an instant, or possibly even less if Dr. Watson did not strangle me while trying to hold to my neck on for dear life." Then looking at me he added, "I really have not had that many close calls with trees, Dr. Watson. You should not be overly concerned."

Sherlock ignored the Unicorn's comments and flatly stated, "I did not lose, Watson, I won, just as I had expected, and in the precise number of moves that I predicted. I had the entire scenario worked out in my head, as soon as we arrived. It played out exactly as I had planned. It was quite elementary. Regarding the old lady, I believe that this was all just a test of our character. And when she found out what she needed, she left."

"But who was she?" I asked.

"I am certain she is the very Morgan le Fey whom we have been following. It appears she has been following us as well."

Chapter 17.

A Very Odd Plan. (And possibly one of Sherlock's most outlandish.)

"What?" I exclaimed. "She was within our grasp the entire time, and you let her escape? What were you thinking? Why would you do that?"

"She did not threaten us in any way, Watson. She asked if we would go out of our way to help her, and we did. That told her something about us and our character. If you have noticed, besides the fact Alfred Lord Tennyson is missing, there has been no evidence that any harm has come to him."

"But what about the fact, that she is holding Nimue prisoner in the domed pond?" I replied "What about that? That does not seem very harmless."

He nodded and answered, "Well, yes, there is that. I do not have all of the answers yet, but I am getting closer, and I am sure there is more than what meets the eye."

"That is an understatement, Holmes," I replied.

"Indeed, Watson, but right now, I suggest we be on our way, as Sir Robert will not be very pleased with his loss, and we do not know what he may do next."

Neither of us was prepared for what did happen next, as Sir Robert, his men at arms, the chess board and gardens, and his entire estate vanished into thin air. One moment they were there, and the next they were gone, leaving a grey mist drifting over the hillside. We stood alone with the Unicorn on top of a barren low hill with only the solitary stairs and platform, that Holmes had directed his chess pieces from. Nothing else remained where the rest of the estate had been just a moment earlier.

I looked at Sherlock and said, "I do not know what you were thinking he might do, but this certainly is not what I would have expected."

The Unicorn looked around and added, "Sir Wizard, when you defeat someone in chess, I must say that you do not leave anything in doubt. There is no possible chance of a rematch here. None at all. Pray tell, how did you accomplish this?"

Holmes looked at us and answered, "It is as I thought; this entire experience was an illusion. The only things that were real were the stairs and platform that I climbed to play the game. You will recall that I never had to touch a chess piece to move any of them. I just called out the moves, and they happened. Or appeared to happen… I did climb the stairs to the platform, so they had to be real, but everything else was an illusion, a projected image. As I said Watson, this entire game was just a test."

I was perplexed. "Well then, is any of this real? Will all of Faerie Realm and Camelot disappear next? What exactly is going on here?"

"My belief is that Morgan le Fey has been observing everything we do and is evaluating us."

"But why?" I exclaimed. "What is the purpose of it all? If she had wanted to stop us permanently, it appears that she could have done so many times by now. After all, she was able to entrap the Lady of the Lake, and she is also a powerful enchantress. Most of the obstacles have been challenging to some degree, I will grant you that, but you have handled them all quite admirably."

"Watson, we will discover the answer to that when we bring this odd adventure to its conclusion, and to do that we must be on our way."

Then turning to the Unicorn, he asked, "Would you happen to know the way to Somerset? That is our next destination."

The Unicorn's eyes brightened, and it nodded affirmatively answering, "Somerset, the location of Glastonbury! It is a very special place indeed. Of course, I do. Every Unicorn worth its name knows the location of Somerset. I can have us there in an instant or perhaps two for your friend Dr. Watson."

"Excellent!" said Holmes, "If you can convey us there to a safe and not too visible location that would be excellent. Then, if you please, find Merlin and bring him to us as well."

I have to say I am not sure which was less appealing, slowly making our away along the trail and encountering who knew what kind of mystical creature, challenging obstacle, or deadly trap, or another ride on the back of a Unicorn at unheard of blinding speeds, narrowly missing trees and other potential obstacles. I did not have long to consider the question, though, as the Unicorn blurred, disappeared, reappeared beneath me, and we were off.

The wind whipped wildly past us as we wove our way through a forest of trees, stone monoliths, and other objects that seemed as if they were trying to jump directly into our pathway. I held my breath and secured my grip while closing my eyes as the Unicorn raced its way there.

We came to an abrupt stop, and the Unicorn calmly stated, "You can stop strangling me now, Dr. Watson. We have arrived."

I released my grip and found myself standing in a sheltered wooded glen not far from an abbey as the Unicorn vanished to go back for Sherlock. I had previously read that Glastonbury had historical connections with Joseph of Arimathea, the Holy Grail, and even King Arthur, but I never expected to actually be here at this time in history.

In 1191, the monks at the Glastonbury Abbey claimed to have found the graves of King Arthur and Guinevere, but historians felt that it was a pious forgery to build up the renown of the abbey and increase pilgrimages to the church. Another belief connected to the area is that Joseph of Arimathea brought many relics to the location including the Holy Grail, but again, it has never been conclusively proved.

Sherlock arrived next with the Unicorn heading back to retrieve Merlin, so I asked him what he expected to find here.

Taking in the surrounding scenery, Sherlock answered, "Pixy Music showed me where the Island of Avalon is located near this vicinity, and that is where the enchanted mirror showed Nimue and Lord Tennyson to be. I asked the Unicorn to retrieve Merlin, since he is the most adept in all of the arcane and unexplainable abilities that we have witnessed on this odd little adventure. It may prove very beneficial to have him present when we do catch up to them."

"When we do indeed

Nimue will be freed."

Merlin's voice proclaimed, as he appeared astride the Unicorn. He then slid to the ground standing beside it and went on.

"You are doing well,

as I did foretell."

Sherlock turned to Merlin and asked, "What did you discover following Morgan's servant? Where did she lead you to?"

Merlin put his hands together, fluttering them like a bird answering,

"To a cage, there she went,

then a raven off was sent,

with a message this I know.

The question is, where did it go?

Into the woods it did fly

Vanishing into the sky,

but pray tell do not fear.

Its destination is quite near.

Yes, it's true, not far from here

the raven landed very near.

The answer soon will be revealed

before the morning bells have pealed."

“That is encouraging,” I responded, adding, “So what are we to do next?”

Sherlock stared silently into the drifting, curling mists that surrounded the area. Then as a shrewd smile crept across his face and an intense glow shown in his eyes, he said simply, “I have a plan.”

We gathered round Sherlock to hear what he had to say. I had previously witnessed, and even taken part in many of the grand theatrical ploys he has used to confound and capture his foes, but what he proposed was beyond my wildest imagination and would end up resounding through history itself.

He looked around, as if to see if there were any creatures in the area that could over hear us and began speaking in a whisper. “We know that Morgan le Fey has both Alfred Lord Tennyson and Nimue on the Island of Avalon. With her arcane skills and abilities, she would most likely be able to see our approach to the island no matter how cleverly disguised we are,” he nodded towards Merlin, “or how incredibly quickly we got there,” and he nodded towards the Unicorn. "We need to craft a plan that will unsuspectingly bring her to us where we can spring a trap that will contain her. Then we can safely rescue Lord Tennyson and Nimue.”

“That is an excellent idea, Holmes,” I ventured. “What did you have in mind? It would have to be something quite profound to draw her away from Avalon. Morgan knows we are on her trail, so she will be suspicious.”

He looked at me and answered, “Yes she will be. That is why it has to be something so significant, so far-reaching and absolute, that she would not even think of staying away.”

Then after a long theatrical pause, he stated clearly and coldly, “That is why King Arthur and Queen Guinevere must die.”

"What?" I exclaimed. "What on earth are you thinking, Holmes?

"That is a rather novel approach, but perhaps a bit extreme, if you ask me." The Unicorn observed.

Merlin's eyes grew bright and he broke out into a wide smile,

"Very clever, clever indeed.

Her suspicions would be freed.

She will walk into our snare

When she hears the news so rare."

Holmes motioned for me to calm myself and went on, "Not literally, of course. It will be a grand ruse. Arthur and Guinevere will drink from their goblets, and then collapse at the table. Merlin will be summoned and pronounce them dead. They will be taken away, and at that time the Unicorn will substitute replacement bodies created by Merlin as he did with Alfred Lord Tennyson when he was passing away."

Sherlock paused a moment to let it sink in and continued, "The word will be sent out that the King and Queen have died, and all those who wish to view the bodies and pay their respects should come to Camelot. It is very near Glastonbury. She will not be able to resist, and we will be there waiting for her. She would not suspect a thing. Merlin can then create the same type of containment sphere that Morgan used to entrap Nimue. Once she is contained, we can go to Avalon and rescue them."

I considered what he was saying, and asked him, "Do you think she would be fooled by the replacement bodies? If she is a sorceress almost at the level of Merlin, I would think she could somehow be able to sense if Arthur and Guinevere are still alive and in hiding somewhere. I don't think there is anywhere in

Camelot or the Faerie Realm that you could hide them without her knowing."

"That is a good point, Watson," he replied, "That is why we need to have the Unicorn bring them to London of our time and hide them in our lodgings at Baker Street."

"Where?" I exclaimed even more surprised than at his first suggestion.

"That is a very novel approach. As long as they are not subject to motion sickness, it could work quite well." The Unicorn replied thoughtfully.

Merlin again smiled broadly.

"Yea, verily, it is so.

To the future they must go.

From her vision they'll be free.

In the future she won't see."

I shook my head in wonder and asked, "You want to send the current King and Queen of Camelot to 1890's London? Just think of all the things that could go wrong. That sounds more like something from a comedic fictional novel that the American humorist, Samuel Clements, would write. Giving them knowledge from the future could end up changing the past."

Holmes answered me, "That is why they would have to stay inside our lodgings at Baker Street the entire time. The Unicorn would transport them there near instantaneously, and they would stay inside and out of sight. As long as they do not read any of my books or periodicals, they should be fine. I really doubt they would be able to read modern English anyway. Mrs. Hudson can fix them a nice meal of tea and kippers with toast and look after them. You know there is no finer host and cook in all of London than she. They will be fine."

"You are certainly right about Mrs. Hudson," I reflected. But should we send a letter of introduction along with Arthur and Guinevere? After all, how will she react to the King and Queen of Camelot showing up in our flat in 1890's London?"

The Unicorn stamped its hoof and interjected, "I am sure that arriving via Unicorn will be more than convincing enough. I need no letter of introduction."

Holmes nodded and agreed. "That is true, quite true. And Morgan will not be able to sense their presence anywhere in this time period, so she will believe them to be dead. It is the perfect plan."

Chapter. 18

A Very Odd Execution, (But certainly not literally speaking, and Mrs. Hudson sends her regards.)

We all agreed that the plan was the best approach to bringing Morgan le Fey out of hiding, as well as freeing Lord Tennyson and Nimue. It would also give us an opportunity to safely speak with Morgan in a more secure environment, and to possibly work out the differences between her and Arthur.

After conveying Merlin back to Camelot, where the wizard begin creating the duplicate bodies of Arthur and Guinevere, the Unicorn returned with King Arthur himself, so Sherlock could explain the plan in secret without anyone in Camelot listening in and discovering what was about to happen.

The Unicorn appeared and bowed regally to allow Arthur to dismount. As he stood before us and I looked upon him, I realized how the myth and legend that surrounded him may have come to be. Arthur was tall and solidly built. His flaxen hair and beard had a golden tinge to them and his eyes burned with fire. He was a vision of perfection. He wanted to lead England to what he thought was the best possible future. After dismounting, he straightened his crown, and rested one hand on the hilt of his sword, Excalibur. He was the very picture of everything that had been written about him.

The Unicorn spoke first and introduced us to him. “My King, may I introduce to you the far-seeing wizard from the future, Sherlock Holmes, and his associate Dr. Watson.”

We nodded our heads to him, and he responded courteously in kind.

“As Merlin explained to you, sir, they are here to rescue your poet and bard, Sir Alfred Lord Tennyson, and they have overcome many challenges and obstacles set by Morgan le Fey.”

"Yes, I have heard of your exploits since you have arrived. They are most impressive. Now pray tell, what is it you have in mind?”

Sherlock drew in close and quietly explained the entire plan to King Arthur. I had wondered what his reaction would be to Holmes’ outrageous scheme. He listened intently without interrupting and smiling nodded his head. He frowned at least once and laughed outright on several occasions. When Sherlock finally finished speaking, Arthur put forth his hand to Holmes, shook it and stated, “You are a brilliant strategist sir. Your plan of attack is well conceived and thought out. I would not want to oppose you on the field of battle. I agree with you entirely on this. I look forward to Alfred Lord Tennyson’s safe return and to finally dealing with Morgan le Fey once and for all.”

Holmes leaned in even closer and said a few words to Arthur that I could not hear, at which the King at first frowned quite sternly but then relaxed, and again nodded his head affirmatively. They shared a few additional words regarding when the plan should be executed, figuratively speaking that is, and how everything should take place.

I turned to the Unicorn and commented, "Sherlock Holmes and I have had some very strange and unusual adventures recently, but never did I imagine I would see him speaking with King Arthur of Camelot."

The creature responded, "I fully understand you, Dr. Watson, I never imagined I would see the King of Camelot and all of England speaking with a sorcerer from a future land of mechanical dragons and more."

The Unicorn returned King Arthur to Camelot with a promise to be back for us before everything was to begin. Merlin had earlier stated he was going to send new disguises for us to be able to blend in better with the citizens of the medieval city, but Holmes had assured him that it would not be required.

Sherlock reached under his robe and from somewhere retrieved several different items of stage makeup and alternate clothing, and after only a few moments, I would not have recognized either one of us.

"That is amazing Holmes," I observed, "You really have a gift at this."

"It is simply a matter of visual misdirection in facial features and attire when it comes to changing one's appearance, Watson. Just take what is and turn it into what isn't. In my little monograph "*An Overview on the Art and Science of Disguises, Theatrical Makeup, and Altering One's Appearance with an Emphasis on Obfuscation, and Concealing the Obvious,*" you can read more about it. It is quite fascinating actually."

Then the Unicorn returned stating, "Your disguises are truly outstanding, Sir Wizard, but your manner of speaking would still give you away instantly if not sooner. When we arrive in Camelot, it is best that you keep your conversation to a minimum, or even better, do not say a word."

It was time to begin. Holmes and I were to be conveyed to Camelot by the Unicorn and then wait in the grand hall until the plan unfolded. The chamber was typically full of people bringing petitions, supplications, requests, gifts, and various invitations to the great King Arthur and his Queen. We were certain that no one would notice us in the crowd.

We arrived in Camelot, and it was the most magnificent city I had ever beheld. The towers were tall and stately. The walls were imposing but welcoming. It was clean and bright and resplendent. It was a city of dreams come true in the most impressive way imaginable. It was golden!

After depositing us, the Unicorn vanished and was preparing to substitute the replacement bodies for the King and Queen. Holmes and I were milling about with the crowd when a peasant approached me and asked, "Good sir, have I seen you in this court before? You look very much like the stranger I met who claimed to be a traveler from a distant place called Connecticut, located somewhere in Yankee Land. His name was Hank Morgan. That is an odd name if you ask me."

I assured the stranger that I had never been to Camelot before and that my name was certainly not Hank Morgan, agreeing with him that it was a very odd name, but not as odd as 'Mark Twain'.

Just at that moment, a great commotion arose at the thrones of the King and Queen. They had raised their goblets in a toast, drank from them, and collapsed. A great cry burst forth from the crowd. People rushed about in all directions. The Knights of the Round Table gathered round their fallen leader and his Queen to protect and help them in whatever way possible, but it was clear they were not certain what to do.

"Merlin! Where is Merlin?" Sir Lancelot exclaimed above the noise.

"I am here.

Help is near.

Silence all

in this hall."

Merlin's voice echoed over the crowds.

Merlin suddenly appeared standing near the throne extending his arms upwards in a gesture commanding them to be still. Then signaling to the knights, he called for Arthur and Guinevere to be carried into the Kings private chambers, and for everyone to leave the room so he could examine them.

The citizens of Camelot were fearful and murmuring quietly. How could this possibly have happened? Who could have been responsible? What was to happen next? What was the fate of Arthur's Camelot? I looked at Holmes and nodded. So far, it was going exactly according to his plan.

After a considerable period of time, the door to the King's chambers opened, and Merlin entered the grand hall with a sad expression on his face. The room fell silent as they waited for his announcement.

He looked out at them and stated simply,

"It is as we feared and dread,

The great King Arthur and his Queen are dead."

He turned and spoke to Lancelot and returned to the King's chambers.

As bells outside began to toll the sad news, Lancelot raised his voice to quiet the crowd and stated that the King and Queen's bodies would be returned to the hall shortly for the citizens of Camelot to pay their respects, and that Arthur and Guinevere would be buried late that afternoon. Messages of the tragedy that had befallen Camelot were being sent across the kingdom as he spoke, and the Knights of the Round Table had vowed that they would not rest until the guilty party was found and punished. Camelot would prevail.

Then I heard the Unicorn's voice coming from behind a nearby tapestry, "Mrs. Hudson sends her regards to the both of you. She is honored by her guests and most happy to receive them, but she wishes you would have given her more advance notice to straighten things up and look her best. After all, how often does one entertain the King and Queen of Camelot?"

Chapter 19.

A Very Odd Turn of Events, (I would imagine Camelot never saw it coming.)

I smiled at Mrs. Hudson's message and breathed a sigh of relief to hear that Arthur and Guinevere had safely arrived at Baker Street. I wondered, what they must be thinking of modern England. What did they think of tea and toast with kippers? It would certainly be a strange experience for them. For that matter, what must they think of Sherlock's flat, which is possibly by far the strangest place in all of London?

After a short period of waiting, the doors of the King's chambers opened, a trumpet was sounded to call for silence. The bodies of King Arthur and Queen Guinevere being carried upon palls of purple satin, accompanied by two columns of Knights of the Round Table were brought into the center of the grand hall.

Leading the procession was Sir Lancelot doing his best to avoid weeping visibly. Accompanying the group was a fair haired young boy dressed in a commoners clothing who silently seated himself on the floor between the two bodies after they had been set in place for mourners to pay their respects. I had never seen the lad before, but there was something very familiar about his eyes. His face was nondescript and plain, but his eyes were both far away and deeply piercing at the same time. They had a clarity that reminded me of something or someone which I just could not place at that time.

Sir Lancelot then spoke to the hushed crowd. "People of Camelot, England's greatest King, Arthur Pendragon, and his beloved Queen Guinevere lie here before you. They have passed on from this life, but their vision of chivalry and justice for everyone is still alive. Let us all pay our respects to them at this sad and tragic time. And let us not forget the wonder of Camelot that King Arthur created with his unequalled strength and skill in battle. Let us not forget the matchless beauty his glorious Queen Guinevere graced us with. There was none fairer throughout the land, and her laughter was the sunshine that made flowers grow and coaxed the blossoms from the trees.

"As Arthur's Right Hand, his first knight, his greatest knight, his best friend, and as the Queen's own champion and escort in her travels, my heart grieves sorely. I share your sorrow a hundred times over. I loved them both dearly. But they are gone. Now let us, with our every breath, go forth to your fields and mills, to your farms and market places, on the streets and in your homes, in all that we do, let us keep King Arthur's glorious dream that is Camelot alive."

Even knowing as I did that Arthur and Guinevere were still alive, I could not help but be moved by Sir Lancelot's heartfelt words, and a tear crept into my eye. He paused as the crowd cheered and applauded his eulogy. One could see him struggling to maintain his composure.

"The King's counselor, Merlin the Enchanter, has already discovered who is responsible for this cowardly act, and is off and away in pursuit of the guilty ones now as I speak to you. As Camelot's greatest knight, I promise you, when he returns with them; they shall be brought to swift and final justice." "But who shall lead us?" a voice cried out.

"Yes, who shall be our king?" another voice echoed.

"A king! A king!" the crowd took up the chant.

Sir Lancelot raised his sword aloft to quiet the group and assured them, "By the Sword of Lancelot, I promise you that will be determined soon. At this time let us in silence pay our respects to our great and beloved leader and his dear sweet Guinevere."

While the Round Table Knights organized the people into orderly lines to pass before their departed King and Queen, Sherlock and I watched the crowd carefully for any sign of Morgan le Fey. I wondered what Sir Lancelot had meant when he said that Merlin was off and away in pursuit of the assassin. According to Sherlock's plan, Merlin was supposed to be right here, right now, ready to capture Morgan when she appeared, but he was nowhere to be seen. Would he actually be gone now, when he was needed the most? If Morgan le Fey did turn up, what would we do? We had no defense against someone of her skills or power. This was not some common street criminal or cut-purse of London that we were dealing with but one the most well-known and feared sorceresses of myth and legend: except in this place and time, she was very much alive, authentic, and very dangerous. Possibly even deadly.

I glanced nervously towards Holmes, but he said nothing. He only nodded back towards the direction of the line of mourners to indicate that I should keep watching and be diligent. All we could do is continue observing and see what became of this day.

Possibly an hour had passed when an elderly lady using a walking stick neared the front of the line. In the same manner that the mysterious young boy, sitting on the floor between Arthur and Guinevere still perplexed me, something about this odd, old woman was somehow familiar. At the very moment she approached them, it suddenly dawned on me. She was the elderly lady who had asked for Sherlock's help freeing her son from Sir Robert in the chess match! She was Morgan le Fey! She was here!

I glanced at Sherlock, trying desperately to get his attention, but he was already aware. He pointed directly at her, and in a loud, clear voice yelled out, "Morgan le Fey!"

Several things happened almost simultaneously, as the old woman blurred and slowly morphed into the younger version of herself, which we had seen in the projected image before she had turned into a bee. Then the young boy that had been sitting silent and motionless the entire time boldly stood up, pointing straight at her, and spoke in a rhyming, ancient language that sounded like Old Celtic. A shimmering, iridescent sphere of energy appeared and began to form itself around Morgan le Fe. With each word of the boy's incantation, the luminous glowing tendrils weaving back and forth grew larger and stronger by the second. Like the tentacles of a nebulous ghostly octopus flowing in and out and all around her, they slowly coalesced into a globe of pure energy that securely entrapped her. At that point, while still maintaining his stance with his hands pointed at the sphere, the young boy began to grow and age rapidly. I watched in astonishment as in less than a minute he aged into a grey haired, bearded old man who was none other than Merlin the Enchanter himself.

Morgan le Fey was absolutely furious and with both arms outstretched wove her hands in a circular pattern while speaking in a language that sounded similar to that in which Merlin had cast his spell. The sphere shuddered and glistened as it resisted her magical attacks. I wondered whether or not Merlin's efforts would hold and feared what would happen if they did not. While Merlin stood his ground in front of her, Sherlock approached the two, removed his improvised violin and bow from beneath his robe, and calmly began playing. An ethereal, haunting refrain that I immediately recognized as Pixy Music, joined his, and the two of them harmonized and interwove melodiously as Merlin's sphere glowed brighter than possible. His energy globe positively radiated strength and security. Though it was near invisible, like a vague shimmering curtain, it was stronger than the very walls of Camelot. As he played, Sherlock spoke to Morgan calmly, "We mean you no harm, Lady Morgan. This sphere is only in place to prevent you from hurting anyone."

"I will show you harm!" She screamed as she turned, raised one hand, pointed it directly at Holmes and spoke once more in that ancient tongue. A bolt of lightning burst against the inner surface of the radiantly glowing globe, crackling loudly, but it held strong, and Sherlock continued to play without flinching, even though he stood mere inches from its outer surface.

"As I was saying, we mean you no harm, as I truly believe you really do not mean to hurt us. You only wish to save and preserve the ancient realm of the Faerie Folk. That is a noble gesture."

She had been just about to cast another spell when she abruptly paused. She gazed at him curiously and intently. She studied him for what seemed like an eternity and finally asked, "What exactly do you mean, Wizard of Words? I observed how you cleverly used distracting utterance to defeat the chess master. Are you using the same tricks on me? Be aware! I can see though them, you know."

While maintaining his musical interlude, he responded, "If you can see through them, Lady Morgan, then you know that I am telling you the truth. You tested my character back on the hill, and I was willing to go out of my way and deviate from our path to aid a helpless old woman. My words during the chess match were my way of ending it quickly and painlessly, to return the captive son to an old woman and to allow us to resume our task of returning Lord Tennyson to King Arthur."

While he was speaking to her, I had noticed that the Unicorn had again disappeared but did not give it any thought. This part of Sherlock's plan had worked brilliantly! Morgan le Fey was captured and securely subdued in Merlin's spell of containment.

The Knights of the Round Table, however, had all at once drawn their swords, but in the resulting confusion and clamor of the crowd, they were not certain what to do or who to point them at. Arthur's knights had stepped back, and the people had scattered in all directions when they realized that it was Morgan le Fey and Merlin who were combating each other. However, when Holmes began playing his improvised violin, with Pixy Music accompanying him, and then Sherlock calmly and peaceably speaking to Morgan, and she actually responded to him in a civil way as well, they all stopped in surprise and listened.

"Yes," she replied, "you do show a most unique character, more understanding and considerate than my poor half-brother. You observe and see things more clearly than he ever did. It was not I that killed them, you know. In truth I am most saddened that he is gone."

Sherlock smiled and replied, "If that is true, Lady Morgan, then you will be pleased to learn that they are not, in fact, gone."

As he spoke, an incredibly bright, silver glow that could only have been the spiral horn of light of the Unicorn returning filled the chamber as King Arthur and Queen Guinevere, astride the majestic white creature, suddenly appeared on the raised platform in front of the thrones. The entire hall fell silent as they beheld their King and Queen alive and standing before them.

Then pandemonium broke out as the crowd began to cheer,

"Arthur! Arthur! Long live King Arthur! Long live Queen Guinevere! Long live Camelot!"

Chapter 20.

A Very Odd but Pleasing Change in Circumstances, (And we avoid the Lair of the Lake Dragon.)

Like everyone else, Morgan le Fey was astonished to see them returned alive and well. “Arthur how is it possible, brother?” She asked. “I could not sense the spirit of you or your Queen still present anywhere in Camelot, or in the Faerie Realm. You were nowhere to be found. I was certain that you both had indeed passed away. I was truly saddened to hear the news. Yes, I have stood against you and vexed your efforts with Camelot, but it was only because you would not honor the ancient traditions of the Faerie Folk. And I was rather angry with Merlin, but I have gotten over that.”

Arthur held up one hand to firmly but courteously interrupt the conversation. “Morgan my sister, pray tell, we will hold these words for a moment while two others of us who are most important to how this adventure concludes, but are not with us here right now, are retrieved."

Then turning to Holmes and I, he asked, "Sherlock Holmes, may I once again call upon you and your associate, Dr. Watson, with the gracious assistance of this most noble Unicorn, to retrieve our missing comrades?"

Sherlock reluctantly stopped his playing and returned his improvised violin to the recesses of his robe responding, "It would be an honor, Your Majesty."

Although Holmes had stopped playing, the enchanting, haunting sounds of Pixy Music's melody still drifted and echoed through the chamber, filling everyone with a sense of serenity. I could tell that Sherlock, while pleased to assist the King in bringing this very odd adventure to a close, was saddened to end this harmonious interlude with Pixy Music. He had truly believed that he would actually meet her before this adventure was concluded. Now it seemed to be coming to an end, and it had not yet happened. Yes, together their song had helped Merlin capture and contain Morgan le Fey, but now it was time to retrieve Nimue and Lord Tennyson, and soon this adventure would be over. Would he never realize his heart's desire? I felt truly sorry for him.

The Unicorn then blurred and vanished from the raised platform and appeared next to Sherlock asking, "Shall we be off to the mystical Island of Avalon? I believe that Nimue and Sir Alfred Lord Tennyson are waiting there for us, and you, Sir Wizard, said that Pixy Music had shown you the way to Avalon.

However, I must request that I carry only one of you at a time. Conveying both King Arthur and Guinevere together, was a very special and rare circumstance and not one that I would choose to repeat, especially considering the nature of the route we must take this time to safely travel there. I assure you, you will understand more fully after we arrive."

Holmes sighed and stated that the requested traveling accommodations were more than acceptable, and with that, he and the Unicorn blurred and disappeared. I wondered how we would free Nimue from the pond, as the enchanted Mirror's image had shown a similar sphere over her, but then I realized that if Morgan was trapped in a sphere herself, then perhaps the one that held Nimue would no longer be effective. I would find out soon enough, as the Unicorn materialized beneath me, and I wrapped my arms frantically around its neck. Everything surrounding me became a multi-hued kaleidoscope like blur of light, color, and objects flying by at less than a hair's-breadth away, with the Unicorn racing like a wind-born spirit through field and forest, over hills and valleys, and astonishingly enough, what seemed like, over the surface of the water as well. I closed my eyes and cringed.

We came to a stop near the cave entrance we had seen in the image shown to us by the magic Mirror, and the Unicorn turned its head to whisper in my ear, "You can stop strangling me, Dr. Watson. We are here and not impaled on any tree trunks. And yes, you did see correctly. I can indeed run across the very surface of the water as well. It is all a matter of moving fast enough. If I had slowed down in the slightest, we would be visiting the Lair of the Lake Dragon right now, instead of basking in the glory of Avalon, thanks to the incomparable speed and swiftness of the Unicorn."

I thought for a moment and tried to imagine what visiting the Lair of the Lake Dragon might be like and decided that in truth, I did not want to imagine it, much less visit such a foreboding sounding place. Instead, I gazed wide eyed in awe at the island that surrounded us. The Unicorn's brief description of "the glory of Avalon" was an understatement. The island seemed to capture all of the mystical enchantment and tranquility of the Faerie Realm, as well as the promise, wonder and magnificence that was Camelot, but in a way that was far greater than both of them combined could ever hope to be. There was a sense of peace and serenity that permeated the very air we breathed. The soft fragrant scent of lilacs danced sweetly in the background, while a delicate wisp of rose played hide and seek. There was no strife or danger here, just an overwhelming sense of eternal endless calm. I understood why Avalon was considered a holy place, a place of rest and healing. I realized why anyone who had ever been there would never want to leave. It was far beyond what mere words could possibly describe.

I looked towards the cave entrance and there sat Alfred Lord Tennyson, England's greatest poet, and Nimue, the mystical Lady of the Lake, calmly engaged in a conversation with Sherlock. I had been correct in thinking that with Morgan subdued, she could not continue to hold Nimue prisoner. In truth, it had appeared that before we left Camelot, her animosity had subsided considerably. Perhaps this entire conflict between her and Arthur would be resolved. Nimue was no longer confined in the pool and appeared to be unharmed and in good health.

Alfred Lord Tennyson also seemed to be well. His greying dark beard and long hair looked no different than in the last photograph I had seen of him taken just before he was spirited away to Camelot at the time that he had supposedly passed away. He did appear rather tired and haggard, probably as a result of his recent travels, but it was still as if he had not aged at all.

Holmes had introduced ourselves and very briefly explained to both of them everything that had transpired and that we were there to safely return them to Camelot where Merlin and King Arthur were waiting for them and anxiously looking forward to their arrival. He also assured them that Morgan le Fey was no longer a danger to them. Nimue sighed in obvious relief and thanked Sherlock profusely saying she would be most happy to be reunited with Merlin, but Lord Tennyson seemed somewhat quiet and withdrawn. All he said in response was, "Well then, let us be on our way… All things must pass."

As we prepared to return and explained to them that the Unicorn would quickly convey each of us back to Camelot individually, the strangest and most wonderful thing occurred. The ethereal enchanting sound of Pixy Music began to emanate faintly from inside the cave. It was almost a whisper at first but gradually increased in volume until it was unmistakable. There was no question at all. It was without a doubt the very song I had first heard in Wonderland, then again on board the Nautilus, and yet again several times here in Camelot when Sherlock played his improvised violin. It was the mesmerizing and melodious song of the third Guardian Queen of Avalon, Pixy Music.

Sherlock stood entranced at the sound of it. He had not been playing his makeshift violin at the time it began, so I am certain it had come as a surprise to both of us. In addition to the celestial music, a golden warm and glowing light began to emanate from within the cave. I had no idea what to do, but Holmes, surrendering unequivocally, as if in a trance slowly walked towards the cave entrance. As he neared the opening, I looked further into the cavern, and it was there that I too finally saw her.

She sat upon a finely carved chair in the center of a dazzling array of quartz crystals that covered the surface of the cave walls and ceiling reflecting a rainbow of shimmering light. Two furry wolves, a reddish-brown coyote with amber colored eyes, some large grey geese, and a few other smaller wild creatures were curled up together, peacefully resting on the ground surrounding her.

As Holmes had stated previously, her exquisiteness was beyond description. I will attempt to elucidate her appearance, although I am certain that words will most assuredly fail me. Dressed in the most delicate of fine lilac colored lace, she was playing a harp of varnished cherry wood. Her graceful fingers lightly danced upon the strings creating the most exquisite music. There were daisies woven into her long dark hair. Bright, sparkling hazel eyes were her most captivating feature. They were a deep crystal pool of liquid aquamarine. One could dive into and lose themselves in her eyes forever. If her eyes were captivating, then her smile was beguiling and tempting. One felt all sense of hesitation or reserve melt away, and one wanted nothing more than to remain endlessly in her presence for all eternity. Now at last I understood why Sherlock had said that for him, there could be no other, why he was so utterly mesmerized by her.

She stopped playing the harp and beckoned him to come closer to her. He drew nearer and stood in total silence. The wild creatures paid no attention to him except perhaps the coyote that raised its head, yawned, and then rested it directly upon Holmes' foot. I only heard a portion of their conversation, and it was heartbreaking. As a Guardian Queen of Avalon, she could not leave this mystical land. She was a part of it, and the island was also one with her. A common spirit dwelled within both of them. She could continue to communicate across worlds and realms, and share musical interludes with Sherlock, but she could never leave. And similarly, she would not ask Sherlock Holmes to give up his life in London of our era. He had done a brilliant job of finding Lord Tennyson, rescuing Nimue and even resolving the conflict between Arthur and Morgan le Fey, but it was not yet his time to be here in Avalon. It is foretold that there is much he has to complete in his London before he could again grace the shores of the mystical isle. He has a great destiny before him, and he must return to it.

They continued speaking softly for an interval, gently reaching out and clasping both of their hands together, embracing warmly, and then she vanished taking the iridescent light with her. The geese other smaller creatures had followed her to wherever she had gone, but the two wolves and coyote remained behind undisturbed. Holmes looked down at the resting coyote who was apparently quite comfortable and seemed to have no intention of removing its head from atop of Sherlock's shoe. Holmes turned to me, sighed and said, "Watson, it is time we went home."

Chapter 21.

A Very Odd Round Table Gathering, (And we slightly alter the path of history.)

I will spare the reader the vivid details of yet another highspeed Unicorn ride, as someone may be reading this after a meal. Suffice it to say, we did arrive safely back in Camelot in less than an instant, and I do recall hearing Sherlock commenting, “That was most invigorating.”

Alfred Lord Tennyson’s opinion was, “Remarkable, simply remarkable! I must capture this experience in a poem.”

Nimue observed. “That was beautiful! What a breathtaking experience. I had no idea Unicorns were as swift as the wind. When can we do this again?”

My personal comments on arrival are really not important, but the Unicorn replied that while it may have been rather close, we did not actually hit the tree.

I will mention to those interested, that if there is any measurable dimension less than a hair's-breadth, which, if you would like to know, is defined as an infinitesimally small distance, it was considerably less than that.

When we were all present, the first thing I noticed is that Morgan le Fey was no longer restrained in the energy sphere but was standing calmly and talking to King Arthur and Merlin.

The second thing I observed is that Merlin was no longer speaking in rhyme. I pointed out both observations to Holmes, and his response was most typical. "Well, of course, Watson, I would have been very surprised had it not been the case. We needed to create an event that would break their barriers and bring them together to speak to each other. There is no real evil in either of them. I saw that in all of the obstacles she placed before us. We were never in any great danger from any one of them. They were actually rather creative, if I do say so. I was thinking of compiling her challenges and adding some of my own creative skill and character tests into a short paper and calling it. *"A Straight Forward Guide to Developing Challenging Tests of Skill, Character, Practical Thought Process, and Fortitude with an Emphasis on Dealing with the Logically Impossible, but Nevertheless, Still Right There in Front of You.*" The title may still need some modification though. I will have to work on that." He paused to reflectively consider the future monograph and then continued speaking. "Regarding Merlin's speech returning to normal, it is quite obvious. If you recall Morgan mentioned that she was angry at him, but she is over that now."

"But what does that have to do with his rhyming?" I asked.

"Do you remember the Unicorn mentioned that in her anger and jealousy, Morgan le Fey had put an enchantment on him to prevent him from speaking to Nimue? Merlin of course found a way around it by speaking in rhyme, something about the heart of a poet and love. Since she no longer desires Merlin and is over her anger, there is no further reason for her to keep the enchantment on him."

Wondering aloud I asked, "Who do you think she is in love with now?"

Sherlock looked at me incredulously and replied, "Really Watson. It should be obvious. It is not so much love, as it is a common, deep shared connection to Camelot and the Faerie Realm. Two hearts beating as one to keep both realms alive. Her new desire is Sir Alfred Lord Tennyson."

"What?" I exclaimed. "He is…"

"Yes, I know. He is old. So was Merlin, and he was her mentor, teacher and guide." He interrupted. "He awoke in her a love for the Faerie Realm. It is not surprising she had feelings for him. She eventually learned everything she could from Merlin and also realized Merlin and Nimue share a different kind of love, so now she desires another with a meaningful association to Camelot. There is no one other than Alfred Lord Tennyson that is so connected to Camelot and now the Fairie Realm. That is why he was so quiet and reserved when we mentioned that there was no further concern or fear regarding Morgan le Fey. It should be obvious that he shares her feelings as well."

I was about to reply when King Arthur signaled us to follow him into the royal hall where the Round Table was located. I waited with my comment and entered the great hall with the rest of our companions. The Knights of the Round Table trooped in behind us and dispersed to their seats. The room was large but not overly so. Colorful tapestries depicting many different scenes decorated the walls with swords, shields, and other medieval weapons mounted on plaques in between them. The famous Round Table of Camelot took up most of the floor space in the room, and it was an emotional experience to behold a representation of such power and legend. The mood was much more joyous and celebratory than earlier. And when we were all settled, Arthur began to speak. “Friends, I thank you for joining me here at the Round Table of Camelot. We have gathered here many times around this symbol of unity and equality among my knights, but I was blind not to realize that my vision should apply to other creatures as well. I have learned much this day, and I want to share it with you."

Morgan Le Fey then began to speak and echoed his sentiment. "I too have realized a great deal and have come to terms with my half-brother. In the past, I stood against Arthur because he did not accept the importance of the Faerie Folk. He felt that the world was changing, and he wanted to bring Camelot and England into this new world excluding the realm of the Faerie.”

"That is true." continued Arthur. "I did not believe that there was a place for magic, or the Faerie Folk, but today I discovered otherwise. Sherlock Holmes crafted a plan to convince everyone in the realm I had passed away in order to bring my half-sister Morgan out of hiding.”

I leaned over to Holmes and asked, “Is that before or after she tried to kill you with a lightning bolt?” but he ignored me.

“But to convince her that I was dead, I could not be anywhere in Camelot as she is able to sense my presence with her arcane skills. Wizard Holmes made it possible for me to visit the land and time that he hails from. It is an entirely different world than Camelot. What I saw in the brief time I was there, showed me that it is a sadder place, a less golden place. It is place with no mystical creatures, no Faerie Folk, no magic at all. If that time is coming and that is what the world eventually becomes, we may not be able to stop it. But while I still draw breath, the Faerie Folk will be a part of Camelot.”

He extended a hand to Morgan le Fey which she graciously received, and they shook hands. Their conflict had ended.

Morgan then resumed speaking and pointed at me. “I too had crafted a grand and multi-layered plan which involved you the scribe, Dr. Watson. While I am not as gifted in seeing the future as Merlin, I did discover that, as his scribe, you collect and record the exploits of your Wizard friend. Your ballads and stories are shared throughout your world, just as the great bard and poet Sir Tennyson’s tales of King Arthur and Camelot are widely shared in your time. My plan was to bring the Wizard and you here, so you could see, experience firsthand, and record the wonder and splendor of the Faerie Realm and the Faerie Folk before we all vanish. Then history will be aware of us and understand that we really did exist. Each of your little adventures led to another, each sharing a different part of this magical realm. That is why Sir Tennyson agreed to come with me. The poet is so important to Arthur and Camelot that Merlin would defy time itself to bring the great Sherlock Holmes and his scribe to Camelot to find him.

Your story of this adventure, Dr. Watson, will keep us alive long after Camelot is gone.”

I did not know what to say. The entire disappearance of Sir Alfred Lord Tennyson was simply a ruse to get me here to witness and record the Faerie Realm before it vanished. Sherlock was just the key to making it happen.

Holmes leaned over to me and stated, “I told you that you had an important role in this game.”

I was dumbfounded. Never before had one of our adventures turned out like this. I could not imagine what would happen next. King Arthur then stood up and answered that question and also altered the course of history for several hundred years.

"Friends, as a part of the Wizard's plan, my counselor, Merlin the Enchanter, created replacement bodies for my Queen and I to convince you that we indeed had passed away today. I am sorry for the grief it caused you, my loyal knights, but it was necessary. Now that you are aware of the truth and of the new life of Camelot, I declare that we shall bury these duplicate bodies. The old Arthur has died. Let him be buried and let there be new life. We shall bury them south of the Lady Chapel near the Abbey Church."

I nearly choked when I heard that and whispered to Sherlock, "Holmes, do you realize that Arthur is placing the duplicate bodies exactly where the Glastonbury monks will find them in 1191? For several hundred years, this was believed to be the very resting place of King Arthur and Guinevere. It was centuries later that historians declared the bodies to be a hoax. Your little scheme to capture Morgan is echoing loudly through history."

Holmes waved his hand dismissively and answered, "Yes, yes, and you are going to record and publish as truth a Sherlock Holmes adventure with Pixies, Gnomes, Dragons, a Unicorn, Merlin, Morgan le Fey, The Lady of the Lake, Guinevere, and King Arthur himself. Tell me Watson, is there any real difference?"

Chapter 22.

A Very Odd Conclusion, (And believe it or not, Sherlock gets outwitted by a Unicorn.)

This was almost more than even I could believe and having accompanied Sherlock Holmes in so many adventures, I have witnessed a vast amount of the strange and unusual. Yet there I was sitting at the legendary Round Table of Camelot with King Arthur and Guinevere. The infamous Morgan le Fey was pleasantly sitting close to England's former Poet Laureate, Sir Alfred Lord Tennyson. Merlin was gazing starry eyed at Nimue, the Lady of the Lake, and all of this had come about because one of the most famous sorceresses of myth and legend wanted me to witness and record it all.

Sherlock leaned over to me again and whispered, "I promise you Watson, you will never publish this adventure while I am still alive. You know my feelings on magic and the unexplainable. I have a reputation to uphold. If you print this, we will have a whole host of literary characters knocking on our door. We could have Dracula show up looking for Bram Stoker, and Frankenstein, his monster, or both of them looking for Mary Shelly. We could even end up with Dorian Grey looking for that Oscar Wilde fellow, and who knows how that would turn out."

I looked at him and realizing he was right agreed. "You are probably correct, Holmes. Not to mention what patient would ever visit a doctor who believes Faerie Land is real?"

The Unicorn who had been standing behind us interrupted, "I don't know about that, Dr. Watson. It could do wonders for you to bring in children and younger patients. It could possibly even increase your business. If you painted scenes of the Faerie Realm on the wall of your office, you might become known as 'The Unicorn Doctor.' Not that Unicorns ever need doctoring. We just focus our energy inwards and heal ourselves. Any Unicorn worthy of its name can do that."

Sherlock turned and faced the Unicorn saying, "That is the second time you have used the expression, 'Any Unicorn worthy of its name,' yet during this entire adventure, you have never once mentioned *your* name. Why is that?"

The creature reflected quietly for a brief period and then answered, "You are most observant, Sir Wizard. I am on a quest, and I have vowed never again to utter my name until it is successfully completed."

"Really?" I responded. "May I ask, what is the nature of your quest?"

The Unicorn gazed into the distance. "Everyone knows the story of "*The Last Unicorn*." Every Unicorn worthy of its name can recite it by memory. It is actually quite well known in your own world, and I am certain it will someday be written down. I am trying to learn the secret story of the very first of my kind, "*The First Unicorn.*" No one has ever discovered it, and it has remained the greatest unsolved mystery of all time. It would be a significant challenge even for you, Sir Wizard."

Sherlock considered the creature's statement and replied scoffing, "I am not so certain about that. There is very little that, with my skills in observation and deduction, I cannot perceive. Why I could most likely solve your little puzzle in my spare time between cases, if I so desired."

The Unicorn's expression warmed considerably and even its horn was glowing brighter. "I sincerely thank you! That is most kind and generous of you, Sir Wizard. It has been a great honor to accompany you and assist in your quest to rescue Lord Tennyson, and help you resolve the matter between King Arthur and Morgan le Fey. It will be even more of an honor to have your assistance in my quest. Now I am certain the mystery will be solved. I must go and tell Sir Percival that I may be away for an extended period of time."

The Unicorn happily cantered off in search of Sir Percival, and I looked at Sherlock while shaking my head. "Holmes! Did the smartest detective of all time and one of the most intelligent and logical people I have ever met just get talked into assisting an imaginary, nonexistent, mystical, creature solve the secret lost mystery behind the first of its kind? What a great adventure story that will make! *"Sherlock Holmes and the Mystery of the First Unicorn*!" I can see it now."

Holmes said nothing except, "Watson, do not even think of it. I did preface my offer with; I could solve it in my spare time *between* cases."

I frowned and said, "Yes you did, Holmes. You certainly did. I imagine we will be quite busy with other cases when we are back in London. I am sure the Unicorn will understand. After all, the swiftness of the creature was only a small part of your success."

Sherlock gave me a somewhat incredulous look and replied, "Watson, you have learned more clever trickery from me than you have let on. Okay, "*The Mystery of the First Unicorn*" it is." And he walked off muttering under his breath.

My attention turned back to the ongoing proceedings. I saw that all was still going well. Arthur, Lancelot, and Guinevere were conversing with Merlin and Nimue on burial arrangements for the duplicate bodies, while Morgan and Lord Tennyson were deep in conversation on the true symbolic meaning of Camelot as it pertained to the society of Victorian England and how she could not possibly fathom the significance unless she witnessed it for herself.

The idea of bringing Morgan le Fey to modern day England was inconceivable to me, and I shuddered at the thought of it.

I focused on the other conversation to hear Guinevere saying that a grand procession would be fitting, while Arthur said that a simple burial just placing the bodies in an oak trunk with a lead cross to identify them would be sufficient.

Merlin stood up and stated that he would inscribe the cross in Latin with the proclamation: "Hic jacet sepultus inclitus Rex Arthurus in insula Avalonia," meaning "Here lies interred the famous King Arthur on the Isle of Avalon."

Nimue pointed out that the bodies were not actually being buried on the Isle of Avalon, and he may want to reconsider. Merlin simply replied, "Satis." Which I believe is Latin for "Close enough!"

He gently took Nimue's hand and the two of them left the room to take care of the arrangements.

King Arthur called Sherlock and me back together, approached us, and thanked us profusely for our help in finding and returning Lord Tennyson. He was even more appreciative to Sherlock for having made it possible for Morgan le Fey and Arthur to resolve their differences.

He did want to let us know that while our England seemed like a much sadder and empty place, Mrs. Hudson had been the perfect host and that she was just delightful. Almost whispering, he also mentioned that if we ever, for any reason, returned to Camelot, could we please bring along with us a good supply of Mrs. Hudson's Earl Grey Tea? He would reward us richly. After trying it while he was there, he had been saddened to learn that tea would not be brought to England for several hundred years. He promised us that if we did bring a quantity back with us it would remain a solemn secret, as King Arthur would never even think of doing something that could alter the course of history.

Holmes and I looked at each other and smiled.

The Unicorn reappeared and asked if we were ready to begin our journey, as we had to first make our way to Stonehenge, then through the portal, and finally back to Baker Street. We said that at last we were, and we fondly bid our farewells to everyone.

Nimue thanked us again for freeing her and reuniting her with Merlin. Morgan also expressed her gratitude and stated that should Sherlock ever want to play a really challenging game of chess, she was always ready and could easily checkmate Sherlock in less than four moves.

Holmes replied, "The only way that could ever happen is if I was asleep, and even then, it would be difficult if not impossible."

In addition, Morgan stated that she was looking forward to reading my account of our brief visit to the Faerie Realm.

"I cannot wait to see "*Sherlock Holmes and the Round Table Adventure*" in print" she stated.

Holmes leaned close to me and whispered, "She has a better chance of beating me in chess than that happening in my life time."

As we were about to leave, a faint echo of Pixy Music's haunting, ethereal melody whispered softly nearby. Sherlock closed his eyes, breathed in deeply, exhaled slowly, and said, "Farewell my dear Pixy Music."

And we were off.

Chapter 23.

A Very Odd Return, (But actually not that surprising when you think about it.

We made it safely back through the Stonehenge portal and to 221-B Baker Street without any overly terrifying near misses; that is, beyond the normal ones that are a part of traveling via Unicorn. It was good to be home again in our familiar lodgings, but the clattering noise and pervasive smells of London seemed odd after the calm serenity of Camelot and the Faerie Realm.

When we arrived outside our flat, Homes asked if, as we had passed by the concert hall, I had noticed the advertisement for the classical music performance that was scheduled for that evening. I responded, "No. What is being performed? Anything interesting?"

With a wry grin, Sherlock answered, *"The Sorcerer's Apprentice."* Would you care to attend?"

I ignored him and did not say a word.

I did notice one slightly odd change though. The outside door of 221-B had a new sign affixed to it. In bold letters it read:

"Mrs. Hudson's Lodgings

Recommended by Royalty."

And in smaller print beneath:

"Unicorns Welcome!!"

And in even smaller print beneath that:

"Please wipe your feet!"

The Unicorn turned to Sherlock and said, "Well, my dear Sir Wizard, we have safely returned from Camelot to your lodgings. When do we begin?"

Coming Soon from MX Publishing:

Sherlock Holmes and the Mystery of the First Unicorn

Shrouded in the misty halls of history, lies the greatest mystery of all time. What ever became of the very first Unicorn?

After resolving the disappearance of Alfred Lord Tennyson in the court of King Arthur, Sherlock Holmes agrees to help solve this timeless enigma, (in between other cases, of course,) and along the way encounters an eccentric inventor, a Scotsman whose lochs have somehow vanished, a mysterious lady in search of a missing journal, a secret society involved in Alchemy, Astronomy, and Horology, and more.

Each new case that crosses the threshold of 221B, Baker Street, leads Holmes and Watson deeper into a labyrinth of questions and answers, that all weave together like the threads of a medieval tapestry revealing a picture and a solution that none of them could have ever imagined.

Also from MX Publishing

MX Publishing is the world's largest specialist Sherlock Holmes publisher, with over a hundred titles and fifty authors creating the latest in Sherlock Holmes fiction and non-fiction.

From traditional short stories and novels to travel guides and quiz books, MX Publishing cater for all Holmes fans.

The collection includes leading titles such as *Benedict Cumberbatch In Transition* and *The Norwood Author* which won the 2011 Howlett Award (Sherlock Holmes Book of the Year).

MX Publishing also has one of the largest communities of Holmes fans on Facebook with regular contributions from dozens of authors.

www.mxpublishing.com

Also from MX Publishing

Our bestselling books are our short story collections;

'Lost Stories of Sherlock Holmes' , 'The Outstanding Mysteries of Sherlock Holmes', The Papers of Sherlock Holmes Volume 1 and 2, 'Untold Adventures of Sherlock Holmes' (and the sequel 'Studies in Legacy) and 'Sherlock Holmes in Pursuit', 'The Cotswold Werewolf and Other Stories of Sherlock Holmes' – and many more……

www.mxpublishing.com

Also from MX Publishing

"Phil Growick's, 'The Secret Journal of Dr Watson', is an adventure which takes place in the latter part of Holmes and Watson's lives. They are entrusted by HM Government (although not officially) and the King no less to undertake a rescue mission to save the Romanovs, Russia's Royal family from a grisly end at the hand of the Bolsheviks. There is a wealth of detail in the story but not so much as would detract us from the enjoyment of the story. Espionage, counter-espionage, the ace of spies himself, double-agents, double-crossers...all these flit across the pages in a realistic and exciting way. All the characters are extremely welldrawn and Mr Growick, most importantly, does not falter with a very good ear for Holmesian dialogue indeed. Highly recommended. A five-star effort."
The Baker Street Society

www.mxpublishing.com

Also from MX Publishing

The American Literati Series

The Final Page of Baker Street
The Baron of Brede Place
Seventeen Minutes To Baker Street

"The really amazing thing about this book is the author's ability to call up the 'essence' of both the Baker Street 'digs' of Holmes and Watson as well as that of the 'mean streets' of Marlowe's Los Angeles. Although none of the action takes place in either place, Holmes and Watson share a sense of camaraderie and self-confidence in facing threats and problems that also pervades many of the later tales in the Canon. Following their conversations and banter is a return to Edwardian England and its certainties and hope for the future. This is definitely the world before The Great War."
Philip K Jones

Also from MX Publishing

The Detective and The Woman Series

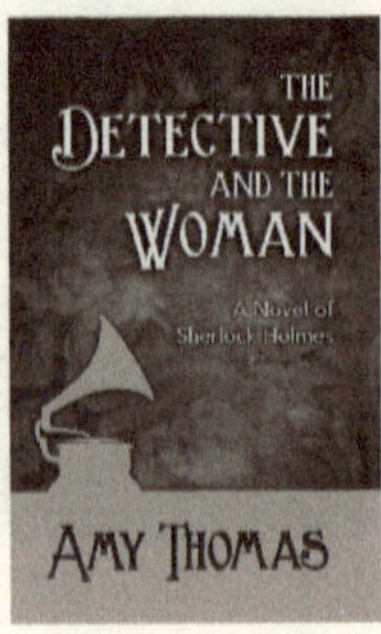

The Detective and The Woman
The Detective, The Woman and The Winking Tree
The Detective, The Woman and The Silent Hive

"The book is entertaining, puzzling and a lot of fun. I believe the author has hit on the only type of long-term relationship possible for Sherlock Holmes and Irene Adler. The details of the narrative only add force to the romantic defects we expect in both of them and their growth and development are truly marvelous to watch. This is not a love story. Instead, it is a coming-of-age tale starring two of our favorite characters."
Philip K Jones

Also from MX Publishing

The Sherlock Holmes and Enoch Hale Series

The Amateur Executioner
The Poisoned Penman
The Egyptian Curse

"The Amateur Executioner: Enoch Hale Meets Sherlock Holmes", the first collaboration between Dan Andriacco and Kieran McMullen, concerns the possibility of a Fenian attack in London. Hale, a native Bostonian, is a reporter for London's Central News Syndicate - where, in 1920, Horace Harker is still a familiar figure, though far from revered. "The Amateur Executioner" takes us into an ambiguous and murky world where right and wrong aren't always distinguishable. I look forward to
reading more about Enoch Hale."
Sherlock Holmes Society of London

www.mxpublishing.com

www.ingramcontent.com/pod-product-compliance
Lightning Source LLC
Chambersburg PA
CBHW030827310726
48980CB00006B/665/J

* 9 7 8 1 7 8 7 0 5 3 3 2 8 *